A CALL TO COLORS

A CALL TO COLORS

A Novel of the Leyte Gulf

JOHN J. GOBBELL

BALLANTINE BOOKS • NEW YORK

A Call to Colors is a work of fiction. Though some characters, incidents, and dialogues are based on the historical record, the work as a whole is a product of the author's imagination.

A Presidio Press Mass Market Original

Published in the United States by Presidio Press, an imprint of The Random House Publishing Group, a division of Random House, Inc., New York.

PRESIDIO PRESS and colophon are trademarks of Random House, Inc.

ISBN 0-89141-890-3

Cover design: Carl D. Galian
Cover illustration: 3DI Studio for AAReps.com

Printed in the United States of America

Presidio Press website address: www.presidiopress.com

OPM 9 8 7 6 5 4 3 2 1

This book is dedicated to the memory of
Alvin P. Cluster, lieutenant commander, USN
1919–2004

A true American patriot and hero.
Unselfishly and often without knowing,
he shaped many lives to carry on.

PREFACE

The battle of Leyte Gulf enabled General Douglas MacArthur to fulfill his promise of "I shall return" to the Philippine people by landing 165,000 troops on Leyte island. Returning to the Philippines was not a frivolous exercise, as General MacArthur pointed out to President Franklin D. Roosevelt in the planning stages. Not only would this archipelago provide a powerful strategic base on the road to Japan, but its recapture had critical political implications as well, in that the United States would develop an important ally for generations to come. Additionally, MacArthur eloquently pointed out to FDR that bypassing the Philippines had sinister implications by saying, "Consigning them [the Filipinos] to the bayonets of an enraged army of occupation would be a blot on American honor."

This set the scene for the last great naval surface battle, far outweighing the battle of Jutland. More than eight hundred ships were committed, the largest naval engagement in the history of mankind.

But the Japanese ingenuously challenged the U.S. Navy at Leyte through their battle plan SHO-GO—victory operation. They engaged the Americans in four phases: the battle of the Sibuyan Sea, the battle of the Surigao Strait, the battle off Samar, and the battle off Cape Engaño. The battle off Samar was perhaps the most critical phase, when Vice Admiral Takeo Kurita and his First Striking Force (Americans called it the Center Force) slipped through the San Bernardino Strait and arrived close to the entrance of Leyte Gulf on the morning of October 25, 1944, with four battleships, nine cruisers, and eleven destroyers.

Standing between Kurita and MacArthur's unarmed amphibious ships and troops was an inferior carrier group code-named Taffy 3, consisting of just six slow (single-screw, eighteen-knot) escort carriers, three destroyers, and four destroyer escorts. Two similar carrier groups, Taffy 2 and Taffy 1, lay farther south, but it was Taffy 3, under the vigilant command of Rear Admiral Clifton A. F. Sprague, that initially stood in Kurita's way. The destroyers in Taffy 3, particularly the destroyers USS *Johnston* (DD 557), USS *Hoel* (DD 533), and USS *Heermann* (DD 532); the destroyer escort USS *Samuel B. Roberts* (DE 413); and the brave aviators of all the Taffy groups opposed Kurita in the most unusual ways—ways that will continue to be discussed in war colleges for generations to come.

This work endeavors to provide an overview of the massive forces committed to Leyte by both sides, and focuses on events leading up to Samar and what happened there. However, there was no USS *Matthew* at Samar—the ship entirely fictitious. She is only on the scene to bring to life what happened off Samar that day and the unselfish bravery and commitment of the sailors who fought there, particularly the courageous men of Taffy 3.

A CALL TO COLORS

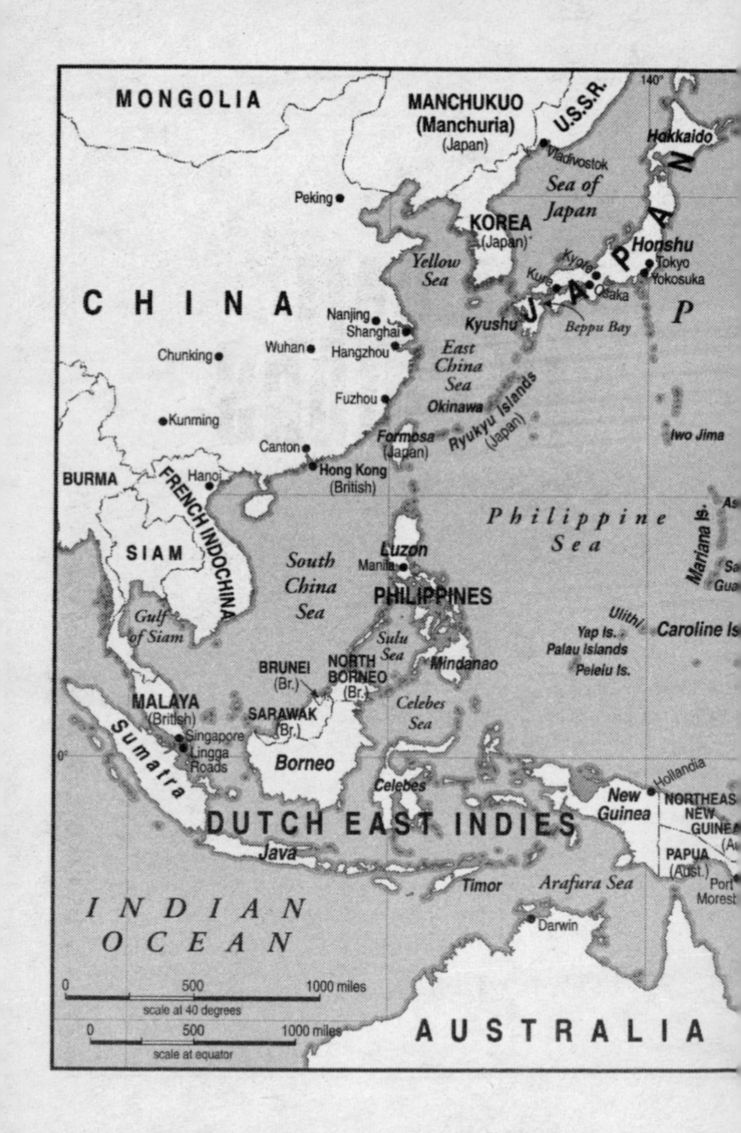
MONGOLIA
MANCHUKUO
(Manchuria)
(Japan)
U.S.S.R.
140°
Hokkaido
Vladivostok
Sea of
Japan
Peking
KOREA
(Japan)
Yellow
Sea
Honshu
Tokyo
Yokosuka
Kyoto
Kure
Osaka
JAPAN
CHINA
Nanjing
Shanghai
Hangzhou
Kyushu
Beppu Bay
P
Chunking
Wuhan
East
China
Sea
Fuzhou
Okinawa
Ryukyu Islands
(Japan)
Kunming
Formosa
(Japan)
Iwo Jima
Canton
Hong Kong
(British)
BURMA
Hanoi
FRENCH INDOCHINA
Philippine
Sea
Mariana Is.
SIAM
South
China
Sea
Luzon
Manila
PHILIPPINES
Gulf
of Siam
Ulithi
Yap Is.
Palau Islands
Peleiu Is.
Caroline Is
Sulu
Sea
Mindanao
BRUNEI
(Br.)
NORTH
BORNEO
(Br.)
MALAYA
(British)
SARAWAK
(Br.)
Celebes
Sea
Sumatra
Singapore
Lingga
Roads
Borneo
0°
Celebes
Hollandia
New
Guinea
NORTHEAS
NEW
GUINEA
DUTCH EAST INDIES
Java
PAPUA
(Aust.)
Timor
Arafura Sea
Port
Moresb
INDIAN
OCEAN
Darwin
0
500
1000 miles
scale at 40 degrees
0
500
1000 miles
scale at equator
AUSTRALIA

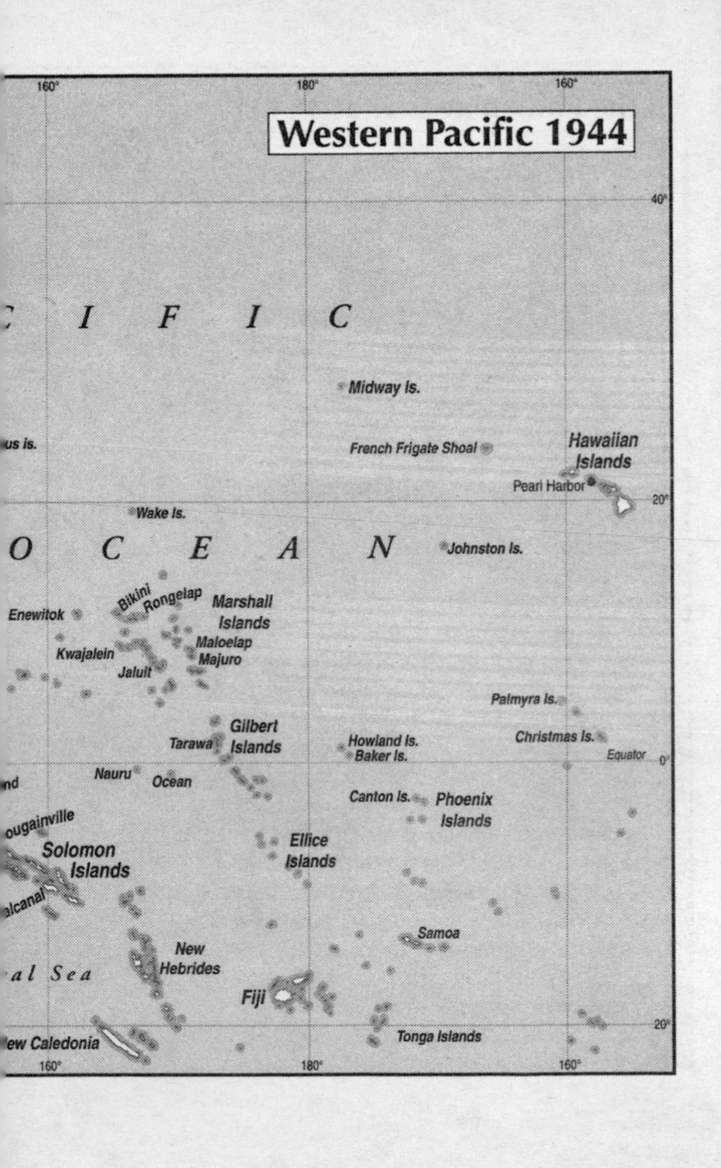
Western Pacific 1944
160°
180°
160°
40°
C I F I C
Midway Is.
us Is.
French Frigate Shoal
Hawaiian Islands
Pearl Harbor
20°
Wake Is.
O C E A N
Johnston Is.
Bikini
Rongelap
Marshall Islands
Enewitok
Maloelap
Kwajalein
Majuro
Jaluit
Palmyra Is.
Gilbert Islands
Tarawa
Howland Is.
Baker Is.
Christmas Is.
Equator
0°
Nauru
Ocean
nd
Canton Is.
Phoenix Islands
ougainville
Solomon Islands
Ellice Islands
alcanal
Samoa
New Hebrides
al Sea
Fiji
20°
ew Caledonia
Tonga Islands
160°
180°
160°

The Philippine Islands 1944
Northern Force - Decoy (Ozawa)
Cape Engaño
Laoag
Tuguegarao
2nd Strike Force (Shima)
Baguio
South China Sea
Luzon
Clark Field
24 Oct. U.S. airstrikes (Halsey) sink superbattleship Musashi, damage cruiser Myoko.
Subic Bay
Manila
Corregidor Island
PHILIPPINES
23 Oct. U.S. submarines Dace and Darter sink cruisers Atago and Maya; damage Takao.
Mindoro
San Bernardino Strait
3rd Fleet (Halsey)
Calamian Group
Sibuyan Sea
Masbate
Samar
Taffy 3 (Sprague)
San Pedro Bay
Paninihian Point
1st Strike Force (Kurita)
Cuyo East Passage
Visayan Sea
Panay
Tacloban
Suluan Island
San José
Bacolod
Leyte
Leyte Gulf
7th Fleet (Kinkaid)
Panay Gulf
Cebu
Negros
Bohol
Palawan Passage
Palawan
Puerto Princesa
Surigao Strait
24–25 Oct. Battle of Surigao Strait (Oldendorf).
Sulu Sea
Mindanao Sea
Dinagat Island
Southern Force (Nishimura)
Mindanao
Davao
Basilan
BRITISH NORTH BORNEO
Jolo Group
Tawi Tawi

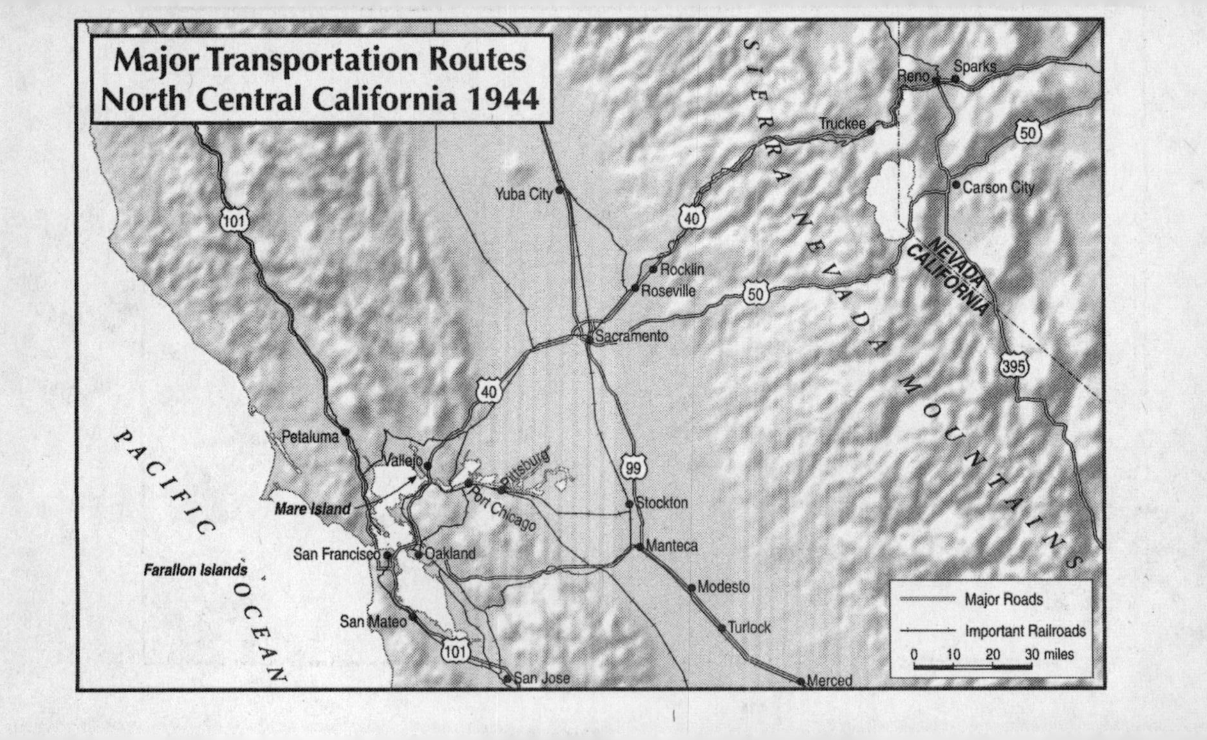
Major Transportation Routes
North Central California 1944
SIERRA NEVADA MOUNTAINS
NEVADA
CALIFORNIA
Reno
Sparks
Truckee
Carson City
Yuba City
Rocklin
Roseville
Sacramento
Petaluma
Vallejo
Mare Island
Pittsburg
Port Chicago
Stockton
Manteca
Modesto
Turlock
Merced
San Francisco
Oakland
San Mateo
San Jose
Farallon Islands
PACIFIC OCEAN
101
40
50
99
395
Major Roads
Important Railroads
0 10 20 30 miles

CAST OF CHARACTERS

U.S. Navy

Forces Afloat

USS *Matthew* (DD 548) (Call sign: Monkey Wrench)

Commander Michael T. "Mike" Donovan, commanding officer
Lieutenant Commander Richard (n) Kruger, executive officer, navigator
Lieutenant Burt T. Hammond, operations officer
Lieutenant Alberto G. "Al" Corodini, engineering officer
Lieutenant Clifford M. "Cliff" Merryweather, gunnery officer
Lieutenant (jg) Howard T. Sloan, supply officer
Lieutenant (jg) Jack (n) Kelso, first lieutenant
Ensign Jonathan M. "Johnnie Hollywood" Peete, torpedo officer
Ensign Rudy J. Kubichek, communications officer, radio officer
Ensign Kenneth L. Muir, III, second division officer
Ensign Steve V. Flannigan, second division officer to replace Muir
Yeoman first class Lucian B. Potter, captain's bridge talker

USS *Tampa* (CA 40)

Ensign Alexander T. "Tiny" Sabovik, John Sabovik's younger brother

Other U.S. Navy

Admiral Chester W. Nimitz, commander in chief, Pacific Fleet, and commander, Pacific Ocean Areas (Cinc Pac)
Lieutenant Arthur H. Lamar, flag secretary to Admiral Nimitz
Admiral William F. Halsey, Jr., commander, Third Fleet
Commodore Arleigh A. Burke, chief of staff to Vice Admiral Marc Mitscher, commander, Task Force 38
Rear Admiral John P. "Cactus Jack" Egan, deputy commander, Twelfth Naval District, special appointee by Ernest King, chief of naval operations
Lieutenant Commander John P. Sabovik, Office of Naval Intelligence (ONI), attached Twelfth Naval District
Captain Alexander (n) "Nitro" Collins, USMC, deputy to LCDR Sabovik, explosives expert

U.S. Army

General Douglas A. MacArthur, commander, Southwest Pacific Area (SOWESPAC)
Lieutenant General Richard K. Sutherland, chief of staff to General MacArthur
Major General Charles Willoughby, intelligence chief to General MacArthur
Lieutenant Colonel Owen Reynolds, intelligence aide to General Charles Willoughby and General MacArthur

Civilians

Franklin D. Roosevelt, president of the United States, commander in chief of armed forces
Diane Logan, MD, intern, Roseville Community Hospital, Roseville, California
Walter Logan, dispatcher, Southern Pacific Railroad, Roseville, California, Diane's father
Milo Lattimer, conductor, Southern Pacific Railroad
Benjamin "Soda Whiskers" Sodawski, engineer, freight train X 4293, Southern Pacific Railroad
Carmen Rossi, Commander Mario Rossi's widow
Vicky Kruger, wife of Richard Kruger

Japanese

Forces Afloat, Imperial Japanese Navy (IJN)

At Lingga Roads (Singapore)

Vice Admiral Takeo Kurita, commander, Central Force, aboard cruiser IJN *Atago*
Commander Yuzura Noyama, favored aide to Kurita, aboard IJN *Atago*
Rear Admiral Seiichi Abe, chief of staff to Admiral Kurita
Vice Admiral Matome Ugaki, commander, Battleship Division One, aboard superbattleship IJN *Yamato*
Minoru Onishi, petty officer third class, Ugaki's valet
Captain Senjuro Koketsu, MD, fleet surgeon, Kurita's physician

At Beppu Bay (Kyushu, Oita prefecture, Home Islands)

Vice Admiral Shoji Nishimura, commander, Southern Force, aboard battleship IJN *Yamashiro*
Vice Admiral Jisaburo Ozawa, commander, Northern Force (decoy), aboard attack carrier IJN *Zuikaku*

At Brunei Bay, Borneo

Vice Admiral Kiyohide Shima, commander, Supplementary Southern Force aboard heavy cruiser IJN *Nachi*

Forces Ashore

Tokyo, Japan

Admiral Soemu Toyoda, commander in chief, Imperial Japanese Navy
Ensign Hiroshi Noyama, IJN, Yuzura Noyama's younger brother, member of the newly formed Tokubetsu Kougeki Tai (kamikaze corps)

Civilians

Masao Noyama, father of Yuzura Noyama
Michiko Noyama, mother of Yuzura Noyama

The suffering, humiliation and mental torture that you have endured since the barbarous, unprovoked and treacherous attack upon the Philippines nearly three long years ago have aroused in the hearts of the American people a righteous anger, a stern determination to punish the guilty and a fixed resolve to restore peace and order and decency to an outraged world. . . .

Franklin D. Roosevelt to the Philippine people
New York Times, 21 October 1944

PROLOGUE

17 July 1944
SS *Quinalt Victory*
Pier 6, U.S. Naval Magazine
Port Chicago, California

Wendell Hamm, third assistant engineer of the SS *Quinalt Victory,* quickly thumped down the gangway beneath a moonless night sky. It was almost ten o'clock, and he'd been delayed for a couple of hours by a meeting with Martin Tuttle, *Quinalt Victory*'s chief engineer. He had a date with Gloria over in Oakland, and now, Wendell was terribly late. On the phone just a minute ago, Gloria had said she could wait at Currie's Ice Cream Parlor until it closed at eleven. If he didn't show up, then she would have to go home. With that in mind, Wendell splurged and called for a cab to meet him at the main gate, a mile and a half away.

Six months out of the maritime academy, Wendell Hamm had become part of the crew of the brand-new 7,212-ton EC-2 Liberty ship when she was being fitted out in the Kaiser Shipyards. And now she was ready for her maiden voyage to the South Pacific. The cargo: five thousand tons of munitions, which included eighteen hundred tons of high explosives.

Blackout conditions kept the pier dimly lit, as a squinting Wendell stepped around six-foot-high pallets of ammunition stacked beside haze-gray boxcars. Steam whistles ripped at the night, often masking the sound of forklifts as they growled past, their drivers yelling and tooting their horns. Wendell jumped off the rail siding as a twelve-ton diesel locomotive emerged from the gloom, pulling six more boxcars stuffed with ammunition. Blue-dungareed chief petty officers shouted and blew whistles while shirtless men cursed and sweated, setting up the pallets to be loaded aboard the *Quinalt Victory,* starting at midnight.

Across the pier, a pallet load of torpedo warheads swung aboard a sister ship, the SS *E. A. Bryan.* The *Bryan*'s loading was just about complete, and tomorrow morning she was to sail for a newly conquered island called Guam in the Marianas. If the crews loading the *Bryan* kept their round-the-clock pace, the *Quinalt Victory* would get underway in four days. Their destination was also Guam, smack-dab in the middle of a war zone. Wendell knew he should be afraid, but he was anxious to get out there; to see how the marines had thrown the Japanese out. Chief Tuttle had said the Nips were still in the hills, that marines went up after them for sport.

Lost in thought, Wendell left the ships and pier behind and headed down a darkened lonely road, the faint gleam of railroad tracks as his guide. Under the watchful eye of Tuttle, Hamm had supervised throttle operations in the engine room when they'd docked earlier this evening. As a reward, Tuttle had given the twenty-two-year-old Hamm a nip out of his hip flask. Later, he had more during the planning conference. And now the buzz continued as Hamm picked up the pace for the main gate.

An excited Hamm checked his watch as he walked past a dimly lit barrack: 2217. The blackout here was far more effective than on the pier. He could hardly see ten feet ahead. Squinting, he made out the gate ahead. And yes! The taxi he'd ordered was just outside, its engine ticking over. Gonna make it.

Even so, Wendell was a little nervous about seeing Gloria. More and more she'd been talking about marriage and— A white light illuminated the sky, and suddenly Wendell Hamm saw foothills clearly outlined in the distance. With a loud *crack,* a pressure wave smacked into Wendell. He was thrown against the barrack. Blinking and unsure of his footing, Wendell rose, bracing himself against the wall. Men cursed inside, stepping on broken glass. Someone was—

Another white light flooded the area brighter than Wendell had ever seen. Again a concussion threw him to the ground, pinning him there for four long seconds. Then it went black, and the sound of the blast mixed with that of screeching metal, screams, crackling fires, and shattering glass.

A marine sergeant rushed outside as Wendell again picked himself up. They looked up to a roiling cloud of fire and smoke and steam rising thousands of feet above them. "Jesus Christ, the Japs have hit!" screamed the sergeant.

"Hell, yeah," Wendell managed.

"Come on," roared the sergeant. Grabbing Wendell's lapel, they ran toward a station wagon parked behind the berm.

Other men poured out of the barracks and gaped up at the cloud. The sergeant pointed at four Marines standing on the landing, wearing T-shirts and shorts. "You men, grab your shoes and get in. We gotta go help."

Shoving Wendell toward the passenger door, the sergeant jumped in, started the car, and backed clear. The others jumped in, carrying boots, shirts, and pants. They struggled into their clothes as the sergeant jammed the gearshift into low and roared off.

Two minutes later he stopped.

"What the hell's wrong?" yelled Wendell. "Keep going!"

The sergeant who'd been so loud was now quiet, his face as white as the dials on the instrument panel. "Can't. Ain't nothin' there," he gasped.

Leaning forward, Wendell saw it was true. The two seventy-four-hundred-ton ships were gone. Locomotives and boxcars were gone. The dock facility buildings were gone. Hundreds of men were gone. The whole pier had disappeared. Water lapped before them just twenty feet away. There wasn't even any smoke.

"My God," gasped Wendell.

PART ONE

Across the sea, corpses in the water;
Across the mountain, corpses in the field;
I shall die only for the Emperor
I shall never look back.

From "Umi Yukaba," Japanese martial song

ONE

20 July 1944
USS *McDermott* (DD 505)
En route Pearl Harbor
Pacific Ocean

Tiny's scream echoed from inside the eight-inch turret. Mingled with other screams, Tiny's was especially loud, ululating, coming right from the depths of his gut. Another powder case cooked off inside the turret, the low-order explosion rumbling. Orange-red flames and smoke belched through the hatches and into the night, lighting up the *Tampa*'s fantail in eerie detail. Tiny's brother, John, stood before Donovan, nose to nose, his gritted white teeth a stark contrast with his smoke-blackened face. John pointed to the turret and yelled, "Get out of my way, Mike." His voice thick with smoke and menace.

"Nobody goes in there!"

"Outta my way or I'm going to—"

—The flashlight flicked over Donovan's eyes. In the dimness, he made out the heavy outline of Rafferty, a boatswain's mate first class. His accent was thick Deep South. "Sir, Mr. Donovan, I'm sorry to wake you. You left orders when to—"

Donovan sat bolt upright in his bunk and yelled, "What is it?" He looked around blinking. Wearing just skivvies, he wiped sweat from his forehead. And it wasn't from the humidity. Rafferty was in here for a wake-up call. Guilt swept over Donovan for snapping at the man. Rafferty was only doing his job. But that damn nightmare. It kept coming back. More and more. And the doc's pills weren't helping.

He rolled his legs out of the bunk, plopped bare feet on the cold deck, and cradled his head in his hands, running fingers through thick, sandy hair. "Sorry, Rafferty. Feels like I just fell asleep." Commander Mike Donovan reached to his desk and switched on the light. The clock read 0541. He'd been asleep for six hours. Yet he felt like a zombie.

"Mr. Jenkins says to tell you we have"—Rafferty held up a crumpled slip of paper and read—"reorientated the formation to a bent-line screen and have increased speed to twenty-two knots." Rafferty studied Donovan for a moment to make sure it had sunk in. "We will be taking our refueling station in ten minutes, sir—uh, Captain."

Usually an officer would report such an evolution. But many of the *McDermott*'s officers were dead. They had been up on the bridge just over four weeks ago when the five-hundred-kilogram bomb smacked into the destroyer. Among those killed was the captain, Mario Rossi, a hotheaded, gum-chewing, lovable little Italian. Donovan and Rossi had crossed swords many times, but they respected each other deeply. Mario was gone, along with the operations officer, communications officer, gunnery officer, fire control officer, CIC officer, and twenty-six enlisted. The whole area was a jumble of bent steel, wood, cork, and rotting flesh. In Majuro Lagoon, they'd only been able to pull out three of the fifteen bodies trapped in the pilothouse and director. Since then, Donovan had been running the ship from secondary conn between the forty-millimeter gun tubs amidships on the 01 level. And now, they were headed home for the States via Pearl Harbor with three other destroyers, the carrier *Alliance,* battleship *Tennessee,* and light cruiser *St. Louis*.

He looked up. Rafferty had called him *Captain.* "Okay, Rafferty. Thanks." He tried to grin. "Give the officer of the deck my compliments. Tell him I'll be up soon."

"Yes, sir." Rafferty started for the hatchway.

"Rafferty?"

"Sir?" He turned.

Donovan managed to broaden his grin. "Can we highline okay?"

Boatswain's mate first class Rafferty's mouth turned up at the mention of familiar territory. Highlining was his bailiwick. "Equipment is all there, Captain. But they still can't repair the forward fueling trunks. So we'll highline forward and take fuel aft. Is that okay, sir?"

"Looks like we have to do it that way. All right, thanks."

"Yes, sir." Rafferty lumbered through the curtain, drawing it shut quietly.

Thirty-two letters to write. Damn. Have to get started before we reach Pearl. Despite their arguments, Rossi had been like his big brother; the other officers, his little brothers. Most of the enlisted he knew—they were brothers, also. Donovan reminded himself that was why he'd picked destroyers. They were small, fast, maneuverable, hard-hitting ships crewed by more than three hundred officers and men. Living in tight quarters, they knew one another intimately. Secrets flashed about the ship in milliseconds. Weaknesses became impurities. Inevitably, impurities were purged by shipmates, sometimes painfully, and suddenly, like reknit bones, impurities became strong points. An amazing process, thought Donovan. Everybody knew everybody. And on destroyers, demarcations between officers and enlisted were vague. But then, he reflected, you can get to know someone too well, officer or enlisted. Like now, with Rafferty, it was almost an algebraic equivalent: knowing Rafferty, becoming friends with Rafferty, will equal pain. Because eventually, Rafferty will die. And that hurts. Of course, Donovan mused, if it's me who dies, it doesn't matter. No pain for me, maybe some for Rafferty.

When are you going to learn your lesson, Donovan? Getting to know your men makes it tougher when you see them die. Now you're nodding and smiling at Rafferty as if he were sitting across from you at Thanksgiving dinner. Dumb. Dumb. Dumb.

He thought he'd learned his lesson after the *Tampa* went down more than two years ago. That time, he had to write forty-seven letters and meet personally seven family members. Several wrote back, most of the letters complimentary. Two were not and that hurt. Forget them. It's over. Let the dead bury the dead. But then he remembered that he'd soon be in San Francisco to take command of a new destroyer.

How you going to be a good CO if you can't sleep? Nightmares. Shit.

He looked again at the papers in his in-basket. A three-page set of orders had arrived while they sat at anchor in Majuro Lagoon: orders to report to the commander of the Mare Island Naval Shipyard in San Francisco Bay to assume duties as the commanding officer of the USS *Matthew* (DD 548), a naval officer's dream.

Captain.

Donovan stood to his five-eleven height, walked to his washbasin, and ran water over his neck and wrists. At 180 pounds, he wasn't musclebound, but he had a well-defined build. A scar from that night aboard the *Tampa* ran across his right shoulder blade. Taking twenty-two stitches, it hadn't healed well, and on occasion, itched and burned, especially on sleepless nights.

Dabbing a towel to his face, he could feel course and speed changes in the way the *McDermott* pitched into the troughs, the way her deck vibrated. The *McDermott*'s engineering plant was doing all right; not bad for a destroyer with mangled topsides. It was a twin-engine Betty bomber that came out of the sun one morning. She must have taken off from one of the nearby Guam airfields, they figured. After a mind-numbing blast, the ship caught fire, and flames burned out the pilothouse, radio central, CIC, and wardroom. For a while, one end of the ship was cut off from the other as the *McDermott* burned like a Viking funeral pyre. Donovan was worried they would lose her. And her chief engineer, Fred Jenkins, was shaking his head while they frantically worked the fire. But they had finally doused it after nine exhausting hours. When it was over, at least thirty-two men were dead; four more were horribly burned, but they pulled through after transferring to a hospital ship in Majuro Lagoon.

That damn ache gnawed at his belly as he bent to tie his shoes. A tingle at first, but he'd been feeling it more and more. Dammit. Of all the things going on, now there was something else to worry about.

"Cap'nonnabrigh," howled Rafferty in his southern accent. It took several weeks for one to get used to Rafferty's accent. Once accomplished, one knew this meant "Captain is on the bridge."

But the bridge was wiped out. So Donovan climbed to the 01 level[1] and walked up to the secondary conning platform. They were well into dawn, but stars still bore through the blackness overhead, and a full moon was setting off their starboard quarter. Easily distinguished were the hulking silhouettes of the three other destroyers charging toward the Hawaiian Islands in a bent-line screen with the fleet aircraft carrier *Alliance* (CV 35) plowing three thousand yards behind. Stationed one thousand yards on either beam of *Alliance* were the battleship *Tennessee* (BB 43) and light cruiser *St. Louis* (CL 49). It was a ragtag formation of wounded ducks headed for repairs. The *Tennessee* had been hit by a shore battery in the opening days of the invasion of Tinian; the *St. Louis* lost her number three propeller and shaft later the same day, thus limiting the formation's speed to the *St. Louis*'s best of twenty-two knots.

Their speed brought a strong blast of relative wind over the starboard bow and ruffled their hair and clothes. But it wasn't enough to blot the occasional odor of burned paint, wood, and human flesh that drifted back from the wrecked pilothouse.

Lieutenant Frederick Jenkins, his thin frame tucked in a light Windbreaker, was outlined against a starry morning sky. Since Donovan had been elevated to skipper, Jenkins was promoted to executive officer, but for now he was officer of the deck during this watch.

"Morning, Captain," said Jenkins.

Damn, it flowed over their lips so easily. *Captain.* "Morning, Fred. All set?"

Jenkins gave a rundown on the ship's status, then pointed to a searchlight jury-rigged to the torpedo director platform on the forward stack. A signalman clicked it furiously. "Morning flight ops are imminent."

"Probably means we're number one to refuel," said Donovan.

"I hope so." Jenkins glanced at Donovan, his brow knit.

"Yes, I've decided."

"Sir?"

"Please announce at morning quarters that we'll have burial at sea for the three men in the locker." During their underway time en route to Pearl, they'd cut a lot of junk away and tossed it over the side, uncovering three corpses in the process.

Jenkins sighed. They'd agonized with the decision of taking the three dead to Hawaii for burial. Right now, the corpses, sewn in canvas bags, were stored in the meat locker below the mess desk. "I think it's the right thing, Captain."

"Let's make it right for them. Officers in clean working khakis. Six-man honor guard in summer whites. The whole crew will be in clean dungarees except those on watch, okay?"

"Yes, sir."

"I'd like to heave to, but we can't of course."

"No, sir."

They looked up to watch two F6F Hellcats take off from the *Alliance* in the early dawn. Beginning their morning combat air patrol, the single-seat fighters winged toward them and growled overhead fifty feet off the deck. Then they pulled up sharply, their exhaust stacks belching flame as they clawed for altitude.

"Too bad we can't have a choir for the ceremony," said Jenkins.

"Ummm."

"I ever tell you I sang in the naval academy choir, XO—er, I mean, Captain?"

"No, you didn't."

"Craziest thing I ever did. Really enjoyed it. But then my grades went to hell. So I had to quit." He turned to Donovan. "You ever do anything like that, Skipper?"

"No. Don't think I ever did. Well, maybe just once . . ."

In 1936, the first week in November was eagerly anticipated at the University of Southern California. It was the height of football season and it was homecoming week, which was celebrated with the annual Trojan Festival. That was capped off Thursday night with songs and production numbers performed on Bovard Auditorium's large stage.

That year the program consisted of fifteen living groups, and the Delta Phi Theta fraternity was scheduled second from the last to perform. It had turned cold, and the men shuffled nervously around the backstage door, waiting to be called. To break the tension, Mike Donovan had hauled a keg down in his car. John Sabovik's younger brother, Alexander Sabovik, now a freshman pledge for Delta Phi Theta, was the one who carried it in and stashed it in the bushes. Unlike Mike Donovan or John Sabovik, who'd missed the cut for USC football, Alexander Sabovik was one of the most promising members of the team and had played varsity second string right away. At six-four, 255 pounds, Alexander was nicknamed "Tiny." And when John and Mike were unable to extricate themselves from predicaments, young Tiny was always nearby to take care of business. Never angry, he merely used his vast muscle to pin an opponent against a fence or wall until things calmed down. And he did it while flashing his toothless grin—he'd lost two front teeth in football—and talking to someone else, in most cases a sheet-white John or Mike Donovan who was picking himself off the ground.

With the keg in place, Tiny became the pledge-class hero, and the brothers were liberally imbued with the stuff by showtime. Upon their cue, the forty-six brothers of Delta Phi Theta, wearing matching blazers, ties, and dark slacks, lined up on stage in three ranks. In the front rank were fourteen seniors, including Mike Donovan, Owen Reynolds, and John Sabovik. Tiny's hulking mass was evident in the third rank. After a pause, house president John stepped out and led them in a deep, rhythmic piece called "Delta Phi Drums." Practice after practice, John had screamed at them for their meandering harmonics. But tonight their voices were beautifully reengineered by Donovan's keg. As the piece ended, the audience roared and stomped and clapped their approval.

John turned, gave a deep bow, and stepped back to blend into center rank between Donovan and Reynolds. On Sabovik's cue, the Delta Phis bowed. As they rose, Mike Donovan looked over the judges seated in the front row: two professors and three senior students. One of the student judges was a drama major, a knockout redhead named Katherine O'Neil. She caught Mike's eye and gave a sultry smile.

"Psst." Donovan elbowed John Sabovik.

Looking quickly from side to side, Katherine winked and shot a subtle thumbs-up.

"Holy cow," whispered Sabovik. "We got it made."

"I'd say so," said Donovan. How could it be otherwise? Kitty O'Neil and John Sabovik were pinned. In fact, Sabovik had borrowed Donovan's fraternity pin to do the job. He'd lost his own. And he hadn't bothered to reimburse Donovan for it.

Fifteen minutes later, the program was over and the Delta Phis were summoned on stage along with two other fraternities for the trophy presentation. The lights came down and a hush fell over the crowd as Professor Rhedd, head of the Speech Department, solemnly mounted the steps to the stage. Paper-thin with a wisp of a mustache, Rhedd was flanked in a tight spotlight by Katherine O'Neil and Lee Ann Bates, another bombshell student judge from the Drama Department. One glance at Katherine's face told Donovan what he wanted to know. They had won. My God, he thought, Kitty might be a man-killer, but she would be terrible at poker.

In a voice cultured by years of practicing with a pencil clamped between his teeth, Professor Rhedd announced the third-place winner and then the second-place. The crowd cheered as Rhedd tried to announce Delta Phi Theta's first place. Gamely, he did his best to shout over them while retaining a semblance of his stage voice. Finally he gave up and nodded to Katherine O'Neil, who handed the trophy to a grinning John Sabovik.

The roar crescendoed as the brothers of Delta Phi Theta lifted Sabovik to their shoulders. Suddenly the crowd roared even louder. Sabovik responded, shaking the gleaming Troy Week trophy over his head. The crowd roared again, many pointing, as a victorious John Sabovik waved the trophy in the air with one hand and pumped a fist with the other.

Katherine O'Neil looked back. Then she threw her hands over her eyes, her face turning red. Rhedd and Lee Ann Bates looked back.

"Oh, dear," said Professor Rhedd, covering his mouth.

The crowd cheered louder.

Donovan stepped out of ranks and looked. "Shit!"

Owen Reynolds peeked around and started laughing. Then Tiny looked and broke into his toothless grin. Perched on his brothers' shoulders, John Sabovik's fly was wide open for the whole world to see. The more they cheered and roared, the more he waved the trophy and pumped his fist.

In retrospect, it was the best thing ever to happen to Sabovik. Two days later, a thoroughly embarrassed Katherine O'Neil returned John Sabovik's fraternity pin, which he promptly misplaced.

After graduation that spring, Katherine O'Neil marched out to Hollywood, where she'd been vowing to go since completing puberty in the seventh grade. She went on a slash-and-burn path leading across a number of casting couches. Plying her skills, she carved out a modest career playing leads in B-westerns and horror movies.

John Sabovik kept forgetting to return Mike Donovan's fraternity pin. Careers were on their minds, and, with the economy in such terrible shape, both signed up for an officer candidate program in the U.S. Navy; they were commissioned ensigns by latter 1937.

Claiming seasickness, Owen Reynolds joined the army. Tiny graduated three years later, in 1940, having made all-American. Instead of going pro, Tiny joined the Beverly Hills office of Merrill, Lynch, Pierce, Fenner & Bean, becoming a retail stockbroker. Right away, Tiny's boss sent him to Dr. Sideman, a Beverly Hills dentist to the stars, who fixed Tiny up with a beautiful set of false front teeth. Tiny's USC football career led to a number of contacts in the movie studios, and by the time the Japanese bombed Pearl Harbor, he'd already made over a half million dollars.

The wind freshened, whipping at everyone's clothes. For sunrise, the ship was at general quarters. Men in the gun tubs and the conning platform walked in place, stamping their feet, looking east into the golden dawn and the promise of Hawaii and, beyond that, home.

Donovan looked aft to the *Alliance.* Her signal light winked at them. "Here we go," he said. Then he stood up in the gun-tub platform, taking the full force of the wind. Definitely, a feel of land, and relief, and relaxation began to grip them. The Marianas business had just about pitched him over. But after burial-at-sea ceremonies this afternoon, he'd be done with it. The pain gnawed in his belly and he massaged it a bit, wondering if he could ever get rid of the stench that drifted from the *McDermott*'s bridge or, worse, from the nightmare of the *Tampa* that now beckoned from six hundred fathoms down in Iron Bottom Sound.

TWO

22 July 1944
Imperial Japanese Navy heavy cruiser *Atago*
Lingga Roads, Java Sea

An oppressive haze hung over Lingga Roads, a vast equatorial anchorage in the Java Sea. The decadent temptations of Singapore lay forty kilometers to the north, where today the sweltering heat had soared to forty degrees Celsius (104°F). This evening it was only twenty-nine (85°F), the humidity still oppressive. Chain lightning sparkled on the eastern horizon, as a quarter moon glimmered on thirty-two anchored warships. Hulking among them were the largest warships ever built, the battleships *Yamato* and *Musashi,* pride of the Imperial Japanese Navy. Their eighteen-inch guns were capable of hurling a thirty-two-hundred-pound projectile for twenty-three miles, but tonight the ships were completely darkened, asleep, and tucked well inside antisubmarine nets. Even so, little sub chasers scurried about Lingga's entrances, making sure American submarines couldn't creep in.

Near the center of the fleet lay the flagship *Atago,* a cruiser of 9,850 tons, her silhouette discernible from no more than three hundred meters. Water gently slapped her boot topping. She looked at rest, like a coyote sleeping in its lair, its snout tucked under a paw. Like the rest of the fleet, *Atago* was at darkened ship. Lights-out had been sounded at 2200, and most of the crew were asleep while security watches patrolled her decks in split-toed sandals. The heat was intolerable belowdecks, despite the grinding of exhaust and blower fans. It was particularly bad in the berthing spaces, with many of the ship's crew turned out on the weather decks, curled up on mats.

Strident voices rang in the flag wardroom five levels above the main deck in the *Atago*'s superstructure. Vice Admiral Takeo Kurita, a slender man of five-seven, 155 pounds, had called a staff meeting after the evening meal. It was still raging at 2248, showing no sign of letting up. Portholes and hatches were clamped shut to keep light from leaking while four overhead mounted fans struggled to cut through thick cigarette smoke.

Seated at the head of a T-shaped table, the nearly bald Kurita heaved a sigh of resignation, frustrated that he could barely control this collection of seventeen men who, with each passing minute, acted less and less like officers of the Imperial Japanese Navy. To a man, they were, eager, desperately sincere, almost overly zealous. Bitterly they argued about how to stop the American advance in the Western Pacific. The Imperial Japanese Navy had taken a terrible drubbing the previous month at the hands of Raymond Spruance's Third Fleet. The losses to the Imperial Japanese Navy were shocking, including more than four hundred carrier planes and their irreplaceable pilots. Worse, the Americans had retaken the Marianas, including Guam, Tinian, Saipan, and Rota.

The question before them was: Where will the Americans strike next? The Philippines? China? Formosa? Once that was known, the Japanese could consolidate their strung-out forces and implement Operation SHO-GO,[2] a brainchild of Admiral Soemu Toyoda, chief of naval operations in Tokyo. Stated simply, SHO-GO was Toyoda's plan to draw out the American fleet and kill it in one decisive blow—no small accomplishment given the Imperial Japanese Navy's dwindling capabilities. Operation SHO-1 was an adaptation for the Philippines, SHO-2 for Formosa, SHO-3 for the Southern Home Islands, and so on.

Rear Admiral Seiichi Abe shot to his feet. "Who says they won't strike the Philippines?" Silence fell; they turned expectantly toward Kurita, who had more time at sea than almost any admiral in the Imperial Japanese Navy. A 1914 graduate of Etajima Naval Academy, he was fifty-six years of age and a proud and humble man, the son of a schoolteacher. Kurita had served his country for thirty-four years. Of this, a solid eighteen years had been at sea, all in surface ships, particularly destroyers, his first love. Also, Kurita was known for leading the navy's night-tactics development to the level that it enjoyed today. The consummate surface warfare officer, Kurita saw no reason to waste time brownnosing his way up the ladder on shore assignments. Before making rear admiral in 1938, he'd devoted his time ashore to either gunnery or torpedo schools, mostly the latter. As a full captain, he was chief instructor at the torpedo school between his stint as commanding officer of the cruiser *Abukuma* and the battleship *Kongo.* After the war's outbreak, Kurita commanded battle groups from the Indian Ocean to Midway to the Solomons to the Marianas. And many of the men gathered here had been with him through all of that.

Now they waited for the Chujo—an honorific for a vice admiral—to speak. Kurita sipped his brandy and said, "I'd say it's the Philippines."

"How can it be?" asked Abe. Rubbing his eyes, he sat. "They can't supply such a large objective over a long period of time. We'd wipe them out."

With a nod, Kurita said, "Consider the size of their fleet—hundreds, we're told. And they've become proficient at replenishment at sea. That's how Halsey and Spruance do it. They never go ashore. They just strike, chase tankers, refuel, and strike again."

Rear Admiral Satomi Takata stood and hitched his trousers. The man was overweight and hitched all the time, a habit Kurita hated in officers. But Kurita looked the other way in Takata's case. He was respected as a brilliant strategist. After a nod from Kurita, Takata said, "Yes, the Philippines. I agree. After all, didn't that egomaniac MacArthur say, 'I shall return'?" Another dark side to Takata was that he was a hothead. He would get so worked up that he'd be virtually tongue-tied. And with the late hour, it was easy to see he was headed in that direction.

But others around the table saw it coming. A few snickered.

Takata's face grew red, his eyes darting from face to face.

"Won't MacArthur be allowed his objective? Isn't he an American favorite? Didn't he try to run for president?"

From across the table, Captain Ryozo Ishima pounded a fist. "Philippines. Nonsense. A no-win objective. They would be bogged down for months, if not years. It's Formosa, I say. That way, they can choke off our supply lines to China and the Dutch East Indies. I say we draw a ring of steel around Formosa. The sooner, the better."

That was the decision before Kurita: how to allocate his dwindling fleet of ships over such a vast area. Right now they were anchored near Singapore because of its proximity to oil. But the Americans would soon be on the move. And he would have to decide. But where . . . where? Kurita chastised himself inwardly. Toyoda wanted a response soon.

In the blink of an eye, Takata and Ishima leaned over the table, yelling, their noses almost touching. If the situation wasn't so dreadful, Kurita would have burst out laughing. Two red-faced, adult senior officers, shrieking at each other, veins bulging in their necks.

A glass toppled over. Water splattered on Takata's sleeve. Enraged, Takata started around the table toward Ishima.

"Enough!" Kurita shot to his feet. He rarely yelled, and his officers sat back in shocked surprise.

Quiet returned. Kurita sat and asked softly, "The first question is: Where are their attack forces? Halsey's Third Fleet? Kinkaid's Seventh? How can you hide two whole fleets like that? Next, where are their amphibious forces? Their troops? We're supposed to have submarine pickets out there looking for them. And yet nobody has—"

A hatch opened. A blast of warm, humid air swirled into the wardroom, carrying the odor of ginger and gardenia from nearby islands. Kurita drew a deep breath. Beautiful.

A full commander, resplendent in dress blues and aiguillette, entered with a limp, a black patch over his left eye, carrying a clipboard. He was Yuzura Noyama, a fighter pilot who'd lost his left eye and nearly lost his leg over Bougainville eighteen months ago. He'd become an outstanding communications officer and was one of Kurita's favorite aides—so much so that the Imperial marines in the passageway automatically admitted him without asking for ID.

Deftly closing the hatch, Noyama walked up to Kurita, bowed, and handed over the clipboard. Then he stood to one side at parade rest.

Kurita took the board, then looked up to Takata and Ishima. Waving the back of his hand, he said, "Sit, gentlemen, sit."

The two officers sat. All eyes turned to Kurita as he read the message. At length, he looked up and said, "Yes, it's from Toyoda." Kurita rose and walked to a bulkhead-mounted chart. Picking up a pointer, he said, "Tokyo intelligence staff have strong evidence that it's either the Philippines or Formosa." Kurita's pointer slapped the chart with a loud *crack*. "They are willing to bet on that. Thus our assignment is to submit plan SHO-1. Our goal is to meet the Americans at the Philippines, draw them out, and annihilate them. Toyoda will plan for SHO-2, the invasion of Formosa. I am to meet him in Tokyo in"—he glanced at the message—"two weeks." He looked up.

Noyama's eyes glistened, and his face was a bit red.

Kurita waved Noyama to a chair. "Your leg bothering you?" Sometimes Noyama was in a lot of pain. But he always masked it effectively.

Noyama sat and exhaled loudly. "No, sir."

The corners of Kurita's mouth raised slightly. "Then perhaps you're up for a bit of mountain climbing tomorrow?" One of Kurita's favorite things to do ashore was mountain climbing. But he seldom got the chance.

Noyama looked Kurita in the eye. "I have the feeling, Admiral, that I'll be working on SHO-1 tomorrow, uh, with respect, sir."

A collective sigh heaved about the room. A sign of relief as the men sat back and nodded to one another. Toyoda's decisions to plan for Formosa and the Philippines were better than no decisions at all. Now they could do something. Now they could plan for a way to get back at the Americans.

Kurita nodded toward Noyama. "Well, maybe no mountain climbing tomorrow, Noyama."

"Thank you, Admiral."

THREE

26 July 1944
Commanding Officer's Quarters No. 5
U.S. Army Fort Schafter
Oahu, Territory of Hawaii

General Douglas MacArthur walked into the bedroom, stripped off his clothes, and tossed them on a chair. Pointing to a bar stool in the living room, he asked, "Grab that for me, Owen?" Then he headed for the bathroom.

"Certainly, sir." Colonel Owen Reynolds stepped into the living room, one-handed the stool, and returned to the bedroom. Just before closing the door, Reynolds put a finger to his lips, gesturing to a signals major, an artillery captain, and two sergeant-valets seated around the living room. Aside from their B-17 flight crew, this was MacArthur's entourage that had flown with him from Hollandia. Reynolds turned to one of the valets—a distinguished Filipino with a full head of salt-and-pepper hair named Navarro—and said, "Begin in two minutes." Then he closed the door.

MacArthur stepped into the shower and fiddled with the valves. Water gushed as he called, "What time did you say we were due there, Owen?" He stretched a hand out the door.

Walking into the bathroom, Reynolds handed the stool over and said, "Fifteen hundred, sir." The general already knew the answer. They'd discussed it many times during the long flight. Now it was 1505. And right now President Franklin Delano Roosevelt, accompanied by a legion of U.S. Navy dignitaries, waited for General MacArthur in Pearl Harbor, fifteen miles away.

It seemed weeks ago that they'd boarded the general's

B-17 in Hollandia, New Guinea, leaving MacArthur's aide and Reynolds's boss, Major General Charles Willoughby, to "take care of things," as MacArthur put it. MacArthur hated leaving Hollandia. He hadn't set foot on U.S. soil since 1937. But now his immediate superior in Washington, DC, General George C. Marshall, had ordered MacArthur to Hawaii to meet with the president.

Over long hours, the flight crew did a good job keeping to the schedule, right up until the last leg from Palmyra to Hawaii. They hit a storm and bounced and jiggled and ground through headwinds all the way to Hickam Field, ending up two hours late. And now Reynolds's legs and butt ached: the legs from lack of exercise, his rear end from a wound on Bougainville.

Steam rose over the transom as MacArthur sat on the stool and sighed, "Ahhh." Then he called loudly, "So we're already five minutes late?"

"Afraid so, General."

"Well, I don't care, Owen. I'm hot and sticky and tired and I'll not go trudging aboard a capital ship of the United States Navy looking like a common bum, ruffles and flourishes be damned."

"Yes, sir."

"Did you know that the president and I are distant cousins?"

"No, sir."

"Out here, doesn't mean anything, does it?" MacArthur began humming. Relative or not, MacArthur ran a veritable kingdom out in the far reaches of the South Pacific. But in Hawaii, he was outranked by his cousin, the commander in chief, who at the moment was most likely drumming his fingers down in Pearl Harbor, waiting. Also waiting, and most likely fuming alongside FDR, were Admiral Chester Nimitz, commander in chief, Pacific Fleet, and Admiral William Leahy, Roosevelt's chief of staff.

This was one of the few times Reynolds actually felt sorry for MacArthur. In most situations, the general was confident, in control, eager for the next challenge. And yet he'd been called to this meeting as a pig to slaughter. It was to be a strategy conference to decide where the Americans would strike next. With the Marianas safely secured, everyone, including FDR, the entire Combined Joint Chiefs of Staff, Ernie King, and Hap Arnold, wanted to invade Formosa next, maybe go even farther north: the Ryukyus, perhaps Okinawa. All were adamantly opposed to MacArthur's plan for retaking the Philippines. They wanted to bypass the seven-thousand-island archipelago, throw up a blockade, and starve out the Japanese garrisoned there. Rumor had it that Admiral King, who had been in Hawaii just last week, had given Admiral Nimitz irrevocable instructions not to back away from the Formosa Plan. Reynolds and the rest of MacArthur's staff knew the navy believed that "Dug-out Doug" wanted the Philippines as a grandstanding issue, to complete his promise of "I will return."

There was another element. Both the navy and army believed President Roosevelt was here for political purposes rather than working with military issues. Just ten days ago, the Democratic Party had nominated FDR to run for president for an unprecedented fourth term. Many felt the only reason the president was out here was to garner votes, grin for his troops, and shake every hand offered.

Maybe that was part of MacArthur's strategy, the wire-thin, balding Reynolds mused. Offer up part of his empire to complement Roosevelt's political campaign. But did MacArthur really have that to give? After all, he was subordinate to his commander in chief. It was to be an enormous contest of egos.

MacArthur's baritone voice echoed through the steam. "Well, Owen, I think you better get out there and put a cork in it for us."

"General?" Like MacArthur, Reynolds was tired. He ran a hand over his chin. He hadn't shaved in two days. And he, too, had been counting on a shower. Moreover, he was famished. Two and a half days of dry bologna sandwiches and lemonade made with brackish water had left him with a sour stomach.

"I mean, Owen, get down there, now. Talk to Nimitz's aide, ahhh—" MacArthur snapped his fingers. "—Lamar. That's it. Lieutenant Lamar. A good man. Just tell him I'll be right along. Then go get yourself a solid meal. Cruisers serve great chow. I love their navy bean soup." Lost in steam, MacArthur gave a chuckle as water splashed over the transom.

Reynolds hated navy bean soup. "Yes, sir. On my way."

"Everything else set up?"

Reynolds ran over to a window and peeked out to see a Buick four-door convertible drawing to the curb. Naturally the top was down, and a four-star general's flag was mounted on each front fender. Atop the right front fender was a gleaming chrome-plated siren. In front of the Buick were four motorcycles, their riders in jodhpurs and shiny boots, dismounting. Four hours out of Hickam, Reynolds had radioed the general's request ahead and their host, Lieutenant General Robert C. Richardson, had come through.

Reynolds checked the bed. Navarro had laid out a fresh set of starched khaki trousers and shirt, the general's four stars pinned on the collar points. Socks and brilliantly shined shoes waited on the floor. His Philippine marshal's hat was perched on the dresser; hanging next to it was his brown leather flight jacket. Good. He grabbed his garrison cap and ran back to the bathroom, finding it clogged with billowing steam. "All ready, General. And your car just pulled up."

"What kind?"

"Buick, convertible. The top is down and you have four mounted escorts. Looks like General Richardson really put his back to it."

"Excellent, Owen. I wouldn't expect otherwise. Now get going and find Lamar. I'll see you there."

"Yes, sir. And may I add, General, best of luck?"

"Thank you, Owen. We're going to need it on this one." MacArthur hummed again.

"Yes, sir." Reynolds dashed through the living room, shouting last-minute instructions to the valets. Then he grabbed a worn leather briefcase, ran for the front door, and exited.

The men in the motorcade looked up expectantly.

"Ten minutes, tops," he shouted. "Then give it all you've got." Like a New Yorker calling for a taxi, Reynolds jammed two fingers on his lips, whistled shrilly, and shot a finger in the air. A four-door olive-drab Mercury sedan pulled from under a grizzled banyan tree and roared up to the curb.

Reynolds jumped in back, surprised that he was out of breath. Dammit. More tired than I thought.

The driver, a balding sergeant, turned. "Where to, Colonel?"

"Pearl Harbor. And step on it!"

The sergeant popped the clutch and stomped on the gas, burning rubber and throwing Reynolds to the back of his seat. He hadn't done that since high school back in California's San Fernando Valley.

"Where in Pearl, sir?"

"USS *Baltimore.*" Reynold's eyebrows shot up. They were headed for the main gate doing seventy. "Hey!" The crazy sergeant wasn't stopping. Frantically, the man waved his hand and blew the Mercury's horn. The guards jumped aside, shaking their fists. Reynolds looked back, relieved they hadn't drawn their guns and opened fire. "Soldier, what's your name?"

"McCormick, Colonel. Don't worry, sir. They know me. More important, they know the car belongs to General Richardson."

"I appreciate your efforts here, but is somebody going to write us up? I mean—"

"Where, sir?"

The man was also rude. "What?"

"Whereabouts in Pearl? I mean, I gotta know what gate to go for."

Reynolds almost said *Baltimore.* But that was stupid. He'd already said that. He reached into his briefcase, shuffled for an agonizing thirty seconds, and pulled out a nine-page agenda. "Here it is: Pier 22-B. That make sense to you, McCormick?"

McCormick jammed down the gas pedal. The Mercury roared for Pearl Harbor at eighty miles per hour. "I can find 22-B blindfolded."

FOUR

26 July 1944
Pier 22-B
Pearl Harbor Naval Station
Territory of Hawaii

Sergeant McCormick made the Pearl Harbor Navy Yard in fifteen minutes. It took another twenty minutes to weave their way through heavy security. The base was crowded with sailors in whites and marines in service C uniforms, the crowd growing thicker as they neared 22-B. "Outta my way," roared McCormick as he raced the engine and honked the horn. At length, a group of men parted and they drew up before a gangway leading to the USS *Baltimore,* which had moored forty minutes previously, carrying the president from San Diego. One of the newest heavy cruisers, she was the lead ship of her class, displacing 13,600 tons. Mounting nine, eight-inch guns, she was painted a menacing dark gray. A soft breeze ruffled her rigging where a number of brilliant official multistarred flags fluttered from her halyards, including the flag of the commander in chief.

Reynolds grabbed his briefcase and looked out, seeing hundreds of men crowded on the pier. Opening the door, he said, "Thanks, McCormick. I may need you later, so stick around. Park the car nearby if you can"—he waved to an ocean of neatly parked official light gray four-door Plymouths—"and go aboard and have some chow. I hear the navy bean soup is great."

"I hate navy bean soup. But don't worry, Colonel. I'll find you when you're ready." McCormick popped the clutch and roared off, men jumping out of the way. Thirty seconds later, he was parking just a hundred feet away in a yellow-striped area beside a fire hydrant.

Reynolds walked up the gangway, remembering to salute the fantail and quarterdeck. The quarterdeck brass was brilliantly polished, the decks and bulkheads clean and free of rust. Wearing the same rumpled khakis he had worn since Hollandia, Reynolds felt like MacArthur's "common bum" as he walked among flag and senior naval officers. Milling about, smoking cigarettes, and chatting casually were commanders, captains, two-star admirals in starched dress-white uniforms with rows of ribbons. Scattered among them were senior marine and army officers also in dress uniform. Their demeanor told him the meeting was in progress, the senior flag officers most likely in the wardroom having an audience with the president. Wistfully Reynolds looked toward the head of the pier, hoping against hope that the general's car would heave into view and put him out of his misery.

The officer of the deck, or OOD, was a lieutenant in whites with two rows of ribbons and two battle stars. A polished brass and leather telescope was tucked under his left arm. Beside the lieutenant stood the junior officer of the deck, a stocky chief bosun's mate, with four rows of ribbons and six battle stars. "Help you, sir?" asked the lieutenant.

"Looking for a Lieutenant Lamar."

"Over there, sir." The OOD pointed to a flag lieutenant, resplendent in whites and aiguillette, engaged in conversation with a two-star admiral, two captains, and a commander. The admiral's hands were jammed on his hips, and the two captains rolled their eyes at each other.

"Thanks."

Reynolds walked over. "Lieutenant Lamar? My name's Reynolds. I come from General MacArthur and would like to extend our—"

"Where the hell is he?" the admiral hissed. "The president and fifteen flag officers are up there right now fidgeting and farting, waiting for your general. The meeting was supposed to begin at 1500, wasn't it?"

Reynolds drew up before the admiral. Overweight, his face was red and puffed with the tropical humidity. And one banal row of ribbons told Reynolds this man was a backwater administrative goldbrick. Evenly, Reynolds said, "That's why I'm here, sir. Headwinds. Our plane was delayed and the general had to change."

The admiral looked him up and down. "Well, *you* got here, didn't you? Couldn't the general have the courtesy to do the same?"

"Well, you see, Admiral, it was a long flight and—"

"And why aren't you in uniform? This is the first time we've put on dress whites since the Japs hit Pearl Harbor. Seems to me the army could do the same."

"Well, Admiral. As I said, we just got in and—"

Their ears picked up at a long mournful wailing sound. Then again. Sirens! Of course. Many sirens. They mixed with one another, the tones growing louder.

"What the hell?" cursed the admiral.

As one, the group jostled to the rail and looked forward to the direction of the commotion.

"I'll be damned," muttered the admiral as the crowd on the pier parted. A pair of motorcycles rounded a bend and hove into view, their sirens screaming. Then two more rounded the curve, their sirens equally strident.

MacArthur's Buick thundered right behind, its red four-starred, fender-mounted flags fluttering in the breeze. The driver was hunched over the wheel, throwing the gear lever up into second to keep pace with the shrieking motorcycles. MacArthur sat alone in the backseat, corncob pipe clamped between his teeth, his Philippine marshal's hat flapping loosely. Smartly, the motorcycles drew to a stop, the Buick right behind, exactly before the gangway, sirens winding down.

"I'll be a sonofabitch. You gotta give it to Dug-Out Doug for showmanship," said a navy captain beside Reynolds.

MacArthur hated the name. Slowly, Reynolds turned his head and gave the man a steely glance worthy of a cadet just before the annual Army–Navy football game. *Dug-Out Doug, indeed.* Then he looked back at MacArthur with pride. Wearing his leather jacket and loose khakis, MacArthur looked like a fighting general, not like the pansies around here with all their damned shiny ribbons. And Reynolds suddenly felt better about his own smelly jungle-rot khakis.

The driver ran around and ripped open the door. As if on cue, the crowd began cheering. Like a bullfighter, MacArthur stood and turned slowly in each direction, waving, grinning, and nodding. The roar grew louder as he continued waving.

"Attention to quarters," growled the chief. "Everyone against the bulkhead, dammit, er please." Eight side buoys fell into place on either side of the gangway, the OOD at the head, the grizzled chief at his side. Behind them hovered Lamar.

MacArthur stepped out of the car and mounted the gangway. Halfway up he stopped, turned, and waved again to the sailors and marines ashore. Again they roared and clapped and whistled. The general milked that one for a long time and then turned and headed toward the quarterdeck, snapping off the obligatory salutes.

A bell rang and the ship's PA announced, "General of the Army, arriving." With perfect tones, the bosun's mate of the watch blew his whistle. MacArthur stepped aboard, saluting the side buoys and OOD. Lamar stepped out from behind, saluted, and accepted the general's outstretched hand. Soon the crowd pressed in, and it seemed everyone wanted to shake hands with MacArthur. Presently, they began walking forward with Lamar leading the way, MacArthur half a step behind. Passing close to Reynolds, the general gave a nod and clapped him on the shoulder.

Reynolds's eyes glistened; he hadn't felt a prouder moment.

Someone else clapped Reynolds on the shoulder. A stocky lieutenant commander with wiry blond hair stood beside him, a lopsided grin on his face. "Owen, my guess would've been the general left you in New Guinea manning a machine gun."

"John. I'll be damned. How the hell are you?" They saluted and shook hands.

"Never better, Owen. You traveling with the general?"

Reynolds made a show of looking in both directions then put a finger to his lips and said quietly, "Shhh. Military secret. Nobody's supposed to know the general is in town."

They grinned. Reynolds was surprised at John Sabovik's

appearance. He looked sallow and thinner than when they'd been fraternity brothers at USC. They'd all gone into the service at graduation; Reynolds hadn't kept up with Sabovik after that. He did learn that Sabovik was aboard the cruiser USS *Tampa* when she was sunk off Guadalcanal in 1942. A quick look at the two rows of ribbons on Sabovik's chest revealed two battle stars and a Purple Heart. Reynolds had his own Purple Heart and battle stars, but the custom in the services was not to wear ribbons on working uniforms. "God, it's good to see you, John. You look great," Reynolds lied. "Last I heard you were on the *Tampa*."

A shadow crossed Sabovik's face. "That's right."

"Where'd you go after that?"

"I was gunnery liaison to the commandant, Twelfth Naval District, in San Francisco. So up until six months ago, I was counting shell casings in San Francisco."

"You're keeping me in suspense."

"Figured I'd been sitting on my ass long enough. So I finagled my way out of the shell-casing business. Transferred to ONI." The Office of Naval Intelligence.

"You what?"

"Gone to school. Everything. Just got out of training at Quantico. Now I'm a spook, so look out."

"That's a career move. You staying in the navy?" Reynolds was surprised. Sabovik hadn't seemed the type to make the navy a career.

He gave a thin smile and said, "Just got my first assignment." He jabbed Reynolds on the chest. "And I got the goods on you, buddy, so watch it."

"Well, that's one for the book. I never thought you'd be such a dedicated citizen." He stuck out his hand, and they shook. "Quantico, huh? Bunch of marines running around, right? They teach you how to march?"

"Speaking of marching, you should have been here half an hour ago." Sabovik waved a hand toward the pier. "A three-star admiral stood out there and lined up ten other admirals in a formation. He was setting them up to march aboard and present them to the president." He nodded to sailors on the pier. "See all those guys out there?"

"Right."

"Well, everybody's watching when this three-star calls, 'Right face!' Two admirals did a left face and screwed everything up. Almost bumped into each other. Sailors and marines out there laughed their butts off." Sabovik gave a low exhale. "But then, I guess they can use a little comic relief. Some won't be coming back."

"I'll say." Reynolds shook his head, then said quietly, "Sorry to hear about Tiny."

Sabovik looked away. "Yeah, we lost a great one, there." His eyes glistened as he turned back to Reynolds. "You know, at the outbreak of the war, he was dating that campus slut I was pinned to?"

"You're kidding. Katherine O'Neil?"

"Can you believe that? She made Tiny think he got her pregnant. Wanted him to marry her."

"I thought she was a movie star."

"Didn't matter. She just wanted to get back at me. By this time, Tiny had made a few bucks pushing stocks. So he hired this Beverly Hills detective and the guy took all sorts of photos of Katherine O'Neil shacking with other guys."

"That shut her up?"

Sabovik looked into the distance. "He even made her pay the detective's expenses: 750 bucks. You know, for such a dumb jock, Tiny really had his head on right."

"Amazing." Reynolds asked, "What's the latest on Mike?"

"Mike who?"

Reynolds smiled. "Mike, Mike, you know."

Sabovik's normally blue eyes turned coal black. "Owen. I don't know anyone named Mike."

An exasperated Reynolds said, "Mike, dammit. Mike Donovan."

Sabovik braced his hands on a stanchion. "Owen, please."

Reynolds started to speak, but someone shouted, "Photo session up forward." With Sabovik, he was swept along as men pressed toward the ship's bow. There four chairs had been placed beneath one of the *Baltimore*'s eight-inch gun turrets. Reynolds and Sabovik squeezed among the officers, seeing MacArthur, Roosevelt, and Nimitz in chairs. Seated with them was Admiral William D. Leahy, Roosevelt's chief of staff. All smiled for three navy photographers, their flashbulbs popping in the midday sun.

Reynolds gasped, "The president looks like hell."

"I'll say," Sabovik agreed. Dark bags ran under Roosevelt's eyes. His face was thin, and his white suit draped about him like a tent. He was seated as if he'd taken his chair like everyone else. In fact, the president had polio and was confined to a wheelchair, now tucked out of sight. He was sensitive about it, and his aides did everything they could to mask the affliction.

"Is it just you, Owen?" asked Sabovik.

"What?" Just then, MacArthur noticed Reynolds and gave a little wave. Reynolds waved back.

"Why isn't General Sutherland here?" Sabovik asked. Lieutenant General Richard Sutherland was MacArthur's chief of staff.

President Roosevelt, his cigarette holder at a jaunty angle, looked over to MacArthur. His expression changed visibly and his face grew red as he stifled a grin. MacArthur's fly was wide open. And the general was distracted, speaking to Vice Admiral Pye off to his right. Reynolds and Sabovik exchanged glances, remembering another time when someone's fly had been open. A very funny time.

Roosevelt beckoned to a photographer and whispered loudly, "Do you see what I see? Hurry, get that shot." He nodded to MacArthur's crotch.

The man fussed with his camera, screwing in a flashbulb. "Trying, sir." The other two photographers were changing film.

Roosevelt giggled. "Quick."

"Right." The flashbulb set, the young photographer dropped to his knee and aimed the camera.

MacArthur looked up and casually crossed one leg over the other, giving the president a steely look. But he made no attempt to zip up.

The flash popped.

"Damn," said a grinning Roosevelt.

"Would have been the shot of the century," said Sabovik.

Reynolds felt a cold rush. There would have been hell to pay if that shot had been taken. And the general would have expected Reynolds to go up there and confiscate the man's film. "What'd you say, John?"

"General Sutherland, why isn't he here?"

"We're traveling light. And they needed someone back in Hollandia to mind the store. So I was elected. Now let me ask you a question."

"Shoot."

"What brings you here?"

"Good question." Sabovik looked around. "You hear about Port Chicago?"

Even though it was classified top secret, Sabovik had seen dispatches. In fact, he'd briefed the general on it just before they took off for their flight to Hawaii. "Of course. That in your bailiwick?"

"Yes, I'm here to brief CinCPac and the president."

"What the hell happened?"

Sabovik scratched his head and lowered his voice. "We're trying to put it together. Five days ago, a Liberty ship exploded while loading ammo at ten thirty at night. All we know is that there was a big bang on the pier. That was bad enough but then six seconds later, the ship blew sky-high. It was an enormous explosion. They felt the shock in San Francisco, all right. Even as far away as in Boulder City, Nevada. Vaporized another Liberty moored across the pier. And she hadn't even loaded yet."

"Good Lord."

"Place looks like a wasteland. Whole damn pier is gone, poof, just disappeared. Buildings smashed flat. Boxcars and trucks thrown hundreds of yards. Ships vaporized. They found a 150-foot section of the *Bryan*'s keel 1,000 feet away, facing the opposite direction. All that remains of anything else is melted chunks of metal, nothing larger than a suitcase.

"And get this. A C-47 was flying over at the time at about nine thousand feet. The flight crew saw the flash of the explosion in the overcast below."

"Yes?"

"They didn't know what was down there. Only that the place lit up brighter than day. And then suddenly, white-hot chunks, the size of automobiles, were whizzing up out of the clouds past them like giant Roman candles."

There was a prolonged silence as Reynolds tried to digest it all. "How many . . ."

"Killed? As far as we know, well over three hundred."

"Any idea what caused it?"

"Well, let's just say that I'm on a team investigating the disaster. My angle is sabotage."

"You think the Japs did it?"

Sabovik shook his head. "Don't know. And after seeing Port Chicago, I have no idea how we're going to figure anything out. I mean, it's like a five-hundred-foot-tall giant jumped up and down on everything. It's all smashed. Nothing recognizable within a thousand yards. Right now I'm just following orders."

Looking off to his right, MacArthur once more spoke to Vice Admiral Pye. Both of his feet were again planted on the deck, his open fly exposed.

Casually, Roosevelt waved at the photographer and smiled mischievously. "Quick, quick, get that shot."

FIVE

27 July 1944
Commanding Officer's Quarters No. 5
U.S. Army Fort Schafter
Oahu, Territory of Hawaii

Fighting a time lag extending over four time zones, Owen Reynolds crawled out of bed early the next morning, a Wednesday. He'd barely wolfed breakfast when a White House staffer called over to ruin his day. Reynolds immediately forgot the man's name, only that he had a squeaky voice and reminded Owen that the agenda called for the president, accompanied by admirals Nimitz and Leahy, and General MacArthur, to tour military installations that morning. The expectation was to wind it up with a parade through Honolulu as if they were grand marshals in the Pasadena Rose Parade.

"Late last night, we discovered the army has provided the president with an enclosed, olive-drab limousine. Not good," Squeaky Voice went on to remonstrate. "The president prefers visibility. He wants an open touring car. What can we do about it?"

"I'll look into it." Owen smashed down the phone and counted to ten. Then he started making calls. He discovered there were only two open touring cars available on Oahu. One was a sedate seven-passenger car owned by the madam of Honolulu's largest whorehouse. The other, belonging to Honolulu's fire chief, was a smaller, bright red five-passenger Buick.

Owen Reynolds and Squeaky Voice collectively decided that discretion dictated the president use the red Buick. Thus the morning tour began with Admiral Leahy climbing in front beside the driver. Stuffed in the Buick's backseat were three of the most powerful men on the planet: Admiral Chester Nimitz, General Douglas MacArthur, and the president of the United States, who waved and grinned to the crowd while puffing mightily on a cigarette jammed in a silver holder.

Things went generally well but the day couldn't end fast enough as far as Reynolds was concerned. He just wasn't used to being an aide—that was General Sutherland's job. But they got through the day without incident, leaving Reynolds free for the evening party. Reynolds looked forward to his first stiff bourbon in six months while someone else worried about whether General Whackety-Whack preferred scotch or gin. The party was to begin with a cocktail hour attended by a number of senior officers from around town—stand-ins, really. After the stand-ins were "excused," there would be a dinner with just ten flag officers. Then the flag officers were to be "excused," the evening capped by a strategy meeting among FDR, Leahy, Nimitz, and MacArthur. Besides a recording secretary, no one else was invited.

The cream-colored stucco mansion was on Kalakaua Avenue overlooking Waikiki's rolling surf. Belonging to Christopher R. Holmes, a millionaire friend of FDR's, it was perfectly laid out to view the golden sunset that greeted Owen Reynolds as he mounted the steps and walked through the ornate front entrance. Voices and laughter beckoned from the living room, but he paused for a moment before a six-foot gold-framed mirror, removed his garrison cap, straightened his tie, and checked the rest of his summer khaki uniform. Satisfied, he stepped in, finding the smoke-filled room jammed with uniforms from all the branches. Large French doors opened on to a patio where more uniforms gathered. A number of women were in attendance, some in uniform, others in evening wear; all were surrounded by officers vying for attention.

Roosevelt sat in a large armchair by the fireplace, chatting and grinning at three marine fighter pilots and a redheaded navy nurse. All fidgeted in the presence of their commander in chief except one marine, who handed his drink to another and began dogfighting with his hands, cheeks puffing with exploding noises as he went. The president's guffaw ranged across the room as Reynolds continued the quest for his bourbon.

"Looking for the bar?" It was John Sabovik. "Army guys never did learn how to find a fueling station." He nodded over his shoulder. "Come on. Orientation exercise."

Looking at Sabovik's drink, Reynolds said drily, "Looks like I have some catching up."

They pulled up before the crowd at the bar and Reynolds asked, "Done your brief on the explosion yet?"

"Ummm, late this afternoon."

"How'd it go?"

"They were as shocked as everyone else. The president especially. He got red in the face. For a while there, I thought he was going to shoot the messenger. He was pretty levelheaded with me. MacArthur and Nimitz, too. But collectively, they are really pissed."

"I don't blame them."

"They're giving the investigation top priority. Right there on the spot, they put me in charge of the West Coast investigation team. And they're giving it the whole works. FBI, everybody."

"Wow. Congratulations. Pretty good for the new guy on the block."

"I know, scares the hell out of me, I tell you."

"But West Coast? You think this is a nationwide plot? Japs? Nazis?"

They reached the bar, and Sabovik stood aside. "Have to consider that possibility." He let Reynolds pass. "After all, we have to—"

Reynolds was puzzled. Sabovik's face was growing red. "What is it, John?"

Sabovik's lips pressed together and turned white.

Reynolds spun. A man stood there, a drink in his hand. A navy commander, he had two rows of battle ribbons and his smile was . . . fading as quickly as John's. Then it hit him.

"Mike. Sonofabitch, Mike Donovan, how the hell are you?" Reynolds thrust out a hand.

Mike Donovan's dark blue eyes darted from Reynolds to

Sabovik. Quickly his expression matched that of Sabovik. "Owen," Donovan said softly, still looking at Sabovik.

Reynolds felt as if he were standing on Guadalcanal's Bloody Ridge between a BAR-armed marine and a Japanese charging with a samurai sword. Strange, he thought, since the three of them were very close. "Mike? What the hell?"

Sabovik spun and disappeared into the crowd.

Donovan looked unfocused for a moment, then said evenly, "Owen, good to see you." They shook.

"Mike . . . I don't understand." Reynolds waved at the crowd where Sabovik had gone.

Donovan gave a polite cough and said, "You look thin as hell, Owen. Doesn't the army feed you?"

"New Guinea. Being at the end of the food chain means you eat scraps, even if you are on the general's staff."

"General's staff. I thought you went infantry."

"I did, then I got shot up on Bougainville. Took a bullet right in my butt."

"Sorry to hear that. Whose staff are you on?"

Just then a hand reached from a curtain and tapped Reynolds on the shoulder. Douglas MacArthur leaned in from the dining room and said, "Sorry to interrupt, Owen. Would you please be so good as to run the slide projector for me tonight?"

"Glad to, General," said Reynolds. "Oh, please meet a friend of mine, Mike Donovan."

MacArthur reached out and shook warmly. "Pleasure to meet you, Commander." Noting Donovan's battle stars, he added, "Whose navy are you in?"

"Yours, I believe, General. I'm en route to San Francisco to take command of the USS *Matthew,* a new destroyer. After a shakedown, we're to join Admiral Kinkaid and the Seventh Fleet in New Guinea."

"Well then, welcome, son."

"Thank you, sir. My pleasure."

MacArthur paused, and Reynolds knew it was time to fill in details. "Mike and I grew up in Southern California. He went to Van Nuys High and I went to North Hollywood High. Our football teams were archenemies." He winked at Donovan.

Donovan grinned. "I was the quarterback for Van Nuys. Score was tied for the big game at seven–seven with two minutes to go. We were on their thirty. I threw a pass. Owen intercepted it and ran it all the way back. I'll never forgive him."

"I see. Who won the game?" asked MacArthur.

Reynolds smiled. Donovan shrugged.

The corners of MacArthur's mouth turned up. "Still playing it over in your minds, eh?"

"Yes, sir," both responded.

"Ummm. And then you"—he nodded to Reynolds—"went to USC and you, Commander, went to . . ."

". . . USC," said Donovan. "We were too small to play varsity football, but we did play intramural. This time, as friends. We were in the same fraternity."

"Perfect. It's the stuff great officers are made of." MacArthur stuck out his hand. "Welcome to SOWESPAC, son. Please let me know if I can do anything for you." The general walked away.

"You're working for him?" asked Donovan.

"Indirectly. I work for General Willoughby, his intelligence aide."

Donovan nodded to the ribbons on Reynolds's chest, the Purple Heart among them. "What happened on Bougainville?"

"Well, let's just say I won't be playing football for a while."

"Come on, dammit."

Reynolds shrugged. "Jap ambush. Got my head down but I couldn't get my butt down far enough."

"You really were shot in the ass?"

"You have two choices when flat on the ground and fired upon. Either your head or your ass. You can't get both down at the same time. Which would you pick?"

Donovan grinned. "It's not what you say. It's the way you say it."

"It only hurts when I laugh," said Reynolds. "You'd be surprised at everything your ass muscles do for you. I can't run and sometimes I have trouble standing. That means I can't go back to the infantry. So instead of getting out, I went to intelligence school. Now I'm a staffer and that's it."

"Not bad. Combat experience helps, I'll bet."

"It really does."

"But you could have gotten a medical discharge, right?"

Reynolds shrugged. "They offered me one. But then I thought about Tiny."

Donovan looked down.

"Why the hell should I sit around on my dead butt when Tiny is . . . is"—he waved toward the Pacific—"still out there?"

Donovan gazed in the distance.

"Sorry, it must have been rough for you and John, being on the same ship and all."

"It was."

"Is that what's at the bottom of this?"

"Owen, I'm famished. You want to go have dinner?"

Reynolds was mystified. "Mike, is there anything I can do?"

Donovan met his gaze. "Let me buy your dinner. You name the place."

Reynolds downed his bourbon. "All right, dammit. But I've got a better idea. Remember, I have to run the slides for General MacArthur?"

President Roosevelt, generals MacArthur and Richardson, admirals Leahy and Nimitz, and six other admirals were inside dining on mahi mahi, a specialty dish prepared by Admiral Nimitz's cook. Alone on the veranda were Owen Reynolds and Mike Donovan, watching the luminescent surf crash seventy-five feet away. They sat at a table, under an umbrella that stirred with the soft evening breeze.

"Troy Week," sniffed Reynolds. "How'd we ever make it through all that nonsense?" They'd been reliving their days at USC.

"Beats me," sighed Donovan pushing away a plate. "Ummm, that was great, Owen." He sipped wine. "Never had mahi mahi before." He relished in the fact that they'd been served the same meal as the president.

Donovan sounded glum, and Reynolds wondered why. There was no moon and the night was dark. With the house blacked out, it was hard to read his face.

A curtain rustled. A white-coated Navarro stepped out and

walked over to Reynolds. In a heavily accented Filipino voice, he said, "General MacArthur sends his respects, Colonel, and asks if you can be ready in five minutes?"

Reynolds replied, "Tell the general the equipment is all set, Navarro, and so am I. Also, please add our thanks for the fine meal."

"I will do that, sahr." Navarro turned and left.

Reynolds sipped and said, "Damn, this wine is good. A taste of home, I'd forgotten what it was like."

"Few and far between," agreed Donovan, smacking his lips.

"So, you still haven't told me what happened," asked Reynolds.

A wave pounded as Donovan looked into the anthracite sky. "It happened on the *Tampa*."

"When?"

"The night she was blown out from under us. Tiny's birthday, November 30, 1942. Right off Guadalcanal, Lunga Point."

Donovan looked up. "John Sabovik has vowed to kill me."

SIX

27 July 1944
Holmes residence
Honolulu, Territory of Hawaii

A ship's horn hooted mournfully in the distance as a wave cracked, shooting a white-luminescent water column fifteen feet in the air. Stars raged overhead in a clear, moonless sky as the odor of drying reef, salt, and decaying kelp drifted across the lawn. An exhausted Donovan sipped lemon-flavored ice water and lowered the cut-crystal glass, hoping Reynolds couldn't see the moisture gathered under his eyes. At length, he risked putting up his hand and wiped it away. Another wave pounded and he managed, "We thought we knew it all. Everything gleaming, the *Tampa* just out of overhaul with a bunch of new stuff: fire control radar. TBS.[3] CIC[4]! In fact, we didn't know our asses from a hot rock . . ."

"So the Japs came in swinging hard."

"Surprised the hell out of us and kicked our butts."

"How?"

"Torpedoes." Donovan shook his head. "We were so stupid. We were firing smokeless gunpowder, you know, the stuff used for daytime shooting. Every time we fired, we lit up the night like it was Hollywood and Vine." He sniffed. "Hell, what a target we were. A kid could have hit us with a slingshot at twenty thousand yards. So His Imperial Majesty sends two torpedoes into us. One opened up a fuel bunker and sprayed fuel oil all over the place. Now we're lit up like a bonfire. With that, the Nips poured the six- and eight-inch into us. Tiny was in the number three turret. They were firing pretty good when a powder case cooked off inside. That was it . . . they were incinerated . . ."

"Did you see it happen?"

"Yes." Donovan gulped more water.

"Mike, dammit. This is ripping you up. How can you command a ship?"

"Um. Compared to this, commanding a ship is easy, believe it or not. This has stayed with me."

"Why? What's different?"

Donovan waved a hand in the dark.

Reynolds leaned over and slapped Donovan on the knee. "Mike, dammit, you know better. It's not your fault."

The living room curtain rustled and Navarro stepped outside, his white coat as luminescent as the waves. "They're ready, sahr," he said in his Filipino accent.

"On my way, Navarro." Reynolds stood and said to Donovan, "Lend a hand?"

"In there? With the president and—"

"You bet. Come on. You'll meet Art Lamar, Nimitz's aide."

"Lamar? I'm supposed to see him tomorrow. All right. I'll try anything once. Just don't blame me if we're busted." Donovan rose, and they walked toward the house.

Reynolds said, "What I'm trying to tell you, Mike, is to let it go."

"I know what you're trying to do," Donovan said. "But I have to live with it. It was me who gave the order for Tiny to be in that gun turret. John wanted him in operations. I wanted him in the gunnery department. We played a sort of tug-of-war, friendly competition. The captain bought my story and . . . Tiny ended up in the aft gun turret."

"Did you pull the trigger for the round that hit the mount?"

"Come on, Owen."

"Of course not. Some Jap did. So go take it out on them, not yourself, dammit." Reynolds swept aside the curtain. It was a light lock; he stepped through another curtain into the living room, now dimly lit. A Secret Service agent wearing a .45-caliber pistol in a shoulder holster was seated behind a card table, stamping documents. He ran his eyes over them for a moment, then went back to his stamping.

Donovan shook his head. "I know, I know. It's just that John—"

"Did he really say that, that he wanted to kill you? I mean that doesn't sound like John."

"You're telling me. But he did say that. It was two days later, aboard a hospital ship anchored in Tulagi. He walked up to me and said, 'Don't get too comfortable, Mike. Because I'm going to kill you for what you did to Tiny.' Then he walked off. That's the last time we spoke. He flew out the next day. All the letters I sent have been returned unopened."

"Damn, I better talk to him."

"You know where to find him?"

"Not until yesterday. He told me he's in the intelligence business now, working for ONI."

"Really? Where?"

"Don't know." Reynolds stroked his chin. "But then I'm in the intelligence business, too. And I work for a guy who knows how to break barriers and get answers." He pitched a thumb over his shoulder toward the room where General MacArthur was meeting.

They eased past two marine guards and walked into a darkened butler's pantry. Three carts were lined up, one with a sixteen-millimeter movie projector, another with the loudspeaker, and the third with a slide projector, film, and paraphernalia stacked on the shelves beneath. Lieutenant Lamar was there with a flashlight.

"All set, Art?" said Reynolds.

Fussing with extension cords, Lamar looked up.

"Say hello to Mike Donovan," said Reynolds.

Lamar flashed a quick smile and whispered, "Of the USS *Matthew*?" They shook.

"*McDermott* now, *Matthew* later. I believe we meet tomorrow afternoon," said Donovan.

"Yes, sir." Lamar gave Reynolds a quick glance and said in a low voice, "Right, Colonel. Cognac has been poured; they're just starting. Are your slides organized the way you want them?"

"Yes. And the gouge[5] over on that table is for you."

"Okay." Lamar opened the door.

Voices drifted in. Roosevelt was saying, "Well, Douglas, where do we go from here?"

"Leyte, Mr. President," MacArthur replied, "we land right here in Leyte Gulf. Once secured, we can easily take Luzon and Manila."

They heard a cracking sound, like a pointer slapping a blackboard.

Reynolds elbowed Donovan and whispered. "We keep our heads down, got it? Like flies on a wall."

"Got it." Donovan stepped behind the cart with the slide projector.

Lamar hunched over the cart with the loudspeaker. "Psst! Go," he whispered.

They shoved the carts into a large room where one wall was dominated by a large world map. Roosevelt smoked a cigarette. Admirals Nimitz and Leahy were seated comfortably in rattan chairs. MacArthur stood before the map, directing a long wooden pointer toward the Philippines. A chief petty officer sat in a corner with a stenography machine.

"But Douglas," Roosevelt said through a cloud of his smoke. "To take Luzon would demand heavier losses than we can stand."

MacArthur shot back, "Mr. President, my losses would not be heavy, any more than they have been in the past. The days of frontal attack should be over. Modern infantry weapons are too deadly, and frontal assault is only for mediocre commanders. Good commanders do not turn in heavy losses."

Reynolds lined his cart alongside the others and stooped to fuss with an extension cord. It was obvious Lamar and Donovan were as fascinated as he was with the general's presentation.

MacArthur continued, "Besides, we can't bypass Luzon, Mr. President. Our flank would be exposed as we press the attack north to the Japanese Home Islands."

"Ummm," Roosevelt said. A poker-faced Nimitz sipped coffee and nodded.

MacArthur's voice rose a bit as he lowered the pointer and looked directly at Roosevelt. "Mr. President, promises must be kept. If we blockaded a bypassed Philippines, the Japanese would steal their food and subject the population to misery and starvation." He doubled a fist and said, "Consigning the Filipinos to the bayonets of an enraged army of occupation would be a blot on American honor. In the postwar, all Asian eyes will be on the emerging Philippine Republic. If her people thought she had been sold out, the reputation of the United States would be sullied with a stain that could never be removed."

Silence reigned as MacArthur reached for a water glass and drank. Reynolds, Donovan, and Lamar stood watching, completely taken by MacArthur's eloquence . . . and his audacity.

The general delivered his coup de grâce. "I daresay the American people would be so aroused that they would register most complete resentment against you at the polls this fall."

Nimitz looked up and shot Lamar and Reynolds a steely look.

"Come on," whispered Reynolds. They filed out into the living room, where Lamar sat and rummaged through file folders.

Donovan grabbed his cover and said, "Whew. Your boss is one hell of a speaker. I thought for a moment there it was Laurence Olivier playing Hamlet."

Reynolds grinned. "He does have his way, doesn't he?" Then he said, "We have a driver outside. His name is Sergeant McCormick. He'll take you anywhere you want. Don't worry about the car, I'll return with the general." Reynolds stuck out a hand. "Good luck with your new ship. And oh yeah, thanks for the help in there."

They shook. "And thank you for the mahi mahi," said Donovan.

"Enjoy your time stateside, Mike. And remember what I said."

Donovan's face went dark for a moment. "Don't worry about me, Owen. You just stay away from Japs. You've done your share. Don't forget to write, will you?"

They looked at each other and laughed. Neither had written since the war broke out.

"Psst! Colonel. They're ready." It was Lamar.

"Right." Reynolds winked. "Don't forget what I said, Mike."

Donovan thumped his chest. "Got it right here." He turned and walked out, looking for Sergeant McCormick.

SEVEN

28 July 1944
CinCPac quarters
Makalapa, Territory of Hawaii

Admiral Nimitz's living quarters were situated a short distance from his headquarters halfway up Makalapa, an extinct volcano overlooking Pearl Harbor. It was a beautiful day, the spectacular view taking in Pearl Harbor to the right and Honolulu to the left. For lunch, Nimitz's cook had scored one of his many triumphs: prime rib with a horseradish that could, as reported by Vice Admiral Charles H. McMorris, Nimitz's chief of staff, peel paint. President Roosevelt sat at the table's head. Admiral Nimitz was to the president's right, General MacArthur to his left. The rest of the combined staffs completed a seating for twelve. As tradition dictated, Lieutenant Lamar, the junior officer, sat at the end of the table opposite the president. Lieutenant Colonel Owen Reynolds sat at the end on Lamar's left. The rest of the diners were either admirals or captains.

Admiral Halsey, just in from an emergency leave on the mainland to visit his wife, Fanny, dominated the table talk. Quite at ease with his commander in chief, Halsey launched into some of the most raucous, off-color stories Reynolds had ever heard. They lasted through the main course and well into dessert.

To Reynolds's left was Captain Tom Anderson, Nimitz's housemate and fleet surgeon, who was explaining how light exercise cured the admiral of the shakes and even amnesia. "It began with pistol shooting prescribed by Gendreau," said Anderson, referring to his predecessor, Captain Elphege Al-fred M. Gendreau, killed a few months earlier in the Munda operation in the Solomons. "Look at the admiral now," said Anderson between bites of lemon sherbet. "Exercise is the best nostrum for tension. He takes long walks, swims, and—"

For some reason, Reynolds turned toward the head of the table. MacArthur looked straight at him and gave a slight nod. *I'm ready.*

Protocol dictated that Reynolds ask the president for permission to leave the table. But the president at the moment was eating sherbet and listening closely to another of Halsey's jokes. Interrupt Halsey and you'll be not just court-martialed, but castrated. So Reynolds turned to Anderson and said, "Excuse me, Captain? I'm being called."

"Of course."

Reynolds rose and stepped into the hall to look for his briefcase. But the hall and living room were crowded, and it was almost impossible to move amid the jumble of aides, stewards, marines, and Secret Service agents. He found Navarro. "The general's ready. Get the car."

"Yes, sahr," said Navarro, walking out the door.

Reynolds was surprised to see an expectant-looking Mike Donovan sitting in a corner. He walked over. "Mike, what in the hell are you doing here?"

Donovan shrugged. "Meeting, remember? They bumped it up from four o'clock with a note saying the admiral would like to see me at one PM, instead. So I thought I'd better get my butt over here."

"Why Nimitz? Is something wrong?"

"No, no. They tell me the admiral likes to meet his skippers. You know, Texas-style." Donovan lowered his voice to a bass falsetto and said, "Kick him and see what he smells like." Nimitz was from Texas and spoke with a slight drawl.

"Well, it's a good time. It's breaking up in there. And the general's taking off immediately. So maybe you'll get in soon."

"Okay."

"Have to go, Mike. Good luck."

"And to you, Owen."

Reynolds found his briefcase and walked back into the

dining room to stand directly behind MacArthur. Halsey had launched into another joke, one quite graphic that had the whole table roaring. Reynolds pulled out two large envelopes and handed them over MacArthur's shoulder.

MacArthur accepted them without looking and then slid his chair back just as Halsey finished his joke. It became quiet. All eyes were fixed on MacArthur as he stood and said, "Please excuse me, Mr. President. I must be on my way." He reached to shake Roosevelt's hand. "Thank you for a most pleasant visit."

Roosevelt shook warmly and replied, "Douglas, I enjoyed every moment. But Chester here was really your host. I hope you two see things differently now."

MacArthur said, "Please be assured, Chester and I see eye to eye, Mr. President. We understand each other perfectly." He reached across and shook with Nimitz. "Thank you for your wonderful hospitality."

Chairs scraped as everyone, except the president, stood.

"Not at all. Hurry back," said Nimitz.

"Right after we meet in Tokyo," said MacArthur.

"I'll drink to that," growled Halsey.

Men around the table nodded and smiled. MacArthur said to Nimitz and the president, "I have something for you." He nodded to Reynolds and then began walking around the table shaking hands.

That was Reynolds's cue. "Mr. President, this is for you." He handed over a large flat envelope. "And this one's for you, Admiral." He passed another flat envelope to Nimitz. Both opened their envelopes to find an eight-by-ten glossy photo of General Douglas MacArthur.

FDR called out, "Thank you for that nice inscription, Douglas." He added, "And please tell your boys out there that Eleanor's and my thoughts and hopes and prayers are with every one of them."

MacArthur replied from across the room, "It will be my pleasure to do that, Mr. President." He nodded to everyone. "Good luck to you all."

He started to turn when FDR called, "And Douglas."

"Yes, sir?"

"I like the Tokyo idea. Don't let up until you get there. And Godspeed to you all."

"Thank you, Mr. President."

MacArthur, Reynolds, and Navarro rode in a command car to Hickam Field. Two motorcycles were in front, no sirens this time. Another command car, loaded with luggage, trailed behind. It was silent as MacArthur fidgeted and muttered to himself during the twenty-minute ride. Once inside the gate, they drove slowly past soldiers standing in formation, MacArthur saluting as they passed. "Magnificent. Just look at these magnificent men," he said.

Soon they were alongside his B-17, the two port engines already turning over. They dismounted. MacArthur strode over to General Richardson and his staff, who stood at parade rest off to the right. While MacArthur dispensed farewells and banalities, Reynolds cursed and sweated as he helped Navarro hand bags, crates, and equipment up to a flight sergeant in the B-17's yawning bomb bay.

Soon everyone was aboard except MacArthur. That was the way the general liked it: last one in. The pilot started the other two engines and still they waited. Finally the waist hatch burst open and Navarro reached to help MacArthur inside. A glance outside told Reynolds that General Richardson was holding the hatch against the windblast from the starboard engines.

The plane began taxiing as soon as the hatch was shut. That was how they'd orchestrated it, General Richardson be damned. Reynolds hoped he'd had time to grab his hat and jump out of the way of the B-17's stabilizer.

MacArthur fell into the seat beside Reynolds, his eyes gleaming. He pounded Reynolds on the knee and shouted, "We've sold it!"

Donovan wasn't supposed to be there when the president was wheeled out the back door. But they let him stay, and Donovan made a show of averting his eyes. Soon they were gone, leaving the first floor a mess. To make things worse, workmen walked in and started pounding and prying boards in the back hall and doorways, the noise incredible.

Lamar walked in and had to shout. "All set, Commander?"

Donovan made a point of screwing a finger in his ear. "Right," he yelled.

Lamar led Donovan out the front door toward the headquarters building. Once outside, Lamar said, "Took ten Seabees to rip up the hallways doorjambs and downstairs toilet to make room for the president's wheelchair. Painted it all late last night and dried it with blowtorches. Now the process is being reversed and they're putting the place back together." He opened a door for Donovan.

Nodding to a marine sergeant, they walked into the air-conditioned comfort of CinCPac headquarters. "Here we are, Commander. Zero Zero has only five minutes."

"Zero Zero is the admiral?"

"His fleet designator. Then he's off to join the president at Aiea"—Aiea was a major naval hospital.

Donovan raised his eyebrows.

"The president wants to see the wounded coming in from Guam. And here, he intends to be pushed in his wheelchair through the wards, showing he knows what it's like to have dead legs and that he has risen above his affliction." Lamar knocked on a door, stuck in his head, and said something. Then he came out. "Okay, Commander. He'll see you now. He's on the phone, but go right on in. He's almost finished."

"Thanks." Donovan walked in. Nimitz, the phone cradled on his shoulder, looked up and waved to a pair of split-bamboo chairs before his desk. Donovan sat, looking around an airy office. The window drapes matched the chair's flowered cushions. The admiral's desk was a busy clutter of papers, a machine-gun model, and a metal bumblebee stamped with CAN DO, the motto of the Seabees. Next to the phone was a framed picture of Douglas MacArthur, the one Owen Reynolds had passed out about an hour ago. Maps were fastened to the walls, and a barometer was attached to a pipe behind the admiral's desk.

Reynolds's eyes flicked to the opposite wall where he spotted a sign:

1. IS THE PROPOSED OPERATION LIKELY TO SUCCEED?

2. WHAT MIGHT BE THE CONSEQUENCES OF FAILURE?
3. IS IT IN THE REALM OF PRACTICABILITY OF MATERIALS AND SUPPLIES?

Nimitz said very little except "uh-huh, uh-huh." But something behind the desk had his attention; he kept reaching down.

Finally Nimitz drawled, "Okay, let me know when we're ready. Very well." He hung up and stood, saying, "Welcome, Commander. Thanks for taking the time to see me."

"Pleasure's all mine, Admiral." Donovan stood and they shook. That's when he saw a gray tail thumping the rattan floor mat beneath the desk.

"Meet my buddy Makalapa." Nimitz reached under the desk and dragged out a gray, sleepy-looking schnauzer. "Spruance gave him to me. What do you think, Donovan? Should I keep him?" Nimitz scratched the dog's ears. Makalapa gave a wide yawn, then waddled beneath the desk and plopped down.

Donovan said, "I'd be the last one to make Admiral Spruance angry, Admiral. Looks like you're stuck."

Nimitz gave a thin smile. "Turns out, I've become attached to the damn thing anyway. Goes everywhere with me. On walks; he even swims with me. Cries like hell when I kick him off the bed at night."

"I'd put that in his fitness report, Admiral."

Nimitz laughed this time. "I like to know my skippers. Makes me feel close to the fleet. But remember this, even if you are going to MacArthur's navy. You're still mine."

"Thank you, sir."

"So you're on your way to the West Coast and your first command. What is it?"

"Destroyer, Admiral. USS *Matthew,* a *Fletcher*-class coming out of Bethlehem Steel in San Francisco."

A shadow crossed Nimitz's face. "Ahh, I heard about that. Too bad." He was recalling that the *Matthew,* after completing her fitting out, had worked up with a fleet training group with a rigorous set of battle problems and had been declared ready for deployment overseas. Then her skipper was killed in an auto wreck.

Donovan looked away. "Tom Drake was a good man. We were ensigns together on the *Mugford.*"

"Indeed, he was," said Nimitz. "But then you have a fine record, too. I'm sure you'll do a bang-up job."

"Thank you, sir." He ran a hand over his forehead, realizing he was sweating.

Nimitz looked in the distance for a moment. "The *Mugford.* Arleigh Burke once commanded her."

"Yes, sir. But we just missed him. We detached just before he stepped aboard."

"But then you served in the Little Beavers." *Little Beaver*—of the radio show *Red Ryder*—was the logo for Destroyer Squadron 23, made famous by Commodore Arleigh Burke in the Solomons campaign.

Donovan caught a gleam in Nimitz's eye. The admiral had done his homework and knew far more about Donovan than he'd suspected. "Yes, sir. When I first reported aboard the *McDermott,* I was the gun boss. We had quite a time."

"Ever hear Burke comment on something being importantly stupid."

"All the time, Admiral."

"He ever talk about the *Vincennes*?"

"No, sir."

"Arleigh was being kind." Nimitz's jaw muscles rippled for a moment. "There were many importantly stupid things we did at the battle of Savo Island." In August 1942 the Japanese had mauled a disorganized American fleet one night in a torpedo-and-gunfire action off Guadalcanal, sinking three American heavy cruisers, *Vincennes, Astoria,* and *Quincy,* and the Australian cruiser *Canberra,* all within half an hour. Astoundingly, the Japanese suffered no ship losses.

"Well, the one importantly stupid example that really takes the cake is when the Japs were beginning to register hits on the *Vincennes* at Savo Island. Her skipper was convinced he was under friendly fire. So he ordered their largest searchlight trained on the flag. Naturally, the Japs really poured it in. The *Vincennes* was gone within ten minutes."

Donovan took out a handkerchief and dabbed his brow. "Hadn't heard that one, Admiral."

"It hasn't been widely disseminated. But I'm sure years from now, when we're all old and sitting around the cracker barrel, the naval warfare schools will feature things like that."

The lesson was obvious. "Thank you, sir."

"Now the shoe is on the other foot. Many Japs in decision-making roles are young and untrained. We're seeing more and more examples of importantly stupid things they're doing. But the Japs aren't done with us yet. They have plenty of fight left."

"I'll say, Admiral."

There was an awkward silence, both realizing what had happened to the *McDermott.*

"You going to take some time off?" asked Nimitz.

"Actually, I have thirty days coming up. But I'm kind of anxious to see my ship, sir."

Nimitz's eyes glistened for a moment. "The young line officer in me says, *Go right now. See your ship.* But that's been tempered by nearly forty years in the service. That voice says, *Go, take your leave. We need you fresh and rested when you take command.*" He fixed Donovan with the same steely glance he'd offered the night before in the Holmes residence.

"I believe I'll take my leave, Admiral."

"Good. And to get things going, we're detaching you from the *McDermott* now and flying you to the mainland."

Donovan was at a loss for words. Home. He hadn't been there in more than two years. And now, instead of riding the slow boat, he'd be home in a matter of days; hours maybe. Yet he hated leaving the *McDermott,* his home away from home for so long. His thoughts flashed to his crew, his officers. They'd been through so much together. "I—"

Nimitz bored in. "Where is your family?"

"San Fernando Valley, Admiral. Uh . . . California. My dad owns a drugstore there."

"Perfect. I'll make sure Art gets you on the soonest air transport to CONUS." Nimitz smiled and looked out toward Pearl Harbor for a moment. "The *Matthew.* Richard Kruger is her exec?"

"Yes, sir. So I've heard."

"And he's in temporary command?"

"Yes, sir. Apparently they're holding her dockside until I report aboard."

"Kruger is a good man. He should keep them in good shape for you."

Donovan was surprised. Nimitz seemed familiar with the *Matthew*'s executive officer. "You know him, sir?" Nimitz steepled his fingers and leaned back in his chair. "Richard served under me when I had the *Augusta.*" Nimitz had been skipper of the cruiser *Augusta* in the mid-1930s. "He's a mustang. Up from chief machinist's mate. Really knows his stuff. Made him our MPA. Did a great job. Trouble was, he knew more than my chief engineer, a full commander. Dick ran the poor fellow's tail off." Staring into the distance, he said, "Hmm, only ten years, but it seems so long ago."

Lamar stuck his head in the door. "Pardon me, Admiral, the president's party is ready to head on over to Aiea. They're accelerating the schedule."

"You mean now?" Nimitz snapped.

"Afraid so, sir," said Lamar.

"Just when I was getting to know—say, are you all right?" Nimitz's eyebrows went up.

A bolt of pain ripped through Donovan's abdomen, and he felt himself on the edge of blackness. *What the hell?* He wanted to double up and grab his belly.

"Sir?" Lamar was beside Donovan, his hand on his shoulder, keeping him from pitching out of his chair.

Nimitz came from around the desk.

Donovan blinked and looked up into their faces.

"Look how white he is," Nimitz said softly. "Call Captain Anderson, Art."

"Sorry, sir," Donovan gasped. "No need to call the doc," he managed.

Lamar, phone in mid-dial, looked up.

"My quinine. Forgot to take it this morning," said Donovan. Actually he did feel a little better.

"What is it, malaria?" asked Nimitz.

"Yes, sir," said Donovan, accepting a glass of water from

Lamar. "Drank some bad water one day on Guadalcanal. Fouled me up for a while, but I'm on the tail end of it now."

Nimitz brightened. "Damn. That happened to me after my first trip out there. Put me on my back for two weeks."

"I'm fine, Admiral. Just need to get to my quinine." Donovan rose, still feeling shaky. His belly felt warm, almost hot, but the pain was gone and his footing was okay. "Thank you, sir."

"Well, all right. But I want you to see a doctor just the same. Make sure all those bugs are out of your system." Nimitz grabbed his hat and steered Donovan toward the door. "Best of luck with the *Matthew,* Commander. Give 'em hell for me, will you?"

"You bet I will, Admiral," said Donovan.

"Don't forget to check in with the doc."

"Yes, sir. Thanks for your time."

"Good-bye." Nimitz and Lamar turned and headed down the hall.

Donovan walked across the shiny green linoleum surface to a scuttlebutt. The water was chilled and felt good going down. Feeling better, he headed for the parking lot. What the hell was that? he wondered. He'd never been ashore at Guadalcanal. And he sure as hell had never had malaria.

EIGHT

1 August 1944
Oak Knoll Naval Hospital
Oakland, California

The doctor was towheaded, had crystal-blue eyes and not a hint of a beard. And yet the diploma on the wall of his closet-size office said the lieutenant junior grade had graduated from the University of Washington's medical school in 1941. Another diploma specified that he'd served his internship at San Diego's Mercy Hospital. Both diplomas stipulated the man's name:

HORACE T. DUBERMAN, MD

A trophy with a bow and arrow sitting on a pile of magazines stated:

HORACE DUBERMAN—SAN DIEGO ARCHERY CENTER
SECOND PLACE

Horace was an archer who tried to make up for his youthful appearance with a somber façade. Donovan only hoped that Duberman was better as a doctor than as a second-place archer.

Donovan offered a hand and said, "Mike Donovan."

Duberman's smile was thin, his hand cold and near comatose. "What can I do for you?"

After Donovan explained his condition, the doctor ordered him to remove his tie, shirt, and lie back. Probing his belly, he asked, "Are you experiencing any pain, Commander?"

"Experiencing pain? Do you mean . . . Lieutenant, *Does it hurt?*"

"Yes."

"Once in a while."

"Now?"

"No."

The doctor probed some more, then said, "Sit up, please." Making a great show of unlimbering his stethoscope, he listened to Donovan's chest and heart. "Breathe deeply, please."

"I'll do my best."

"Thank you."

So much for this guy's bedside manner.

Duberman pushed his stethoscope around and then said, "Okay, you can relax."

"You want to put that thing against my head, Doc? Might hear the latest hula music from Hawaii."

The doctor didn't blink as he checked Commander Donovan's eyes, ears, and nose. Then he stepped back. "You can put your shirt on."

"Thanks."

"I see from your file that you've had, ahhh, extensive combat experience."

"Experience?"

"Well, yes, you know, combat. Contact with the enemy."

"Contact?"

"Please, Commander, I'm trying to help you."

"Let me put it this way, Lieutenant. The Japs have done their best to separate my ass from the rest of my body. But somehow, I've foiled their plot and survived."

"Ummm." The doctor nodded solemnly while flipping pages in Donovan's medical record. "How's your appetite?"

"Now that I'm home, I can report that I'll be eating like a pig."

"I see. And how about your sleep?"

"Well, it's like I said. Sometimes I have nightmares that scare the daylights out of me. I wake up sweating."

"What are your dreams about?"

Donovan ran his tie under his collar and began the four-in-hand knot. "Same one. We're aboard the *Tampa,* John and Tiny and me." He explained the nightmare.

"I see. Your medical file here says you've been in combat, more or less, over a period of twenty-one months."

"More or less."

Dr. Duberman ran his finger down a page. "See here. You had a ship blown out from under you. The cruiser *Tampa*."

"Lieutenant, that's what I've been telling you."

Dr. Duberman looked up with curious blue eyes. "Have you ever had a mental evaluation?"

"You think I'm a head case?"

"Well, it could help to—"

"Bullshit! Just give me something for a restful night's sleep. I've got a ship waiting for me." Donovan finished with his tie and turned to face the doctor, fists jammed on his hips. "That's all I need."

Young Dr. Duberman rubbed his chin. "Very well. Report to the lab. I want to see some blood work and a urinalysis. If they're okay, then we'll put you on something."

"Like what?"

Duberman shrugged. "Belladonna, possibly."

"What's that?"

"Stomach tranquilizer. Helps you sleep, too."

"You think that will take care of it?" He began to straighten his tie.

"Yes, it should work." Dr. Duberman scratched on a form and handed it over. "Here's your lab slip. Go down there now, give the samples, and then report back here tomorrow morning at 0900. If everything's okay, I'll give you a six-month supply."

"Thanks, Doc." Donovan reached to shake the man's hand, but Dr. Duberman had walked out.

That afternoon, Donovan got a priority telephone clearance from the Alameda Naval Air Station switchboard and put a call through to his home in Sherman Oaks, California. His mother, Mary, answered and was overjoyed to learn her oldest son had returned to the States. But soon she broke down, and Donovan thought he was going to start crying as well. Fortunately, the phone booth was in the bachelor officers' quarters lobby; people walked to and fro, giving a detached sense of reality.

"When can we expect you, son?" she asked.
"Right after I see Carmen Rossi in Rocklin."
"Who's that?"
"Skipper's wife. We, ahhh, lost him out there. I was the closest to him; it's my job to talk to her."
She sniffed for a moment. "Mikey, I'm so sorry. Are you all right?"
"I'm fine, Mom."
"Do you have to go far?"
"Oh, no. Rocklin is southeast of Sacramento, about thirty or forty miles. I take the train there."
"Oh."
"Mom. They're giving me command of a ship, a destroyer."
"Oh, your dad will be so proud."
"How is Dad? How's the store?" Ray Donovan owned Donovan's, a popular neighborhood drugstore on Ventura Boulevard. He'd been one of the first to install a soda fountain and jukebox, making the store popular with teenagers.
"I wish I knew."
"Pardon?"
"The store is doing fine. I work there a lot since my boys are gone." Mary Donovan was also a pharmacist.
"Working your fingers to the bone, is he?"
"He wouldn't know."
"What?"
"Right now, Ray's out buying real estate."
"What for?"
Mary Donovan's voice turned to a whisper. "Remember the panic after Pearl Harbor?"
"You bet." After the long string of Japanese victories in the Pacific, many local landowners were convinced the Japanese were going to strike California next. Quite a few sold homes and businesses, especially near the coast.
"There's a lot of storefront property available on Ventura Boulevard out in Tarzana and Woodland Hills. Last week, he bought a city block in Encino. He wants to build a Signal gas station at the corner of White Oak and Ventura. That's phase one."
"What's phase two?"

"A new Donovan's drugstore, right beside it. Phase three will be a bowling alley on the other side. Doesn't that sound keen?"

"Mom, that intersection is out in the sticks. He'll lose his shirt."

"That's what I keep saying, but you know your father: firing both barrels all the time."

"Well, I hope Hopalong Cassidy's horse burns ethyl."

The family had survived the Depression fairly well with the drugstore, even at a time when a lot of friends and neighbors had been hit hard. Now Donovan visualized his white-haired, cigar-chomping father losing it all, ending up in the poorhouse. He could see his dad digging ditches for a TVA dam or something. "Mom, are you okay?"

"Goodness' sakes, we're fine. How about you?"

He decided to pop the question. "Mom, what do you know about belladonna?" He pulled the bandage off his arm where the lab technician had drawn blood.

"Well, it—say—who wants to know?"

"Ah, a buddy of mine has to take it. He's worried that it could cut into his ability to make decisions and be alert."

"Well, it's used for patients with nervous stomachs. Doctors like it because it decreases acid secretions in the stomach and reduces the risk of burning the lining and causing ulcers. We don't hear of complaints of drowsiness, either. Is that what you want to know?"

"Basically. Thanks, I'll tell him."

"You can also tell him that his mother misses him and wants him to get down here."

He never could fool his mother. "Mom, I—"

"Can you get here by Saturday?"

"Try to, why?"

"Because on Sunday, your father leaves on the train for New York."

"Good God. What for?"

"To line up financing for all that property. He wants to—he calls it bundling the loan."

"I think so. I'll try, Mom."

It was silent, so Donovan asked, "How's Pat doing?"

Donovan's younger brother, Captain Patrick Donovan, was a P-51 pilot with the Eighth Air Force in Britain.

"Last we heard he had thirty-eight missions."

"I thought he only had to do twenty-five."

"That's what we thought, too, but he's going for fifty."

"He'll be the youngest general in the air force. Either that or the youngest pilot in a German prison camp."

"Mike, don't say that!"

"Just pulling your leg, Mom. See you Saturday."

They rang off.

Donovan pushed open the phone booth's accordion doors and stepped out into the lobby. *A day to kill before I shove off for Rocklin tomorrow morning.*

It was a Tuesday, and he didn't think much would be doing in Oakland or over in San Francisco, for that matter. Besides, he was still tired from the flight. He'd bounced and jiggled in the air for fourteen hours, arriving early this morning. Maybe tomorrow night, he'd go into San Francisco or possibly out to the Claremont Hotel in Berkeley with its fine view of the bay. Tonight he just wanted to sleep. But what to do for the rest of the day?

A bus rumbled up to the front door. Air brakes squealed as its accordion doors opened. A marine captain and a navy ensign alighted and walked into the BOQ lobby. A sign over the bus's front window announced it was the hourly shuttle for Mare Island.

What the hell. Nimitz wouldn't mind.

As often happens in August, it was a cold, blustery late afternoon in the San Francisco Bay Area. The wind roared though the Golden Gate and fanned out, raising goose bumps on those brave souls trapped in summer garb. Unaccustomed to this winter-like onslaught, Donovan walked down the pier at the Mare Island—derisively called Nightmare Island—Naval Shipyard wearing working khakis, a light foul-weather jacket, and a garrison cap. Donovan cursed himself for not taking the bus at the front gate or even checking out a pool car, but he wanted to see the *Matthew* for himself. To sort of amble up and look her over without anyone knowing.

Fairbanks Morse "rock-crusher" diesel engines rumbled

as he walked past four *Gato*-class fleet submarines moored in a nest, menacing in their gray-matte and black camouflage patterns. Forklifts and stake trucks darted about while a massive overhead crane clanked and ground its way down the pier. Shooting beneath was a little 0-2-2-0 steam-switcher engine shoving two gray, ammunition-laden boxcars.

Destroyer tenders, APAs, a light cruiser, another nest of submarines, five this time: the ships were alive with men bustling about, carrying crates and boxes, hooking up steam or electrical hoses, while radar antennas and gun mounts spun, their strident warning bells clanging at sailors to stand clear. Men hung over the ships' sides, chipping paint, while other men on deck bent low, wearing protective safety hoods with Martian-like cobalt lenses, performing their artistry with welding torches.

He found the *Matthew* jammed at the far end of the pier, forty feet of her fantail sticking into the fairway, the wind whipping her ensign. Moored portside-to, she hulked all by herself, not nested with other destroyers; alone, like a forgotten orphan. Donovan walked along the opposite side of the pier in the shadow of a large seaplane tender and studied her from a distance. The hair on the back of his neck bristled, and it wasn't from the wind. In fact, it was calm in the lee of the high, slab-sided seaplane tender.

Just look at her. Sleek, graceful. She was at cold iron,[6] her stacks covered with black canvas. She wore a camouflage pattern of dark gray on light gray, not the dappled pattern popular in the South Pacific during the early part of the war. Her prominent features were a superstructure rising a third of the way aft of the bow and twin raked stacks; all were surrounded by five single five-inch 38-caliber gun mounts, each gun capable of hurling a fifty-four-pound projectile eighteen thousand yards, or nine nautical miles. A quintuplet torpedo mount lay between her stacks on the 01 level; another was nested just aft of number two stack, each mount carrying five mark 15 torpedoes with an 825-pound warhead of HBX. The rest of the ship bristled with forty- and twenty-millimeter cannons and depth charges.

One of 175 *Fletcher*-class destroyers, the *Matthew* was a brand-new greyhound, ready to leap and bound. But she wasn't tested, Donovan knew. At this stage of her young life, he wondered if she would be mature enough to run with fast carriers and battleships; mature enough to dish it out to the enemy.

Maybe so, maybe not. He wouldn't know until he stepped aboard. Right now she was quiet, still in mourning for Tom Drake, her skipper. Automatically his eyes whipped to the port yardarm, seeing the "absentee pennant"[7] two-blocked there. Tom Drake, you're absent forever, he mused. But then, I'm absent, too, and that must be for whom the pennant is flying.

Unlike frenetic activity aboard other ships, the *Matthew*'s decks were empty; nobody was about except the quarterdeck watch, where an ensign and a white hat, both wearing holstered .45s, paced up and down, trying to keep warm. From the looks of her, Donovan figured Richard Kruger must have sent half of the crew either on leave or to school while waiting for the new skipper.

Something wasn't right. It was near sunset as Donovan walked to the end of the pier and eyed her mast. She carried a starboard list of about five degrees. No big deal, but it looked sloppy.

The ensign on the quarterdeck spotted Donovan and watched, his hands on his hips. Casually Donovan eased back across the pier and deep into the shadow of the seaplane tender, where he ambled to a portable reefer shed.

The ensign turned away and bent to work on his quarterdeck log.

Two sailors smoked in the lea on the other side about ten yards away. Unaware of Donovan's presence, one commented, "Just look at that damn can. Sleek, fast, she looks like she's just aching for a fight just sitting there."

"Not that one," said the other sailor.

"Huh?"

"Ship's a hangar queen. High and dry on coffee grounds. They call her '*Matthew* the Motionless.' "

"Wonder why?"

"Hard-luck ship. Skipper was killed. Something's always going wrong."

"I'll be damned."

"Nice looking, isn't she?" It was a woman's voice.

Donovan nearly jumped. "What?"

She was beside the reefer shed in shadows where the fan exhausted warm air. A woman in her late thirties, her graying brunette hair pulled back in a bun. She was in a wheelchair, a blanket over her legs. "I'm not going to bite," she said, her eyes narrowing as she studied his silver oak leaves. "Commander." Her smile was genuine. But it was a smile hard earned and carefully dispensed. Her eyes were deep set, with crow's-feet, and her chin was sharp. She was a good-looking woman who had survived well over time.

"I didn't see you." Donovan walked over, wondering what she was doing. Looking around, he asked, "Are you all right? Do you need anything?"

She fumbled a Lucky Strike from a pack and worked at a book of matches. Clamping the cigarette between stained teeth, she tried to light it, but the fan's blast kept blowing it out. "Damn," she swore softly.

"Here." Donovan took the match and lit it between cupped hands while she bent to ignite the cigarette and puff.

"Guess I'll never make a sailor, Commander."

"Takes practice." He handed her matches back.

Taking a big drag, the woman exhaled and looked at the *Matthew.* "Husband's over there, finishing up some work. He's the exec." She looked up with glistening eyes and patted the wheels on her chair. "Tough to get around in this thing. I been in it six months. But we're going out to dinner tonight. First time in quite a while."

"That sounds wonderful."

"Well, I just want you to know that my Richie is working his butt off for you, Captain."

She had figured out who he was. "How did you know?"

"I seen it in your eyes. Your mettle. The way you sort of snuck up on her without wanting anyone to know. I seen plenty of skippers, and you can tell right away which ones care and which ones don't give a damn."

"How can you tell, ah, Mrs. Kruger?" He tipped her a salute and they shook.

"Vicky."

"Okay, Vicky."

Just then the *Matthew*'s loudspeakers clicked on and a metallic voice announced, "First call, first call to colors."

Vicky continued, "Well, the ass-kissers just walk up the gangway and expect everybody to bow down and grovel. Now, bullshitters do the same thing, except instead of making everybody grovel, they try to make 'em laugh." She looked in the distance. "Come to think of it, I haven't seen too many bullshitters since the war started."

Donovan laughed.

Vicky pointed up to him and took another drag, all in one motion. "Now, guys like you. You appreciate good horseflesh. You don't want to startle them at first. Just watch 'em flick their tails to see how they swat the flies off."

Then she nodded to the other side of the shed. "Don't let those kids steer you wrong. She's a good ship."

"I can see that."

"But you spotted that list, didn't you?"

Donovan was astounded at this rough-cut woman. "You sure know your stuff."

"That's what Richie's doing right now. Transferring fuel. Maybe pumping a bilge or two. Going to take another hour or so. Then we can go out. And your ship will be straight up and down, like a plumb bob."

"He's down in the hole?" Donovan referred to the main engine room.

"In his coveralls. Chief engineer is on leave," she replied.

"Once a snipe, always a snipe." Donovan looked at her. "You are one hell of a navy wife. How long you been married?"

"Six months."

He stepped back. He hadn't expected that.

"It's a long story."

Donovan checked his watch: 2005. The sun, he knew, would soon be at the horizon. The wind hadn't dropped, and it was getting colder. "I've got to get back. Enjoyed talking to you, Vicky."

"You're not going aboard?"

"No, you caught me fair and square. I was in the area and I couldn't resist sneaking a look. And I like what I see. You can tell Richie that."

The *Matthew*'s loudspeaker squealed again, the metallic voice announcing, "On deck. Attention to colors."

Donovan faced the *Matthew*'s fantail and drew to attention, his right hand snapping to a salute. A pair of gulls squawked at each other, water lapped at the pier pilings as two white hats on the destroyer fantail slowly lowered the national ensign. From the corner of his eye, Donovan saw a man on the fo'c'sle haul down the union jack.

"Two. Carry on," called the loudspeaker.

Donovan relaxed as Vicky took a final drag on her cigarette and expertly flicked it over the pier into the water. "He'll be disappointed," she said. "After all. He's flying the absentee for you." She nodded toward the pennant flying from the port halyard.

"I wouldn't go that far, Mrs. Kruger."

"I beg your pardon?"

Donovan leaned over and gave her his best Irish grin. "This will be our little secret, okay?"

"I don't understand."

Her chin was raised and Donovan realized this woman was not used to being upbraided. He would have to go gently. "Regulations state that if the captain is gone for more than seventy-two hours, then the absentee pennant is flown for the executive officer's absence."

"Oh. That means it shouldn't be up there at all."

"Right. But don't worry, Vicky. I'm not going to jump on him for that. At least not right away."

The look in her eye told Donovan that Mrs. Kruger would do the jumping for him.

"Also, I'm not going to jump on him over the fact that the man on the fo'c'sle was without his hat."

Her eyes narrowed. Richie Kruger would hear about that as well. Welcome to this woman's navy, thought Donovan.

"Nor that the forward stack cover is loose and hanging down. A good wind will carry it away." Donovan was about to mention sweepers on the fantail, leaning on their brooms, shooting the breeze, but he figured that wasn't her problem.

She fumbled for another cigarette. Donovan took the pack and helped her light it, saying, "I know many a skipper who would make a big deal out of all that. And maybe I will. But what I'm really interested in is if this ship can fight. That's what I need to know. Can she lick the Japs."

She took a long drag and said, "I think Richie can help you with that."

"That's what Chester said. He also told me to go on leave, and that's what I'm going to do."

"What? Who's Chester?"

"Chester. Admiral Nimitz. Your Richie knows him. They served on the *Augusta* together. Please tell him that, and give him Chester's compliments. Mine, too. I enjoyed talking to you, Mrs. Kruger. Enjoy your dinner this evening." Donovan saluted her and walked away.

NINE

2 August 1944
321 Elm Street
Rocklin, California

"Let me get you some coffee, Mike. Please, sit anywhere." Carmen Rossi's petite frame whisked into the kitchen. Furnished with large, old pieces, the living room was small and rectangular, a fireplace at one end and an upright piano at the other. A gold star hung prominently in a window by the front door, white lace curtains drawn behind it. A clock ticked near an unlit staircase. Cluttered atop the piano were silver- and porcelain-framed pictures; one was an eight-by-ten glossy of Carmen and Mario Rossi on their wedding day. A grinning lieutenant junior grade, Mario Rossi was dressed in navy whites with sword, Carmen in a formal white gown. They stood before an old church with a dark brick façade. Donovan wasn't sure, but it looked like St. Mary's Catholic Church in San Francisco.

Donovan was left alone with Mario's father, a stooped old man who sat in a rocking chair in the corner. It squeaked as he rocked back and forth, looking out the window.

"Nice day, huh?" said Donovan.

The old man nodded and rocked and squeaked and gazed out the window, a cane resting in his lap.

"He doesn't hear so good, Mike," Carmen called from the kitchen. Dishes clanked. "Won't be a minute."

"Hokay," the old man gasped. He waved to Donovan and went back to his rocking.

Donovan waved back. "Okay."

"He thinks his son is still alive." A voice echoed from the

staircase, startling Donovan. It was a boy, twelve or thirteen perhaps, sitting halfway up in darkness. His two prominent features were jet-black hair and dark eyes big as saucers, resting in a heart-shaped face. Just like Carmen his mother, thought Donovan, but not as delicate. Except the boy's voice was uncharacteristically deep, almost having completed its puberty. That's what made Donovan jump, he realized. The boy's voice was much like Mario, his father. Especially the inflection.

"That's your grandfather?" Donovan called up.

"Luigi Humberto Rossi," the boy confirmed.

Scary. Donovan heard Mario's voice and it made him feel strange.

"Hokay." The old man apparently recognized his name and gave a toothless grin. He reached out to Donovan.

"Okay." Donovan stood and walked over and shook Luigi's hand. God bless you and your wonderful son.

"What do you do in the navy?" asked the boy.

Donovan walked over to see better. An enormous head of hair flowed over the boy's ears and almost down to his shoulders. That's right. Mario had complained how much trouble it was to get the kid to cut his hair. "Executive officer on a destroyer. I was on—"

"—my dad's ship? What happened to him? The telegram didn't say anything."

Donovan nodded to the old man. "Maybe—"

"He doesn't listen. Anyway, he'll be asleep soon."

Carmen walked in, carrying a tray of cups and a carafe. "You take sugar, cream?" Her smile was bright, her face devoid of what he knew she was suffering. For all her feminity, Donovan knew Carmen Rossi was tough. She wouldn't crack in front of him.

"No, thanks, just black."

Smiling, she said, "Navy-style," and poured. "I see you've met Dominic," she added, nodding to the boy.

"Nick," the boy said.

"We've been talking," said Donovan. He felt uneasy, and his stomach growled.

"Can I have some?" asked Dominic.

"No," said Carmen, sitting back and pouring. She sipped

her coffee, set it down, and twisted her wedding rings around her finger.

"Why?"

It was difficult for Donovan to listen to the boy whine in his father's voice.

"You know, caffeine. You must wait till you're seventeen," said Carmen, still twisting her rings. One was a large emerald-cut diamond engagement ring, the other a silver wedding ring. Donovan wondered why she hadn't tossed them into the collection plate.

"Seventeen, shoot. I can handle caffeine, Mom. Look at all the Cokes we drink."

"I said no." She turned to Donovan. "You're nice to come. And such a distance. This is hard for you, I know."

"Mario was the best skipper I've served under," blurted Donovan. "I wouldn't have done otherwise." That was maybe true, Donovan thought. But they had argued a lot, almost to the point of yelling at each other in front of the other officers. Still, hotheaded as Mario was, he was a good skipper, a good teacher, and one hell of a ship handler. It seemed a miracle that a hotheaded Italian and a hotheaded Irishman could get along in the same ship.

Carmen nodded in a business-like fashion. "Thank you. Tell me, Mike, can you answer Dominic's question?"

"It's Nick," the boy called from the staircase.

"Shush," she called over her shoulder. She fixed Donovan with a stare.

"About how it happened?" asked Donovan.

"Yes, we'd like to know. I mean you were there, weren't you?"

She'd emphasized the word *were* as if to question Donovan's presence aboard ship.

Ignoring that, Donovan asked, "What about Rosa?" Rossi's other child was an eight-year-old daughter.

"Piano lesson. I'll tell her when it's time," said Carmen. Big round eyes and black pupils dominated her face. Looking at him curiously, she began twisting her ring again.

"And . . ." He nodded to the old man.

"I don't think he knows. At least he's never said anything

since the telegram. He keeps to himself. I think he's back in Napoli."

"Is that all he does?"

"Retired now from the power company. Fly-fishes in the morning and rocks away in the afternoon. Has dinner and goes to sleep."

The clock ticked for a moment.

"Okay." Donovan shrugged. With a look at Dominic, he began. "Jap air raid. Fifteen or twenty dive-bombers in the Marianas."

"Is that where Guam is?" asked Dominic.

Donovan nodded. "We were about twenty miles southeast of Guam. Off by ourselves, running escorts for a bunch of AKs—uh, cargo ships. Anyway, they caught us flat-footed without air support. But"—Donovan grinned—"you should have seen them at first. They were so screwed up. Couldn't hit the broad side of a barn. Mario and I were laughing. Their aim was terrible."

"Where was my father's post?" Dominic called from the staircase.

"On the bridge."

"Where were you?"

"In CIC."

"Where's that?"

"Inside the ship, main deck."

"Where you were safe."

"Dominic!" yelled Carmen.

A wave of outrage flashed over Donovan, then was gone. He took a deep breath and said, "Young man, we do that for a reason: to make sure someone qualified can take over in case something happens to the captain. Also, the exec sees the big picture with the radar plot and all the radio circuits. He's in contact with the captain by sound-powered phone all the time. Together, they fight the ship." Donovan was surprised to find he was on his feet. Taking a deep breath, he lowered his hands from his hips.

Dominic's eyes were wide open. And he drew back.

"Apologize," said Carmen. Her eyes glistened.

"I'm sorry," said the boy, his voice wavering.

It seemed strange to hear Mario's voice like this: subordinate, rather than what he was used to. But then this Mario had a lot to learn. "It's okay."

"Go on, please," said Carmen.

"Not much to tell." Donovan sat. "A bomb hit the bridge. I heard this loud *bang*. Then everything went black. It was smoky. And then flames. We got out." Donovan called up to the boy. "We lost twenty-six people with that bomb. Took us all day to put out the fires. But we did it and we brought the ship home."

"Where is it now?" asked Dominic.

"I left her in Pearl Harbor. After temporary repairs, they'll send her back to Mare Island."

"In San Francisco Bay?"

"Yes."

"Can I see her?"

Unusual question, Donovan thought. Carmen averted her eyes. She didn't know what to think about it, either.

"I suppose so," said Donovan.

"That's keen."

"Your father died a hero's death, young man. Never forget that." He lowered his voice and patted Carmen on the arm. "And I know this. There was no pain. It was instantaneous."

She wiped a tear, and then to his surprise, reached up and wiped one from Donovan's cheek. "Here." Carmen gave Donovan a handkerchief.

"Dammit." Donovan honked and gave a grin. "Sorry."

She took his hand. "You two were a great pair."

"We argued like cats and dogs but . . . dammit . . . I loved the guy. Behind our backs they called us the Spic and the Mik."

Carmen shot a quick, efficient smile. "I hadn't heard that." She reached down and began twisting.

Donovan blew again.

"Mario said in his letters you were like a young brother. Always defying him. Usually right."

Donovan looked up. "He said that?"

" 'Crazy Mike,' he called you."

"Yeah, that's Mario. Off by ourselves he called me 'Crazy Mike.' But dammit. Nearly floored me when I found out he recommended me for command."

"You deserve it." A pause and then, "You haven't touched your coffee. Want me to warm it up?" Donovan's belly felt strange. Dr. Duberman's belladonna must have been doing some weird things. And it still ached. "No, thanks. Here." He pointed to the corner. "That's Mario's B-4 bag. All his stuff is in there. There's some medals on top."

"I don't care about those," said Carmen. She looked up at Dominic.

"Maybe," said the boy.

"I'd a lika see 'em." Again, Donovan was startled. It was the old man speaking in the voice of yet another Mario, a deeper timbre, a self-assured and heavily accented voice.

Carmen drew in her breath. "Pappa."

The old man pointed a bony finger. "My boy's medals. Can I see my boy's medals?"

"Pappa, you . . . you know?" asked Carmen.

"Whadda you think, I'ma stupid?" Luigi pointed to the B-4 bag. "Just lay it over here, please."

"Of course." Donovan walked over to the B-4 bag, unbuckled it, and opened it flat on the floor at Luigi's feet.

The old man reached out and patted Donovan on the shoulder. "Thank you for coming," he rasped.

Donovan looked up to speak. Instead, he blew his nose.

"Carmen, we got dinner for a hungry boy?" said the old man.

"Yes, Pappa." She rose to her feet.

"Then get out there and fix us something." With a glance at Donovan the old man said, "You minda stay for dinner?"

"My honor," said Donovan.

"Come sit over there and tell me about my boy's medals," said Luigi, his voice stronger. "In fact, I wanna know everything. What you guys did, about his ship, where you went. Canna you do that?"

"Yes, sir."

"Good. Now Dominic, get down here where we can see your damnda face. And your name is a Dominic. You unnerstand?" He pointed a long bony finger at the boy.

The boy walked down the stairs and emerged into light. "Yes, Pappa."

TEN

2 August 1944
Southern Pacific Westbound Special 533
Rocklin, California

It was a late, warm evening as they gathered on the passenger platform under a sharp cobalt-blue sky. Luigi stood between Carmen and Dominic, his arms around them.

Luigi reached out and pumped Donovan's hand once more. "You woulda made a great Italian."

Donovan said, "Hey, what about the Spic and the Mik?"

". . . Hokay, hokay." Luigi waved him off

" 'Board," yelled the conductor.

"Thanks for coming, Mike," said Carmen. "Please write. Let me know how you're doing." She stood on her tiptoes and kissed him on the cheek. Then she stepped back, still twisting her wedding rings, her eyebrows knit.

"You take care of yourself, Carmen." Donovan turned to Dominic, grabbed his hand, and clapped him on the shoulder. "You're the man of the house now, Dominic. Take good care of your mom and Rosa and grandpa. Okay?"

Dominic's voice squeaked a bit when he said, "You bet, Mike. And you go out there and get some Japs for us, huh?"

Donovan grinned.

"Maybe send me a sword or a pistol?" the boy asked.

"I'll see what I can do."

The engineer blasted his whistle twice, and the conductor scooped up the little stool beneath the front of the door. "All aboard. Last call."

"Gotta run. Good-bye, everybody. Thanks for everything." He ran for the car just as the train jerked.

The conductor, a thin, owlish man in his late fifties, helped Donovan aboard the car then closed the door and secured the vestibule, setting the stool on the floor and clipping the window open. "Leave it open for a while, maybe cool the place off," he muttered.

Couplings clanked as the engine's drivers spun on the rails against a consist of eight passenger cars. Gray-white smoke puffed into the sky as the engineer yanked a handle, spilling sand onto the tracks. The big engine's drivers grabbed hold, and the train pulled out slowly.

Mike found a seat and looked out to see Carmen walking alongside the car. She raised her hand: *Open the window.*

With some effort, Donovan got it up.

"Here, take them." She reached up to him. She walked quickly as the train gained speed.

Donovan extended his hand palm-up, having no idea of what to expect.

She dropped something in his hand as the train went faster. She was almost running as she called hoarsely, "There'll be a day when you'll meet a good woman, Mike. That'll be the wedding present from Mario and me." She was puffing and stopped abruptly at the end of the platform.

Donovan opened his hand to find a gleaming one-carat diamond engagement ring and a white-gold wedding band. He leaned out and called back, "I'm speechless."

"God bless you and bless you and bless you, Mike." She blew a kiss and wiped at her eyes.

"And you, too," called Donovan, too flabbergasted to think of anything. Then he waved to Dominic and Pappa Rossi, standing on the platform. "Thank you."

Dominic waved and the old man started yelling something, but the engineer blew the whistle, its mournful wail drowning out Pappa Rossi's voice.

The train lurched around a bend and suddenly Rocklin was gone as they rattled over a crossing and into the twilight. Pushing down the window, Donovan sat heavily, feeling tired and strangely devoid of energy. Carmen's dinner had been wonderful, spaghetti with a tomato sauce flavored by beef, red wine, chopped olives, mushrooms, and spices that had been simmering in a crock all day. They'd started with a Caesar salad, and the meal was attended with a bottle of local Chianti. Everyone ate and drank with vigor, except Donovan, who wasn't hungry. But he put on a good show of apologizing for having a heavy, gravy-laden pot roast for lunch. Actually, he'd only had half of a dry tuna sandwich at the Sacramento station.

Fortunately, the car was only half full, the seat next to Donovan unoccupied. He pitched his cap on the seat, undid his blouse, and spread out, wondering why he hadn't been hungry. Or thirsty. The Chianti was excellent, but he'd had only one glass as Carmen watched curiously. He clinked glasses with them as they finished off the bottle, toasting the liberating armies of the United States of America, a free Italy, the pope, and the president. They poured a glass for Dominic, over Carmen's protest. The boy gulped and coughed as Luigi and Donovan grinned at each other, the old man silently thanking Donovan for helping to validate the boy's coming of age.

He studied the engagement ring for a moment—beautiful—its emerald-cut facets gleamed. He remembered Mario telling about the fantastic luck he'd had buying it on a trip through Panama.

He dropped them in his pocket, amazed at Carmen's sacrifice. She could have sold them, kept them in the family for Rosa when she was ready to be married, given them to friends, dropped them in the collection plate at church, or simply heaved them in the river. But then he remembered the time he'd almost married. She was a southern girl with a cute accent. Nancy Stringer was a nurse whom Donovan had met at San Diego's Balboa Naval Hospital. The invitations were out. John Sabovik, who was to be the best man, put together a lavish bachelor party at the Hotel del Coronado. Three days before the wedding, Nancy gave back the ring. It turned out she wanted to marry her childhood sweetheart from Memphis. Later, after he'd thrown the ring in San Diego Bay, he discovered this man from Memphis had made it big in soybean futures, a miracle in the midst of the Depression.

Donovan pat the rings in his pocket. Sabovik; Nancy. What would Carmen say if she knew about his tattered relationships?

The train whistle wailed into the night. *Stop moping, dammit.*

He felt woozy; his belly ached, and it wasn't the spaghetti; he hadn't had that much. This was a different, almost throbbing discomfort. Running his hand over his forehead, he realized he was clammy, and he wondered if he was running a fever. Maybe the flu?

The conductor entered the car and started taking tickets. He was bending to reach for the ticket of the man sitting opposite Donovan when a shadow crossed his face. The conductor looked up and said, "I'll be damned. Milo Lattimer, SP's finest conductor. What brings you aboard?"

"Hi, Charlie. Just deadheading back to Roseville. You up for a game?" Lattimer's voice was a resonant baritone. He was tall, six-three at least, Donovan figured, but not heavy. In fact, Donovan judged him to be on the thin side, except that his back and shoulders were broad beneath a blue chambray work shirt, and powerful. His hair was short, curly, and unparted, and as he nodded Donovan noticed he had a bald pate.

The train was up to speed and rumbled into the dusk, the car rocking gently from side to side. Charlie, the conductor, leaned over, took Donovan's ticket, and punched it, hardly giving him a glance. "Thanks, Navy," he muttered as he turned back to the big man. "Sorry, Milo," Charlie said. "You're too good for me. Besides, I have to work up the manifest."

"I'll give up my queen." Lattimer grinned through crooked teeth.

Charlie's mouth twisted into a guarded smile. "Hogwash. You'd still clean me out. Let me take a rain check. We're due in Roseville in thirty minutes and that wouldn't—hey—"

"Sorry." Donovan stood and lurched past the two men. His face felt like it was on fire, and something surged in his belly. He wasn't sure if he was going to vomit or if he just needed air. When at sea, a blast of air over his face always had a calming effect. That's where he wanted to go, into the vestibule between cars, where he could open the big window and stick his nose in the wind. "Is the head up there?" he asked.

"Right at the front of the car," said the conductor. "Jeepers, navy guys." He turned to Lattimer and grinned. "In my lingo, a head is on top of your shoulders and a toilet is where you take a crap. How'd they ever get it so screwed up, anyway?"

The two laughed as Donovan lurched forward, keeping his feet while the car rocked and bumped into the night. His destroyer legs didn't seem to help as he hand-over-handed his way along. With difficulty, he opened the door to the vestibule and stumbled inside, standing over the coupling platform. His stomach seemed fairly alive, and a second-place archery trophy came to mind as he tugged open the window and clipped it in place. The trophy became the image of Dr. Duberman as he stepped on the stool, leaned out the window, and retched into the cool night air.

What the hell is wrong with me? he wondered as he retched again. Just then the train roared over a crossing as an eastbound freight blasted past in the opposite direction. The noise was incredible, the air filled with the pulsing, red-hot energy of the passing locomotive and the odor of burned fuel oil. He had a sensation of falling, that maybe it was all right to let himself go . . . that everything was okay now. The image of Dr. Duberman became that of Luigi Rossi smiling and nodding, his arm around young Dominic, both wearing baseball caps and gloves. The pain hit again, searing inside his belly. Mercifully, there was blackness. . . .

"There's no time. I'll take him." The voice was deep, resonant; he'd heard it before.

"What the hell's wrong with him?"

Fingers probed around his belly. A fire raged inside. "Ahhh." Donovan's eyes fluttered open. Several silhouettes stood over him in darkness. A baggage cart. He was lying on a baggage cart.

"Man, he scared the shit out of me. I never thought I'd see a guy puke so hard. Standin' on the stool, he almost fell out of the car. Can you believe that? Hell, Milo, you saved him."

"Ummm." The fingers probed. ". . . maybe chronic appendicitis."

Donovan remembered now. It was the big man on the train. The chess player who was going to give up his queen.

"You mean he's gotta have an operation?" It was the conductor's voice.

"Can't tell. These things are tricky. You don't know until—"

"Hey, Charlie! We gotta highball, dammit," a man shouted.

The conductor said, "We're pullin' out." He leaned close to Donovan and patted him on the shoulder. "You take it easy, fella. You're lucky Milo's so damn strong. Saved your life. Then he carried you off the train all by himself." Charlie looked up. "Gotta go, Milo. Thanks." The man dashed away just as the engine gave two blasts of its whistle. The couplings clanked and the engine took the strain, pulling the train out.

"Roseville?" asked Donovan.

"Just hold on, my friend. Yes, Roseville."

It was the way he said *Roseville* that gave Donovan the impression Lattimer had a European accent, perhaps Dutch.

"Ah, here we go," said Lattimer.

A station wagon crunched in gravel beside the baggage cart. A man stepped out and said, "Here we go, Milo. Best I could do."

"It's perfect," said Lattimer.

"Backseat is down so you can slide him over the tailgate. Want me to take his feet?"

Lattimer's arms slid under Donovan and he said with a grunt, "That's fine. I have him. There, grab his hat." Donovan was lifted into the night air. It felt wonderfully cool on his forehead and cheeks, and for some reason, he smelled a mixture of burned fuel oil and orange blossom. Lattimer's booted feet crunched in gravel as he carried Donovan to the station wagon. "That's okay, step aside, please," he grunted.

Apparently someone didn't move fast enough, for Lattimer said, "I said step back, dammit!"

Donovan's feet smacked into the doorpost. Pain ranged in his stomach. "Ahhh."

"See what you made me do?" Lattimer said as he eased Donovan onto the station wagon's floor.

A voice echoed in the dark "Sorry, pal."

A train rumbled through the station without stopping, its whistle blaring. Then nothing . . .

* * *

The light was bright. White-clad figures in surgical masks stood over him. He was still supine, but now all his clothes were off and he was covered by a thin blanket.

"Hey everybody, he's up and about," reported a figure behind his head.

"How are you feeling, Commander?" asked a white-clad figure.

It hit Donovan that the man was a surgeon. "Place smells awful," he said.

The man chuckled. "You're right. It does smell awful. That's ether, and not my wife's perfume, unfortunately." Gray-black eyebrows over intense blue eyes stared down at him. "Good evening, I'm Dr. Finnigan." He nodded to his right. "And this is our team at the Roseville Community Hospital. The disrespectful man behind you is our gas-passer and chief anesthesiologist, Dr. Ross."

The voice behind Donovan mimicked a thick Count Dracula accent: "Velcome to my laboratory, Commander."

Dr. Finnigan continued, "Very funny. Across from me is Dr. Logan, who will be assisting me. Now, right away, I want you to know that you're going to be just fine."

Dr. Ross, the anesthesiologist behind Donovan, was barely a shadow, perched on a stool, ready to flip valves and fill him full of ether.

Donovan smacked his lips. His mouth was dry as he rasped, "Okay." Then he realized that the assistant surgeon, Dr. Logan, was a woman.

She must have caught Donovan's glance, for she said, "Good evening, Commander. Welcome to Roseville." She wore thick glasses, but the voice beneath the mask told him she was smiling, something that helped moderate the panicky feeling building in his chest.

"What's wrong with me?"

"We figure chronic appendicitis," said Dr. Finnigan. "And yes, you do need surgery. The blood type on your dog tags is in good supply here. Now. Do we have your permission to proceed?"

Donovan gulped, thinking this was his last glance at humanity. "What's chronic appendicitis?"

"Your appendix becomes inflamed but is walled off in its

own sac, so to speak, becoming abscessed inside. A nasty little infection sets up in there. Hard to detect. Actually, your buddy on the train figured it out."

"Lattimer?"

"That's right."

Ironic. Donovan wondered how a railroad conductor could diagnose his condition while a doctor of medicine at the Oak Knoll Naval Hospital completely flubbed it.

"So, ah, do you want us to go ahead?" It was the woman, Dr. Logan. Her glasses were thick, so he couldn't see her eyes well. But she had gentle eyebrows and her voice was full, compelling. A voice that he felt he would enjoy over cocktails.

"Commander Donovan?" she asked. Right now her inflection was clipped and professional.

"I think so."

"Next of kin?" asked Finnigan. At the same time, he nodded to Dr. Ross behind Donovan's head.

Donovan gave his mother's name and phone number in the San Fernando Valley.

Dr. Logan laid a damp towel over his forehead. It felt wonderful. "Any other next of kin?" she asked gently.

The rubber mask came down slowly. He saw the light overhead and drew a breath, feeling as if he were rising in a balloon. Only the straps held him from floating to the ceiling.

". . . Admiral Nimitz," he stammered. Then he was gone.

He gagged and then let it go, spittle dribbling down his chin. And his head ached. "Ahhh."

Someone sat beside him cradling his head. "It's okay . . . shhh." It was a woman.

That voice. "Dr. Logan?" he rasped.

"That's pretty good. Now here." She cradled his head against her and stuck a straw in his mouth. "Try this. It'll settle your stomach."

Donovan sucked. It was cold 7UP in a glass filled with ice cubes. It tasted wonderful.

"Easy. Not too much at one time, Commander."

He spit out the straw. "Do I still have all my arms and legs?"

"Ummm." Something scratched. She was writing with her right hand, a clipboard balanced on her thigh, her left arm still cradled around his head. Green ink flowed from her pen. Then he looked into her eyes. They were as green as what flowed on the paper. Her auburn hair was pulled back under a finely sculpted neck. Her cheeks were prominent, and he recognized the delicate eyebrows. She glanced down, caught him looking, and gave a quick, efficient smile.

"Dr. Logan?"

"That's right, Commander." Her fountain pen scratched as she resumed writing.

"Call me Mike."

"Ummm." Her pen scratched.

"Is that my chart?"

"Yes it is, Commander."

"Well, like I said, are my arms and legs still attached?"

She eased her arm away and stood. "Yes, they are, and you're going to be fine." She wore a lab coat over a skirt, and he looked down to see perfectly shaped legs. Ignoring him, she went on, "It was as Dr. Finnigan suspected. Chronic appendicitis. We drained it as best we could and put you back together. You weren't under for more than an hour."

"Did the appendix come out?"

"Yes, you're lucky. We got it. Sometimes we have to go back again and redrain the abscess. I think you'll be okay now. How do you feel, Commander?"

He looked around, finding he was in a four-bed room. It was hard to focus, but he saw the vague outlines of other men in their beds. A blue sky sparkled outside. "What time is—?"

"It's Wednesday, Commander. Welcome back to the world. You're in Roseville Community Hospital." She walked over to the window and raised it. "Ummm, pretty warm outside. This okay with you?"

A dry heat flowed in the room, caressing him. "Feels wonderful. What's your first name?"

She walked over and reached for his wrist. Instead she knocked over a paper cup, water splattering on the floor. "Shoot." She picked up his wrist, taking his pulse while stooping, grabbing the cup, and refilling it. Again she scratched on the chart with green ink. "You needn't bother, Commander. There's only one thing that should concern you now."

She'd been so friendly last night at the operating table. Why the deep-freeze act now? "What's that?"

"Getting well. Now lie back and get some rest. We'll get you on your feet later this afternoon." Dr. Logan walked out.

ELEVEN

3 August 1944
SS *Empress Anne*
North Pacific Ocean
En route Honolulu, Territory of Hawaii

Third mate Karl Strauss smacked his lips and lightly patted his belly. Homer Yates, the cook, had once again performed his magic. Strauss had started lunch with a bowl of split pea soup. That was quickly followed by breaded pork chop, mashed potatoes, thick gravy, and carrots. Strauss polished it off with a dish of custard and coffee. After a second cup, he rose, stepped into the midships passageway, and walked to the hatchway on the starboard side. The hatch was clipped open and he propped a foot on the coaming, leaned against the bulkhead, and reached for a pack of cigarettes while taking in the Pacific.

Amazing! It was difficult to believe there was a war on. The sun was shining. The day was crisp, and a warm wind tickled his face, hair, and blue chambray shirt. This was his third trip to Pearl Harbor. He'd learned to recognize the moisture-laden trade winds that would caress them all the way to Hawaii. And the color of the ocean. Now that they were well away from land, the Pacific had turned to a deep, shimmering blue. He wished he could jump in.

Also amazing was that old *Annie* was doing twelve knots. A pace unheard of before the war. The ship's engine had been reworked, her bottom cleaned, and now her screw joyously churned through a glassy sea. There was very little groundswell; only occasionally did the Pacific heave as if in a deep slumber, producing a slow, majestic five-degree roll aboard the *Empress Anne.* Otherwise, King Neptune left them alone.

The *Empress Anne* was part of a five-ship convoy three days out of San Francisco, sailing for Pearl Harbor in a circular formation. *Empress Anne* and the three other cargo ships were on the two-thousand-yard circle; the *Regina Dalmatia,* a C-2 cargo ship deeply laden with ammunition, was in the formation's center as guide. Six newly minted destroyers from DESRON 63 on their way to the war zone were arrayed around them on the four-thousand-yard circle. The destroyers proudly wore their dapple-gray war paint and were ever vigilant: radar antennas twirling, gun mounts exercising, sonars pinging for enemy submarines.

Strauss lit his cigarette and blew smoke out the hatch, watching it whip aft to be captured by the wind. A sense of pride surged through him as he felt the ship move easily beneath his feet. He'd calculated the cargo load perfectly, and the ride so far had been nice. They hadn't rolled or pitched too much in the storm they'd hit just outside of San Francisco. The destroyers, of course, had bucked and bounced furiously. Strauss and Captain d' Angelo both agreed they'd rather be on a plodding merchant ship than be known as the fastest dog on the block. As cocky as they were, the poor sailors aboard those tin cans paid dearly in rough weather, the strongest of stomachs eventually giving in. He wondered if . . .

"Hey, Strauss!" It was Roberts, the tan, heavily muscled second mate, yelling from the deck above.

"Yeah?"

Robert's voice rumbled, "The old man wants you onna bridge."

"Dammit, what'd I do now?" Strauss flipped his cigarette over the side and started up the ladder for the bridge. A charming conversationalist in the wardroom, Peter d' Angelo was hot-tempered and often flew off the handle at his men on the bridge. Strauss said a silent prayer he wouldn't be d' Angelo's next victim. He reached for the rail on the next deck when—

—a brilliant flash of light. A loud, almost simultaneous *crack* pinned him against the bulkhead, slamming his head against a pad eye. The thunderous roar that followed was worse than the pain from hitting the pad eye as he tripped, fumbled, and bumped back down to the main deck. A world of sound roared through his essence for a good twenty seconds. The world turned a whitish gray, and the next thing he knew he was sitting up and groaning.

He felt around. No bones were broken, but his head hurt like hell. He ran his hand over his scalp and brought away a bright glimmer of red. With another groan, Strauss grabbed a bulkhead-mounted rail and pulled himself to his feet.

Someone ran past. It was Yates, the cook, pointing, his mouth working.

"What?" yelled Strauss.

Yates kept pointing, his mouth open wide, jaw muscles straining, his face red.

It dawned on Strauss that his hearing was gone. Then he remembered the explosion.

Yates jerked at his sleeve and pointed to starboard.

White mist. Oil-scummed water. The destroyers turning in slow circles. White mist.

"What?" rasped Strauss.

"What the hell was that explosion?" demanded Yates.

Strauss's hearing was coming back. "I don't know." His head throbbed and he wiped away more blood. It was worse than he thought.

Yates shouted, "Never heard anything like it—say, are you all right?"

The mist was evaporating. A destroyer on the opposite side of the formation had sped up and was headed toward them, a bone in its teeth. Then it hit him. Where was the guide? The ship in the center? The *Regina Dalmatia*! "Sonofabitch!" he said.

"You better sit down," said Yates.

"Lookit that," bellowed Strauss. "She's gone."

"Karl, set your ass on the ladder here and let me take a look at you."

Strauss sat, his mouth open. Incredible. The 7,952-ton *Regina Dalmatia* had moments before been plowing through the sea at twelve knots. And now she was gone. The mist was rapidly clearing. He could see all the other ships—except the *Regina Dalmatia*. He looked up at Yates. "What the hell happened?"

TWELVE

8 August 1944
Headquarters, Twelfth Naval District
San Francisco Bay, California

Yerba Buena Island was headquarters to the Twelfth Naval District and lay right in the middle of San Francisco Bay. The main building had begun life in 1939 as the site for the ultramodern World's Fair. Done in art deco, the building was situated at the base of the three-hundred-foot Yerba Buena peak. Since taking it over, the navy had run four tunnels deep inside the hill to, among other things, house the command center for its West Coast radio intelligence and cryptographic network. An adjoining landfill gave rise to the Treasure Island Naval Base with a complex series of docks, warehouses, and berthing facilities.

Tunnel 2A ran for 275 feet beneath Yerba Buena peak. And three laterals, or offshoots, were situated along the way. The first lateral held a large conference room, the next had offices and an infirmary, the last was a cavernous armory originally intended to house six-inch ammunition for the defense of inner San Francisco Bay. Now it just contained small arms and ammunition.

The door to room B-6 in the "Baker" lateral opened and John Sabovik walked out, a manila folder tucked under his arm. Quicky he walked down the hall to the corner of Tunnel 2A and Lateral B and drew up before the door of conference room 2A-B-1. Standing at the door were two marine sergeants dressed in fatigues and duty belts with .45 pistols. Sabovik knew both of them: Saunders and Evergreen. He gave a thin smile and said, "I'm back."

"Excuse me." A tall, thin navy captain walked up. His hair was salt and pepper, and he looked as if he continually struggled with a five o'clock shadow. He looked at Sabovik. "Any luck yet? I've been waiting quite awhile." It was Captain Samuel Doyle, commanding officer of the Port Chicago Naval Magazine. A former heavy cruiser captain, he wore dress khakis and held a garrison cap in his left hand, slapping it against his leg.

Sabovik sighed inwardly. Everyone knew Doyle would be pilloried whether or not he was responsible for the explosion. "I'll check again, sir, and let you know."

Apparently not satisfied, Doyle grunted and started for the door. Sabovik stepped before him and said, "Pardon me, Captain."

They glared at each other until Sergeant Saunders reached down and opened the door for Sabovik, giving him just enough room to slip through. "I'll let you know, Captain," Sabovik promised.

Saunders stepped behind Sabovik and pulled the door closed with a soft *click*.

Sabovik walked into a smoke-filled room twenty by twelve feet. A conference table was covered with a green baize cloth and littered with books, papers, coffee cups, and brass butt kits[8] made from five-inch shell casings. A slide projector stood at one end, a carousel of slides poised on top. It reminded Sabovik of the old submachine guns with the round, drum-type magazine used by gangsters. A slight, wiry, balding man sat at the table's head, his blouse off and sleeves rolled up. The organization chart stated that two-star rear admiral John Egan's title was deputy commander, Twelfth Naval District. But it was a trumped-up title, since Egan had reported aboard just two weeks ago. In actuality, he'd been appointed by Admiral Ernest J. King, chief of naval operations in Washington, DC. Everyone knew "Cactus Jack" Egan was Ernie King's hired gun and troubleshooter. His presence here meant that King, and perhaps someone higher, intended to get to the bottom of things quickly and that his authority had the full backing of Admiral King, which included access to highly classified ship, train, and aircraft dispositions and movements. Also, King made sure Egan had access to the highest priorities for sending radio messages along with complete wiretapping capabilities, if needed, and the full cooperation of the FBI.

On Egan's left were two navy captains. The first was a thin, dark-haired man whose place card read CAPTAIN HENDERSON. On Henderson's right was a heavyset navy captain with thinning straw-colored hair. His place card read CAPTAIN DANBURY. Next to them was an empty chair where Sabovik had been seated. To the right of that was a balding marine colonel. Beside the colonel was Alexander Collins, an EOD[9] marine captain with a light, almost anemic complexion. His hair was in a tall crew-cut style. His eyes were light blue and were nearly perfect circles, as if they were propped open in perpetual surprise. Sabovik guessed that the combination of Collins's EOD work and his eyes gave rise to his nickname "Nitro"—as if he were perpetually occupied with something so sensitive that it could blow up at any instant.

To Collins's right was a cigar-chomping Army Air Corps colonel whose place card read COLONEL SPARKS. An army brigadier general by the name of Cartwell sat at the end, opposite Egan.

Seated to Admiral Egan's left, across from Sabovik, were two civilians. The place card of the first man, in coat and bow tie, read LARRY PINDAR—BUORD, ALAMAGORDO. The other civilian was a balding man in a dark blue suit. His place card announced he was ROGER STEWART—FBI. On Stewart's left were five army officers ranging in rank from full colonel to a first lieutenant sitting at the end, who tapped a stenographic machine. All the officers' coats were off and their ties were loosened except for Sparks, the air corps colonel, who kept his on, sporting a Fifteenth Air Force shoulder patch, three rows of ribbons, and five battle stars. Wall-mounted fans whirled furiously in the room's opposite corners, only succeeding in shoving the blue cloud of tobacco smoke in a counterclockwise direction.

"Excuse me, gentlemen," Sabovik said quietly and took the seat beside Captain Danbury.

Egan looked up to Sabovik, his question unspoken.

Sabovik replied, "Captain Doyle is still out there, Admiral, pacing up and down."

"Dammit. I told him to go get a cup of coffee. Is he getting impatient?"

"An understatement, sir," replied Sabovik.

Egan nodded. "That's Sam Doyle, all right. Chomping at the bit. Can't wait to get things done. I have to say this. He's a good man, but somebody's going to nail his ass to a hitching post and he knows he can't stop them." He eyed the group. "That's not what's going to happen here, gentlemen. Our job is to get our arms around this situation now and take names later. Most of all, I'm not going to sanction a kangaroo court against Sam Doyle." Egan checked his watch. "We'll get him in here shortly and listen to what he has to say, and then figure out what to do. In the meantime"—he looked at Sabovik—"you got what you need?"

"Yes, sir." Sabovik handed the folder over to Captain Danbury, his boss. "These are the load-out figures on the *Regina Dalmatia,* sir. We still don't have an accurate crew manifest, though."

"Mmm," said Danbury. He flipped pages, then waved the back of his hand at Sabovik. "Continue, please, John."

"Yes, sir." Sabovik looked around the table. "The *Regina Dalmatia* was loaded with 2,476 tons of high explosive. Most of that was composed of, let's see"—he flipped a sheet—"sixteen-inch, fourteen-inch, eight-, six-, and five-inch projectiles of various types, most of it armor piercing. That was in number two hold. All of it is semi-fixed, which means there were accompanying powder bags or canisters. Those were loaded in the number three hold. Also in number two hold were warheads for mark 14 and 15 torpedoes. Most of the stuff in the forward hold was 75-, 105-, and 155-millimeter projectiles for the army. The aft hold held smaller stuff. Aerial rockets, twenty- and forty-millimeter ammunition, some depth charges."

"The crew?" asked Cartwell.

"We don't have a full tally yet, General, but they were from the Higgins Navigation Company of Newark, New Jersey. The captain had been licensed for twelve years. And they had a navy gun crew aboard."

"What happened?" asked Egan.

At a nod from Danbury, Sabovik turned to another report.

"Eyewitnesses aboard the destroyer *Reveley* say the weather was perfect—visibility unlimited. Sonar conditions were five thousand yards, and there was no sonar contact from any one of the six destroyers. They were zigzagging on a base course of two-two-six at twelve knots. The *Regina Dalmatia* was the guide." Sabovik eyed the army officers. "In other words, she was right in the center of the formation, which means she was encircled by four other merchant ships and six destroyers."

"Difficult to get a torpedo in there," offered Captain Danbury.

Egan added, "And with perfect sonar conditions and all those ships around her, we can pretty much exclude that a submarine got the *Regina Dalmatia*."

"Where was the *Reveley* in relation to the *Regina Dalmatia*?" demanded Henderson.

"Let's see, here it is. The *Reveley* was in station five, bearing one-four-five from the *Regina Dalmatia*. In other words"—Sabovik nodded to the army officers—"they were on her starboard quarter."

"Okay," said Egan. "That means the people on the *Reveley* were looking almost right at her when she went up."

"Yes, sir," said Sabovik. "We also have a report from the *Phillips,* which was in station six on the opposite side of the formation; they also had a full view of the *Regina Dalmatia.*"

"And . . . ," asked Egan. "Anything we don't know?"

Sabovik shook his head. "Eyewitnesses pretty much concur that she went up in a single white-hot brilliant flash. No one saw what could have been a torpedo hit. Nothing like an explosion plume up the ship's side. No torpedo wakes. And as we said, no sonar contacts before or after."

"A brilliant flash?" asked Pindar, the ordance expert.

"Just one great big flash, a shock wave, a loud boom lasting twenty to thirty seconds, and then everything was gone," said Sabovik. "Same as Port Chicago," he added.

With a glance at Stewart to his left, Pindar sat back and steepled his fingers. "Keep in mind, Commander, that there was a double flash at Port Chicago. A minor explosion was observed. The major detonation occurred four to six seconds later."

"Yes, sir. Excuse me, sir," said Sabovik.

"Any damage to other ships?" asked Stewart.

"No, sir."

Egan asked Pindar, "Larry, what was that gadget you were waving around Port Chicago yesterday. You called it a Geiger . . ."

". . . counter," said Pindar.

"What the hell is that for?"

Pindar picked up his briefcase and shuffled papers. With another glance at Stewart, he said, "We use that to measure different levels of ambient light."

"What?" asked Egan.

"Light, you know, ambient light. Something that might have been leaking out that would have attracted a saboteur."

"Are you bullshitting me?" retorted Egan.

Stewart said, "Admiral, let me—"

Nitro Collins raised his hand.

"Yes, Captain?" said Egan.

Collins said, "Excuse me, Mr. Pindar. But isn't a Geiger counter used to measure radiation?"

"Well, yes, that too." Pindar sat back, folded his arms, and shot Collins a steely glance.

"That's what I thought," said Egan. "Why did you have it there in the first place?"

"The best thing we can tell you, Admiral, is we used it to make sure there aren't any dangerous residuals around the explosion site. And we found none," said Pindar.

"Tell us again what you boys do down in Alamagordo?" asked General Cartwright.

Pindar looked at Stewart, who said, "As we said before, General, we measure the physics of explosive forces and determine the best compositions for munitions of the future."

Egan snapped, "More bullshit. Our ordnance labs do that. What the hell are you guys really doing?"

"Well, I must admit, some of it is classified," said Pindar.

"Horseshit!" said Egan.

Stewart said, "Admiral Egan, the director personally asked me to convey to you and this committee that Alamagordo has no gravity in this situation."

Egan shot back, "Perhaps we better ask Mr. Hoover to speak with Admiral King."

Stewart steepled his fingers. "They have."

Egan sat back and lit a cigarette.

Cartwright kept at it. "How does what you do in New Mexico relate to what we're doing here?"

Pindar sputtered for a moment, then said, "Nothing, I hope. We're just checking."

"What?" said Egan and Cartwright simultaneously.

Stewart sat forward and said, "What he means is that they have technologies that will help you trace the origin of the explosion."

Egan and Cartwright traded glances. Finally Egan said, "This isn't getting anywhere. We'd better get back on track." He turned to Sabovik. "Is that it?"

"Yes, sir, for now." Sabovik sat back, lit a cigarette, and exhaled, feeling a bizarre satisfaction that he was contributing to the density of the cloud in the room.

General Cartwell snorted. "Poof. That's it? Scratch one ammo ship? Come on, we need more than that, Jack. Dammit, I've got an invasion coming up and I'm supposed to have bombs and bullets on hand for 170,000 men. Now the question from General MacArthur is, what the hell is going on? He wants to know if his supply lines are secure."

Egan butt-lit a fresh cigarette. "Easy, Tom. We have five ships loading right now. You'll have plenty of stuff." He exhaled, the smoke in the room growing thicker.

Colonel McTierney of the Army Transportation Corps was seated across from Sabovik. "Rumor is that the darkies won't load any more ships. They're scared. I've heard talk about mutiny."

Egan drew a long face and replied, "Colonel, there's truth to that, I'm afraid. I'm ashamed to admit we've botched it. The loading gangs in Port Chicago were all black and now nobody wants to talk to them, buck them up. They're scared to death. Worse, somebody stuck them on a barge and everybody is ignoring them like they're guilty or something. We're going to take care of that."

"Poor bastards," said McTierney. "Who's supposed to be responsible for them? The sonofabitch should be cashiered."

He swung his eyes to Egan. "Doesn't this lie at the feet of your Captain Doyle?"

Egan said, "Probably so. We'll ask Sam when he comes in. But remember this. It's not every day that 1,780 tons of high explosives goes up in your face. We're trying to unravel this thing a step at a time, and right now we're making the rules as we go along. And the first rule is to keep the stuff moving." He darted a glance at Cartwell.

McTierney bored in with, "Who's to say one of the darkies didn't do it on purpose?"

"Highly unlikely," said Egan. "But then we're leaving no stone unturned." He nodded to Danbury. "That's his job."

Danbury steepled his fingers and went, "Mmm."

Egan turned back to General Cartwell. "Tom, Port Chicago is still a mess, and, for the time being it's unusable. So your ships are being loaded out in Mare Island. We're getting it done. You'll have your stuff."

"I'll take your word for it," said Cartwell. Then he asked, "Where do we go from here?" All eyes turned to Egan. After a moment, he tapped his finger on the tablecloth and said, "I recommend we attack this from three main standpoints. First, we want assurances that the ammunition is stable. Is it coming from the factories in a satisfactory manner? Does it comply with safety regulations? Is it safe to handle?" He turned to Pindar. "That's your job, Larry. You say you and Roger and your boys know your science? So prove it. I want you to go after the munitions manufacturers on a round-the-clock basis. Especially the boys making the big stuff. I don't think small arms could touch off explosions like we've been having. So go for the companies making five-inch stuff and up. Let's see if we can validate what they have."

"Right," said Pindar.

Egan turned to the navy captain on his right. "Regis, you've got to look into ammunition handling and loading procedures. Also, I want complete background checks on all Port Chicago personnel."

"Yes, sir," said Henderson.

Egan continued, "This talk of work stoppage and mutiny is bullshit. I want you to put a halt to that. I have special powers and I can do anything I damn want, legally and otherwise.

Right now, I want those ships loaded properly and swiftly. But I don't want people to go after the loading crews just because they're black. We'll look into this in our own time and if we find something wrong, then we'll figure out what to do. In the meantime, put 'em to work." Egan thumped his forefinger on the table.

"Yes, sir," said Captain Henderson. "We have discovered one thing."

All eyes turned to Henderson.

He continued, "The supervisors have been running the loading gangs against one another on a competitive basis. In other words, the team with the fastest loading time, or the one that moves the most tonnage, gets more liberty and extra privileges, et cetera."

"Do you think that led to carelessness?" asked General Cartwell.

"We're looking into it," said Henderson.

"Anything else, Regis?" asked Admiral Egan.

"That's it for now, sir."

Egan stubbed out his cigarette and laid a fresh one on his lower lip. He lit it with a giant Zippo, exhaled, and said, "Find out what those loading gangs are doing right and what they're not doing right. See if we can improve things for them, and for efficiency."

"Yes, sir," said Henderson.

Cartwright asked, "What's the third point, Jack?"

Egan laid both hands flat on the table. "The supply line. I want to see what's happening to the stuff along the way."

McTierney straightened a bit. "Why, that's a job for transportation corps security, Admiral. And believe me, we've been working our butts off since all this began. No way a Jap spy can get to one of our trains."

Egan gave McTierney a long look. "I'm sure there isn't, Byron, but just to make sure, I'm assigning Commander Sabovik here to check the supply routes. And I understand our biggest railhead is in Roseville, California. Is that right, Colonel?"

"Well, yes," said McTierney.

"Place is full of people running around, switching cars and engines and all sorts of equipment?"

"Well, yes."

"And what about the Sierra Nevada route?" asked Egan.

"Pretty tight," said McTierney. "We have guards in every snowshed and at least one every mile. And that's over a 139-mile route from Sparks, Nevada, to Roseville, California."

"Is that so?" asked Egan. "Well, Colonel, I want it checked and double-checked and then taken apart and checked again."

"Yes, sir," said McTierney. He took out a handkerchief and mopped his brow.

Egan added. "Also, don't you think we should bear down on that as well as points east? Say, Nevada and Utah and Wyoming and so forth?"

"It's an enormous task," sputtered McTierney.

"Well, yes, and we've had two enormous explosions. We have to start somewhere, so I say we start with Roseville. Okay? Then we look farther east." Egan darted a glance around the table. Nobody objected.

"Good," said Egan. He turned to Captain Danbury. "Roger, can you help Colonel McTierney and take that on?"

"Mmm." Danbury rubbed his chin and looked at Sabovik.

"Yes, sir. Roseville, sir," said Sabovik.

Danbury looked at Collins, the EOD marine captain. "You mind joining us?"

"Be glad to, sir," said Collins.

"How can he refuse?" said General Cartwright.

Egan grinned. "Damn, I appreciate men who know how to follow orders. You run a tight ship, Roger."

"Mmm," said Danbury.

"*Mmm.* Is that all you can say, Roger?" asked Egan.

Danbury tapped tobacco into a pipe, looked directly at Egan, and said, "Glad to be of service, sir."

Egan grinned again and tapped a fist on the table. "See that? People who follow orders. Military courtesy. How can we lose?"

The men chuckled.

Egan turned to Sabovik, "Okay, John, go on out there and bring in Captain Doyle. Let's see what he has to say."

THIRTEEN

10 August 1944
Roseville Community Hospital, room 206
Roseville, California

Donovan felt better than he had for a long time. Blood tests showed that he was responding to treatment, and chances were good that he would be discharged tomorrow. The only problem was that Diane Logan continued to act like an icebox.

Roseville Community Hospital turned out to be a comfortable two-hundred-bed facility with a bored Donovan walking the halls the past few days, looking out, taking in the town. One thing for sure. Roseville was a railroading town, the second largest hub in the United States. Whistles and chuffing engines, day and night, confirmed that. Often he was awakened by the strident racket of an engine pulling out, couplers clanking down a line of eighty or one hundred cars.

He was in a four-man room; the tag at the door read MORGAN, MUMFORD, SODAWSKI & DONOVAN. The names rolled off the tongue as if they were a law firm, and indeed, the nurses had a grand time with them as they made rounds, especially in the evening.

Roland Morgan, the oldest, was a grandfather of five children and half owner at Barclay's Hardware Store on Oak Street. The war had been hard for the retail hardware business, and an overstretched Morgan and Barclay were mortgaged to the hilt. Ulcers and the doctor's demand for complete bed rest is what put the thin, bespectacled Roland Morgan in Roseville Community Hospital.

Stanley Mumford was a lawyer who worked for the Southern Pacific Railroad. Poor hearing kept the young Stanley unmarried and out of the service, which frustrated him endlessly, especially in the presence of uniformed men like Donovan. Mumford had undergone surgery for a double hernia and had moaned for the first three days, the others having a difficult time sleeping. But now he seemed better.

Benjamin Sodawski was admitted for an unspecified illness. But soon it became apparent that Sodawski had had bouts with alcohol and was on the edge of delirium tremens.

Donovan had slept the entire night of his surgery and a good part of the next day. He'd heard later that Sodawski, who was admitted the same night as Donovan, had groaned a lot and had to be strapped in. But after two days, Ben Soda Whiskers, as he was called, became the life of the party in room 206. A slight man, no more than five-seven, he sported a flowing salt-and-pepper beard and, like Mumford, worked for the Southern Pacific. Soda Whiskers was a perpetual fireman. Like the second-class gunner's mate in the navy always getting busted down to seaman, Soda Whiskers should have been promoted to engineer a long time ago. Instead, minor infractions held him back: drinking on the job, talking back to supervisors, fighting, gambling. Even so, Soda Whiskers was a free spirit, Donovan sensed. Someone you could bet your life on when the chips were down. One thing about Soda Whiskers that caught your attention: he had one dark brown eye. The other one, the right, was a bright duck-egg blue. If one saw just the left, Soda Whiskers looked rather ordinary. But if just the right eye was revealed, the railroader appeared bright and intense, almost as if some hidden source of energy burned from within nearly out of control.

It was eight in the evening when Soda Whiskers reached in the bedside drawer and pulled out a canvas bag. "You pussies up for a game?" he growled. The bag contained the cards and chips they'd used for poker over the last three nights. Without waiting for a reply, he tossed aside his covers and shuffled over to Mumford's bed. They gathered there for a reason. Mumford kept to himself most of the time and didn't smile or laugh at Sodawski's crude jokes, which at times had the others roaring. During the day, the young attorney stared off into space and didn't join in their conversations. But poker seemed to buck him up. The others let him win at times.

Soda Whiskers reached over and turned off Mumford's radio.

"Hey . . ." As usual, Mumford had been unfocused, staring at the ceiling.

"Don't need no bullshit longhair music," said Soda Whiskers, plopping the bag on Mumford's bed.

"I told you, it's Mozart, you clod." Radio station KGEI in San Francisco played classical music at night. They often went to sleep by it. He clicked it back on.

"C'mon, Junior," said Soda Whiskers, "we don't need no—"

Morgan raised a hand. "It's okay, Stan. Just turn it down a bit."

"That crap gives me a pain," grumbled Soda Whiskers. Then he clapped his hands. "Okay. Time for some real recreation." He shook chips and cards from the bag and yelled at Donovan, "Hey, Commodore, shake a leg. What the hell's wrong with you? You afraid we're gonna clean you out again?" Donovan and Soda Whiskers had conspired to put Mumford up by twenty dollars the previous evening. Like an eight-year-old, Mumford had squealed in delight as he gathered in chips.

Donovan was sorting gear, getting ready to check out in the morning. "On my way." He eased off his bed, pulled up a chair, and sat at Mumford's bed, Morgan on his right, Sodawski across.

"You guys want to play some serious poker?" asked Sodawski.

"What?" they asked.

"None of this *joker, split-bearded kings, and one-eyed jacks are wild* bullshit. Let's play some down-home, sho 'nough stuff poker."

"Such as?" Donovan sat back, trying to stifle a grin. Sodawski was scheduled for release tomorrow as well, Morgan the next day. It seemed Sodawski was intent on regaining his losses before everyone split up.

"Five-card stud. Guts to open," said Soda Whiskers. He passed the deck to Mumford. "Cut."

The young attorney did as instructed.

With a grunt, Soda Whiskers took the deck and began dealing.

"I can't remember, does three of a kind beat a straight?" asked Mumford.

Flipping cards, Soda Whiskers gave a ghoulish smile. "Wait and see."

Morgan lit an enormous cigar. "Damn right it does."

Mumford said to Morgan. "I thought I heard Dr. Logan say no tobacco."

"It's my first one since I've been here," squeaked Morgan.

"Your third," said Soda Whiskers.

"Well, what she doesn't know won't hurt her," Morgan said. Oblivious, he finished lighting and blew smoke. "Ummfff, ahhh."

Donovan began to gather his cards when he looked up, noticing the men had stopped and were looking over his shoulder. It became quiet. In fact the whole hospital corridor was quiet; almost like before an earthquake.

Donovan turned around. Silhouetted in the doorway was a man, his face indistinguishable. Powerfully built, he was about six feet with broad shoulders and must have weighed nearly two hundred. He had a tight crew cut and an absolutely square face and wore the summer khakis of the U.S. Navy, his combination cap clamped under his left arm. Two and a half stripes on his shoulder boards told Donovan this man was a lieutenant commander. In the hallway behind the figure was a woman in a wheelchair.

The man knocked on the doorjamb. "Commander Donovan?"

"Uh-oh. The cops are here," said Soda Whiskers.

"Come," said Donovan. He tossed his cards on the bed. "Deal me out for now, Ben." He stood to meet the lieutenant commander.

The man walked in, extending his hand. "How do you do, sir? I'm Richard Kruger." His face was lightly pockmarked, very tan, square, with thin lips and white even teeth. But what struck Donovan was that his eyes were close together, giving the impression that Kruger was cross-eyed. Or was it intense concentration? Donovan couldn't tell.

"Good to finally meet you, XO. What a nice surprise."

Donovan took Kruger's hand and was greeted with a crushing grip. He actually felt as if his knees were going to give way before Kruger released his hand. Pain radiated up Donovan's arm, but he did his best to appear nonchalant, saying, "What brings you out here?"

"Thought I'd better pay my respects, Captain. Please forgive me. I didn't hear anything from the medics until yesterday."

"Not to worry. There's plenty of time."

Kruger turned and said, "Here, may I present my wife, Vicky?"

Vicky Kruger wheeled through the doorway offering a hand. "Good to see you again, Captain." She wore a very heavy perfume.

The other men caught it, too. Soda Whiskers gave a low whistle.

Donovan said, "What an honor. My word." He ran a hand over stubble. "I'm afraid—"

"Captain. We're only here for a moment. We don't want to disturb you. And our train leaves in"—he checked his watch—"forty minutes. So we won't be long."

"Please, sit," said Donovan, waving to chairs around his bed. "Can I get you something, coffee perhaps?"

"No, thank you, sir. We had gallons of coffee on the train out here, and to tell you the truth, my eyes are floating," said Kruger.

"Pardon?"

"That means he has to go potty," laughed Vicky.

Kruger grew red and Donovan chuckled. "Outside and to your left," said Donovan.

"I believe I'll take you up on that, Captain," said Kruger. He walked out.

"You look a lot better than you did the last time," said Vicky, pulling a pack of Luckys from her purse.

"I do?" Donovan looked around for matches. "Let me ask—"

"Yes, you do." Expertly, she flicked a match one-handed across the strike board, lit the cigarette, and inhaled. "I can tell you now. You looked like a pile of crap. What happened?"

Donovan opened a drawer and handed over an ashtray as he gave her the extended story.

"Well, that's no fun. When do you get out?" she asked.

"I think tomorrow."

From across the room, Soda Whiskers yelled, "Shiiiit. Where'd you get them aces?"

Donovan looked over to see Mumford raking in chips.

Kruger walked back in, saying, "Sounds like the mess decks in here."

Mumford giggled.

"Can't concentrate with that damned Vichinsky playing," said Soda Whiskers. "Here, you earned the deal."

"It's Mozart," said Mumford, shuffling the cards.

Kruger looked up and said, "Actually, it's Haydn."

"I beg your pardon?" Mumford looked across the room to him.

"Joseph Haydn, I believe," said Kruger.

Donovan wouldn't have predicted a solidly built boxer like Kruger to come up with something like that. He caught a glance from Vicky. Her eyes were gleaming.

"I don't know," said Mumford. "I didn't realize Haydn did that kind of—"

"Who cares? Deal," growled Soda Whiskers. They went back to their poker.

Kruger paced for a moment. "Captain, do you need anything?"

"Nothing, thanks. Right now I'm supposed to be on leave. And off the ship, the name is Mike. Okay?"

"Yes, sir."

"Yes, Mike."

"Mike."

"Now tell me, uh, do you go by Dick?" asked Donovan.

"Richard, sir."

"Okay, Richard. Admiral Nimitz sends his best," said Donovan.

"So I heard." Kruger glanced at Vicky. "I'm quite surprised, actually. He busted me once."

"What?" said Donovan.

"You'll see it in my jacket. It was for—"

"He was very specific with me and spoke highly of you. Said you ran rings around the *Augusta*'s chief engineer."

"Well . . ."

"As far as the other stuff, that was long ago and you were enlisted then. Now you're a lieutenant commander."

Kruger nodded. "That's true."

"How's our ship?" asked Donovan.

Kruger twirled his combination cap on a short, powerful finger and said, "She's in good material shape. It's the crew I'm worried about."

"In what way?" prodded Donovan.

"She needs to get under way and stretch her legs. We've got a lot of green kids who are getting bored with nothing to do."

Morgan said, "I'm out." His cards hit the bed.

"Beats me," said Soda Whiskers.

"Keen," said Mumford.

Soda Whiskers yelped, "All you had was a pair of sevens? Sheeyat!"

The radio concert ended. In cool, soft tones, the announcer said, "You've just heard Joseph Haydn's One Hundredth Symphony, the Military, part of his London Symphonies, played by Arturo Toscanini and the NBC Symphony Orchestra."

"You were right, Commodore," called Soda Whiskers to Kruger. "At least there's something the kid can't do."

Vicky shot Donovan another glance.

There was a scuffle across the room. "What the hell?" roared Soda Whiskers.

Morgan dropped to his knees, a hand clutching his throat; he spun in a half circle, gasping. A pile of books fell off the bedside table and crashed to the floor.

"Call the doc," yelled Soda Whiskers. "He's having a heart attack!"

Kruger dashed out the door.

Morgan gave a loud gasp and sank to his haunches. Horribly blue in the face, he fell forward, his body twitching.

"Dammit." Donovan dashed over and kneeled by Morgan. "He's not breathing. Ben, help me flip him over."

Soda Whiskers came around the bed and dropped to his knees. Mumford eased out of bed and kneeled beside them.

"Here we go, guys. Easy now," said Donovan. They rolled Morgan to his back. His face was blue. His eyes were wide open. So was his mouth. "I wonder . . ." Donovan stuck a finger in Morgan's mouth.

"What the hell you doin'?" said Soda Whiskers, eyeing Donovan with a glistening light blue eye.

"Hold on," said Donovan. "Yeah." He reached farther down Morgan's throat.

"Leave him be. Wait for the doc," said Soda Whiskers.

"Not for long," said Donovan. "Just a little farther. Here, fellas, roll him to his side a little."

"What the hell for?" yelled Soda Whiskers. Then he called over his shoulder, "Where's the doc?"

Donovan barked, "Do it! Now!"

Mumford reached under Morgan. Soda Whiskers helped and they got Morgan to his side.

Donovan said, "Okay, that might work. Ah!" With a jerk, he pulled a false-tooth stay plate out of Morgan's mouth. "Stuck in his throat, must have gone down the windpipe."

"Geez," said Mumford. "He took a big puff on that cigar and started hacking. That must be when it happened."

Donovan said, "Roll him all the way over. See if we can get him going again."

They rolled Morgan onto his stomach, and Donovan slapped his back. Then he straddled the prostrate man and began pushing on his lungs, giving artificial respiration. "Come on, come on, old man."

Morgan wheezed.

"That's better, Roland. Come on, you can do it," urged Donovan.

Morgan gave a prolonged gurgling gasp.

"Atta boy," said Donovan. He sat back, and they watched as Morgan's chest heaved time and again.

"Shit. Lookit that. His color is coming back," said Soda Whiskers. He looked up to Donovan. "How'd you know?"

"Just a guess. I knew he had a flipper," said Donovan. He picked it up off the floor and tossed it onto Morgan's bed. "Let's get him back into—"

"Excuse me." Dr. Logan kneeled beside Donovan. "Let's sit him up and let me listen to him."

They moved Morgan to a sitting position. "Who . . . ," he gasped.

Donovan patted the man's hand. "Easy Roland. You're fine now."

Diane moved her stethoscope around. "Sounds fine. Pulse is a little weak, but he sounds okay." She looked up to two nurses. "Let's get him into bed." She reached up to his bedside table, fumbled her grip, and knocked over a large glass vase full of flowers.

"Damn," she said softly. "I'll, I'll go out and get . . ."

Morgan lay a hand on her sleeve. "It's only the tenth time today," he gasped. The others chuckled. Dr. Logan was notorious for knocking things over. "Now can I finish my poker game? I'm down fifteen bucks."

"No, I mean really . . ."

They laughed.

"Forget it. The damn things were nearly wilted anyway."

With the help of two nurses, Morgan shuffled over and flopped onto his back. He pointed a bony finger at Mumford. "Guy's a ringer, I tell you. Soda Whiskers. Don't you know when you've been taken?"

"Sheyyatt," grumped Soda Whiskers.

Diane Logan bent over and picked Morgan's burning cigar off the floor. Jamming a hand on her hip, she asked, "Whom, may I ask, does this belong to?" She walked to the sink and turned on the water.

"Hold it," Mumford said. "It's mine, actually, Dr. Logan. Hope you don't mind."

Diane Logan stopped, looking from Morgan to Mumford. "Fine." She gave the cigar to Mumford. "Here, smoke it."

"Thanks, Doc." Mumford took the cigar and puffed mightily.

Diane Logan went over to Morgan and took his pulse. Then she ran a hand over his hair, smoothing it. "Poor Roland. That was not fun. But you're okay now. You be careful with that stay plate. It's getting too loose. Better have a dentist fit you for a new one." She leaned close, sniffed at his face, and gave a churlish smile. "You're a good man, Roland, except you have awful taste in tobacco."

"Huh?" said Morgan.

Diane leaned over and kissed him on the forehead. "If you're going to smoke, smoke a good cigar. Not cheap stuff like that one. That way, you won't gag so much. And only one a day."

"Awwww," went Morgan.

"Wheeeouw!" whooped Soda Whiskers.

"Hubba-hubba," said Mumford.

"Okay, Doc. Thanks," grinned Morgan.

"Don't thank me, Roland. Thank Commander Donovan. He's the one who saved you," said Diane.

"He did?" asked Morgan.

"That's right. Okay, see you later, fellas. Lights-out in fifteen minutes." She gave Donovan a quick smile and said, "Your blood work looks good. You can go home tomorrow." She started to walk out.

"Doc?" said Donovan.

"Yes?"

He caught her at the doorway and said quietly, "Can you give me some of those pills to take with me?"

"Are you still having nightmares?"

"Not really." The "Tiny" nightmare had been recurring about twice a week before his surgery. Then three nights after it, when the anesthetic wore off, the dream returned in vivid horror, Tiny's screams echoing in his head. Morgan and Mumford awoke white-faced as Donovan sat up in bed, shouting, "Clear the mount! Clear the mount!" Sodawski snored through it all as the night nurse calmed Donovan. The next day, Diane had prescribed something that helped him sleep.

Kruger looked at him curiously, and Donovan turned his back, saying, "But they help sort of, you know, smooth things out."

Diane said, "I can give you a few, but you should really take it up with your own doctors. That's something you don't fool with."

"What shouldn't I fool with?"

"Well, they call it a number of things. Around here it's—"

He didn't want to hear her say *battle fatigue* so he said, "Come on, Doc, I'm not that far gone."

Diane and Donovan looked over to see everyone watching. In almost a whisper, she said,

"Well, have them take a look at you. Okay?"

"Doc," he protested.

She grabbed his elbow. "Come on now. Promise."

"All right."

"Okay. I'll give you some stuff to tide you over. Sleep well." She tapped a finger on his nose and walked out.

Donovan walked back in the room rubbing his nose absently, not realizing that the corners of his mouth were turned up.

"Wow wheee," said Soda Whiskers. "You have a date?"

"No," muttered Donovan.

"So it's still not too late. What do you think I have to do to get a date with her?"

"Jump out the window and break a leg, sucker. Now deal," said Mumford. Vicky slapped her hands over her face and began laughing.

Kruger asked, "Would you like to start with the personnel records, Captain?"

Donovan sat on his bed. "Just the officers for now, Richard." He picked up a small hand mirror and looked at his nose. What the hell is it about her?

"Sir?" asked Kruger.

Vicky's grin spread from ear to ear.

Ignoring her, Donovan said, "You see, Richard, Admiral Nimitz told me to take it easy and not do anything strenuous."

"Yes, sir."

"Mike."

"Mike, sir. Yes, Mike."

FOURTEEN

11 August 1944
Ugaki suite, flag officers' quarters
Yokosuka Naval Shipyard
Yokosuka, Japan

Commander Yuzura Noyama limped to the blackout curtain, lifted a corner, and peeked out. The sky was clear, the moon overhead full. Even under a complete blackout, the massive Yokosuka naval base with its insect-like cranes, the city beyond, the surrounding hills, and the glistening waters of Tokyo Bay, stood out in stark detail.

"Arrrrgh!" A painful cry drifted from the bedroom where Vice Admiral Matome Ugaki sat in a chair while Captain Saguaro Mishima, the fleet dentist, filled a cavity. Earlier, Mishima had filed into Ugaki's suite followed by a rat-faced assistant lugging two heavy suitcases. Together they'd set up a mobile lab in the bedroom and gone to work on Ugaki. The only reason Ugaki permitted Dr. Mishima to work on his mouth in the first place was that he was also being fitted for a new set of false teeth.

"Careful with the curtain, Yuzura. The air-raid wardens would love nothing more than to throw a bunch of flag officers in the pen. I hear they work on a point system these days." It was Vice Admiral Takeo Kurita, Noyama's boss and mentor. Along with Vice Admiral Ugaki, a renowned battleship sailor, Kurita was one of five top seagoing admirals gathered in the suite. The other three were Vice Admiral Jisaburo Ozawa, Vice Admiral Shoji Nishimura, and Vice Admiral Kiyohide Shima. Four of them sat around a low table playing a game of mah-jongg while Dr. Mishima ground away on Ugaki in the next room.

Ugaki's outburst made it difficult to keep third-class petty officer Minoru Onishi, one of two valets, from kicking in the door and going to his aid. Onishi was well over six feet, weighed 340 pounds, and had no neck. A brute of a man, his eyes were so close together they often looked as if they were fused into one. And he had a thick lower lip that often hung open, exposing a jagged lower row of tobacco-stained teeth. Onishi was a gunner's mate who'd been demoted to seaman first class several times and was known more for eloquent grunts than for words of two or more syllables, which he distributed with great effort. But Onishi was strong, determined, and very loyal. And he always got his task done—that was why Ugaki liked him and selected him for a valet. There were occasions, too, when Onishi's great strength came in handy, the most recent a barroom brawl in Singapore when Ugaki sent him looking for girls. Today only the constant sharp commands from one of the admirals in the room kept Onishi from charging through the door.

The admirals had been called to Tokyo ten days ago for a strategy meeting on Operation SHO-GO[10] by the plan's innovator, Admiral Soemu Toyoda, commander in chief of the Combined Fleet and overall commander of the Imperial Japanese Navy. There was no doubt the meeting was needed, but politics were rampant. Last June, the Americans had taken the Marianas with its three large islands Guam, Tinian, and Saipan. This caused the downfall of Prime Minister Hideki Tojo and his cabinet on 18 July with civilian and military officials scrambling to save themselves. Absent that, some committed seppuku.[11] Senior flag officers in the army and navy knew what was to come. Using Tinian and Saipan's three-thousand-meter runways, American B-29s could now strike major cities in Japan at will, including Tokyo. It was only a matter of time. That was why Noyama was looking out the window—checking firebreaks. Using everything from bulldozers to donkey carts, civilian defense workers frantically cut large open swaths throughout the Tokyo-Yokohama-Yokosuka complex.

For the past four days, Toyoda and his admirals had been

war-gaming in Meguro, a Tokyo suburb near the Navy Ministry and Imperial Palace. Intelligence reports had been gathered. The mutual conclusion was that MacArthur would go for the Philippines instead of Formosa, Okinawa, or possibly the Home Islands. Hence, they concentrated their efforts on the Philippines, and the plan was formally designated Operation SHO-1, as Kurita had in mind. But they'd lost so much of the fleet—in particular, seasoned carrier pilots—in the disastrous Marianas campaign. Without saying it, all present sensed Japan had her back to the wall, that a brilliant stroke was required to throw MacArthur back.

On the first two days, Admiral Toyoda, more a politician than a seafarer, went through the motions of running the gaming sessions, but he was oftentimes shouted down by Navy Minister Mitsumasa Yonai and Admiral Kantaro Suzuki, head of the privy council and close adviser to Emperor Hirohito. Worse, Ugaki, one of the referees, cheated when the red team (America) sank two blue-team (Japan) aircraft carriers. Instead of nine hits and two carriers sunk, he arbitrarily recalculated the score to three hits and only one carrier damaged. Even at that, the red team went on to win both days' matches, with General Yoshijiro Umezu, the army's chief of staff, scowling at Admiral Yonai, the privy council officials scowling at those two, and the Jushin[12] scowling at the privy council.

They had concurred on two things: First, MacArthur would strike in Leyte Gulf, a large natural anchorage on Leyte's east side that yawned invitingly to attackers from the east. Second, nothing short of the total commitment of all of Japan's remaining ships could stop him. One blue-team innovation on the SHO-1 gaming board was a pincer movement. Nishimura and Shima would lead battle groups through the Surigao Strait and attack MacArthur from the south, thrusting up into Leyte Gulf. Simultaneously, Kurita would lead another battle group through the San Bernardino Strait and drive down along the eastern shore of Samar, rendezvousing with the Nishimura/Shima force off Leyte Gulf, and together wipe out MacArthur's troopships. But the blue team lost each time because they had no air cover. While the hapless Toyoda sat back, watching others vent their rage, Ugaki rushed around, changing rules, mitigating blue-team losses. Today they adjourned to their quarters at six o'clock with two major questions unanswered: how to stop Halsey and his carriers, and how to gain air superiority.

Noyama mused over the admirals and generals he'd watched the past few days: grown men yelling at one another. For the most part, Kurita, Nishimura, Shima, and Ozawa, battle veterans, kept cool and remained detached, working with their staffs. But even the veterans couldn't answer the two key questions, the latter perhaps more important, since it was the lack of air cover and nearly four hundred irreplaceable planes and pilots that had lost them the Marianas.

". . . it's only a matter of time," Noyama muttered, thinking of the air raids that were sure to come. If only the people knew. He wondered what would happen then. He let the blackout curtain drop.

"Uhhhh!" It was Ugaki again, growling in pain.

Onishi tensed but forced himself to relax under a withering glance from Vice Admiral Ozawa.

Nishimura pushed a tile across the mah-jongg board and said, "Better send in a bottle of Johnnie Walker."

"Uhhh, Johnnie Walker?" grunted Onishi. Providing a square fifth of Johnnie Walker Black Label Scotch was one of Onishi's standard tasks. He began to head for a bar set up on a side table.

"I don't think so," said Kurita. "We need him sober." He snapped his fingers at Onishi and said, "Asahi. Frosted glass for the admiral."

"Uhhh." Onishi walked out.

"Ummm." Nishimura sat back to take another bite of katsuboshi, a salami-shaped stick of dried bonito fish. "This stuff is delicious, Noyama. Where in the world did you get it?"

"Well, sir—" Noyama began.

"On the base or off?" prodded Nishimura.

"Off, sir."

"Excellent. Where?" demanded Nishimura.

Kurita raised a hand. "Yuzura, I don't want you to answer any more of Nishimura's questions. He may buy the place and ruin it for the rest of us." The others chuckled. Nishimura's family was well off. He could have afforded to buy anything.

"Owwww!" screeched Ugaki. "*Kono BaDianearo*[13]." Something crashed.

Ozawa leaned forward, "First it's false teeth, now he's having a . . . root canal?" He looked up to Kurita.

Kurita shrugged. "A filling, I thought."

The door was wrenched open and Ugaki strutted out bare-chested, his trousers held up by suspenders. He massaged his jaw, wiped his face with a towel, and muttered, "Man is a sadist." Walking over to the side table, he grabbed a bottle of Johnnie Walker Black Label Scotch.

Dr. Mishima walked out, his assistant close behind, staggering with the two cases of the mobile dentistry unit. Ugaki stood with his back to them and filled his glass halfway with scotch. Dr. Mishima and his assistant bowed. Ugaki continued to ignore them, so they backed silently out the door while he downed his scotch in three gulps.

When the door closed softly, Ugaki turned. Finding Noyama the nearest, he shouted, "That fool couldn't get the motor to work on his stupid drilling machine."

"Sir?" said Noyama.

"Had to use a foot pedal." Ugaki waved a hand in the air. "*Zzzz, zzz, zzz.* Up and down, up and down. The damn fool couldn't get the thing to spin fast enough. Then, then—" Realizing the others at the mah-jongg table were smirking, he walked up to Noyama and sputtered, "The idiot ran out of novocaine!"

"Your new teeth look marvelous, Ugaki," quipped Nishimura. "I hope they smell better."

"What?" Ugaki spun.

"Your halitosis. Will new teeth keep your mouth from smelling so bad?" asked Nishimura, tossing a die in the air and catching it.

Ugaki pulled a face.

"Or is it all that *miso*[14] you suck up?" asked Kurita. The others laughed.

Ignoring them, Ugaki stepped closer to Noyama. "Do you smell halitosis, son?"

The man had been sweating and smelled of body odor.
"No, sir," said Noyama.

"Here, Kurita!" shouted Ugaki. "Watch." He grabbed Noyama's cheek and pinched hard.

"Owwww!" protested Noyama.

Ugaki kicked Noyama in the shin and then released his grip on Noyama's cheek.

Noyama stepped back, rubbing his cheek while the others sat at the table watching Ugaki. He had their full attention.

"It came to me," Ugaki said, "with that incompetent dentist." He reached up and patted Noyama's cheek softly. "Sorry, son. But tell me, what did you feel?"

"Sir?" asked Noyama.

"What did you feel, Commander? That's all I asked you," said Ugaki, leveling a gaze at Noyama.

"My cheek, it . . . well, it . . ."

"Hurt, didn't it?" prodded Ugaki.

"Well, yes, sir," replied Noyama.

"How about your leg, your shin?" asked Ugaki.

"I don't know. I don't think so. It was my cheek that I was thinking of," replied Noyama.

"Ummm," said Ugaki.

Just then Onishi walked in silently, carrying a silver tray with a frosted glass and bottle of Asahi beer. He walked up to Ugaki and held out the tray with a bow. "Uhhhh."

"Thank you, Onishi." Ugaki sounded as if he was speaking with a dear old friend. He picked up the glass and bottle and poured, carefully nursing the foam to the top. Then he put the bottle to his cheek. "Ahhhh." He looked up, saying, "Isoroku loved Johnnie Walker. Taught me to love it, too." He held up the glass. "But I couldn't talk him into Asahi." He spoke of Admiral Isoroku Yamamoto, Toyoda's predecessor and CinC of the Combined Fleet. Architect of the Pearl Harbor attack and brilliant strategist, Ugaki had been Yamamoto's chief of staff until April 18, 1943, when both were shot down by American P-38s off Bougainville's coast. Yamamoto was killed, but Ugaki miraculously survived, although seriously injured. After a long recovery, he returned to seagoing commands.

And from this distance, Noyama noticed, grisly scars and burns were in stark evidence.

Ugaki sipped his Asahi and again pushed the glass to his cheek. "That dentist taught me something. You notice before they jab you with that novocaine needle, they first pinch your cheek to mask the pain?"

"Works all the time with me," agreed Kurita. "But what's all this have to do with Meguro?"

"We'll pinch Halsey's cheek," said Ugaki. "Offer him something." He darted a glance at Ozawa. "Then we shove the needle into MacArthur all the way."

"What?" the four admirals said in unison.

"A diversion. That's what the dentist does. He diverts you with the cheek pinching. Then he sticks the needle in. So I say let's offer Halsey what he wants. We divert him away with a piece of the Imperial Japanese Navy while we jab the needle into MacArthur and let him have it."

"Aircraft carriers?" gasped Ozawa. "My aircraft carriers? Preposterous."

"It's what Halsey wants," said Ugaki. "Isn't he the one who says, 'Hit hard, hit fast, hit often'? Well, let's give it to him. He can hit hard and as fast as he wants while we're stirring up the pot elsewhere. Look at it this way, what use are your carriers to us now if you don't have pilots?"

Kurita, Nishimura, and Shima turned to look at Ozawa. Kurita said it for them all: "Halsey has an ego bigger than MacArthur's. He would fall for something like that all right, Ozawa."

"Not that I'm afraid to die for the Emperor, but what if they sink us?" said Ozawa.

"For sinking two or three of your carriers, we sink fifty, a hundred of MacArthur's ships in Leyte Gulf," said Ugaki.

"But these carriers are all I have," protested Ozawa.

"What good are they without pilots? Where are your pilots?" Ugaki repeated.

"I . . . I." Ozawa raised his hands and flopped them to his side.

Ugaki stepped close to Ozawa. "Think of it, Ozawa. If you divert Halsey"—he nodded to Kurita, Nishimura, and Shima—"they would have the time of their lives. Damn!" Ugaki smacked a fist into his palm. "We'll send everything we've got in there. Even the *Musashi* and *Yamato*."

Ozawa's voice was strident. "And does that include you on *Yamato*'s bridge."

Ugaki stood to his full height, his scars red, almost glowing, "Better there than sucking it up with all the shore-based idiots here in Imperial Headquarters. You can—"

There was a collective intake of breath. Everyone's eyes were focused over Ugaki's shoulders. Admiral Toyoda had silently entered the room from an adjoining suite. He was followed by two aides, a rear admiral and a captain, carrying a huge briefcase.

Ugaki turned. All stood with him and bowed to Toyoda in unison. The others softly said "Gensui," an honorific given to the commander in chief of the Imperial Japanese Navy. Ugaki refused to say it. The only Gensui he'd respected was Admiral Yamamoto, a fighting, seagoing admiral. To Ugaki, the two CinCs following Yamamoto were worthless bureaucrats.

It was silent for a moment. Without a shirt, Ugaki felt naked standing before his commander in chief, even though he was in his own suite and even though Toyoda had walked in unannounced. Dammit. The man was dressed for dinner and even wore all his medals. "Would you like a drink, sir?" Ugaki nodded to the bar. "Perhaps some beer or some Johnnie Walker Black?"

"Ummm," said Toyoda. "That seems to be the preferred libation this evening. Just two fingers, please. I have to be sober for tonight's meeting with Umezu."

Noyama, standing closest to the bar, was surprised when Ugaki nodded casually to him. *Pour the CinC a drink.*

Noyama picked up a glass and poured as Toyoda said, "I heard part of what you were saying, Ugaki. Could you try it again for me?" He accepted the drink from Noyama, saying, "Thank you, Commander." Then he sat and waved with the back of his hand.

"Seats, gentlemen, please."

Everyone sat, except for Toyoda's aides, who backed to a corner.

Ugaki sat a meter across from Toyoda and said, "Admiral,

we need two things for this to happen." He waved to Onishi, who brought over a dress shirt.

"Which are?" Toyoda sipped. "Ummm, excellent."

Kurita moved to a chair beside Ugaki and said, "I think he has something, Gensui."

"Have you gamed it?" asked Toyoda.

"We'll have it up first thing tomorrow morning," said Ugaki.

"Very well. Now, what are your two things that must happen?" asked Toyoda.

Ugaki counted off on his fingers, "First, we have to get rid of Halsey and his carriers. Second, we need air cover. Lots of it." He went on to explain the rest of his plan. When he finished, the room was silent. Toyoda pierced Ugaki with a stare that would have killed a king cobra. But Ugaki knew Toyoda well enough to know that nothing was in his head at the moment. Most people were intimidated by the fierce stare and did everything from backpedaling to outright resignation. Ugaki knew better. Strictly a defense mechanism, the fierce stare meant Toyoda was vulnerable.

Casually Ugaki stood, finished buttoning his shirt, and waved a hand. Onishi passed over his tunic and helped him slip into it.

Toyoda steepled his fingers.

Noyama glanced at the CinC's glass and was amazed to see it empty. He stepped to the bar and waved the bottle. At a nod from Toyoda, Noyama walked over and poured three fingers this time.

Toyoda sniffed the scotch appreciatively. "We don't get enough of this stuff. Damn war." He looked over his shoulder at Ozawa. "You can do this? You can draw Halsey off?"

Ozawa sat forward in his chair and looked up to Ugaki, who finished buttoning his tunic. The two glanced at each other. Noyama realized a concurrence had passed between them; that Ozawa had bought into Ugaki's plan. Ozawa said, "Yes, sir, I can do this. Additionally, I can throw in 100, perhaps 150 planes as well."

The admirals murmured, even Ugaki. Toyoda spun to face Ozawa directly. "I thought you didn't have any pilots?"

"None to speak of, at least not right now. But we have an intensive recruiting program going on. We're giving them a truncated training program as well. The people over at Toho[15] have been doing great simulations for us, which saves a lot of time and, I might add, fuel. Some of our lads are doing well. I believe we can put on quite a show for Halsey when the time comes. Maybe do some damage."

Ugaki said, "Think of it, Admiral. With the attacking force"—he waved to Kurita, Nishimura, and Shima—"in a pincer movement, it would be a killing field. American bodies floating everywhere. MacArthur, if he lives through it, would have to draw back and regroup. That would take at least six months; maybe a year. It would gain us invaluable time. Think of world opinion." Ugaki lowered his voice, "Think of *Dai Nippon*."[16]

Toyoda nodded and sipped his scotch. "It could work."

"*If* we get air cover, Admiral," cautioned Ugaki. "We need General Umezu to give us everything he's got in the theater, and then some."

"How many?" asked Toyoda.

Ugaki and Ozawa exchanged glances. Ugaki said it for both of them: "Three hundred fifty to four hundred planes. We'll base them on Formosa, Luzon, and Samar."

Toyoda looked over at Kurita. "Would you like a scotch?"

Everyone knew Kurita was a teetotaler. Even so, he said, "No, thank you, sir."

Toyoda asked Kurita. "With Halsey gone, you can do the rest? Wipe out MacArthur?"

Kurita replied, "Yes, sir. I believe we can. Also, the air cover would hold MacArthur's capital ships at bay. That's when we wipe out his amphibious fleet."

"How many of you?"

"Everything," said Kurita, getting a nod from Nishimura and Shima. "We have about fifty ships among the three of us. We can smash them in one decisive blow."

A light flickered in Toyoda's eyes. He leaned forward and slapped his knees, then tossed off the rest of his scotch and stood. Chairs scraped as the others stood with him. "I like it. This version of SHO-1 has possibilities. Very well, gentlemen. I'll discuss it with General Umezu tonight. Yonai will be there as well, so perhaps we'll have some additional influence." To Ugaki he said, "I'll be at Meguro tomorrow to watch the games. No cheating this time."

"I wouldn't think of it," said Ugaki.

The admirals left for their dinners and Noyama helped the other staffers clean up. Then he walked down to Kurita's room and arranged the admiral's papers for tomorrow's session at Megura. By eleven-thirty his leg hurt terribly. He'd been standing too long and the knee was swollen, so he sat in an easy chair to massage it. The next thing he knew, it was four-thirty. Someone had draped a blanket over him; perhaps Kurita, perhaps second-class petty officer Kurusu, his valet. Whoever it was had gone to a lot of trouble. His shoes were off, his collar loosened, and a pillow was propped behind his head. He was surprised he'd slept through it. A plain cream-colored envelope with the Imperial family chrysanthemum emblem was on the side table near his right hand. He opened it, finding a single cream-colored page in Kurita's impeccable hand:

N

Umezu has given full permission for us to use army planes. Toyoda is pleased and operation SHO-1 is official. So, set up our section of the game tomorrow—the First Striking Force—to take that into account. The next day, I'm climbing Mount Fuji with Nabuko, as you suggested, war games or not.

I want you to take three days' liberty and trust you spend them with your family. A green-car rail pass is included. Also, I've left a signed chit for you in the flag mess to draw two ducks, courtesy of the Emperor's Royal Aviary. Please give your parents my regards with hopes you enjoy the ducks.

K

Noyama sat back, a strange, long-forgotten sense of calm and peace sweeping over him. At last they were decided, and none too late, for they would have to commit soon. The fleet intelligence reports gave every indication the Americans were on the move. Most of all, they were unified. He thought of Ugaki's aside about *Dai Nippon,* and it gave him a warm feeling. Maybe there was hope after all.

FIFTEEN

12 August 1944
Yamashina train station
Kyoto City, Japan

Kurita had given Commander Yuzura Noyama a rail pass to a green car, a first-class car where he had the luxury of his own compartment. But the train was two hours late—a wreck, the conductor said, although Noyama had not seen any trouble along the way. The four-hundred-kilometer ride was supposed to be an express taking six hours; instead it took eight.

He fretted over his parents, whom he hadn't seen in more than two years. They'd be waiting two hours most likely, and his mother, Michiko, was a fidgeter. She did it constantly at the dinner table, tearing napkins into tiny pieces or twirling hair around her index and middle fingers, worrying about her boys or finances or her husband's job. Noyama's father often shouted her down. Then she would pout, and the table would become silent, nobody speaking. Even his younger brother, Hiroshi, who took after his mother and babbled a lot, became silent. No one dared to speak until—

The train jerked to a stop. He reached for the door handle but it was yanked open before he could touch it.

A little man, no more than five-two, stood before him, wearing the same assistant stationmaster uniform Yuzura had grown accustomed to all these years.

"Father!"

Masao Noyama mounted the steps, and they hugged. He stepped back and let his son alight with duffel bag and two packages clamped under his arm. "You look marvelous," said Masao. "And that eye patch makes you look like a true warrior."

"Father, please."

Masao took a step back and reached up and touched his son's hair. "My goodness, you're becoming gray. What in the world is the navy doing to you? I always said you would be better off in the army." Masao's smile was infectious. A gold tooth gleamed, and the corners of his eyes crinkled. But his eyes were close together, and for some reason he often looked cross-eyed. Even though proven mentally competent, time and time again people talked behind Masao's back, labeling him the village dope. It was what had held him back in his job. At fifty-nine, Masao Noyama was frozen as assistant stationmaster at the Yamashina train station, a position he'd held for twenty-two years. Younger men were jumped over him, his current boss just thirty-eight. The irony was that there hadn't been an accident in the Yamashina train station since Masao became assistant. But his supervisors always took the glory. It didn't seem to bother Masao. His lightheartedness and his broad grin were compelling. The serious family worrying was always left up to his wife, Michiko, the fidgeter.

Carrying bag and bundle, Noyama followed his father through a throng of soldiers and sailors. Wounded men were in strong evidence, some on crutches, some without limbs. Beside the strident noise of trains chuffing and rumbling through, the human noise seemed louder than before. Having grown up just a kilometer away, he'd spent many days in here as a youngster. Over in the corner was the same decorative urn. It was so large that he and his little brother, Hiroshi, had hidden in there for two hours, laughing and giggling while their father and mother rushed about, screeching their names. But oh, did they pay for that over the next two weeks, which began with a whipping from their father.

Today was strange, though, he thought. No one was seated. Everyone seemed to be hurrying to or from something, their eyes fixed on the ground, unmindful of anyone else around. Then it hit Noyama. *Kempetai*—secret police. His eyes darted over the familiar platform, where he picked out two pair of medium-size men in civilian clothes at opposite ends of the platform. Even though the crowd's eyes were fixed on the ground, they still afforded the *Kempetai* wide berths, as if the men had been miraculously detected by some sort of radar.

Father and son stepped from the station platform and into the sunlight. Noyama took in Kyoto's Higashiyama ward, the Eastern Mountain area where he grew up. There were many days when he and Hiroshi ran its slopes and played in little ditches. They built a makeshift hideout in one of the ditches and spied on old Usui, a retired potter. They stole apples from his modest orchard, were caught, and were turned over to the police, who promptly dragged them home. There Masao and Michiko were aghast to learn that the apples mysteriously appearing on their doorsteps in the early morning over the past few weeks were not gifts from friendly neighbors, but had been stolen from old Usui's orchard by their sons. But each time, there were only two apples—one from Yuzura and one from Hiroshi—no more. Even at that, Masao was too overcome to do the whipping. That was left up to Michiko. But in later days, the boys referred to themselves as her "two apples." They even designed their own insignia: two red apples on a square, white field, bordered by gold filigree.

Noyama and his father walked down Route 1 toward town, Noyama hobbling to keep up with his father. Masao looked back to see his son's cheeks puffed, his face a bit red.

"Say, what's wrong?" He stopped, his hands on his hips.

"I'm fine, Father," said Noyama. "Just a stiff leg from a long train ride." He hadn't told his parents about the severity of his wounds at Bougainville. Only that he'd been removed from flying status and bumped upstairs, working on a flag officer's staff.

"What is it you're not telling me?" he asked.

"Can it wait until we get home?"

"As you wish." There was an edge to Masao's voice as he fell into pace with his son.

Realizing he'd handled it badly, Noyama asked lightly, "Aren't you working today, Father?"

"They've given me the day off in your honor."

"That's very nice, Father," Noyama said, as he took in Mount Kazan to their right, Mount Rokujo to their left. And ahead was Mount Otawa with the ancient Kiyomizu Temple and its wondrous, meticulously kept grounds. Oh, how he wished he could play again here in springtime: tumbling down the grass slopes, Hiroshi giggling, Masao pushing them along faster.

They turned up a lane and were soon at the modest four-room wooden structure where he'd grown up. He'd no sooner kicked off his shoes than his mother, Michiko, stood before him. He leaned down to kiss her and was surprised by the severity of her hug. "We miss you so much," she said. Then she stood back, cupped his jaw, and examined his face. "You've been hurt. What is it that you haven't told us." Her voice had that penetrating effect he'd known as a child. Except this voice held no contempt or admonition or threat of punishment: only compassion.

"Oh, Mom, it wasn't—"

Someone moved behind her. "Hiroshi," Noyama fairly yelled and wrapped his arms around his little brother. Pounding each other's backs, Noyama finally stepped back and grinned. "Look at you. An ensign in the navy. And here: pilot's wings. I didn't know, Hiroshi. How did you qualify so quickly?"

At age nineteen, Hiroshi Noyama had graduated from Etajima Naval Academy after just two years. From age four, he had buzzed through the house with wooden gliders and other flying contraptions, wanting to be a pilot. "They jumped me over a bunch of kids because I had the best eyesight and best coordination. And if you don't watch out, they're going to jump me over you, make me a full captain so you'll have to salute me! Finally, my big brother paying the respect he owes me. Hah!" He thrust a fist in the air.

Father and two sons laughed. But Michiko still wore her sober expression. "I see it in your face, my son. Tell me what happened."

Noyama said, "Make you a deal?"

Michiko's eyes narrowed, "Don't forget who you're talking to."

"I'll never do that, Mom." He hobbled over to a chair and sat heavily. "Uhhh."

Masao and Michiko sucked in their breath.

Noyama massaged his leg and looked up. "Buck up, you

people. This is a present from Admiral Halsey and his boys over Bougainville. I jinked right when I should have jinked left. A P-38 got me. But I got the plane back to Buin. You should have seen the holes. Damn thing never flew again.

"Here, Mom." He handed up the package. "Present from Admiral Kurita. Two ducks for dinner tonight, all plucked and dressed. All you have to do is pop them in the oven. And these ducks are fatted, right from the Emperor's Aviary."

Michiko kneeled before her son and threw her arms around him. "My two boys together, I can't believe it. A special dinner, a special moment. Please thank the admiral for us."

"It's okay, Mom."

She wouldn't let go. The others sat.

"Please talk some sense into your brother," she said in his ear.

"What is it, little man?" he called across the room to Hiroshi.

"What, me?" he replied. "Just going into advanced training soon. Dive-bombers. Can you imagine that? Four thousand meters and then you push over"—he gestured with his hands—"*vrooom.* There goes an American tank. Oops! Big mistake. I hit Imperial army headquarters instead. Too bad. Back to primary training."

Noyama and Masao laughed while Michiko stood and accepted the packages. "I'll do your deal. We'll have a nice dinner, then it's off to the Suji's for therapy." She referred to Sujiyama's Onsen—public bathhouse. "Something tells me you've rushed things and something hasn't knitted properly."

She wiped at her eyes, flashed a look at her husband, and walked toward their small kitchen. Masao followed, muttering to himself.

Hiroshi gave a wan smile. "You off flying status?"

"All done."

"You should have let them know, I mean, about your wound. I bet it was really serious. It's not nice to keep secrets."

"I didn't want them to worry." He leaned forward. "Now tell me, Hiroshi."

"What?"

"What is it that you haven't told us?"

* * *

Noyama's parents and young Hiroshi hadn't enjoyed a delicacy for at least three years, let alone two fatted ducks from the Emperor's private game preserve. With a little scrambling, Michiko made a navy bean soup. The duck followed, basted with a ginger and teriyaki sauce and rice on the side. Masao surprised them all with three bottles of Asahi beer that he'd been hoarding. After tea, they walked down the road to Sujiyama's onsen. Over light protests, Noyama paid for them all, and they went to their respective rooms to prepare.

Noyama took his time, sitting on his stool and thoroughly washing himself with soap and water. He did it three times, making sure he was squeaky clean, and then limped into the great room where the ofura—the soaking tub—was situated. Fortunately it was a Thursday night, and only one other couple occupied the other end. His mother and father and Hiroshi were already fully immersed in the water up to their necks, steam lightly wafting around their faces.

Here comes the hard part. He casually tried to drape his towel over his leg and even turned his back. But it was of no use; the towel didn't cover enough. His mother gasped at the sight of his mangled leg. "Yuzura!"

"Easy, mother, it's all right," said Noyama, quickly hobbling into the ofura. He drew in his breath sharply and got to his waist without too much trouble. Then he reached over and pulled up the thermometer: thirty-eight degrees Celsius. He took his time settling; finally the water lapped over his shoulders. Its warmth caressed him, penetrating every pore of his body, in a way giving him a sense of being lifted. "Mmmm."

"What happened?" Masao asked. "Is that why you're no longer flying?"

"Like I said, Father, I was shot down over Bougainville. I was lucky to live. The plane never flew again." He chuckled with a look at Hiroshi. "And the doctors had great sport patching me up." Actually, the doctors wanted to amputate. But Noyama had resisted, and it eventually grew better.

The others looked away, but Masao glanced quickly at his left eye patch.

"This is good therapy, I'll bet," said Hiroshi.

Noyama nodded. "I've tried it a couple of times. But one doesn't find many ofura at sea, nor in Lingga Roads." He settled back. "And ahhh, you're right. It does feel wonderful."

Noyama looked to Hiroshi. "Tell me little brother, now that you have wings, where are you stationed?"

Hiroshi fixed him with a gaze. "Suzuka."

An unsettled feeling surged in Noyama's stomach. Then he had it. Ugaki had briefed them in their Meguro war games. New special attack squadrons were being formed at Suzuka, Kochira, Tokushima, and Kanoya air bases. This was because Japan no longer had pilots skilled enough to get close to bomb enemy ships. And there was no time to fully train new ones. Thus, the Shiragiku Special Attack Squadrons were getting ready to send able young volunteers against the Americans, their planes loaded with a torpedo or a single five-hundred-kilogram bomb—on a one-way mission. They were to deliberately crash their planes into American ships—preferably aircraft carriers or battleships. They had gamed it on the last day when the blue team scored two Shiragiku hits on a red-team carrier, forcing it to retire. He sucked in his breath. "You?"

Hiroshi nodded.

Their parents smiled politely, not realizing what they were discussing.

"I'm in the *Wakagiku* (Young Chrysanthemum) Squadron. We're shipping out to the Philippines early next week. This is . . . my last time." He looked down to the water.

"Now you've done it," said Noyama. Hiroshi, always the flamboyant one. Always wanting to grow up fast, to be like his big brother and fly fighter planes. Hiroshi was eager to get in the war when he still should have been in school. And now he'd joined the kamikaze corps, the divine wind.

"What would you expect me to do?" said Hiroshi. "It's over, anyway."

"What?" said their parents.

"Maybe not," said Noyama.

"It's true," said Hiroshi. "Except now, I can do it with honor."

Hiroshi stared at the water, so Noyama asked, "What are you flying?"

"A B5." Hiroshi referred to a Nakajima B5N2 single-engine torpedo bomber. "I'm not afraid."

"No, little brother, I don't doubt that," said Noyama. He looked to his mother and father. Their smiles were still there, but now they looked confused. They weren't following what Hiroshi was saying. And Michiko was fidgeting, twisting her hair.

"I'll tell them," Noyama said.

"Thank you, Yuzura," said Hiroshi.

Noyama turned to his parents. "Mother, Father. Hiroshi has joined a Shiragiku squadron. He is—"

"—not coming back, is he?" barked Masao Noyama, his chin up.

"Aoooww," gasped Michiko. "I knew it. It was in your face."

Hiroshi looked to the ceiling with gritted teeth. "How does she know these things?" He turned to her. "Mother, I'm sorry. It's my duty."

Michiko nodded and looked away. Then she asked, "Are you sure? Do we ever see you again?"

"I'm afraid not, Mother."

"When do you go?"

"Day after tomorrow."

Michiko twirled her hair and turned to her youngest son. "Well, then. I'll fix you a nice dessert tonight and we'll have to have a picnic tomorrow. Maybe at the palace."

"That would be nice," said Hiroshi.

Michiko nodded and leaned back, the decision made. She twirled her hair and, almost as an afterthought, said, "We'll need a lock of your hair."

"Of course, Mother," said Hiroshi.

They passed the hour pleasantly and then walked home as if returning from a summer evening stroll.

Noyama didn't sleep well that night in his little room. He heard Hiroshi tossing and turning in his own little room. And the thin walls couldn't mask the low moans of their mother, nor the muttered phrases of their father in futile attempts of comfort.

Two days later, Hiroshi was gone, leaving his older brother to spend a dismal day at home. Late that afternoon, they were surprised to hear a knock at the door. It was the bewhiskered Usui, owner of the apple orchard, now barely able to walk.

"Yes?" demanded Masao.

"I have a present for you," the old man wheezed. The half-kilometer hike had been difficult, and he still hadn't caught his breath. He held up a paper bag. "Actually, it's for Michiko. It's from Hiroshi, who bravely goes off to war." His eyes glistened, and he handed over the bag.

Masao was astounded as the old man bowed, turned, and wobbled away on his cane. He slid the door closed, muttering, "How would Usui know what Hiroshi is doing? Michiko," he called.

She walked up. "What?"

Masao growled, "Old man Usui is up to his tricks again. He says this is for you from Hiroshi." He handed over the sack.

She took it and opened it. "Hiroshi," she chirped. Inside were two apples.

Looking in the bag, Masao growled, "I wonder how much Hiroshi paid the old man?"

SIXTEEN

17 August 1944
Roseville Community Hospital
Roseville, California

"Ouch, dammit," growled Donovan. "Are you sure you can see what you're doing?"

"Easy, Commander. These are special glasses." Diane Logan bent close to his belly to pull sutures. "And right now, this is all looking pretty good." She snipped another suture, clipped forceps on the knot, and pulled it from the incision site.

"Uhhhh."

"Don't tell me that hurt."

"You must have attached the damn stitch to my spinal cord. It's like—ouch!"

Diane Logan stood and lay a gloved hand on Donovan's shoulder. "Would you please relax? You know, I took twenty sutures out of a kid's forehead this morning. Eleven years old. Not a peep. What's wrong with you, anyway?"

Donovan grinned. "I figured this way I'd get to know you better."

"What?" She bent to do the remaining sutures.

"Look at it this way, Dr. Logan. What was that kid's name?"

Diane looked to the nurse, who shook her head. "Don't remember," Diane said.

"What's my name?"

"Commander Scaredy-Cat," she said.

"I rest my case."

Diane laughed, then the nurse joined in. At length, Diane threw a set of forceps in the stainless-steel tray and said,

"You're all done, Commander. And everything looks good. Just make sure you check in with your regular doctor every month or so. Wait—don't get up yet—Gloria is going to do one last pass."

The nurse lightly swabbed Donovan's incision with antiseptic. With that, she looked up. "They need me down the hall, Doctor."

"Please, go," said Diane.

"Thank you, Doctor." The nurse walked out.

"You can put your shirt on," said Diane, jotting notes on his chart. She flipped a page and looked up, frowning. "Question, sir?"

"Uh-oh. I'm in trouble."

"Have you seen anyone about your nightmares?"

He flushed a bit. "Actually, no. When I checked out of here I stayed at my folks' house in the San Fernando Valley and slept like a baby. Our doctor gave me more sleeping pills, but I didn't have to use them."

"Well, let's hope that's the end of it."

"You bet."

"Another question?"

"Shoot."

"Why didn't you have your own medical people remove your sutures?"

Donovan stood, putting on his shirt and tucking it into his pants. "Four reasons. First"—he held up a finger—"Dr. Duberman looks and acts like he graduated from medical school about ten minutes ago." What he didn't say was that he'd returned here without checking in at Oak Knoll Navy Hospital in Oakland.

"Well, can't you just ask for another doctor?"

"Second," Donovan plunged on, "you're far more familiar with the case, and I trust your judgment."

"Well, that's nice, but there are other doctors who—"

"—Third, I had to come back anyway to recover the dop kit I left behind." He didn't say Carmen Rossi's diamond rings were in there and that he didn't trust the mail. "And fourth, will you have dinner with me tonight?"

She looked down. "Oh, I don't know. I'm so busy here."

"Busy? Busy? They have you working seven days a week?"

"Well, no, but . . ."

"But what? You have a husband? A boyfriend? Someone you're engaged to?"

"To tell you the truth, no, no, and no."

"Then three nos make a yes. What time do I pick you up?"

"Will you stop this? I haven't decided."

Donovan snapped his fingers. "Damn. I forgot. You haven't decided and you need time. Well, okay. How much time do you need? Three seconds? Five? A whole minute?"

She waved her hands in the air. "All right, all right. You certainly know how to wear someone down."

"Thanks. Six o'clock? Where do you live?"

"Four-six-one Cypress Avenue. And make it six thirty."

"Done."

Massive poplar trees lined the parkways on both sides of Cypress Avenue, sucking heat out of the air, making the ninety degrees seem tolerable. An ice-cream truck tinkled and clinked its way down the street. Kids chased after it, waving nickels, dimes, and quarters. Women watered their lawns, their men working overtime on the railroads—or off to war.

The Logans' house was a 1920s two-story Craftsman with a wraparound front porch. A garden hose fed a sprinkler that shot water back and forth. It would have been a quiet, pastoral little street except for the sound of the rail yards four blocks away. There, massive compound engines spun their sixty-three-inch drive wheels, searching for a grip in the rails, lumbering forward as ninety-pound couplers took up slack on mile-long trains in a mind-racking five-second cacophony.

He walked up the driveway, seeing her sitting on a swing on the front porch, gazing into the distance. At her feet was an ink-black Labrador retriever. One of the dog's big yellow eyes opened as Donovan took a step. Its tail thumped on the porch with a hollow sound. Just then a tree limb wavered in the breeze, allowing a last shaft of golden sunlight to sweep across her face. *Good God, she's beautiful.*

The pounding of the dog's tail caught her attention, and she looked up.

"Am I late?" he asked.

"You're on time." She stood, wearing a simple navy-blue linen sleeveless dress and spectator shoes. Her rich auburn hair was pulled back in a French twist. Around her neck was a string of pearls. The evening's golden light emphasized her eyes, making them look bigger than life.

Donovan made a show of checking his watch. "It was six thirty, wasn't it?"

"Yes, it was six thirty. Someone caught wind I was going out tonight, so they kicked me out early."

"You mean interns really do have friends?"

"Few and far between." She beckoned. "Come on up. There's someone I want you to meet."

"Okay." He mounted the steps, pulling off his cap and tucking it under his arm, thinking, *Oh my God. It's time for the stiff-necked parents and the bratty little brother.* The dog walked over, stood on its hind legs, and looked up to Donovan.

"Hey, Rex, er does he bite?" asked Donovan. He petted the dog, and its tail wiggled rapidly.

"No. He's fine. Down, Blackie," she commanded.

The dog kept at it, his front paws on Donovan's chest.

"Hey, Blackie, good boy." Donovan petted and the dog licked, slobbering up his hand.

"Great watchdog. He hardly knows me."

"Good judge of character, I guess." She walked through the door, holding it for him. Pushing the dog aside, Donovan followed her into the parlor and back to the dining room, where two men sat concentrating over a chessboard. "Here he is," she said.

Chairs scraped as they rose. Diane said, "Commander Mike Donovan, meet my father, Walt Logan."

Walt Logan had a full head of gray hair combed straight back. His face was red; his enormous nose looked as if it had been through a wood chipper. Stocky, he stood about five-ten and puffed mightily on a pipe. He extended his left hand. Walt Logan had no right arm below the elbow.

"Pleasure to meet you, sir," said Donovan.

Logan shook vigorously, his left-handed grip strong. "The pleasure is all mine, Mike. But only if you call me Walt."

"Thank you, Walt."

Diane continued, "And I think you know this man."

"You look so much better now, Commander." The man extended his hand. Thin, tall, he wore the same chambray blue work shirt and denims he'd seen that night on board the train bound for—

Donovan gasped, "You. That night on the train. You're the one who—"

"Say hello to Milo Lattimer," said Diane Logan.

With broad shoulders, Lattimer's shirt barely concealed the power that lay within. Donovan had an uncomfortable moment, trying not to grimace as the man gave him an iron squeeze. "Damn, I don't know what I would have done if you hadn't carried me off the train. I owe you my life."

Lattimer gave a small bow. "It was nothing," he said in a slightly accented voice.

"Forgot something," said Diane. "Won't be a minute." She walked past her father, knocking over his beer glass. "Oh, Dad, I'm—"

In a flash Lattimer caught the beer glass before it fell all the way over. With an extraordinarily long reach, he grabbed a dish towel and had the spilled beer covered before it spread.

"How's that for speed?" said Logan. "But then he's had lots of practice."

"I'll say," said Lattimer, casting a sidelong glance at Diane. "How'd you ever get through med school?"

Walt Logan jumped in with, "Hey, hon, we got time to show the commander here your baby pictures?"

"Stop it, you two," muttered Diane. "Be right back." She ran up the stairs.

"Hah! Got her." He turned to Donovan. "Well, now that I need a refill, how 'bout you? Coke? Water? Beer? Maybe something more challenging?"

"No, thanks," said Donovan.

"Have a seat," said Walt. "You must be hot in that uniform."

"You walked over from . . . ," asked Lattimer, tossing the soaked towel through the kitchen door into the sink. He grabbed a fresh one, wiping up the rest of the beer.

"Barker Hotel," said Donovan.

"Ummm, you were lucky to get a room," said Lattimer, pronouncing it *woom.*

"I'll say," said Donovan, cocking his head at Lattimer's accent. "Had to slip the clerk an extra sawbuck."

Lattimer caught Donovan's look and said, "That's right. I'm from Austria. We got out in '37 when that damn Schicklgruber began making noise all over Europe."

Walt Logan returned, fresh beer in hand, and sat before his chessboard. Blackie sat beside him, and Walt began absently petting him. "How 'bout you, Mike? Say, look at all those medals. Three battle stars. What do you do in the navy?"

Donovan gave them a rundown on his destroyer career.

"Where you serving?"

"Pacific."

"Yep," said Walt. "We get a lot of stuff for you boys through here. See it every day."

"Well, keep it coming, Walt. We need it all."

Logan knit his brow. "You ever been through the Solomon Islands?" He cast a look at Lattimer.

"Where in the Solomons?"

"Bougainville?"

Donovan pursed his lips. "Went by it plenty of times." He looked up, seeing they watched closely. "Why?"

Walt lowered his voice and said, "That's where Stan went down. Dive-bomber pilot with the marines."

"Who?" asked Donovan.

"Her fiancé," said Lattimer softly. With his hands he mimed a plane crash. "Almost a year ago."

"Ohhh," said Donovan. "I didn't know." Suddenly, he wanted that beer.

Diane's feet thumped toward the landing upstairs. "Has . . . has she been going out . . . you know?"

They shook their heads. "One or two, but nothing serious," said Walt. "By the way," he whispered, "she loves Chinese food."

"Thanks."

Diane's footsteps cascaded down the stairs and she walked into the room, flipping a leather case in the air. "Couldn't find my regular glasses . . . say, why such sour faces? Must be one heck of a chess game."

"Milo's beating me as usual," groused Walt. "You lost your glasses again?"

"Lose 'em? No. I just can't find them right at the moment," said Diane. "Could you keep a watch out?"

"Do I have a choice?"

Donovan stood.

Logan asked, "You play chess?"

"A wee bit," said Donovan.

"Say, how 'bout a game sometime?"

"Maybe so," said Donovan, "but I'm afraid even Blackie could beat me."

"Well, let's see what happens," said Walt. He stood and took Donovan's hand. "Sorry we didn't have time for all the baby pictures. Maybe next time."

Donovan shook. "Can't wait. The ones of Diane in the bathtub were great. I look forward to seeing more."

"Come on—" growled Diane.

Walt said, "You two better go before she knocks over the refrigerator."

They moved into the parlor with Donovan saying, "Well, then, thank you Walt. See you—"

There was a knock at the front door. Outlined in the evening light was a man in uniform.

"Hello?" he called through the screen.

Logan walked ahead. "Captain Collins?" He opened the door and shook the man's hand.

"Good to see you again. You remember my daughter, Diane?"

"Ma'am," said Collins. Wearing summer khakis of the U.S. Marine Corps, Collins was pale with a tall crew cut and wide, light blue eyes that were near perfect circles.

"This is Commander Donovan," said Walt. "And you remember Milo Lattimer?"

"Sure do. Evening, Commander." They shook.

Walt continued, "Captain Collins is working with the army on a special project." He held a finger to his lips. "All very hush-hush."

Diane took Donovan's hand and squeezed. *Let's go.*

Donovan took the cue. "Well, gentlemen. Thanks for your

hospitality. We'd better be going." He headed for the stairs with Diane in the lead, still tugging.

"Come back soon, Mike," Walt said, waving.

As they walked down the steps, Collins said, "Sorry to barge in like this, sir, but Commander Sabovik wants to know if we can see the manifests for tomorrow."

"Don't see why not," said Walt. "They're in the top right-hand drawer."

Donovan stopped short.

"Mike?" asked Diane.

Donovan turned and asked. "Captain. Is that Commander John Sabovik you mentioned?"

Collins turned. "Well, yes, sir."

"Do you mind if I ask what your MOS[17] is, Captain?" asked Donovan.

"EOD, sir," said Collins. A bomb disposal expert.

"Do you know him?" Walt asked Donovan.

"Well, yes. Is he in town?" asked Donovan.

"Practically lived here the past week. Even had him over for dinner. And then of course he and Diane—"

"Father!" called Diane.

"Sorry, hon." Walt turned to the marine captain. "How 'bout you, Nitro? You want to stay for dinner? Of course my paid help"—he nodded to Diane—"is taking the night off, so I hope you don't mind chili and beans?"

"Thank you, sir, but we're doing a late one tonight. My next stop is the Brown Mug for take-out burgers."

Donovan took Diane's arm and began walking.

"Mike, are you okay?"

"Never better."

"Your face is red. Maybe you should go back in and sit down. Let me take a look at you."

"No, thanks, I'm fine. Come on. I hear you like Chinese food."

SEVENTEEN

17 August 1944
New China Café
Roseville, California

The New China Café occupied the second floor of a classic turn-of-the-century building on Church Street. Situated on the first floor was the Owl Club, one of the best nightclubs in the area. At the moment, both establishments did a thriving business, half the customers civilian, the rest military. The difference was that many of the civilians in the Owl Club were railroad workers, the combination with servicemen sometimes brittle, while upstairs patrons tried to eat peacefully.

Donovan and Diane Logan had a window table looking down on the street, where they watched the Thursday-night crowd. A group of police and MPs stood around a lamppost across the street, poised to assault the Owl Club in case of trouble. Like cabdrivers queued up at a train station, MP jeeps and a paddy wagon were parked around the corner on Lincoln Street. Whenever a serviceman staggered out, unable to coordinate his movements, an MP across the street would pump a fist. Within ten seconds, an MP jeep would roar around the corner and pull up before the hapless soldier. IDs would be examined, the soldier sometimes hauled off.

"Not funny, is it?" asked Diane.

"No," agreed Donovan. "Lonely eighteen-year-old kids from Smackover, Arkansas, or Downpayment, Iowa, away from home, out looking for a good time, trying to forget it all. Instead, they land in the clink."

Another jeep screeched to a stop below. Without pulling

their clubs, the MPs spoke with two army privates, then motioned *Get in.* The men stumbled into the backseat, and the jeep roared off.

"Not bad," Donovan said. "No handcuffs. Door-to-door service to the main gate." They sat back as the waiter set bowls of wonton soup before them. Donovan had barely lifted a spoon when something thumped beneath. Glass tinkled and the floor shook. Four MPs and two policemen dashed across the street and through the Owl Club's front door.

"Railroaders versus the army, you suppose?" asked Donovan.

"Probably."

Something thumped again on the first floor and there was a muffled shout, making Donovan feel uncomfortable. "They should declare the place off-limits."

"They did a couple of months ago. Up to that time, I was sewing up one or two heads a night. With the 'off limits,' things quieted down. Now it's been lifted." She rolled her eyes. "Here we go again."

"Why so much army around here?"

"Security troops for the Military Railway Service. Many are assigned to outposts guarding the railroad here and up on the High Sierra. They get lonely up there. At times it's snowy and bitter cold. And the rail workers don't really help or take pity; of course they have their own problems just keeping the stock rolling. So the Owl Club is one of the first places the army guys hit when they come down for rest and relaxation."

"Reminds me of Tijuana." He finished his wonton soup.

"What's that like?"

"Not fit for mixed company."

"Can't be that bad." She reached for her water glass and knocked over a tall saltshaker. "Damn." She shot him a look.

Donovan's eyes glistened.

"Don't say it."

"Your secret's safe with me."

"I'll bet. How was your soup?"

"You're changing the subject."

"And you're laughing at me."

"I am. I'm sorry. Actually, the soup was excellent." He dabbed his mouth with a napkin as they heard another thump downstairs. This one heavy enough to make plates on the wall rattle. "I wonder who's winning?"

"Army fourteen, Railroaders fourteen."

The shouting grew loud on the sidewalk below, where MPs and policemen wrestled two soldiers and a brawny civilian in overalls to a paddy wagon and threw them in. It reminded Donovan of a time more than two years ago when he was a lieutenant aboard the heavy cruiser *Tampa.* En route to the Solomon Islands, they were taking on provisions in Pearl Harbor and half the crew was given liberty. Unlucky at the draw, Donovan was assigned to shore patrol duty one night. Worse, he wasn't given the Honolulu beat. Instead they sent him to Pearl City, a pesthole replete with sleazy nightclubs and whorehouses, concentrated on Hotel Street. Donovan's only consolation was that Tiny had also drawn SP duty and was assigned to work with him.

A disturbance had been reported at Club Hollywood and Lieutenant Michael Donovan and Ensign Alexander Sabovik walked in, flanked by three burly SPs. They found a marine slugging it out with a torpedoman from the *Tampa.* Frantically Donovan tried to work his way to the middle as the yelling, cheering crowd closed tighter around the men who, by this time, were bare-chested, trading blow for crushing blow.

The crowd roared. Donovan pushed hard. Someone threw a punch. Donovan found himself on his rump, more surprised than in pain. His enlisted SPs charged in, brandishing their clubs. Ignoring the mêlée, Tiny leaned down to Donovan, his hands on his knees. He shouted, "You okay, Mike?"

"You get the license number of that truck?" Donovan rubbed his jaw and extended a hand. Tiny yanked him to his feet.

The enlisted SPs were clubbing away, but they didn't seem to be making progress as their adversaries fought back, shoving them to the rear of the room. Tiny looked at Donovan, his face a perfect image of *Please, please, oh please?*

Donovan yelled, "Hold on." He grabbed a chair, stood, and blew his whistle. "Settle down!"

His reward was a beer bottle flying right at him. He ducked

at the last possible instant. When he came up he saw one of his SPs go down; the other two fighting a losing battle.

He looked at Tiny. "Go!"

With a roar, Tiny grabbed the nearest man, a marine, and threw him onto a table. The table cracked in half, sending the marine, splintered wood, and chairs caroming into a corner. Next, he grabbed two white hats by their collars, butted their heads together, and threw them on top of the marine. Another burly sailor leaned back and cocked his arm for a roundhouse punch. Tiny merely grabbed the sailor's arm, spun him around, and sent him over the bar, the sailor shrieking in pain.

Apparently the man's scream and the tinkling glass caught the crowd's attention, for the fighting petered out within seconds. Looking up at Tiny, they edged back. Roughly shoving men aside, Tiny worked to the center, where he found the sailor and marine on their knees, having beat each other senseless. One man's eye was swollen shut; the other's lip bled profusely. They were too exhausted to raise their arms. Tiny and Donovan got their SPs organized and threw twelve men into the brig that night. The longest part of their evening was filling out paperwork.

"Hello?" she asked.

"Pardon?"

"Who's Tiny?"

"A friend." He nodded down to the street as the police threw another overalled civilian into the paddy wagon. The rear doors were slammed shut, and it drove off.

He said, "Just kids. Unfortunately, they'll grow up."

"Yes, unfortunately."

The waiter cleared their bowls and set a plate of roast duck in a plum sauce before Diane. Donovan had tender sliced beef smothered with onions and green peppers. It was quiet, and he looked up to see she ate with vigor. But it wasn't a ravenous hunger; she just enjoyed her food.

She looked up in midbite. "You're staring."

"How's your duck?"

"The best. You?"

"Great, except it's been marinated in a garlic sauce that could repel two-pound mosquitoes on Guadalcanal."

Her face darkened.

"Did I say something?"

"Welcome to the New China Café: lots of garlic." She looked in the distance.

"I'm sorry." He put a hand over hers.

She withdrew her hand and looked away. "Thought I'd forgotten all about Guadalcanal and the Solomons."

"You and me both." Donovan felt stupid the moment he said it.

"Pardon?"

Donovan tried a smile. "Sounds like we both left ghosts in the Solomons."

"Those times are past." She resumed eating.

"Make you a deal. I won't—"

Someone walked up to their table. "Mr. Logan," Donovan said, shooting to his feet.

"Daddy?" Diane started up.

"Thought I'd find you here. Sit down, you two, I'm on my way to the yard." Walt Logan gently pushed on Donovan's shoulder, easing him back into his chair. "Look, Mike. There's a problem at the Barker Hotel."

"What sort of problem?"

"You're not registered."

"What?" He tried to rise again, but Walt eased him back down.

"Someone screwed up," said Walt. "When did you get there?"

Donovan said, "My train got in about twelve. I went over there to sign in, but they said I couldn't do it until checkout time, which is 1:00 PM. But I was due at the hospital, so they said they would hold a room for me anyway. Pre-registration, they said. And I gave him a tip. In fact," Donovan snapped his fingers, "I went back after seeing Diane at the hospital and the guy said I was all set."

Logan shook his head. "They lost track of it somehow. Now the place is full."

"What? I don't believe it."

Walt said, "The Barker sent a kid over to the house with the bad news. And there's more bad news. They tried to set you up at the Rex Hotel, but no dice. It's full, too."

"I'll be damned, there goes my sawbuck." Donovan sat back. "What else is there in town?"

"Nowhere you'd want to be," said Diane.

"Look, Mike," said Walt. "The kid left your duffel at our house. And what the hell? You might as well stay there. We have plenty of room."

"Oh, no, I couldn't." Donovan started to rise.

Walt pushed him down again. "Besides. Think of the money you're saving." He checked his watch. "My shift starts at ten." He cast a glance at Diane. "His duffel's in the downstairs room."

Diane dipped a finger in her water glass and flicked it at Walt. "Thanks, Dad."

"I knew you wouldn't mind. Gotta go. See you tomorrow at breakfast. Diane makes great French toast. So long." Walt Logan walked off.

They looked at each other like a couple of wary animals. Donovan said, "This is ridiculous. I can't put you out like this. I'll take the next train for Oakland."

"Don't be silly. There's an extra room, my brother's," she said, pushing away her plate.

"You didn't finish your duck."

"I'm done." She drummed her fingers.

"Coffee? Dessert?"

She shook her head.

"What would you like to do? Hit a movie, maybe?"

She sighed, "I don't know. It's been so long since I've been out."

"Hey, we can always go downstairs and get drunk. Bash in some heads. Throw chairs through the window. Maybe end up in jail."

"Yes, of course."

"I didn't know you had a brother."

She squared Donovan with a look. "Younger brother. Wild. Used to run away a lot."

"And?"

"Something happened after Mom died. I had just started medical school. Ralph ran off. Once in a while he would send postcards. That stopped two years ago." She looked at him.

"It really ripped up Daddy. Blackie, too. Ralph was his master."

"Walt works for the SP?"

"Dispatcher. Been doing that for thirty years. As a kid, he had me so stoked up I wanted to become a dispatcher, too. But then I went to medical school instead. Even more so, Daddy really wanted Ralph to work for the SP but he wouldn't have any part of it. And then the double whammy. Mom dies and Ralph runs off. And now Dad doesn't use his name. It's just *the downstairs bedroom.* Not *Ralph's room.*"

Donovan took her hand into both of his. "I'm sorry."

She withdrew her hand. "I could kill the little bastard."

"No contact at all"—he snapped his fingers—"just like that?"

"The last postcard we had was about twelve months or so ago. Nothing since then."

"You know, you really look like you need some coffee."

She cocked her head. "Mmmmm . . ."

"Dessert?"

"Actually, the green-tea ice cream here is fabulous."

The radio played a soft Woody Herman while she made hot chocolate in the kitchen. They sat and stirred, listening to trains in the distance. He closed his eyes and sighed.

"You okay?" she asked.

"This sure beats the hell out of the Barker Hotel."

"The Barker is the best one in town."

"I just found one that's better."

"Don't wear out your welcome."

He opened his eyes to catch her giving him a look. A freight hooked up to a long line of cars, the couplers rattling for five long seconds. "Ever get tired of hearing that?" he asked.

"People around here are so used to it, they don't hear it. Me, I love it. I can tell the type of engine from the sound. I can just about tell how many cars the engine's pulling and whether it's passenger or freight. I can tell what kind of diesel engine it is or what kind of switch engine they're using in the yards. In fact, I know the numbers on the switchers and can almost pick 'em out by their sound." She cocked her head to the sound of a locomotive working its way through the Roseville yards. "Now, that's a compound engine."

"Like two engines on one chassis?"

"Sort of. Two engines receive steam from one boiler. The forward and rear units are hinged or articulated so the whole mess can go around curves."

"Shows you how much I know."

She let that pass with, "We call them Mallets." She pronounced it *Malleys*.

"How about that?"

"Invented by a Swiss engineer, Anatolle Mallet."

"I thought he was a private detective on radio."

She gave a look and said, "They're big things. Sixty-three-inch drive wheels. Listen." She cupped a hand to her ear. "Hear the syncopated *ch-chuff, ch-chuff, ch-chuff* sound they make?"

He listened. "I do."

"That's an AC class, meaning articulated compound class. That's probably an AC-10 4-8-8-2 cab-forward locomotive."

Donovan sipped. "You know your stuff." He had no idea what all the numbers meant. "I guess you have to grow up in a place like Roseville to appreciate all this."

Fixated on the sound, Diane went on. "Now listen. She has a long consist. Maybe seventy or eighty cars. You'll hear two other helpers soon, one in the middle and a pusher at the back. They're headed east, up over the mountain, which means they're probably shipping lettuce back east. Chicago, New York, maybe."

"You really do know your stuff."

"Fresh, refrigerated lettuce anywhere in the United States. All you want; all within ten days."

"Maybe you should have gone into the railroad business."

She gave another look.

"On second thought, you're a hell of a doctor. I'm glad you went into medicine."

"I have to admit I'm still a kid at heart. But thanks." She finished with her cocoa and stood to wash out the mug. "You grow up here, you learn a few things. Finished?" She stretched an arm for his mug.

Donovan rose. It was the way she reached; the way she

held out her arm, an eyebrow raised. "With this, yes." He set the mug on the sink, took her into his arms and kissed her. Her arms went around his neck then began working up and down his back. She'd melded into him so perfectly. It felt right as he kissed her cheek, her neck, then the tip of her nose; then her lips once again, deeply. He looked in her eyes. She'd taken off her glasses and she looked so damn good, so—

—She shuddered and drew back.

"Diane?" He brushed hair off her forehead.

"I . . . I better not."

He pulled her close. She pushed away. "It doesn't work for me right now."

"Who is it?" asked Donovan. Walt and Lattimer had given him a tip. But he wanted to hear it from her.

"I'm sorry."

He took her chin in his hand. "Is there someone else? If there is, I'm sorry."

"Not now."

"What happened?" He kissed her forehead.

"Guadalcanal. That's in the Solomons, isn't it?"

"Right." Come on, let it out.

"And Bougainville?"

"That's at the western end of the Solomons," he said, stroking her hair.

Gently she pushed away.

"Bougainville? You lost someone at Bougainville?"

"I said, *not now.*"

"You don't want to talk about it?"

She folded her arms.

My God. She still carries the torch. "I'm sorry. I'm making a mess of this. I didn't know."

She gave a short laugh.

Donovan was surprised at the incongruity. "What?" he coaxed.

"I don't know what reminded me of this."

"Of what?"

"The tenth grade. When I lost my first boyfriend."

"Who?"

"His name was Mortimer."

"Like in Snerd?"

She nodded, a smile stretching across her face. "Mortimer's father owned five thousand acres of delta bottomland. Made a fortune in wheat farming. Look what I gave up."

He cupped her chin. "You made the right decision."

She stepped away. "Of course I did. Mortimer turned out to be a drunk." She headed for the door. "Please kill the lights when you're done. Good night." She walked out.

It was eleven o'clock when Donovan walked into Ralph's little bedroom. Blackie was already there curled up in a corner on an old throw rug. He opened one yellow eye and flopped his tail for a moment. Then he groaned and rolled onto his back, his legs in the air, exhaling deeply. Donovan opened the window and crawled into Ralph Logan's bed, a comfortable twin. He snapped off the light and lay back as Blackie gave a softer groan. Donovan cradled his hands behind his head, listening to the sounds of the night. The evening was cool and the music of the rail yards drifted in: *Ch-chuff. Ch-chuff. Ch-chuff.*

EIGHTEEN

18 August 1944
461 Cypress Avenue
Roseville, California

Screams. That's all he heard. Hot and sweaty. And darkness.

"Arrrrgh!"

There it was again. "Tineeeee!" He threw off the covers.

"Mike, come on."

"Not my fault!"

"It's okay." She held him close.

His eyes snapped open and suddenly, Donovan realized where he was.

It was Diane, sitting against the headboard, gently rocking him. "Really, it's all right," she murmured.

". . . sorry."

"Shhhhh."

He lay back against her chest; her warmth, her scent enveloping, caressing him as she wrapped her arms around him.

He looked up as she ran a hand over his forehead. "Was I yelling?"

"A little bit."

"What happened?"

"I was down for a glass of milk and heard you. You okay now?"

Donovan realized she was in just a nightgown. Under his back, he felt her bare thighs and just about everything else through the thin fabric. He became aroused and started to turn over.

"Yes, you're better." She slipped away and stood. "You want something? A glass of milk?"

"Forgive me." He ran a hand through his hair. It was damp. And he knew that even though he was tired, he didn't want to go back to sleep. Ruefully, he admitted to himself he was scared and checked the radium dial on his watch: two twenty-five. "Yes, milk sounds just right."

"Be right back."

A locomotive whistle beckoned, and he sat up to listen. "What kind of engine is that?"

The refrigerator opened. "Sounds like a Big Boy: a 4-8-8-4."

"A compound engine?"

She walked back in with the two glasses of milk and set them on the bedside stand. "A monster. Union Pacific uses them for troop trains. We only see them around here at night." She opened a closet, fumbled for a moment, and drew out a bathrobe. After working into it, she sat at the edge of the bed and handed over the milk. She held hers up and clinked glasses. "Your health, Commander Donovan."

"And to you, Dr. Logan." He tried to keep the disappointment out of his voice when she'd put on the bathrobe. Dr. Logan had one great figure. But then he reminded himself, Donovan, you're a guest here of some very nice people, so grow up.

He swallowed. It tasted wonderful; it was always a marvel how good milk tasted in the United States. When overseas, the best they could do was a reconstituted condensed milk that tasted like ground-up cardboard. Within seconds the glass was empty. "Wow," he gasped. "Thanks." He nodded to the robe. "That belong to Ralph?"

"Can't you tell?" She held out her arms, the sleeves drooping well over her hands.

"Ralph's a big boy. I'd better not tangle with him."

"More?"

"Okay."

She was soon back with a refill.

"You haven't touched yours."

"Give me a moment." She sat and drank, looking at him. Her glasses were on, and she examined him as if he were lying on one of Roseville Community Hospital's operating tables.

"What?"

"You want to talk about it?"

He checked his glass: half empty. "Damn, this is good stuff." He looked up to see her eyebrows raised. "I don't think so. Thanks."

"You're sure? My rates are cheap this time of night."

He looked away and shook his head.

She patted his knee. "Okay, Commander. Early rise tomorrow." She stood, grabbed a magazine off the dresser, and pitched it in his lap. "Maybe this will put you to sleep."

It was a November 1941 issue of *Popular Mechanics.* He flipped pages. "Look at this. A garbage disposal right in your own kitchen sink. What'll they think of next?"

"Good night, Mike." Incredibly, she bent over and kissed him on the forehead. Then she tapped him on the nose. "Sleep well."

"Diane?"

"Ummm?"

"Okay. I'll talk." He patted the edge of the bed. "And turn off the light."

"Are you sure?"

He downed the rest of the milk. "It's dark where we're going. Yes, turn it off."

She clicked off the light and sat. "More milk?"

"No, thank you. . . ." He wove his fingers behind his head. "Almost two years ago. It's Guadalcanal." In the dark, he shot her a look. "My Guadalcanal. Off Tassaforonga Point on the night of November 30, 1942. The Japs were desperate to resupply Guadalcanal and their troops." He raised up on an elbow. "You see, their destroyers would shoot by the beaches and kick crates of ammo, food, medicine, over the side without stopping. They even pitched their troops over and made 'em swim ashore. Well, that night we were trying to stop them. . . ."

NINETEEN

30 November 1942
USS *Tampa* (CA 40)
Iron Bottom Sound, off Tassaforonga Point
Guadalcanal, Solomon Islands

The night lit up brightly to port. An instant later, an explosion walloped director 82, Donovan feeling as if he were trapped inside a fifty-five-gallon drum with a five-hundred-pound ghoul swinging a sledgehammer outside. The heavy cruiser USS *Tampa* shook and vibrated and whipsawed, reminding him of a San Fernando Valley earthquake that had thrown him out of bed. Director 82, a mark 31 gun director, was one of two main-battery tank-like directors for acquiring targets and controlling the ship's eight-inch gun mounts. Atop each director was a brand-new mark 3 fire control radar so highly classified that they were airbrushed from photographs except those classified secret and above. The two directors were located high in the superstructure: Director 81, in the forward section of the ship, was two levels above the pilothouse and usually controlled the two forward eight-inch gun mounts. Donovan's director 82 was in the after section, five levels above the main deck, overlooking the aft eight-inch gun mount and the fantail.

There was a shocked silence; then everyone seemed to yell at once. "What the hell was that?" shrieked Shinglar, a chalk-faced third-class radar firecontrolman sitting in the back of the director.

Also in the back of the director was Ensign Tiny Sabovik, who growled, "Easy, Shinglar, don't wet your pants."

Shinglar heaved a sob, fell silent, and drew into a corner,

trying to disappear in the gloom. For Shinglar, at five-six and 135 pounds, that was easy to do. And as cowardly and shriveled as he was, the little man was a genius with electronics. Director 82 had always beaten director 81, the forward main-battery director, in target acquisition. In large part, that was due to Shinglar's genius, so nobody beat up on him too hard.

Tiny had only been aboard for two weeks and Donovan had swept him into his division and appointed him assistant illumination officer, a made-up job to break him in and keep an eye on him. The real illumination officer was chief fire-controlman Foley, a twenty-two-year veteran. "What's going on, Mike?" Tiny asked in a calm voice.

"Wish I knew," muttered Donovan as he spun the sound-powered telephone barrel switch. Panic ranged along the sound-powered telephone circuits as everyone chattered at once.

Finally Lieutenant Nichka, the fire control officer in director 81, yelled on the fire control circuit, "Silence on the line, dammit!" Voices trailed away, then Nichka said, "Bridge says we took a torpedo in the forward fireroom. It also punctured a fuel-oil tank, which sprayed the ship with the stuff. So we're pretty well lit up. But never mind. I want everyone to hunker down and do your jobs."

Shinglar cranked open the after hatch and looked out. "Oh, my God." Light danced and flickered on his face.

A wide-eyed Donovan rose out of his hatch. "Sonofab . . ."

As Nichka had reported, the ship was afire. Flames consumed the main mast and cross-arm, making them look like a giant crucifix planted by the Ku Klux Klan. Instead of the rich aroma of Guadalcanal's jungle rot, the ripe odor of naval-standard fuel oil coursed through his nostrils.

"Mike, what is it, for crying out loud?" asked Tiny.

Donovan stammered, "We're lit up like a Christmas tree."

Even as he spoke, the whole forward section of the *Tampa* caught fire from her number one gun turret back to the midship section break. Screams filled the night as bodies tumbled from the hatches of the two forward eight-inch gun mounts. Some men, their clothes on fire, jumped screaming over the side, while others with fire hoses sprayed water on the flames.

The bridge was afire, and it looked as if it was creeping down to flag plot, two levels below the bridge. John Sabovik was in there, serving as a staff intelligence officer with the admiral. *My God, get the hell out there, John.*

"Lost communication with mount 83," said Palovich, their thick-chested pointer.

Donovan rolled his barrel switch to the three circuits guarded by the aft eight-inch mount. "All of 'em dead." Then he connected with Lieutenant Tim Sullivan in main-battery plot, who reported they also had no communication with mount 83 and didn't appear to be receiving signals from the computer. "We need to get word to 'em somehow to shift to local control and start acquiring targets by themselves," said Sullivan. "Any ideas?"

"I'll take care of it," said Donovan. He turned and spotted Tiny's hulk in the glow of gauges. "Tiny, think you can get down to mount 83 and tell 'em to shift to local control?"

Tiny stood and unhitched his sound-powered phones. "I'll put a man right on it. You want me to stay?"

"Come right on back. I'll want you to be here when we start cranking out illumination. And keep your helmet on. There's a lot of crap flying around outside."

"Okay." Tiny squeezed his considerable bulk through the narrow hatch and disappeared.

Moments passed and a ghostly silence fell while the *Tampa* staggered through the night. It seemed to Donovan as if she was losing speed, which was probably the case, since she'd been hit in the forward fireroom.

"Director 82?" Nichka's voice was weak.

"Eighty-two, aye!" Donovan shouted back. "Walt, what the hell's going on up there? What do you want me to do? We need some target designation. Where the hell is CIC?" The phone circuit gave a scratching sound.

Another blast shook the ship, this one far worse than the first. Shrapnel clanked against the director, two pieces tearing ragged holes just above Donovan's head. Picking himself off the deck, Donovan wondered, *How'd the Japs find us?* We have radar, they don't. Smoke poured into the director as he called, "Everyone all right?"

His question was greeted with coughing and curses as his men pulled themselves up. Tiny!

The ship lurched to port. And she was indeed slowing. Worse, the director was as black as the night sky outside, the gauges dark and silent. "Power?" Donovan shouted.

"Nothing. Ain't got a pissant thing," gasped Palovich. The director was trained out to port, but he couldn't see because the night sky was lighted with their own fires: a massive one forward, a smaller one aft, breaking out in the seaplane hangar. It dawned on Donovan that the heavy cruiser USS *Tampa* had become a perfectly illuminated target for whatever was out there.

As if in confirmation, six freight-train sounds rumbled overhead. Six luminescent white splashes rose just two hundred yards to starboard. "Geez," he shouted into the phones, "We're a damn beacon."

"Don't I know it," Nichka yelled back, his voice suddenly clear. "Do you have a target, director 82?"

With the flames forward, it was impossible to see anything beyond fifty yards. "Negative, director 81. The whole damn director is dead. And mount 83 is dead."

"Jesus! Get 'em local control."

"I sent Tiny down there to take care of that."

"Okay. Now find a target, Mike," said Nichka.

"Working on it, Walt. But can't see a damn thing with all these flames. I haven't heard a word from CIC. What the hell are they doing?"

"Abandoned. Too much smoke, four dead."

"Good God. How about you?" asked Donovan.

"Flames are getting close. We're gonna have to jump pretty soon."

"Roger and good luck," Donovan yelled inside the director. "Shift to manual. Come on, you guys, we need targets."

Just as Donovan spoke, five shells landed close aboard to port while a sixth hit directly on the *Tampa*'s bridge, making the fuel-oil-fed fire rage even brighter.

"Good God . . ." was all he could manage. Icy fingers of fear reached up from his lower bowel, through his intestines, and into his chest. *Get a grip on yourself.*

A loud explosion erupted below. Donovan looked down to

the main deck. The after eight-inch gun had been hit. Impossible as it seemed, the mount seemed to jump and vibrate on its turret ring as explosions racked it again and again.

"Powder cases cooking off one by one!" said Foley. "Amazing they haven't all gone off at once." Then he said, "Uh-oh."

"What," demanded Donovan.

"Lost the fire control radar," said Foley.

"Well, switch to optics and fix it, quick," said Donovan. "Shinglar, can you get that thing going?"

"Those poor guys," muttered Shinglar. "What about Mr. Sabovik?"

Tiny! Shiiiiit! Donovan had forgotten. Checking his watch, he calculated that Tiny had had time enough to get down the mount and start back. He barked, "Shinglar, dammit, all you have to do is to plug in a tube or something. Now hop to it, dammit!"

"Sir." Shinglar rummaged around a repair kit.

Donovan was fighting for control. He knew he had to keep things on an even level while finding a Japanese target for the eight-inch guns to obliterate. But his mind swarmed with thoughts of Tiny. Where is he? Donovan yelled back, "Shinglar. Do you see Mr. Sabovik coming up?"

The hatch squeaked open then clanged shut. "Not yet, sir," reported Shinglar.

"Keep looking." Donovan's mind reeled with the thought that Tiny might not have gotten out of mount 83 in time. He looked at the gun mount again. Thick reddish smoke gushed out of its hatches, her right gun at a bizarre angle high in the air, the other two level with the horizon. Donovan realized the *Tampa* had no operable eight-inch guns. The only remaining guns of consequence were the five-inch guns on the port side. Two of those were in flames—and they were hopelessly out of range for five-inch, anyway.

Donovan shrieked into the night, "Get out of there."

"They're dead, Mr. Donovan. And we better scram before the whole ship blows," yelled Shinglar. The aft hatch squeaked open.

"Shut up, Shinglar, and get back to your post," hissed Foley.

Whump went another powder bag in the turret, as if to underscore what Shinglar had just said.

"Tiny . . . ," Donovan mouthed.

The smoke was thick. Screams drifted up from the main deck as firefighters drew back from the erupting eight-inch mount. Each time a round cooked off in the mount, smoke and flames shot out blown-open hatches, the center gun barrel, and the optical sighting apertures.

The *Tampa* listed farther to port. She'd lost way and was almost dead in the water.

An after five-inch gun cranked out two quick rounds. The muzzle *crack* snapped Donovan awake. "Target? Sure." Concentrating on his binoculars, he said to Palovich and Laughlin, his trainer, "Come on, you guys, come up with something."

More shells screeched past. Two rounds slammed between stacks one and two. Steam, smoke, and flames roared into the night as bits of lifeboat, canvas, deck plating, and human parts swirled high into the air.

Donovan could hardly hear with all the screaming from inside and outside the director. Smoke billowed into the cramped compartment and his men coughed and gasped.

Someone vomited.

". . . director 82 . . ."

Donovan shouted into his mouthpiece, "Louder, I can't hear you, Walt."

The phones squeaked again; Walt Nichka's voice was faint. It sounded as if he was coughing, too. "Abandon."

"Abandon ship?" repeated an incredulous Donovan.

"Affirmative. Word from Brubaker in secondary conn." Commander Brubaker was the *Tampa*'s executive officer. "Almost everyone on the bridge is dead, including the captain. No power. Fires are out in all boilers. Magazines are flooded. We're taking on water."

"Flooded?" Donovan felt cheated. He hadn't fired a shot.

"I repeat. Abandon ship. Brubaker is abandoning after conn. He asked for you to secure the scuttles to the after magazine before you jump. He doesn't want the fire to spread."

"What about the people down there?"

"Goners," wheezed Kelso. "Now get with it. See you in the water." The circuit went dead.

"Roger." Donovan turned and shouted, "Everybody out. We're abandoning ship. Everyone to their lifeboat station."

The coughing and hacking men in the director needed no further urging and began scrambling down ladders and companionways. The way down was easy, most of it lighted by the flames consuming the ship forward.

Donovan stumbled onto the main deck, finding the *Tampa* dead in the water, her list at least thirty-five degrees. Another powder case cooked off in the after eight-inch turret with a *whump.* Donovan swore the turret jumped three feet off its ring. But the scuttles were closed.

Someone grabbed his shoulder. "You okay?"

Donovan spun, finding John Sabovik standing before him. A gash ran across his forehead, and blood ran down his cheek and neck. "John, thank God. How about you?"

"I'll live." Sabovik's eyes darted in his sockets as flames flickered on his face. "Tiny! Where's Tiny?"

Donovan tried to speak, but it didn't come out.

"Mike? Mike, what the hell? Where's Tiny?"

Donovan pointed to mount 83. "He's . . . he . . . I mean . . ."

"What?" Sabovik shouted. "You're shitting me."

Tears ran down Donovan's face and it wasn't from the smoke. "I'm sorry, John. Direct hit. They didn't have a chance."

"What the hell is he doing in there?"

". . . I . . ."

Whump. Another powder case cooked off.

"Maybe they're stuck in a compartment or a void or something. Come on. Let's go see." John Sabovik turned and bolted for the mount.

Donovan dove and caught a foot, tripping Sabovik. "Nobody can survive in there."

The mount exploded again. Smoke and flames shot out the hatch right over their heads. At the same time, the *Tampa* lurched farther to port.

Sabovik struggled to his feet. "Why was he in there? He's supposed to be in the director with you."

"We . . . I . . . had to send him . . ."

"You what?"

"We needed someone to tell them to shift to local control."

"So you send my brother? You . . . you stupid sonofabitch," Sabovik screamed.

Men ran past shouting as Donovan rose to his knees and grabbed Sabovik's arm. "Come on, John, she's gonna capsize."

Flames flickered on Sabovik's face as yet another round cooked off. He swung at Donovan, the blow glancing off the side of his head. "You stinking bastard," Sabovik yelled. "That's my brother in there."

"John, I couldn't . . ."

"You dirty, stinking bastard." Sabovik's face was a malevolent orange as he charged after Donovan.

Three sailors grabbed Sabovik and wrestled him to the deck. One of the sailors looked up and pointed. "Lifeboat 27, Mr. Donovan. We got room. But we gotta scram; the ship's a goner."

Flames roared. Smoke clouded the ship. Another shell hit forward, throwing Donovan and the others to the deck. They gained their feet, the sailors tugging at Sabovik, who kept yelling at Donovan, "You bastard, you dirty bastard."

TWENTY

19 August 1944
Alameda Naval Air Station
Alameda, California

Sabovik gazed out the Plexiglas window. It was scratched and oil-smeared, and nothing but morning mist swirled about the R4D[18] as it waddled down the taxiway. A wind sock drooped at its mast, the washed-out orange matching the mood of the foggy whites and anthracite grays of the early morning. The pilot stomped in right brake and goosed the port engine, swinging the twin-engined cargo plane into what little wind there was. Seated beside Sabovik on the hard wooden bench was marine captain Alexander Collins who, for the moment, was fast asleep, his head back, mouth wide open. Sabovik chuckled over Collins's nickname: Nitro. Yes, the marine did look as if he were handling nitroglycerin that was ready to explode at any moment.

The crew chief, a redheaded second-class aviation bosun with headphones jammed over his ears, stuck his head out from the pilot's compartment. Unlike Sabovik and Collins in fatigues, boots, and garrison caps, he wore an airman's overalls. "Ready for takeoff, sir?"

Sabovik drew his belt as tight as it would go and nodded. It had been clipped the moment he sat. He hated flying and dreaded today's journey to Nevada: a flight sure to be bumpy over the Sierra Nevadas. "Check."

The bosun frowned at Collins.

Sabovik glanced over to see Collins's seat belt dangling in his lap. "Nitro."

"Huh?" Collins's eyes flipped open and he looked quickly about.

"Time for takeoff. Fasten your belt."

"Yes, sir." Collins's belt clicked loudly as he buckled it in place.

"Coffee coming up soon." The aviation bosun waved and disappeared forward, closing the door behind him. In seconds the pilot firewalled the throttles, and the R4D surged forward. The plane was light; there were no other passengers or cargo, just a few mailbags. The tail rose almost immediately and they were off the ground in ten seconds. Ten seconds later, the overcast enveloped them as they climbed in a right bank, the pilot cutting his throttles to climbing power. Rivets rattled as the engines growled. Condensation trailed over the window, but there was no sensation of flight as the R4D rose into the overcast, an opaque miasma.

Sabovik turned to speak with Collins but the man had fallen back to sleep, his mouth again wide open.

Nitro.

The young captain was a marvelous find. A ninety-day wonder, he'd been in the Marine Corps for just eighteen months. While others went on to become platoon leaders and "mud marines," Collins was held stateside because of his knowledge of explosives. With a degree in chemistry from Northwestern University, he'd worked for Dupont's explosives section before signing up for the marines. But wisely, a detailer had sidetracked him for stateside duty, despite his repeated protests that he deserved to have a crack at the Japs like everyone else. For Sabovik, the captain was indispensable. He had a sixth sense and an inquisitive mind that had led them down some very promising paths, while eliminating other time-consuming possibilities.

Today they were headed for the naval air station in Fallon, Nevada. After landing, they would hitch a ride to Sparks, Nevada, where they were scheduled to board the engine of train number X 4293 westbound, departing at 11:59 AM. One hundred and six cars were in the consist, all destined for the Roseville freight yards. The cargo manifest listed everything from large-caliber ammunition to torpedo bodies, torpedo warheads, air-to-ground rockets, small-arms ammunition, aircraft engines, aircraft fuselages and assemblies, packaged food, dry goods, and various electronic and engine parts. Also, there were fifteen tank cars containing aviation fuel, ten flatcars each mounting an M4 tank, along with thirty-two empty reefer cars that had been used to ship produce, mostly lettuce, to the eastern seaboard. In Roseville, the train would be broken up, its various components forwarded to the Bay Area or Southern California.

Bouncing in air currents, the plane rose through the overcast into crystal-blue skies. Shafts of sunlight pierced the cabin with brilliant golds and yellows. Sabovik hardly noticed. Despite his dread about flying, he'd been looking forward to the 139-mile, eight-hour return trip to Roseville. He hadn't slept well last night, just thinking about it. Even so, the plane continued to jiggle, reminding Sabovik that he was at the mercy of elements created by God—while trapped in a machine designed and built by mere mortals.

The door opened and the bosun waved a thermos, his eyebrows raised.

"Please, just black," said Sabovik.

"Be warned, Commander, I didn't make this. It's thick stuff."

"Go ahead."

The bosun poured coffee into a paper cup and handed it over while nodding at Collins.

Sabovik took the cup. "Thanks. Maybe later for him."

"Yes, sir." The bosun went forward and closed the door behind him.

Sabovik sipped. "Yeaach." His stomach rumbled in protest. Yet he sipped again with that never-ending hope that the coffee might suddenly taste good. The trick with navy coffee, he'd learned, was to let it sear your tongue a bit while it was still piping hot. Then you couldn't taste it and had only to wait for the caffeine to hit your system.

They were headed east, nearing foothills. The horizon was hazy, but he knew they'd be over the Sierras' tallest peaks in another forty-five minutes. With a sigh, he reached in his briefcase and drew out a book: *Man Against the Mountain* by Burton T. Chase. Sabovik wanted to check a few things about the railroad's beginnings . . .

* * *

It was 1854 when Theodore Dehone Judah came to California to realize his dream. Aware of Congress's objective to establish a railroad running from the Mississippi Valley to the Pacific Ocean, Judah wanted to play a major role. The young civil engineer decided to survey the High Sierras and build a railroad from California's Central Valley over the mountains to the high plains of Nevada. His ultimate dream was for his railroad to connect to one of the many sprouting from the eastern seaboard as Congress mandated. East meets West; a unified country. That was his dream.

Judah arrived in a time of fervent gold-rush activity and headed up California's first railroad in the Sacramento Valley. At the same time, he began looking for an optimum rail route over the Sierra Nevada mountain range.

Judah completed the Sacramento Valley Railroad in 1856 and then began surveying the High Sierra mountain passes in earnest. He rapidly became an expert on the area and, by 1859, had been selected to represent West Coast interests in Washington, DC. Given the politics of the time and the threat of war on the horizon, Congress was reluctant to allocate money to the project and couldn't give Judah a definite commitment. But they did give him strong encouragement to proceed. Judah returned in 1860 with plans for a final route over the rugged seventy-five-hundred-foot Sierras. And to his delight, Congress was still interested. He returned to California and began looking for financial backers. In Sacramento, he found a group that included Leland Stanford, a wholesale grocer; Charles Crocker, a dry goods dealer; and Mark Hopkins and Collis P. Huntington, proprietors of a local hardware store. The "Big Four," as they became known, agreed to finance Judah's preliminary surveys.

By the spring of 1861, Judah had completed his survey work, and the Big Four incorporated their operation as the Central Pacific Railroad on 28 June of that year. Newly elected California governor Leland Stanford was elected the railroad's president, Collis Huntington became vice president, Mark Hopkins the treasurer, and Charles Crocker the construction manager.

Again Judah went East to solicit backing from Congress. The Civil War had broken out and Judah found a change. Congress was more receptive than it had been before, as railroads were now considered critical to winning the war. Judah laid the foundation for the Pacific Railroad Bill in May 1862, and it was signed by President Lincoln the following July. The major provisions of the bill stated that the Cental Pacific Railroad would be constructed over the High Sierras, thence continue east until it met the Union Pacific Railroad, which was authorized to build west from Missouri.

The project officially began on 8 January 1863 at Front and K streets in downtown Sacramento, with the first eighteen miles of road being completed northeast to a little town called Central, California, later becoming Roseville. When this was done, it turned out that the Big Four only wanted government funding to build a local infrastructure. The first forty miles of track satisfied a government requirement, and with coffers full of government money, the Big Four reduced their activities.

But Judah wanted to complete his vision of building the great continental railroad. So again he sailed for the East Coast, via Panama, with the idea of finding new investors to buy out the Big Four. But tragedy visited the ship carrying Judah. He contracted yellow fever in November and died.

Judah's dream didn't die with him, however. Enthusiasm in California for the railroad resumed among the Big Four. By the following spring, track reached Rocklin, California. By 1864, construction of the Central Pacific Railroad was well up the hill, with the Big Four in full control.

As the Civil War wound down and more money became available, the workforce on the mountain shot up—from twelve hundred to two thousand. By July 1865, it was up to four thousand men. One problem was that the railbed was now striking deep into gold country. Many men seeking to work for the railroad were actually looking for free transportation over the mountain so they could jump ship and prospect for gold. Soon only one in four remained, giving Charles Crocker a terrible labor problem. It was the exasperated Crocker who came up with the idea of employing Chinese as a more stable workforce. At the peak of construction over the mountain, Crocker's workforce exceeded ten thousand men, many of them Chinese.

Enormous challenges faced Crocker and his construction crew: bridges, trestles, and tunnels had to be built. There were an amazing fifteen tunnels in all—one 1,659 feet long. Slowing them were avalanches, bitter-cold blizzards, and sweeping snowslides. Sometimes Crocker's Chinese accomplished superhuman tasks. For example, at Cape Horn, overlooking the gorge of the North Fork American River, they were lowered down cliffs for initial rock cutting, dangling from bosun's chairs twenty-five hundred feet above the river.

The logistics were phenomenal. At any one time there were at least thirty ships at sea, bringing materials around to San Francisco and up the Sacramento River Delta. More than five hundred kegs of powder were used each day to blast tunnels, passes, and railbed for the grade. Fighting the elements, and oftentimes each other, the Central Pacific crews reached the summit of 7,032 feet on 30 August 1867. By the following December, the track extended to the Nevada state line. Waiting out a bitter winter, track was laid to what became Reno, Nevada, by May 1868. The track reached Wadsworth, Nevada, by the following July.

The race was on. Fully energized construction crews of the Union Pacific drove west from Omaha while the Central Pacific crews drove east from Wadsworth. Crocker's workforce swelled to nearly twenty-five thousand, supported by more than five thousand teams delivering six hundred tons of supplies daily. In nine months, a blink of the eye, the Central Pacific crews laid track more than five hundred miles to link up with the Union Pacific in a little-known whistle-stop in Utah named Promontory. There, the golden spike was driven on 10 May 1869.

The mountain was conquered; the transcontinental railroad was completed in record time. An instant success, it more than paid for itself. Many grew rich, including the Big Four in California. Double-tracking over the mountain began almost immediately. But this presented incredible engineering challenges, the whole program not completed until 15 October 1925. Even so, traffic on the mountain grew with each passing year.

* * *

They hit an air pocket and Sabovik put down his book. It was eight thirty and the clouds were white and broken, the day promising to be clear and beautiful. Nitro was up and looking out the left-side windows. He turned, waved, and resumed his spectating.

Sabovik looked out his own window. Off to the right, Lake Tahoe glistened in the sunlight, the magnificent sharp-edged Sierras beyond, seeming to extend forever. Closer in, the town of Truckee drifted beneath their right wing, where flashes of railroad track snaked down the mountain into Nevada. About five miles east, a train worked its way upgrade toward Truckee and the summit. It was incredibly long, with two engines in front, two more "helpers" in the middle, and a single at the back. The wartime traffic ran over the mountain at an unprecedented rate, almost every other block[19] occupied, in addition to many of the sidings. The Donner Pass route was the single most important rail line in the Western United States. Sabovik reckoned that if there was any funny business to be done, a saboteur would begin here; just too many tempting targets. But his reports said the grade over the mountain was well protected. The U.S. Military Railway Service, part of the U.S. Army, provided a security force consisting of guard shacks at strategic locations manned on a twenty-four-hour basis. They observed bridges, tunnels, underpasses, and the like. But that was not Sabovik's concern. What he wanted to know was if anyone could tamper with the cargo while it was en route.

The R4D hit another pocket. The plane lifted suddenly.

"Whoops." Collins staggered across the aisle and took his place beside Sabovik, threading his belt buckle. "Lumpy seas," he grinned. "I knew there was a reason I couldn't become an anchor-clanker."

Sabovik muttered, "Jarheads don't know what's good for them."

Nitro pulled his belt tight just as the plane jiggled again and nodded to Sabovik's book.

"Too bad," he said.

"Have you read it?"

"Ummm. It's a good book. You can't help but feel sorry for the guy."

"Judah?"

"Right. This guy is the ultimate jarhead. I mean, he knew how to march. Think of all the time he spent tramping around those mountains down there, surveying for the best grades. Dragging around mules and horses, living around campfires, bitter-cold blizzards, fighting snowstorms, and wind, and hunger-crazed gold diggers out to kill for their next meal. Hell, the Donner Party had just cannibalized each other a few years before—when was it?"

"In 1846."

"Yeah, 1846. People eating each other to stay alive." Nitro shook his head slowly and pointed out the window. "Look down there. Donner Lake. Now we just fly over it"—he snapped his fingers—"easy as that."

Sabovik sighed. "Okay, Nitro, he was a jarhead."

"Right. I mean, this guy has a really powerful vision and puts it all together. Then his California backers start screwing with him and he travels east with his wife to find new money. He already has the support of Congress. All he needs are a few investors to jump in and take the place of these California jerks. But fate deals him a terrible card. He catches yellow fever and dies a couple of days after his ship docks in New York." Nitro Collins shook his head. "The poor guy set everything in motion but didn't get to see it happen."

Sabovik looked forward to the Nevada plains stretching before them. "Well, it did happen after all, didn't it?"

Nitro lay back his head. "I just feel sorry for the poor bastard, that's all."

Nitro really felt it, Sabovik could tell. He wondered why he couldn't summon the same basic feeling. "Yeah, poor bastard."

TWENTY-ONE

19 August 1944
Southern Pacific Freight Yards
Sparks, Nevada

The R4D, bucking headwinds, was ten minutes late to Fallon. En route to the Sparks freight yards, their jeep waited at a grade crossing for five minutes while an impossibly long train rolled out of the yard on its way to Omaha. Then Sabovik and Collins ran around the yard for another fifteen minutes looking for X 4293 amid an enormous array of rail equipment.

The two were easily distracted as engines snorted, cars rumbled, and whistles hooted. At one heart-stopping moment, Nitro yanked Sabovik out of the way of a pounding troop train. An embarrassed Sabovik had forgotten to look both ways after a freight train ripped past in the opposite direction.

At 1156, they trudged out of breath up to a quietly hissing black cab-forward locomotive, the numbers 4216 stenciled on her sides and front. Behind that was her oil tender, the letters SOUTHERN PACIFIC down its side. After 4216, another cab-forward engine, number 4205, patiently waited, also hissing. Sabovik spotted two more cab-forward engines about two-thirds of the way back. Clearly a lot of power was required to drag this 106-car consist over the Donner Pass.

Sporting a silver façade, engine 4216, the lead engine, was a behemoth. In the railroader's lexicon, she was an AC-10 class 4-8-8-2 locomotive. The *4-8-8-2* meant that a set of four wheels in front was followed by sixteen massive sixty-three-inch-diameter drive wheels arranged in groups of four—two groups, or eight wheels, to a side. Each group of drive wheels was powered by a common driveshaft connected to a steam chest driven by two enormous twenty-four-inch-diameter pistons. The *AC-10* stood for the tenth design in a proud series of "articulated compound" engines specifically built to haul freight over the Sierras. The cab-forward design was unique in placing the smokestack in back, which meant that stack gases didn't asphyxiate engineers or firemen in tunnels or snowsheds. Moreover, the articulated engine's drive wheels were hinged separately from the after section, allowing the 125-foot-long engine to negotiate curves more easily. The weight of the after section was supported by a set of two rear wheels.

A bearded man with an engineer's cap leaned with both forearms at the right-side window, smoking a cigar.

"Looking for X 4293 westbound," panted Sabovik.

The man puffed on his stogie. "Right."

"Are you the X 4293 going to Roseville?"

"Right. You our riders today?"

"Affirmative."

The man reached over his shoulder and called into the cab, "Rudy, you got those train orders?" Oil-stained papers were jammed into his hand. "Names?"

"John Sabovik, commander, United States Navy; Alexander Collins, captain, United States Marine Corps."

"Okay." The man checked his watch, took another puff, and looked back at his train. "Come on up." He picked up a walkie-talkie, spoke, and then leaned out his window and waved toward the rear of the train. "Better hurry, we pull out in another minute." He reached up and pulled a lanyard, sounding four loud short blasts on the whistle. The engine behind answered. The two down the line answered as well.

Sabovik twirled a finger in his ear and said to Nitro, "Now, *that* whistle has the sound of authority."

"I'll say." Nitro grunted as his boot caught the post of a yellow rectangular signboard.

"Easy, Nitro." Sabovik looked back. The signboard was posted with two digits: 60/45.

"Least of my problems. Lucky I haven't been run over."

"Let's not press our luck." Sabovik walked up to the locomotive, grabbed the ladder, and scrambled up through an open doorway. Inside, he was greeted by a maze of hissing pipes and gauges. Everywhere, heat and raw energy enveloped him. And his nostrils were assailed with the odors of hot oil, raw steam, and hydraulic fluid.

Two overalled men regarded them curiously. Sabovik shook hands with the bearded one. "John Sabovik."

"Welcome aboard, Navy. Ben Sodawski." He was no more than five-seven and wore an engineer's cap, his beard heavily salt and pepper.

The fireman, a portly man in a black cap, pumped Sabovik's hand once and said in a German accent, "Bergman. Rudolph Bergman." Then he gave a broad gap-toothed smile. "Please call me Rudy."

"You the engineer?" asked Sabovik of Sodawski.

Sodawski checked his watch and looked backward out the window. "One and the same," he said, looking directly at Sabovik. They were within a foot of each other and Sabovik almost jumped. The engineer's combination of one brown eye and one blue was a bit unsettling.

To break the silence, Sabovik nodded outside to the signpost. "What do those numbers mean?"

Sodawski and Bergman traded glances. Then Sodawski said, "It's a speed board. The *60* is the speed limit for passenger trains, *45* the speed limit for freight trains."

"Oh."

The walkie-talkie squawked. Sodawski picked it up and said, "Roger." He turned to Sabovik and said, "Excuse me, we just got a highball." He yanked a lanyard over his head, sounding two blasts on the whistle. He grabbed a giant lever, then pulled back on another. On the cab's left side, Bergman began twisting valves and easing a set of levers.

It hit Sabovik that the cab crews in the three other engines were doing the same thing. Despite all the heat and smells and sweat, he realized this was a well-orchestrated dance, as each six-thousand-horsepower locomotive dug in its driving wheels. The cab-forward's four great steam chests blasted into the noontime sky as the engines took the strain. Couplings clanked down the line, the helper engines gathering their part of the load. The 106-car train began its journey to California.

As a boy, Sabovik had stood in awe of the cab-forwards as they thundered through the San Fernando Valley, hauling long trains up over the 3,799-foot Tehachapi Pass and into the San Joaquin Valley. Even now as an adult, it was difficult to suppress his excitement as the engine wound through a dizzying combination of switches, snaking its way out of the Sparks freight yard. Soon westbound X 4293 was on the main double-tracked grade heading west toward the state line. The day was warm, and before them the dark blue Sierra Nevadas jagged peaks were topped by duck-egg-blue skies.

Looking about the cab, Sabovik was reminded why he never liked naval engineering. As with boiler rooms aboard ship, he was greeted with an impossible array of valves, gauges, levers, all surrounding the waist-level firebox. A malevolent red glow emanated from a peephole.

"You see she's oil-fired . . ." Rudy Bergman was explaining the workings of the locomotive with exaggerated hand gestures. Nitro caught Sabovik's glance, rolled his eyes, then went back to nodding and smiling at Bergman.

Sodawski yelled, "You been aboard one of these before, Commander?"

"No, I haven't. By the way, my name's John."

"Call me Ben. Or my friends call me Soda Whiskers." He yanked his beard.

"Which do you prefer?"

"Don't matter." Sodawski waved to a thermos on a small shelf. "Coffee?"

"No, thanks." Then Sabovik asked, "You and Bergman been teamed up for long?"

"No. Actually, this is our first time."

"Really?"

"More to the point, John, it's my first time. They just promoted me to engineer. Not only that, they made me lead engineer. Now, that's gotta mean something." Sodawski looked over and tossed a smile, his one blue eye glinting. "Before that, I was a fireman, just like Rudy."

Sabovik didn't know what to say except, "Congratulations."

"You sure you want to ride with us?" He jabbed a thumb toward the rear. "We're carrying ammo, you know." His hands wiggled out an explosion. *"Kaboom!"*

"No, this is fine, thanks."

"Why are you here, anyway?" Sodawski pushed a small lever. Air hissed.

"Security check. Making sure the ammo doesn't go *kaboom!"*

"Well, glad you're not one of those top-of-the-mountain boys."

"Who?"

"Military Railway guys. Got nothing to do but freeze off their asses up there and pester us for hot coffee."

"When do you—"

"Lookit that damn fool." Sodawski pulled his air horn lanyard, sounding two long blasts, a short and another long. "It's Popovits."

A man in an ancient stake truck was racing them on an adjacent road. Thick black smoke poured out the tailpipe as its driver hunched over the wheel. A faded label on the door read, POPOVITS FARMS. Half a mile ahead, Sabovik saw where the road crossed over the tracks. His eyes darted about the compartment, looking for a speedometer. There: forty-five miles an hour.

"Dammit, he's pulling ahead," growled Sodawski. With a fisted hand, he bumped a massive lever, then sounded five blasts on his whistle. Engine 4041 answered. So did the others, although Sabovik hardly heard them with all the noise.

The speedometer worked its way to fifty, and they pulled even with the truck. It was going to be close if Nitro's eyes were any measure. Right now, they were wide open, perfectly round, and his Adam's apple jumped up and down as he peered out the window.

"Hah!" Sodawski pointed at Popovits's stake truck. "Guess what's for dinner?"

"Last time it was rabbit," said Bergman. He turned to them, grinning. "This time it's chicken."

Indeed, Popovits's stake truck was loaded with crated chickens. Feathers trailed in its wake as Popovits matched the great cab-forward's speed. They zipped past a speed board: 60/45.

Bergman jabbed a thumb at the stake truck and said, "Ben, maybe ve should take it easy. Popovits is crazy man."

"Not me," growled Sodawski. "They're paying me to keep a schedule." Once again he yanked his lanyard, the whistle rendering four blasts: a mournful long, long, short, long.

"Come on, Ben!" yelled Bergman, thumping the arm of his chair with a thick gloved fist.

Ahead, Sabovik plainly saw that the grade-crossing barricades were down. Yet the truck raced on, Popovits concentrating at the wheel, occasionally glancing over at them.

Soda Whiskers's blue right eye glinted in the sunlight. He blasted the horn again and said, "Idiot trying to get hisself killed."

Less than five hundred feet, Sabovik reckoned. "You can't stop now, can you?" he asked.

Soda Whiskers shook his head. "We could slow down, but nah. Gonna teach him a lesson."

"Ben," yelled Bergman. "Don't press your luck. Slow down."

"More steam, Rudy, dammit." He reached up and sounded five more short blasts on the whistle.

"Ben!" shouted Rudy.

"Don't look at me, he's asking for it!" yelled Sodawski.

The walkie-talkie squawked. Bergman grabbed it. "Yeah?" Then he said to Sodawski, "It's Elmer. He vants to know vat the hell you're doing?"

Sodawski yelled back, "Tell him to pay attention and give me more steam." He yanked the whistle lanyard five quick times.

"He vants to talk to you," said Rudy, handing over the walkie-talkie.

"Sure, sure." Sodawski grabbed it and threw it in a metal cabinet, slamming it shut.

Sabovik ventured a question to Sodawski. "Who's Elmer?"

Sodawski jabbed a thumb toward the engine behind. "Hogger[20] behind us. Gone cold feet on me."

"Vat vill Milo say?" asked Rudy.

"Who cares, now give me steam!" Again, Sodawski yanked the whistle cord, giving five short blasts.

"Okay, okay." Rudy twirled valves. The engine surged ahead, the speedometer jiggling to sixty.

The stake truck lost ground. But then more black smoke gushed out the tailpipe. It started to catch up, then slowly pull ahead.

"Shiiiit," yelled Nitro, his Adam's apple bouncing.

They thundered past another speed board: 70/50. Sabovik glanced at the speedometer: sixty-five.

Suddenly a Packard four-door sedan pulled onto the highway from a side road and rolled to a stop before the barricade. A split second later, the Popovits Farms stake truck screeched to a halt just behind the Packard in a flurry of dust, flying pebbles, and feathers. The engine blasted through the intersection.

"Jerk does that all the time," said Sodawski. "First time we've beaten him. You'd think he has a death wish." He reached up and sounded four short blasts.

Sabovik offered, "That means to change speed?"

"That's right," grinned Sodawski, kicking back on the regulator. "Four to slow down, five to go faster, six to shut up." In moments, the speedometer jiggled back to forty-eight miles per hour.

Bergman called across the cab, "Ben, I vas supposed to tell you to take it easy."

"It's okay, Rudy."

"Vat do I tell Milo?"

"He's back in the buggy, Rudy. Don't worry." Sodawski gestured to the cabinet. "Or you can call him. I'm sure he wants an explanation."

Rudy shrugged.

"Who's Milo?" asked Sabovik.

Sodawski's face darkened for a moment. "Our boss, the conductor. And I'm hogging today because we're shorthanded."

Sabovik had read the file on Soda Whiskers. The man had been a fireman for years, long after his peers were promoted to engineers. But he'd been in trouble for minor scrapes. And once in a while there was an incidence of drinking on his record. He'd recently been in the hospital for an undisclosed illness. From the way it was written, Sabovik figured the supervisor was being kind to him and was glossing over the fact that he'd been in Roseville Community to dry out. "Do you ever see him?"

"Oh, yes. I'm sure I'll hear about this at our next water stop."

The walkie-talkie squawked in the cabinet, its tone strident.

Sabovik looked at Bergman and then shrugged.

"Okay, okay. I get it." Rudy walked over, drew out the walkie-talkie, and pressed it to his ear. He thumbed the switch and said, "It's Milo, all right." After a moment, he grinned and put it back on the shelf.

"What?" asked Sodawski.

"Milo says your skills aren't up to par."

Sodawski's blue eye glinted. "The hell you say!"

Rudy's grin broadened. "He says your timing vas off. He vants to know vy you didn't hit the sonofabitch?"

Sodawski sat back in his chair and shook his head. "Next time I'll try harder." Then he looked up to Sabovik. "All right. Our fun for the day is over. Now, what is it you want to know about this monster?"

"Anything you can tell me." Sabovik didn't add that he was really interested in the route. Sodawski grabbed his pipe and began puffing. "Well, you're riding in one of the most innovative engines in North America, if not the whole world." He pointed out the window. "As you can see, we have clear visibility down the line. And we don't breathe fumes when we're pulling through tunnels because the stack's behind us. You'll see that today. Now, as far as this engine goes, it's an AC-10 class compound engine, two-hundred-pound plant generating six thousand horsepower with superheat—"

"What's that?" asked Nitro, edging over.

"Superheat?"

"Er, yeah."

Sodawski looked at Nitro with half an eye roll: *Everybody knew what superheating was!* "Superheating is where you take the steam generated in the steam drum, run it through some pipes, then let the fire hit it again, which makes the temperature and pressure go up. *That's* when you shove it to the pistons. Much hotter, far more efficient, 25, maybe 30 percent. Far more power."

"Superheat," said Nitro.

"Right, superheat," said Sodawski.

TWENTY-TWO

19 August 1944
USS *Matthew* (DD 548)
Moored, Mare Island Naval Shipyard
Mare Island, California

". . . I said the plant is superheated, Mr. Peete; 815 degrees. You do know what superheating is, don't you?"

"Uh, I believe so, sir," was the muffled reply.

Sitting at his desk in the captain's day cabin, Mike Donovan listened to the banter drifting from the wardroom on the other side of the bulkhead. It was the deep, corrugated voice of Lieutenant Burt Hammond, the ship's operations officer, pulling Ensign Jonathan Peete through a knothole. The irony was that this was the first time Donovan had heard Jonathan Peete sound unconvincing. Before the war, the man had been a budding movie star, playing in westerns and detective stories. More recently, Hollywood had discovered that Peete could sing, and he was given a supporting role in the musical *One Swell Summer.*

It turned out that Jonathan Peete's luck was attributed, at least in his early days, to his father, Michael Thomas Peete, a major star pre- and post-talkies. But now Michael Peete's star image was on the wane, as evidenced by the very paternal role he played in *One Swell Summer.* That was 1942 when the draft board in North Hollywood, California, began breathing down young Jonathan Peete's neck. Armed with a degree in drama from Yale, he enrolled in an officer candidate program. Only when Jonathan was about to graduate from OCS did he learn that father Michael had pulled strings, trying to secure for him a full lieutenant's commission with a Hollywood assignment.

Jonathan balked. He'd stormed into his commanding officer's office and requested—no, demanded—assignment to the fleet, preferably overseas to the war zone. Michael became furious, and father and son hadn't talked since. Jonathan couldn't have been happier. After receiving his commission, he put in for the navy's prodigious destroyer fleet and was ordered to the *Matthew.* Once Kruger had seen the orders, he'd sent Peete on to gunnery and torpedo school before the young ensign reported aboard.

Donovan hoped he'd fit in. In this war, he didn't need a movie star as a leader. He needed leaders to lead and they were damn hard to come by, especially experienced people.

Hammond was still at it with Peete. He bored in: ". . . because if you don't know about superheating, Mr. Peete, Mr. Corodini here will be happy to send along the ship's engineering specs for you to go over before we next get under way.

"You do know who Lieutenant Corodini is, don't you, Mr. Peete?"

"Ship's engineering officer, sir."

"Very good, Mr. Peete. Now, I imagine that if you can read lines in a screenplay, you surely can read a few lines in the ship's engineering doctrine."

Two or three officers chuckled.

"Mr. Peete?" demanded Hammond.

"We had instruction in naval engineering, sir. But I can't—"

"You mean they didn't teach superheating to you in Ninety-Day Wonder school?"

Donovan didn't mind the hazing. All junior officers endured it from one aspect or another. But hazing was only good if it was constructive. Burt Hammond's hazing was demeaning, particularly since there were chief petty officers in the wardroom waiting for the meeting to begin. Donovan needed an officer and chiefs corps that pulled together, not one busy dodging bullets.

Where the hell is Kruger? he wondered. It was early afternoon, and Donovan fidgeted. He needed Kruger to let him know if all the officers and chiefs were gathered for the meeting. Despite Admiral Nimitz's admonition to take his full thirty days' leave, he'd decided to report aboard early, assess the ship's needs over a few days, put them into motion, *then* take the rest of his leave.

Diane Logan had advised him not to return to duty for at least another week, but he felt much better and was getting agitated about his first command. The Logans were putting him up, and both he and Diane knew they had unfinished business. He'd gone through a catharsis of sorts, telling her about that horrible night off Tassaforonga Point and how Tiny was killed. He knew he had to keep talking. But there was something at a deeper level that he sensed, and he wanted to pursue that as well. Also, he had to admit that the feminine scent he'd caught that first night lay fixed in his subconscious.

One thing that he and Nimitz hadn't discussed—and that Diane didn't realize—is that a ship that doesn't get under way is a dead ship. And with Tom Drake, her captain, killed in an auto wreck, they'd kept the *Matthew* dockside pending a new skipper. Donovan needed to take over before the *Matthew* atrophied to a shriveled wreck. He'd seen signs of it this morning when he overheard sailors on the reefer ship across the way. They were laughing about "*Matthew* the Motionless," saying it was impossible to get her under way since she was stuck high and dry on coffee grounds.

To everyone's surprise, he walked up the gangway unannounced at 0900. It was worse than he'd seen that evening when he'd stood out on the dock with Vicki Kruger. Little things: petty officers standing around drinking coffee, talking with nonrated men who were supposed to be working. Cigarette ashes littered the deck, and the men's uniforms looked dirty, their shirts not tucked in. Elsewhere, inspection plates lay open, the areas unattended. A young bosun striker was painting over rust. Donovan shuddered to think what he'd find on his captain's inspection.

After telling an apologetic Kruger to go back to work, he spent the morning reviewing service jackets, having lunch sent to his stateroom where he ate in seclusion. He discovered that only sixty of their enlisted complement of 341 had been to sea; of that, only thirty-seven had combat experience. It was just as bad with the officers. He could count on just six qualified men for top underway watches, seven if he included Kruger. It was not just going to be a long day, it was going to be a long year.

A knock on the door.

"Enter."

Kruger walked in. "All set, Captain."

"Chiefs, too?"

"Just about everybody. Except Chief Dudley, who's standing the quarterdeck watch."

"Let's get in there before"—Donovan looked at a personnel file—"lieutenants Burt Hammond and Alberto Corodini rip Mr. Peete to pieces."

Kruger stopped in the doorway. "It's Al or Lieutenant Corodini. He's adamant about that. No one but his mother or grandmother calls him Alberto."

"He hates Alberto?"

"That's what he tells me."

"I wonder what else he hates?"

Kruger remained tight-lipped.

"Let's go, Mr. Kruger." Donovan eased past his executive officer and stepped into the wardroom.

"—tention on deck," someone called. Chairs scraped, men shot to their feet. Coffee cups clanked, and blue tobacco smoke cascaded about the space as three rubber-bladed fans tried vainly to disperse it. The wardroom, with a long athwartships dining table, was designed to accommodate twelve men at meals. The compartment was packed with about thirty, half of them jammed against the forward and port bulkheads, all straining to see their new skipper.

"Seats, gentlemen, those of you who can find chairs." Donovan took his chair at the table's head, while Kruger slipped into the chair to his right. Corodini, the next senior officer, sat to his left. "Smoking lamp is lit."

It grew silent. Expectation, concern, and foreboding were written over the officers' faces. The chiefs, older men, far more experienced, were more passive, expressionless, professional. Donovan knew he could depend on them. It was the officers he worried about.

It hit him that he was seated in the captain's chair—not the chair to his right, where he'd sat before, aboard the *McDermott*. That was the exec's chair and it now belonged to Kruger. He was seated where Mario Rossi had sat. It was where Mario had so easily dispensed justice and wisdom and discipline and confidence.

Mario's smiling face flashed before him. *Get it rolling, you crazy mik.*

"Well, now, it can't be all that bad, gentlemen. I've only been aboard for five hours. She's still afloat, isn't she?"

Chuckles ranged about the space.

He shrugged and then said, "Tom Drake was a good man. Last month I had the good fortune to meet with Admiral Nimitz, and he said as much. He sends his condolences."

He shook his head. "It doesn't make sense, I'll admit. The pinnacle of your career and zap, an auto wreck. But as the Good Book says, 'Let the dead bury the dead.' It's time to move on and bring this ship back to fighting trim. By that I mean she's got to be worthy of joining the Big Blue.[21] And right now, I don't think this ship is ready for a division officer's inspection, let alone a captain's inspection. Am I right?" He looked into their eyes. "Anybody have anything to offer to the contrary?"

Silence. Lieutenant Corodini took a drag on his cigarette. Immediately he broke into a deep-seated, lung-twisting smoker's cough that lasted thirty seconds. He grew red in the face and wheezed, ". . . sorry, Captain." Someone shoved over a glass and he gulped water.

Kruger reached over and stubbed out Corodini's cigarette. "That's why they call 'em coffin nails."

"Sorry, Captain," said Corodini. He was a massive man, at least six-four, 250 pounds, with fiery red hair.

"You play football, Mr. Corodini?" asked Donovan. He'd already read Corodini's service record and knew the answer.

Corodini straightened to his full height. "Fullback, Ohio State, sir."

"Glad to have you in the lineup."

"Thank you, sir."

It grew quiet. Donovan continued. "The hell with inspections. Here's what I'd like to do. I intend to read my orders at

1500, assume command, and then get this ship under way tomorrow at 0800."

Outside, it was bright daylight, but the wardroom suddenly seemed to grow dark. "Holy smokes," murmured one of the chiefs.

"Anything wrong with getting this ship under way?" asked Donovan. "I mean those three bladed things hanging off the fantail are meant to go round and round, aren't they?"

Corodini cleared his throat. "Captain, there's a few things you should know about the plant first."

"And what are those, Alberto?"

Despite the little red flecks that quickly flashed at the corners of Corodini's eyes, he did a good job keeping his temper. "Well, sir, we have a lube-oil problem to the main feed pump in the after engine room. Also, the fuel-oil service pump in the forward fireroom is—"

"Estimated time of repair?" asked Donovan.

Corodini blinked and looked at Kruger. "Well, sir. If the parts get here on time possibly by 1800 this evening."

"What if the parts don't get here until 1900? Will you be able to work on it then?"

". . . uh, well, if need be."

"And what if the duty section can't finish the job by then?"

"Well, sir. With the ship's company back aboard, we'll finish the job tomorrow morning, sir," said Corodini.

Donovan stared at Corodini.

Corodini cleared his throat and continued, "Besides that, there's a failure in the after steering port ram, and we've—"

"We have a starboard ram, don't we?" asked Donovan.

"Yes, sir."

"Can you fix the port ram by 0800 tomorrow?"

"If we get the parts." Corodini gazed darky to the end of the table.

The seat at the other end was occupied by Howard Sloan, a redheaded, freckle-faced, thin lieutenant junior grade. Sloan said nothing, his lips pressed.

Donovan said, "Thank you for your candor, Mr. Corodini. Are there any other casualties of note to the engineering department."

Corodini sat back and exhaled. "Not right now, sir."

"And will the boilers generate superheated steam?" For some reason, Donovan fixed his gaze on Peete. He was a good-looking kid, with lanky, straight brownish hair flopped on his forehead. Absent makeup, he seemed to have no pretense. He looked like any ordinary twenty-three-year-old.

"Well, Captain, we can light them off and see what happens," said Corodini. Immediately he flushed with the realization that he'd given the wrong answer. "I mean, we'll have superheat ready to go, sir."

Corodini had the makings of a good engineer, Donovan decided. There were good fitness reports in his personnel jacket. His qualifications were excellent. He'd been an engineering major at Ohio State University and had indeed played football there. But he had no combat experience, and Donovan could tell the man needed to be goosed occasionally. In a way, he felt sorry for Corodini. He was giving the man a terrible beating before the other officers. But he could tell they were used to making excuses—being victims—and that had to change. Corodini would survive, and these men would view Mike Donovan as a bastard. That's what he wanted. He caught a glint in Kruger's eye for just an instant. Kruger knows what I'm doing. *So be it.*

Donovan turned to Corodini. "Very well. Do we have enough fuel oil to leave the dock and do a couple of circles around the Farallons?"

"Yes, sir," said Corodini.

Donovan looked at the other officers. "Anybody else have a reason not to get under way?" He turned to Hammond. "Operations department?"

Hammond was in the process of lighting another cigarette. With great panache, he waved out his match and exhaled through his nose. "Everything except the gyro, Captain."

Donovan knew about this. He'd read the report. "When will it be fixed?"

"Well, it's a ship-alt, Captain. We've been waiting on parts now for three weeks." Hammond looked to the end of the table. "Mr. Sloan?"

"Not a word yet," said the supply officer.

"Mr. Hammond, how about the watch, quarter, and station bill?"

"Yes, sir?"

"When was it last updated?"

Hammond's resonant voice softened a bit. "Let's see. Two weeks ago."

"I see. And if I read the service records correctly, we've had at least a dozen new enlisted posted here, and two officers that I can think of. In fact . . ." Donovan turned to Ensign Peete at the end of the table. "Mr. Peete, where's your general quarters station?"

"I don't, er . . . torpedo director, I think, Captain."

"How about special sea detail[22]?"

"I don't know, Captain," he said softly.

"Is your name posted on the watch, quarter, and station bill?"

"Not yet, sir."

Hammond glared at Peete and then at Donovan. "I'll take care of it, Captain."

"You bet you will. It's now"—Donovan checked his watch—"1347. I expect to see the updated watch, quarter, and station bill on my desk prior to ceremonies at 1500."

"Yes, sir," Hammond said evenly.

Donovan caught the glance of a balding towheaded heavyset lieutenant with thick glasses. "You're Mr. Merryweather, our gunnery officer?"

"That's right, Captain."

"How's gunnery?"

"Five men AWOL, Captain."

"What?" said Donovan. He exchanged glances with Kruger, who gave a shrug.

"They're in the brig. You see, there was a big fight at the Paradise Bowling Alley last night over in town. Wrecked the place. So we're waiting for the Mare Island SPs to assess damages before they deliver our boys back to us."

Again, the wardroom was silent, the three fans whirring gleefully. Donovan let them stew for a moment.

Kruger spread his hands and offered, "Crews from three other tin cans were there. Started calling us '*Matthew* the Motionless.' It got to them. Got to where they stood back to back fighting for their ship. Finally the SPs showed up and hauled them off. Won't let them go until damages are assessed. I think we should—"

Donovan raised his hand. "I get it. Are there any other equipment casualties or crew problems?"

Again the chiefs sat passive, stone-faced, their arms folded. The officers leaned forward in their chairs, eyebrows raised.

"Very well." Donovan lowered his voice. "As mentioned, we'll meet on the fantail at 1500 and I'll read my orders and take command. There will be a captain's inspection at 1600. All spaces are to be opened except voids."

Kruger made notes. "Very good, sir. What time shall we call liberty?"

"There will be no liberty," said Donovan. He listened for the collective intake of breath.

"But, but . . . ," said Corodini.

"What is it, Mr. Corodini?" asked Donovan.

"Nothing, sir."

"Very good. Now that we have all of our manpower on board except five men AWOL"—Donovan fixed Merryweather with a glare—"I expect all the casualties to be repaired by the time we get under way tomorrow. Do you understand me?"

They looked at one another.

"I can't hear you."

"Yes, sir," they said.

"Very good," said Donovan. "By 1500, I want this ship looking like a ship topside. Right now it looks like a whorehouse." He pointed to Lieutenant (jg) Jack Kelso. "And I'll hold you personally accountable. I don't care who is responsible for what space. Clean her up, now."

"Aye, aye, Captain," said Kelso.

Donovan turned to Kruger. "When was the last time you sounded GQ?"

"Well . . ." Kruger's eyes darted about the wardroom. "About two weeks ago. You see—"

"That's okay," said Donovan. "Since Mr. Hammond is so kindly providing us with a new watch, quarter, and station bill, we'll sound general quarters at 1700. Pass the word to all hands."

Kruger's eyes wandered to the overhead. "Yes, sir. GQ at 1700, sir."

"Very good. Now everyone is dismissed, except department heads."

They shoved their way out as if the ship were afire. Kruger and the ship's four department heads remained: Corodini for engineering, Merryweather for gunnery, Hammond the operations officer, and Sloan the supply officer.

Donovan said, "I won't take long, gentlemen. We have a lot to do between now and 0800 tomorrow. I'm sure it's no news to you that this ship is pathetic. Material condition is poor, attitude is poor, everything is poor."

Hammond said, "Sir, we can't help it if—"

"No excuses," barked Donovan. "Look, maybe it really isn't your fault. But I don't care."

He paused for a moment, reveling in their incredulity. "The system is screwing you, and now you have this new sonofabitch who is treating you unfairly. Well, war is war, and we've got to be ready, no matter whose fault it is. Good God. Do you expect to ask the Japs not to open fire because we're not ready? It's just not our fault? They don't give a damn about what's fair."

"No, sir."

"I don't care about faults. Somehow, we've got to get around all this crap and get these things fixed." His gaze whipped to Sloan. "You see the *Bridges* across the way?" He referred to a shot-up *Benson*-class destroyer that had just returned from the war zone.

They all nodded.

"Well, everybody's on leave except for skeleton crew. What does that tell you?"

They looked at one another. Corodini rolled his eyes.

"Dammit, we're getting under way tomorrow morning, Mr. Corodini. That means you're going to have to go out there to the midnight auto supply and find parts. Same with you, Mr. Hammond. Just don't get caught."

"Yes, sir," they said.

"And Mr. Merryweather. I want you and the exec to go over to the brig and bring our boys back."

"What if they don't let them go?" asked Kruger.

"Draw some money from the welfare and rec fund and pay off the damages, whatever they are. We can have a captain's mast for them later, but I want all hands back here by the time we get under way."

Donovan stood. "Main feed pump, fuel-oil service pump, gyro, steering ram, men AWOL—I want that rectified tonight, not next week. Is that clear?"

"Yes, sir," they said.

Corodini said, "Captain?"

"What?"

"My wife, she's pregnant, due anytime now. I should really be . . . home these evenings."

"Mr. Corodini," Donovan said. "The navy recognizes that it was necessary for you to be present for the laying of the child's keel. However, your presence is not required for the launching. Moreover, the Imperial Japanese Navy has greater demands on your time, my time, all of our time that requires us to forgo personal items. Do you understand me?"

Again, the little red flecks flashed at Corodini's eyes then were gone. "Yes, sir. Sorry, sir."

"Very well, 1500 then." Donovan walked out.

Donovan walked into his day cabin, closed the door, and sat. The porthole was open and he heard an incredulous sailor gasp, "No shit? Under way tomorrow? How the hell we gonna do that?"

The response was muffled.

". . . what a horseshit sonofabitch. We'll be lucky to get past the Golden Gate."

"You eating on board tonight?"

"This swill? Not on your life."

Their voices drifted aft. ". . . woddaya say we mosey over to the *Tingey*. I got a buddy there. She serves good chow. Real ice cream, too. Then we . . ."

Sailors leaving the ship to find a decent meal? No wonder they don't want to get under way. How bad will it be when we're at sea? Donovan thought. Lousy food. Poor material readiness. All this damn squabbling. Not exactly the way I planned it. But there you have it. Wait until we meet the Japs.

His eyes wandered up to the overhead, and again he thought of Mario Rossi. *What would you do, Mario?*

Then it hit him. His own admonition. *Let the dead bury the dead.*

He had nobody but himself.

TWENTY-THREE

22 August 1944
USS *Matthew* (DD 548)
Moored, Mare Island Naval Shipyard
Mare Island, California

There's something in the air when a ship is about to get under way. On the surface, one could call it a brittle tension combined with the thrill of going to sea. But far beneath, there have been hours of preparation, refueling and reprovisioning, the meticulous lighting off of boilers, bringing up the generators, the energizing of the ship's gyro and electronic equipment. Awakening from her "cold iron" state, she becomes a living, breathing thing. Vents and exhaust blowers howl around the ship, providing fresh air inside. Uptakes in her stacks whine as boiler tenders raise steam, and perhaps lift a safety valve once or twice, the noise an ear-racking hiss heard for hundreds of yards. On board, raw heat radiates from her decks as one feels the vibration from pumps and motors whining within her, sending life-giving steam or electricity or hydraulic fluid throughout the ship. Inside, the odor of steam and condensation and hydraulic fluid combine with the morning pancakes and eggs, giving an unmistakable sense of purpose and direction. She's alive and, in a way, exerts her own will, tugging at her dock lines, anxious to get to sea.

With an hour to go the ship is ready, and then they wait. Everyone seems to stand around, bored. And yet they're not. Massive tonnage underfoot is about to move, and almost everyone—from machinist's mates to boiler tenders to enginemen, boatswain's mates to line handlers, quartermasters to signalmen, radarmen to radiomen—is part of getting her safely away from the dock and into the element for which she was designed. Men fidget with cigarettes and lighters, some spill coffee, others sniffle and blow their noses while pacing the decks, waiting for word from the bridge to do something. Inevitably someone runs about on a last-minute emergency; a rush for something—anything—stark anxiety. Novices, officers and enlisted, pace up and down, oftentimes asking inane questions. The pros stand back, their eyes darting everywhere, quietly double-checking, making sure everything is right.

Donovan sat in his day cabin waiting for them to finish their jobs. He'd been waiting nearly all night and had only two hours' sleep while keeping track of the repair jobs. Sloan was a bit more ingenious than resorting to the midnight auto supply in the tempting form of the USS *Bridges* across the way. Tomorrow was Tuesday, a payday, and Sloan walked to the supply center to draw currency to pay the crew. Normally he would take a storekeeper to carry the satchel full of cash. Both would be wearing .45 pistols strapped to their hips. This time, he took six of the tallest, burliest boatswain's mates, suited them up in dress blues, leggings, and duty belts, and strapped .45s to their hips. After drawing the cash, Sloan and his entourage marched over to the main-base supply office. Crowding around the desk of a thin, balding supply corps lieutenant commander, they exacted all the parts from him as requested, the man's eyes popping at the hardware crowding his desk. The parts were aboard by 1700, and they began installing them. The engineering jobs were finished by 2300; the gyro alteration was going nicely but, due to tedious calibration procedures, was not slated to be finished until early morning.

Donovan turned in at 0015. He read for a while, then rolled over and flicked off the light. But his eyes were fixed to the bulkhead. He slept for an hour, then awoke sitting bolt upright in his bunk, sweating.

Fire.

He felt heat and choked on smoke and cordite while flames seared his flesh. Then the ship started capsizing, men pouring out of the engineering spaces below. Some were scalded, their skin blistering horribly all over their bodies. Their mouths opened to flattened ovals as they screamed. Except he couldn't hear their silent screams; he could only see their faces.

"Stop!"

He jumped from his bunk, padded over to the washbasin, and rinsed his face with cold water. He was almost afraid to go back to sleep, so he took the chair and put up his feet, listening to the sounds of the shipyard, well into the third shift. Diane had held him in her arms and rocked him that night. He wondered if he could have a pure moment like that again with her, trusting, giving. My God, he realized. Not only had she patched up his abdomen, she'd played a role in stopping the nightmares. Except . . . they hadn't stopped entirely. And he knew he couldn't go to sea like this. He'd be a physical wreck after two or three nights.

It grew light and he stood to look out the porthole. Fog. He couldn't see more than a hundred feet. *Now, ain't that a pip?*

He showered, shaved, and got dressed. Then he had breakfast sent in: powdered eggs, which tasted like cardboard, and greasy bacon. After a few bites, he sat back and drank coffee, aimlessly flipping pages of an impossibly thick technical report.

Special sea detail was set at 0730 and he longed to be out there, looking over his ship. Making sure all was ready. Becoming part of her. But as captain, he had to step aside and give them their heads; let them work out the kinks. Let them learn. That's what Mario had done, and Donovan could do no less. He owed it to them.

He turned back to the report. It was labeled TOP SECRET and laid out new specifications for modifications to the mark 63 fire control radar system, which unfortunately had been installed under an obsolete procedure, a minor embarrassment for a new *Fletcher*-class destroyer that was supposed to have the best available. But he couldn't concentrate. He was simply killing time, flicking pages, waiting for the knock.

It came at 0752.

"Enter."

Wearing parka and binoculars, Burt Hammond, the operations officer, stuck his head in. "Ship's ready for sea, Captain." Hammond was officer of the deck for special sea detail.

"All respects?"

"Yes, sir. Boilers one, two, three, and four are on the line. So are generators one and two. Main control requests permission to shift from shore power to ship's power?"

"Granted. Now, how's the gyro?"

Hammond crossed his fingers. "It's spinning, Captain. Yardbirds are finishing calibrations and are wrapping it up. Should be gone by the time we shove off."

"The fuel-oil service pump?"

"Done."

"Starboard ram?"

"All set."

". . . and the main feed pump?"

Hammond's face darkened. "Mr. Kruger reports it's ready to go."

"And where is he?"

"Down in the hole, Captain," Hammond said offhandedly.

The executive officer belonged in CIC during sea detail, watching the plot. "Who's in CIC?" Donovan asked.

Hammond looked at the deck, kicking aside an imaginary piece of dust. "Mr. Talbert, sir. He's the CIC officer."

Donovan glanced at the bulkhead clock: 0754. "Very well. I'll be up in a minute."

"Yes, sir." Hammond closed the door.

Donovan yanked the phone from the bracket and punched MAIN CONTROL.

"Kruger." Turbines and the cacophony of a number of whining pumps shrieked in the background. Kruger would have a finger jammed in his unengaged ear, Donovan knew.

"Dick, it's Mike. What are you doing down there?"

"I beg your pardon?"

"Sea detail. You belong in CIC," said Donovan. Outside he heard the 1 MC[23] click on. The bosun's metallic voice echoed throughout the ship. "First call, first call to colors."

"I'm sorry, Captain. This is where I've always been."

"Where's Corodini?"

"Right here. You want to speak with him?"

Donovan hadn't spoken with Corodini since he'd ripped him apart in the wardroom yesterday. "Not at all. I want you in CIC."

"But who's going to take care of main control?"

"Mr. Corodini. That's what we're paying him for."

Kruger paused. A loud horn bleated in the background. "Captain, we're not entirely certain of this main feed pump."

"Then tell Corodini to get on it. It's his job, not yours."

"Sir—I really think we should—"

"CIC, now, Mr. Kruger. I don't care if you're in your overalls or in your underwear. Get up here and let Corodini handle main control."

"But, Captain—"

"For crying out loud, Rich. How do you expect the man to learn his job with you hovering over him? He'll figure it out. And if he doesn't, we'll fire him and get someone else. Now get up here. That's an order." Donovan jammed the phone in its bracket, stood, and looked out the porthole. He didn't know if Kruger realized it, but he really needed his XO up here. It was foggy as hell. He couldn't see more than a hundred feet.

Once again, he splashed water on his face and patted it dry with a towel. Leaning close to the mirror, he saw that his eyes were red. In fact, he looked as if he'd been on an all-night drunk.

Hey, Crazy Mike. Time to be captain.

Shut up, Mario. Grabbing his foul-weather jacket, he opened the door and stepped into the passageway.

Khaki-clad officers and chiefs, signalmen, quartermasters, and boatswain's mates jammed the pilothouse and open bridge. Climbing the ladder, Donovan eased among them, looking for Hammond. Fog swirled as he stepped to the starboard bridge wing. A sailor, a first-class yeoman, blocked his way as he went to stand on the pedestal. "Can I help you, sailor?"

The man looked bewildered. "Well, er, no, sir. You see—"

"What is it then?"

The man chewed gum and clacked it loudly. "Er, I'm your

talker, sir." He was tall and stringy, with tufts of wheat-colored hair sticking out from under his sailor's cap.

"You ever comb your hair, sailor?"

"Well, er, I was in a hurry, this morning, sir." His Adam's apple bounced, but he had a generous resonance in his voice.

The bridge became quiet. It was as if Donovan and this sailor were the only people there.

"You ever been a bridge talker before—what's your name, anyway?" demanded Donovan.

"Yes, sir." The man's gum clacked. "Been a talker for six months now. And my name's Potter, Lucian B." He stood almost to attention.

"All right, Potter. Spit out the gum, comb your hair, and stand right here. I'll relay orders from atop the pilothouse."

"Yes, sir!" Potter leaned over and expertly ejected a giant wad of gum into the oily water between the ship and the pier.

"Mr. Hammond?" Donovan called.

Hammond walked out carrying a mug of coffee. "Yes, sir?"

"I notice the gangway is already gone. Who gave permission to do that?"

"Er, I did, sir. I thought—"

"Henceforth you'll ask the commanding officer for permission to take in the gangway. Do you understand?"

"Yes, sir!"

"Now, who do you recommend to get this ship under way?"

Hammond did a double take. "I thought it would be you, sir. I mean, Captain Drake always . . ." His voice trailed off.

"Who is your JOOD[24]?"

"Why, it's Mr. Peete, sir."

Donovan walked to the ladder. "Have Mr. Peete join me on top of the pilothouse. I'd like you down here to relay orders directly to the helm and lee helm."

"Mr. Peete?" Hammond's hand went to his hips.

"Yes, send him up, please." Donovan climbed the ladder rungs to the open platform atop the pilothouse. The only items up here were the tank-like structure of the main-battery director and two twenty-millimeter cannon mounts. Aside from that, the platform offered a fine view of the whole ship, bow and stern. It was his favorite area from which to conn the ship in close quarters. Trouble was, with the fog, he couldn't see more than four or five hundred feet. But just then a soft breeze tickled the back of his neck. The San Francisco Bay fog, so typical for this time of year, was about to be swept away.

Ensign Peete walked up wearing a heavy foul-weather jacket. Binoculars dangled from a strap around his neck. "You sent for me, Captain?"

A cold, damp zephyr curled around Donovan's cheek and into his shirt. *Ah, yes.* He turned to Peete. "You ever get a ship under way, son?"

Peete stepped back, his eyebrows raised, "Me, sir?"

"I take that as a no."

"That is correct, sir."

He stepped close to Peete. "First time at sea?"

"Well, first time on one of these things, Captain."

Donovan looked from side to side. He needed to build on someone and decided to start with Peete. He grinned and said, "Half the trick is making people think you know what you're doing."

"I beg your pardon?"

"Shhh. Look, dammit. You're not going to wreck the ship. I won't let you do that. Look at it this way. Do you realize how much fun you can have with sixty thousand horsepower?"

"Haven't thought of it that way, Captain."

"Right. Here's what you do. Relax. Enjoy it. Just do what I tell you to do. You'll get the hang of it. Okay?"

"Well . . ."

"You ever do Shakespeare?"

Peete straightened up. "At Yale, sir."

"Very well. Now go over there, lean over the rail, and pretend like you're Laurence Olivier." He nodded to a racked megaphone. "Use that if you have to."

"I think I can do without, Captain."

"Very well. We begin by telling Mr. Hammond you have the conn and to single up all lines."

"Now, sir?"

"Right now." Donovan walked to the opposite side of the

platform, a good ten feet away. He called softly, "Okay, Mr. Peete, take one; the camera is rolling."

Peete's eyes had that *Don't-leave-me-now* look. "Yes, sir." He stepped to the starboard rail, braced his hands, and bellowed, "Mr. Hammond. I have the conn. Single up all lines and prepare to get under way." His tones were electric: pure, resonant, compelling. And damn, Donovan stifled a grin: Peete sure didn't need a megaphone, and he did sound like Olivier.

With the captain out of view, the men milling below looked up in disbelief at the apparently lone Ensign Jonathan Peete, the newly minted ninety-day wonder. Three seconds passed.

Hammond recovered first. "Mr. Peete has the conn," he yelled into the pilothouse. Then he said to Potter, "Tell fo'c'sle and fantail to single up all lines." That done, he looked up to Peete, his face saying, *What's next, kid?*

Peete looked to Donovan.

Donovan strolled past and, covering his mouth, said, "Now you say 'Tell main control to stand by to answer all bells.' "

Standing tall, Peete barked the order then asked softly, "Now what?"

"Wait."

A voice in the pilothouse echoed, "Main control answers nine-nine-nine turns for maneuvering bells, sir."

Donovan walked by casually again, looking up in the sky, and whispered, "Very well."

Again, Peete braced his hands on the rail and looked down. "Very well."

Donovan moved beside him and said, "Your next command is 'Rudder amidships.' "

"Rudder amidships," bellowed Peete.

By now everyone had caught on, but Peete's performance was compelling, the timbre in his voice near charismatic.

"My rudder is amidships," hollered the helmsman in the pilothouse.

Hammond repeated it.

Without prompting, Peete said, "Very well,"

Donovan walked around the main-battery director and again stood beside Peete. "What do you think now, Mr. Peete?"

Ensign Jonathan Peete said, "I wish I knew, sir."

Donovan clasped Peete's elbow. "Come on, figure it out, son. Look." His hand waved at the sky. "See that? Wind. The fog's blowing away."

"Yes, sir."

The 1 MC gave a metallic screech, and the bosun's mate of the watch announced, "On deck, attention to colors."

Along with everyone topside, Donovan and Peete faced aft, stood to attention, and saluted as the national ensign was raised on the fantail. At the same time, the jack was raised on the fo'c'sle jackstaff. The same announcement echoed from the other ships as topside personnel honored their flag.

"Ready, two," called the boatswain's mate of the watch.

"And what kind of wind is it, Mr. Peete?" asked Donovan.

"Uh, an offshore wind, sir. Right on our beam."

"Very good, Mr. Peete. So tell them to take in lines one, two, three, four, five, and six. Then let Mother Nature take care of the rest."

The resonance in Peete's voice could have ripped lumber as he bellowed the order. The lines were taken in.

The last line left the pier and the boatswain's mate of the watch announced on the 1 MC, "Under way, shift colors." The union jack was lowered from the foredeck, the national ensign was lowered aft, and a new national ensign was run up the halyard and to-blocked at the mainmast.

They had drifted out about a half a ship's length from the pier when Donovan said, "Very good, Mr. Peete. What do you think so far?"

"Nothing better than to wind up sixty thousand horsepower, Captain."

"Well then, Mr. Peete. Go over there, check your ship's heading, and tell the helmsman to steer five degrees to the left of that course. Then we'll put some of your horsepower to work as you ring up all ahead one-third."

"All ahead one-third, sir."

"That's right."

Peete rendered the maneuvering orders in a clipped, metallic staccato; the *Matthew*'s screws bit the water and she gathered way.

"Well, what do you think so far, Mr. Peete?" asked Donovan.

"Really keen, sir. When do I get to use all sixty thousand?"

"Sooner than you'd think."

Ensign Peete gave more orders and Hammond relayed them crisply into the pilothouse, where the helmsman and lee helmsman executed them perfectly. With a prolonged blast of her whistle, the USS *Matthew* gathered way for the first time in sixty-two days.

Ensign Jonathan Peete wore a thin smile as Donovan kept feeding orders.

The crew on the bridge took it all in, marveling at Peete's immediate command presence. All except for Burt Hammond, who had trouble imagining why the captain had picked this Johnnie Hollywood to conn the ship for their first time under way. Getting a ship under way was an honor, a gift the captain usually gave to senior officers. Why not me? Hammond wondered.

TWENTY-FOUR

25 August 1944
Southern Pacific railroad station
Roseville, California

The evening was balmy, the temperature a dry eighty-eight, with plenty of twilight in a deep amber sky. It was a little after eight as a dog-tired Donovan jostled among other servicemen toward the street, looking for a taxi. The devilish train ride epitomized everything he'd heard about milk trains. This one, the 532, had stopped every mile or so, either on a siding to let a freight train roar past, or simply . . . to stop and wait, and do nothing. The maddening trip from Oakland took four and a half hours, arriving two hours late.

He reached the platform's edge, finding three taxis. But all were stuffed with five or six men sharing rides. Scratching his head, Donovan looked in vain for another taxi, realizing he would have to take the bus. Even the damn bench was full.

On Mare Island he'd found a sympathetic operator, who'd placed the call to Diane. She'd invited him for a home-cooked meal at six. He was welcome to stay the night, but she was due at the hospital at eight, working until six the next morning.

He checked his watch: nearly eight fifteen. Diane would be gone, and the next bus wasn't due for another half hour.

Start walking.

He'd taken only a few steps when he heard, "Hey! Mike! Hold on a minute."

"Hello?" He turned to find Walt Logan rushing up. "Walt, it's good to see you."

They shook left-handed as Logan nodded to a control tower across the tracks. "On duty, so I don't have much time.

Look, Diane says you two were supposed to have dinner, but then I gave her the lowdown on the 532."

"So she knows?"

"Right. There was a derailment near Fairfield. That's why everything was so fouled up. We're working around it. Look, go over to the house. There's a key above the doorsill and meat loaf is in the icebox."

"Wow, meat loaf!"

"It's her recipe. Spicy. Makes your hair stand on end."

"Here's to the 532."

"Best we can do. I'll be home around midnight, so leave some for me."

"Maybe not."

"Don't be a pig. Say, how about a game of chess tomorrow?"

"I'm not sure. I'd be playing among excellence."

"Hah! Excellence. You should see what Milo Lattimer does to me."

"Now, that's something I'd like to see."

"Well, he'll be there, too."

"Okay. That'll give me a chance to thank him properly. Feel like I owe him my life."

"Nah. I'm sure he's forgotten it by now. Look, I have to go. See you tomorrow. Here." He tossed a set of keys. "Take my car. It's the dark blue Chevy two-door in the SP parking lot next block over. You'll need lots of choke to get her started."

"Thanks. You want me to pick you up at midnight?"

"It's okay. Ken Taylor will give me a ride. And don't forget to leave me some meat loaf."

"I'll think about it."

Logan grinned, tipped his hat, and, crossing four sets of tracks, began scrambling up a ladder to his control tower just before a sixteen-driver Mallet clanked past, pulling an interminable string of refrigerated fruit cars.

Five minutes later, Donovan mounted the Logan front porch, found the key, and opened the door. Diane's meat loaf was indeed wonderful, and it took all his willpower not to wolf the entire dish. Then he walked into the living room, flipped on the radio, and sat in a deep armchair. *Fibber McGee and Molly* was playing on radio station KGEI all the way from San Francisco. He rubbed his face, realizing he was tired and could really hit the sack without any trouble. He let his mind wander over the week. Luckily, they let the *Matthew* steam independently, getting the kinks out of a ship that had only recently been worked up to fighting trim. There had been the usual screwups, but they had done fairly well, he had to admit. They'd been eager to please, and that made him feel good with hopes that soon they would overcome the "*Matthew* the Motionless" sobriquet.

But a dark moment came the last night out. Kruger let on that he and Sloan had been investigating the food situation and had irrefutable proof that Watson, a first-class commissary man, was selling the ship's food on the black market. That's why the food had been so horrible. Watson had been watering it down and thinning out portions. Kruger and Sloan had the chief master at arms bring Watson to the wardroom. After two minutes, the tall, athletic, and well-liked commissary man first-class Elmer Watson broke down and admitted all.

The next morning, they held captain's mast on the way in from the Farallon Islands. When the question of mitigating circumstances came up, it turned out Watson's younger brother had polio. The kid was in an iron lung, and Watson was selling the ship's food to pay medical bills. With all the evidence presented, Donovan didn't have to think long about Watson's punishment, but he hesitated before pronouncing it. Watson's career was wrecked; he'd been due for promotion to chief, but now everything was over for him. Innumerable seconds passed in the wardroom as Donovan searched for a way out. There wasn't any. Despite the younger brother's dilemma, Watson had broken the law, stolen from his shipmates, and jeopardized the ship. It was up to Donovan to finish it. Everyone's eyes, even Watson's, remained fixed on the bulkhead when Donovan sentenced Watson to six months in the brig and a dishonorable discharge.

Later, Donovan climbed to the bridge just before they slipped under a fog-shrouded Golden Gate. It was quiet. The word on Watson's sentence had flashed around the ship like wildfire. Now it was sinking in, the jocularity of the homeward voyage lost in the screaming silence.

Right after they docked at Mare Island and doubled up, Watson was led to the quarterdeck in handcuffs and leg chains. Activity topside turned deathly still. Even people on the ships around them stopped what they were doing. The sailor cried while marines led him off the ship, shoved him in a paddy wagon, and rattled off for the brig. Donovan walked off the gangway next and headed down the dock. Feeling their eyes on his back, he thought, Mike, it sure didn't take long for you to make your mark.

That took care of the food problem, but two issues lingered in his wardroom, and he wasn't sure how to handle them. One was that Kruger was inclined to stay with things most familiar—his engines and boilers. He spent far too much time in the hole, rather than acting as a true exec and absorbing the administrative details for Donovan. As Admiral Nimitz said, Kruger was a great engineer—but except for the Watson investigation, he'd fallen short as an exec.

The second problem was more volatile. Burt Hammond and Jonathan Peete were like two of Diane's enormous compound locomotives rushing head-on at 120 miles per hour. The two were similar in demeanor, and both were handsome; in a way they could have passed for brothers. Both had strong intellects, athletic frames, and quick minds. The main difference was that Hammond was more inner-directed and analytical. He never acted without examining things from all angles. Peete, on the other hand, seemed to do things spontaneously. He had a broad smile and got along with officers and men alike, something that infuriated Hammond. Hammond often pulled rank on Peete, sometimes in front of the enlisted, doing his best to embarrass the young ensign. Two days ago, Donovan watched from the bridge as the two went at it just beneath on the 01 level. Hammond became strident and drew close. Peete smiled. Then openly grinned. Hammond braced Peete to attention and began circling the ensign, yelling, chewing him out.

When Donovan saw Peete's fists balling and unballing, he sent for Kruger to break it up. Later, Donovan and Kruger discussed transferring Peete to keep the peace and keep from wrecking two naval careers.

The *Fibber McGee* show broke for a commercial. Donovan heaved himself up from the armchair and walked to the back bedroom to unpack his things. He opened the closet to hang up his blouse and found Ralph's bathrobe. It was the one Diane wore that night he'd told her about the dream. His mistake came when he picked up a sleeve and drew a breath. She was there: that delightful combination of perfume and shampoo and female; her aroma, her essence.

In the living room, Fibber McGee opened his closet. The whole world tumbled and crashed out, the audience roaring with laughter.

But something different had tumbled from this closet.

Diane.

He checked his watch. The *Fibber McGee* show had another fifteen minutes to go. But Walt's car keys were still nestled in his pocket.

Diane.

With luck, it would be quiet at the hospital. They could have a cup of coffee or something.

He grabbed his blouse and cap, knowing that he would probably make a fool of himself. But then he didn't have that much time. Right after the marines hauled off Watson, the guard mail truck pulled up to the gangway. Packed with updated codebooks, operations manuals, and official mail were orders for the USS *Matthew* (DD 548) to get under way the following Friday to escort a convoy to Pearl Harbor, whereupon they were to report to commander, Destroyer Squadron 77, now swinging at anchor in the Ulithi Atoll.

The evening was still warm, but when Donovan walked into the Roseville Community Hospital lobby, it felt cold, stark. A sharp tinge of alcohol grazed his nostrils, reminding him of his recent surgery. Outside, he'd chatted with two MPs who lingered near their jeep. They were both from the Deep South, and he enjoyed their accents as he felt the heat and heard the trains making their racket over in the rail yards. Cars zipped past, and people bustled about.

In here, it was quiet.

Good. She's got nothing to do.

"Help you, Commodore?" It was a gray lady, a volunteer; a fifty-plus redheaded, corn-fed woman close to two hundred pounds. With a name tag that read GLADYS, she was seated at a desk in the corner behind a neglected ficus whose leaves had dropped on the floor.

He walked up to the desk. "Right, Gladys. I'm looking for Dr. Logan."

"Dr. Logan's in emergency." Gladys's jaws worked industriously as she chewed gum while thumbing a tired copy of *Colliers*.

"I know that. Can I speak with her?"

Gladys lay down her *Colliers* and scooted forward. "Dear boy. I never go into emergency. You'll never know what you'll find."

"Telephone?"

"Only if you have an emergency."

This is going nowhere. "How do I find emergency?" It seemed a strange question since that was the way he'd first entered this hospital fifteen days ago. But then, he'd been unconscious.

Gladys looked him up and down and said, "Is there an emergency, Commodore? You look okay to me."

"Please?"

She gestured to an urn behind her desk. "Like some mud? You know, real navy coffee?"

It looked as thick as bottom paint. "Maybe later, Gladys. Now, where's emergency?"

"Hmm," she snorted. Gladys nodded over her shoulder to her left. "Down that hallway, through the set of double doors, and then through the next set of double doors. But you won't find a reception nurse there. Just a bunch of people milling about, half of them bloody and groaning, the other half sitting back and drinking coffee." Gladys seemed to think this was funny and gave a short laugh.

Donovan looked off into space.

Again, she looked him up and down. "Say, you aren't a bill collector, are you?"

Pointing to his commander's stripes, Donovan said, "Do I

look like a bill collector to you?" He plopped his hat on for emphasis.

"Good luck, Commodore."

Donovan bucked through the two sets of double doors, walking into a room surrounded by six curtained-off beds. Here, the alcohol-ether smell was far more pronounced. Two nurses rushed pass, ignoring him, pushing a cart laden with gleaming surgical instruments and dressings. Swishing aside the curtain, they disappeared into the space. A young voice groaned from inside. A woman cooed, "It's okay, Bobby. We'll be home soon."

A boy whimpered.

Donovan found a chair next to an oxygen bottle, eased it behind an empty metal desk, and sat. There was nothing on the desk, no telephone, nothing in the drawers.

Bobby cried out.

The woman soothed, "It's okay. It's okay, hon."

A man said, "That should take care of the pain. Now we can get to work. Oops, forgot something. Be right back." The curtain swooshed aside and a balding doctor with a thin mustache walked out, his lab coat spattered with blood. He walked to a cabinet next to Donovan and began rummaging. "Come on, where is it?" he muttered. Then he looked over. "Hi, Navy. You looking for something?"

Donovan stood. "Dr. Logan?"

"Ahhh. The green-eyed monster."

"I beg your pardon?"

He smiled. "An in-joke. Sorry, Dr. Logan is in surgery with that young marine. Are you next-of-kin? A friend perhaps?"

"Well, no. But—"

"Well, are you his commanding officer?"

"No, I'm afraid not. You see—"

The double doors opened and a man wearing fatigues walked in. Donovan's heart jumped. It was John Sabovik. His face was darkened with some sort of dust, and his shirt and trousers were grease-smeared. Sabovik's eyebrows went up momentarily when he spotted Donovan. Then he whipped off his cap and walked up to the doctor. "Where is he?"

The boy groaned again, and the nurse stuck her head out the curtain, her brow furrowed.

"In a moment," the doctor said to her. Then he turned to Sabovik, his voice all business. "What do you want?"

"I was told Nitro is in here," said Sabovik.

"Who?" asked the doctor.

"Captain Collins, the marine," replied Sabovik, his voice tight.

"Ahhh, yes," said the doctor, his face darkening. "The marine. He's in surgery right now with Dr. Finnigan and Dr. Logan."

"Diane?" asked Sabovik, his hands on his hips.

"Yes, I hope that meets with your approval."

"Well, yes, that's great," said Sabovik with a sidelong glance at Donovan. "But how is Captain Collins?"

The boy groaned. "Just a few more minutes, Bobby," said the woman.

"I have work to do, gentlemen," said the doctor. "Now I must ask both of you to wait in the reception room." He palmed their elbows and began walking them to the double doors.

Sabovik jerked his arm away. "But I must see Nitro, I mean—"

"You'll see him after we're done, Captain—"

"Commander. Actually lieutenant commander," said Sabovik.

"I'll get word to Dr. Logan that you're waiting. Now please." The doctor waved a palm toward the double doors.

"I'd at least like to—"

Bobby began crying. The doctor jammed his hands on his hips. "I'm giving you a count of three to get out of here. Then I start calling in the artillery."

Donovan said, "John, you always were blockheaded. Come on, you'll find out soon enough." He headed for the doors.

Sabovik stood rooted to the spot.

"Are you coming, Commander?" said Donovan.

Sabovik exhaled. "I'm sorry, Doctor. Of course I'll wait in the lobby. Please let Dr. Logan know I'm here at your earliest convenience." He walked past Donovan and through the double doors.

TWENTY-FIVE

25 August 1944
Roseville Community Hospital
Roseville, California

Donovan followed Sabovik through the double doors to the main lobby. Gladys spotted the utility-rigged Sabovik and said, "Hey, soldier. How 'bout a cuppa joe?" She poured dark, steaming liquid into a paper cup and shoved it across her desk.

"No, thanks," muttered Sabovik. "And I'm navy, not army."

"Touchy, touchy," said Gladys, munching gum. "How 'bout you, Commodore?" she asked Donovan.

"Sure." Donovan took the cup and pitched a quarter across. "Thanks."

Gladys picked up the quarter. "Gee, now I get to send my kid to college." Her jaws worked her gum for a moment. "On second thought, keep it. It's supposed to be on the house." She flipped the quarter back to Donovan.

"You're a doll." Donovan sipped and nearly gagged, thinking maybe it really was bottom paint. He walked over to Sabovik. "Come on, John, time to talk." He laid a hand on Sabovik's arm and extended his right hand, offering to shake.

Sabovik jerked his arm away; coffee splattered on the floor. "Get away, you sonofabitch," he hissed.

Donovan glanced out the front door, seeing the two MPs still lingering. Carefully, he set down the coffee cup and drew to his full height. "You better be careful who you're talking to, mister, or I'm going to brace you, call in those MPs, and have them shove your dead ass into the brig." They'd joined the navy at the same time. Donovan supposed he'd advanced more quickly in rank because he was a line officer. And now he'd taken advantage.

A wide-eyed Gladys pushed back her chair. "Shit—I mean, dammit. I mean . . ." She knocked over a cup of coffee. "I'm sorry, I didn't mean to . . . I mean, this is supposed to be a hospital, isn't it?"

"It's okay, Gladys. Relax. The commander here has just had a bad day, haven't you, Commander?"

Sabovik's eyes were slits, his pupils burning coals.

Donovan looked over Sabovik's shoulder. "Say something, Commander, or I snap my fingers and have those two corn-fed boys come in here, hook you up, and shove you in solitary."

Sabovik exhaled, rested his hands on his hips, and bowed his head for a moment. "Okay, Mike. Here's the deal. I'm not going to kill you. I've gotten over that part. But I don't have to talk to you and I don't want you around me because I think you're one rotten sonofabitch."

"What are you talking about?"

"My God, you still don't understand. If it weren't for you, Tiny would still be alive."

"John, I couldn't help it."

"Bullshit!" Sabovik shouted.

"Oh," peeped Gladys, her fist to her mouth.

Donovan rasped, "I couldn't help it if that Jap round hit the mount."

"But Tiny belonged in the director, didn't he? What the hell was he doing down in the mount?" shouted Sabovik. "You lived and he died."

"I . . . I sent him down there. I had to."

"What the hell for?"

"We'd lost communications. The whole system went down. I sent Tiny to tell them to shift to local control."

"And then what?" yelled Sabovik.

Gladys bolted from behind her desk, knocked over her chair, and scooted out the double doors.

"Keep your voice down, sailor," said Donovan.

A barely controlled Sabovik said, "And then what? Why didn't he return to the director?"

Suddenly the lobby no longer felt air-conditioned. Donovan's uniform was too tight, and he wanted to unbutton the blouse and loosen his tie. His hands felt clammy, and he wiped his brow. Sabovik had asked a question that had been buried almost two years ago with the battle off Tassaforonga Point.

Sabovik stood close, his eyes even more intense. "You haven't answered me, Commander Donovan. Why didn't Tiny return to the director? What the hell was he doing in that gun mount?"

In a flash, Donovan knew the answer. The nightmare became reality and engulfed him.

He stepped back. "No."

"No *what,* you dirty bastard."

"Oh my God, I . . ."

"Spit it out. And it better be good, Captain."

The words spilled out before he could contain them. "I forgot. Jesus, the ship was on fire. Everyone was screaming. It was all happening so fast, I forgot Tiny was in the mount. Damn, I . . ."

"You forgot because you turned yellow and lost your nerve, didn't you?"

"No!"

"How the hell do you live with yourself?" Sabovik shook his head in disgust.

Two large orderlies in white coats burst into the lobby. Gladys followed, her hand pointing to Donovan and Sabovik.

"Everything all right here?" asked the taller one, a baby-faced man; his cheeks and hands were pink and he had a short crew cut.

"Nooo." Donovan hardly realized the orderlies were there. His stomach turned as he relived the horror of that night. The abject realization that he'd forgotten to recall Tiny sunk in. The thought disappeared for a moment as he tried to suppress it. Then it washed over him again with all its terrible finality. I forgot to recall Tiny. And Tiny died because of it. He looked up. Everyone's eyes were on him. "I need to sit." He walked over, righted Gladys's chair, and sat heavily.

The larger orderly followed Donovan over. "Maybe I should call you a cab, buddy."

He'd forgotten about Tiny. Donovan couldn't decide which

was worse. The fact that he'd forgotten about Tiny or that he'd suppressed it all this time.

The orderly shook his shoulder. "Hey, Mac. I'm talking to you."

"What?"

"Maybe I should call the cops, or maybe them MPs outside," said the orderly.

Sabovik stood across the lobby regarding him curiously, his arms folded.

"What's the word, Mac?" demanded the orderly.

Donovan stood. The orderly was taller and looked down at him. Aside from a bit of drool leaking from the side of his mouth, the orderly looked fit. Donovan wondered why he wasn't in the service. Then one look into his dull, lifeless eyes gave the answer. "I'll bet you have flat feet."

"Huh?"

The other orderly giggled.

The taller orderly said, "Maybe you should—"

A loud female voice called, "Captain Collins is going to be okay." It was Diane Logan wearing light green scrubs, cap and all, the double doors swinging closed behind her.

Donovan and Sabovik walked over to her, the orderlies in tow.

"Thanks, Luther, we're all set here," said Diane. "You, too, Rex."

"You sure, Doctor?" asked Luther. "This guy's bothering people." He glanced at Gladys.

"Go," said Diane. "They need you back in the commissary."

"Yeah, I heard they's cookin' hamburgers tonight," said Rex.

"Hamburgers," said Luther. With a nod, he backed away and the two walked out.

"Gladys, could you please make us a fresh pot of coffee?" Diane asked over her shoulder.

"Yes, ma'am." Gladys began fussing.

"Everything okay here?" asked Diane, looking the two over.

"What's the word on Nitro?" asked Sabovik.

Donovan found the way he addressed her to be curious. They knew each other.

"Hi, Mike," said Diane.

"Evening, Doctor," said Donovan. *I knew I shouldn't have come here.*

"Nitro should be fine." Diane whipped off her surgical cap and ran a finger through mussed auburn hair. "He has two broken ribs, a broken left arm, and several lacerations."

"Whew," gasped Sabovik. "Not bad for a dumb jarhead. Is that it?"

"No, unfortunately, that's not. Nitro also has a concussion. He's conscious now, but he's not talking clearly. I think he'll be all right after time, but for now, we're erring on the side of caution."

"Which means?" asked Sabovik.

"Which means we want to keep him for a day or two until we're certain there's no permanent damage. And that'll help hold down chance of infection with the broken arm and ribs."

"Okay," said Sabovik. "How about—"

"Mind if I ask a question?" Diane interrupted, taking off her glasses. She exhaled on a lens and began polishing. To Donovan, her eyes were greener than her scrubs.

Sabovik said, "Shoot."

"Nitro was wet and muddy. But we cleaned him up and got him into some dry garments. So what went on? Some sort of interleague football game?"

"I wish it were that simple." Sabovik rubbed his jaw. "We were riding the 4293 westbound. We were delayed in Truckee for two hours and it wasn't till after dark that we reached the summit and started down. Right after that, Nitro saw something that didn't look right. We were going pretty slow, so I asked Soda Whiskers if he could slow a tad more to let Nitro—"

"Ben Soda Whiskers?" Donovan and Diane said in unison.

Sabovik gave them a *how-the-hell-do-you-know-Soda-Whiskers* look. "Yeah, so what?"

Donovan shrugged.

Diane said. "He's been a family friend for a long time. Gave me my first ride in a locomotive when I was nine years old. Daddy could have killed him."

Sabovik said, "He's a crazy bastard, I'll say that."

"And a love," said Diane.

Sabovik scratched his head. "Well, I wouldn't put it that

way, but okay. Anyway, Nitro jumped out of the engine and grabbed a freight car ladder about ten cars back." He paused.

"Yes?" asked Diane.

"But something was wrong. He didn't come up on the walkie-talkie."

"Where were you?" she asked.

"Jasper Flats, where it levels out."

"Umm," she mused. "Lots of boulders and rocks in there. Then what happened?"

"It was almost pitch black and I wouldn't have seen anything. Except an eastbound was coming round a bend. The eastbound's headlight caught Nitro flying though space. It looked like he'd jumped . . . or was pushed. But that's almost impossible. Nobody else was around. We'd picked up speed by then and I thought he was a goner."

Gladys stepped up with a tray of coffee. Nodding their thanks, they each picked a cup and drank. Much better, thought Donovan.

Sabovik sipped again and continued, "You're right. It is all boulders and rocks in there. If he'd hit one, we'd still be scraping him off."

"What happened?" asked Donovan, his curiosity up.

"We ran over a trestle. Nitro fell right over the side and into Jasper Creek, about a twenty-foot drop. I yelled to Soda Whiskers and he slammed on the brakes right away. But it took the damn thing forever to stop so I jumped off and ran back to the trestle. A guard shack was there and I found the sonofabitch asleep. So, I kicked the kid in the butt and we ran down and found Nitro on the riverbank, slithering in mud. He was about ten feet from some rapids and, jeepers, he's lucky he didn't fall into that. Otherwise—" He drew a finger across his throat. "So we wrestled Nitro back up to the guard shack about the time Soda Whisker got the engine back to us. Luckily, we were about two hundred feet from Highway 80. So the guard dialed up an ambulance and we had Nitro down the mountain pretty quick."

"What were you doing there to begin with?" asked Donovan.

"Just intelligence stuff."

"Like spies?"

Sabovik ignored the question and asked Diane, "Can I see him?"

"For just a minute. No trip-hammer questions. He's woozy."

"But I have to talk to him."

"I'm afraid not. A minute and that's it," said Diane.

Sabovik nodded and turned to Donovan, "Now let me ask, what the hell are you doing here, Captain." He spit the word *Captain*.

Donovan stammered, "Saying hello to my old friend Ben Soda Whiskers."

"How do you know him?"

Donovan waved to Diane. "We bunked in the same ward. I had an appendix attack and Soda Whiskers was in for something else. The good doctor here took care of us. We played some poker, and I ended up owing him money." Actually, that wasn't true. Soda Whiskers owed everyone else money, Donovan about twenty dollars. He had written IOUs, but never paid.

Sabovik stepped closer. "You sure they didn't operate on your head?"

Donovan said, "John, for crying out loud. Don't you think—"

"Okay, okay." Diane stepped between them and pushed them apart. "Commander Sabovik, down the hall, turn left to room 131. Commander Donovan, out. Go back to your hotel."

Hotel, that's a good one. Donovan said, "But—"

"Go. Now." She pushed on Donovan's chest until he stepped away. The she turned. "Follow me, Commander Sabovik." They walked through the double doors, leaving them swinging.

Something rustled the side of his bed. Startled, he sat up quickly. "Battle stations!" he shouted.

She gave a low chuckle and pushed him back down to the pillows. "Easy, Captain. The ship's still afloat."

Donovan checked the radium dial on his watch: 0517. It was still warm outside, and he was covered with just a sheet. He'd had trouble sleeping the last three days. The images of that horrible night aboard the *Tampa* two years ago off Tassaforonga Point kept racing through his mind. The ship, saturated with fuel oil, burning brightly, men screaming as they scrambled up from the engineering spaces; Tiny's lopsided grin as he crawled out of the director and willingly walked to his death in that damn eight-inch turret. And now he wished Sabovik had carried out his promise to kill him.

But she was here and he relaxed a bit. "Some habits are hard to break," he said. "You're late." Her hair was down and mussed around her face. She wore just a bathrobe and . . . and . . . smelled wonderful.

"Guy fell through a window. Lot of sewing there. And then there was an auto wreck out on 99." She looked down. "One of them didn't make it. An old man."

He sensed she wanted to get it out and drew her down to him, wrapping his arms around her. "Not your fault."

Her voice rose. "Damn drunk hit him. Head-on. You should have seen the bastard. All he needed was fourteen stitches in his forehead. He sat there and kept laughing."

"It's okay."

"I wanted to do it without novocaine but they made me."

"Shhhh." He stroked her hair, then her back. She raised her legs to the bed and nestled beside him. He kissed her neck, then her ear as she moved closer.

"We have to do something about you and John," she said.

"First thing we have to do is to put me up in a decent hotel."

She gave a low laugh. "Best I could come up with for the moment."

He kissed her cheek, her hair, and began running his hands up and down her back. "That okay?"

"Helps."

"Good for what ails you after a long day at the office." He rubbed harder.

She moved closer, throwing a leg over him. "You bet."

"You know John?"

She tensed. "Why do you ask?"

"I just had an impression."

"He's taken me to dinner."

"More than once?"

"Twice."

"Wow, Sabovik gets around."

She rose up, looking down to him. "Is it important?"

"Depends." He pulled her head down, kissing her fully on the mouth. She yielded, and with no urging rolled all the way atop him. Running his hands up and down, he found the front of her robe and slipped a hand inside, finding her belly, then her breast. They kissed again, fuller, more deeply, urgently. "Mike," she murmured.

The kitchen light snapped on. Light knifed through the doorway and into Donovan's eyes as if it were a sword. The light also fell on Blackie, who lay in his spot in the corner. He raised his head and looked at the doorway, his tail thumping on the floor.

"Damn," Diane muttered. She rolled off, crouching in the opposite corner.

"It's okay, Blackie. Shhhh . . ." A hand reached in and silently pulled the door closed with a *click*.

She came to his side and kissed him. "Daddy must have worked late. Thought he was already in bed."

"After your meat loaf."

She kissed him again. "Gotta go, Mike. We'll talk tomorrow."

"I hope so." Donovan's heart was beating fast. Her scent was there and he ran his hands though her hair. Phenomenal. He stretched and exhaled, trying to relax. "Why don't you crawl under the sheet and wait until he leaves?"

"Mike, dammit . . ."

He kissed her hard.

". . . gotta go." She slipped away and moved to the foot of the bed. Raising the window all the way, she said, "Haven't done this in years." Her teeth flashed with a wide grin. "Did this when Ralphie and I were kids." Easing up the window, she crawled out.

She reached back in and tapped Donovan on the foot. "I'll fix you breakfast. Sleep well." Then she was gone.

With a graceful leap, Blackie was after her. Moments later, he gave a short bark.

"Blackie, dammit, shhhhh." Leaves rustled as Diane scrambled a tree limb up to her bedroom window directly above.

Moments later, the pitch-black apparition leaped back

through the window. He walked over to his bed, spun around twice, then settled down and exhaled with a groan.

The floorboards creaked softly above and Donovan whispered "Thank you" to the ceiling. In a way, Walt Logan's interruption was providential. The way he felt, he didn't think he could consummate an act of love; he'd been so overwhelmed with the memory of that damn night two years ago. Even now, it flashed before him again, and he knew he wouldn't sleep. But then the lovemaking had taken his mind off it. Diane had seemed willing and he was still breathing hard. Could be. "Thank you," he said again.

The refrigerator door closed softly in the kitchen. A plate clanked in the sink. Walt Logan belched, and the light under the door blinked off. Feet shuffled off to the stairs. Donovan lay back, his hands laced behind his head. A warm zephyr eased through the curtain and teased his nostrils with a combined scent of summer wheat and locomotive fuel oil. The floorboards again creaked above. And in the distance he heard a Mallet's mournful whistle followed by *ch-chuff, ch-chuff, ch-chuff.*

"Thank you."

TWENTY-SIX

25 August 1944
Logan residence
Roseville, California

A terrible smell blew across Donovan's face. His eyes snapped open.

Blackie's head was inches away, his tongue lolling to one side.

"What have you been eating?" Donovan raised a hand to pet the dog.

Blackie rose on his hind legs. His paws flopped on Donovan's chest and he slobbered on his hand. "Easy, easy," soothed Donovan. Again, he whiffed the dog's breath. "You need to brush more regularly.

"Holy cow!" He checked his watch: 0927. He hadn't slept this late in years. Donovan sat up, scratched, and stretched, seeing an envelope under his door. He reached to pick it up, seeing it written in her classic green ink.

M

Got a call. Back to the hospital. A lot going on, I'm afraid, and we're understaffed. I was supposed to be off today. I might be able to spin away for lunch. Does that sound all right?

XO XO
D

"That sounds just fine," he said wiggling into his T-shirt and trousers.

His brow furrowed as he realized he was getting in deeper than he thought possible. But he didn't want to make any decisions yet, and he knew she didn't, either—they'd spent so little time together. Then the grim thought came to him that war forces decisions. In a way, that makes it easier than civilian life, when you have all the time in the world. In wartime, you decide—right or wrong—and go on. No fooling around. But in another sense, quick decisions were the bane of the serviceman. Like getting engaged or going all the way with marriage. She'd already lost one guy over Bougainville.

Absently, he reached to his B-4 bag and unzipped a compartment. He found Carmen Rossi's engagement and wedding rings and drew them out. The diamond's facets glittered brilliantly in the morning light. Was it providence that Carmen gave him these just a short time ago? Stupid, Mike. Hell, they'd only known each other three weeks. He lay the rings on the bedside stand, took Blackie's head in both hands, and rubbed the dog's ears. "What do you think, big boy?"

Blackie's eyes closed as Donovan rubbed.

"Come on, tell me."

The black Labrador groaned appreciatively.

"Hi!" Diane plopped her arms on the windowsill and leaned in.

"Ah. You startled me. Good morning."

Warm sunlight glistened on her auburn hair. She looked gorgeous. "Haven't seen you since last—"

"—ahh, yes. You just getting up?"

"About time, don't you think?"

Blackie barked.

Someone knocked. "Good morning!" Walt Logan's muffled voice came through the door. "Can I come in?"

"Might as well. Seems like a town meeting," Diane called into the room.

Walt Logan eased the door open and walked in. "Well, hello, Miss Nightingale," he called to the window. "What brings you back?"

"Forgot my glasses," said Diane.

Donovan's heart jumped. Her glasses lay on the bedside stand, and Walt hadn't seen them yet. And the damn wedding rings were there, too. Fortunately, they were on the other side of the lamp, out of her sight. He jumped to his feet and stood before the bedside stand. "Morning, Walt."

Blackie barked again

Walt leaned over. "What's into you, old fella? Didn't I hear you last night?" As he bent to rub the dog's ears, Donovan glanced at Diane, seeing her redden for a moment. Blackie slobbered Walt's hand and wagged his tail. "You ready for some water, boy?" asked Walt.

Blackie's tail beat faster.

"How 'bout some coffee, Mike?" asked Walt.

"Sounds great." Casually, Donovan eased close to the table, reached down, and grabbed Diane's glasses. He held them out behind him toward the window.

She snatched them away.

With a bark, Blackie rose on his hind feet and thrust his paws on Walt's chest, his tail wagging in great sweeps.

"Dammit, Blackie. Diane, why can't you train this dog?" asked Walt.

"He's Ralphie's," she called back. "I have to go upstairs." Diane stepped away.

"Down, Blackie," called Logan, pushing the dog away. Blackie's tail wagged vigorously as he turned to follow Logan. Just then his tail swept across the bedside stand. The lamp, Donovan's watch, loose change, an ornate Southern Pacific Railroad coaster, and everything else went flying through space and hit the floor with a clatter.

"Dammit," cursed Logan.

Lowering his head and tail, Blackie slinked to the corner and sat.

"It's okay," said Donovan. He and Logan dropped to their knees.

"We all right?" Diane poked her head through the door.

"Damn mutt is like a gorilla in a dentist's office," said Logan, picking up the lamp.

Donovan's heart jumped in his chest. Before him lay Carmen Rossi's rings. Looking quickly from side to side, he realized they hadn't seen them.

Yet.

He grabbed at them, fumbled a grip on the wedding ring, and stuffed it in his pocket.

"Anything else?" asked Walt, looking around.

"Nope." With his forefinger, Donovan quickly flicked the engagement ring under the bed, where it bounced off the wooden molding with a light *ting*.

Later.

"China store," corrected Diane. Behind Logan's back, she winked and flashed her glasses to Donovan. "Be right back." She ran down the hall and up the stairs.

Logan put the lamp back on the table and snapped on the light. "Working okay. No harm done. Got your stuff?"

"No harm done," said Donovan. He leaned back and pet the dog. "Good boy."

Once again, Blackie's tail thumped proudly.

Diane clattered down the stairs. "Found 'em," she called, holding up her glasses.

Walt said, "First time that's ever happened. Usually, they disappear for days, if not weeks."

Donovan walked her to the door. "See you for lunch?"

"Unfortunately, I can't go out."

"You're kidding."

"I'm sorry."

He took her hand. "Okay, I'll wait till dinner."

"No, lunch is fine, but I have to stay at the hospital." She tapped a finger on his nose. "I'll treat you to one of our cafeteria sandwiches."

Donovan's stomach rumbled at the thought of hospital food. "Maybe I better bring along Chinese food."

"Watch it, buddy. Roseville Community Hospital has a world-class selection of peanut butter. See you later." She dashed out the door.

John Sabovik walked through the double doors and down the hospital corridor, a leather pouch under his arm. For the first time in weeks, he wore dress khakis with combination cap. It felt good not to be thumping around in heavy brogans—and, clean for a change. He didn't smell like a combination of fuel oil, hydraulic fluid, and engine smoke. He didn't know how the train crews stood it. The snowsheds, built to ward off avalanches in bitter winters, smelled terrible as one engine after another left its calling card. The AC-class cab-forward locomotives were built with the smokestack in back so the engine crews wouldn't suffocate. Still, there was enough leftover smoke from other engines to make a man cough and hack for weeks. Once they had to stop in a tunnel and wait for half an hour. Sabovik thought he'd go crazy with the smoke.

He found room 131 across from the nursing station. It was a private room with equipment for monitoring critically ill patients. Sabovik walked in, finding Nitro sitting up in bed, pillows braced behind his back, reading the *Sacramento Bee.* A large dressing ran around his head, his arm was in a sling, his chest wrapped tightly. "Morning, jarhead. You ready to drop to the deck and give me fifty?"

Nitro lay down the paper. "Not at the moment, sir."

Nitro's crew cut stood tall, and his eyes were as round and blue and intelligent as Sabovik could remember. "How do you feel?"

"My head's fine. Everything seemed to kick in this morning. It's my damn chest that's killing me. Hurts to breathe. I can only sit a certain way, like this. They're going to put a cast on my arm today."

"It'll only hurt when you itch."

"Yeah, thanks."

Sabovik set the pouch on a bedside stand. "Our mail."

"Okay." With a grimace, Nitro reached for the pouch.

"In a second, Nitro. First, can you tell me what happened?"

"I wish I could. It all happened so fast."

"Do your best."

Nitro sat back and arranged himself. "Well, I jumped from the engine and watched as the cars went by. One car zipped past and, damn, the door was open, just as I thought. So I jumped aboard."

"Which one?"

"Forgot to get the number. It must have been ten or twelve back."

"I'll check the manifest. Then what?"

"Hell, it was dark. I reached for my flashlight, but something conked me. Next thing I know, I'm spitting up water on a riverbank."

"How'd you get there?"

"Don't know."

"Do you think someone pushed you?"

"Don't know. But then, thinking about it, I don't see how it could have happened otherwise." Nitro scratched and looked up. "Where did you find me?"

Sabovik told him, then asked, "What else?"

"That's it."

"Come on, Captain, you should have—"

"Good morning, everyone." Diane Logan walked in and headed for the foot of the bed, pulling the chart.

"Hi, sweetheart," said Nitro. "I see you found your glasses."

"Umm. Enough to see you're doing pretty well." She walked over and picked up his wrist, taking his pulse.

"Beating fast for you, honey," said Nitro.

"Watch this." She ran her fountain pen toward his eyes, twice, then felt his forehead.

"You wanna go to the movies tonight?" asked Nitro.

She took a final look, then said, "They'll be over for you this afternoon to cast the arm." She looked at Sabovik. "You're looking fine this morning, Commander. You look like a real navy officer for a change. My, look at all those ribbons. What's that one for?" She pointed to a ribbon with a star.

"Doesn't mean anything," said Sabovik.

"Come on," said Diane. "That indicates you were in combat, doesn't it?"

"Nope, got it at the YMCA," said Sabovik. "It's for second place in the hundred-yard dash in high school."

"Nonsense," said Diane.

"Nonsense is right," said Nitro. "It's an action ribbon for the battle of Tassaforonga Point. The commander here put his butt on the line, protecting our marines on Guadalcanal."

"That's enough, Captain," snapped Sabovik.

It grew quiet. Diane said, "I'll be across the hall if you need me." Her eyes fell on Nitro.

"You're looking much better. We'll probably discharge you tomorrow or the next day." She walked out.

"Thanks," Nitro called after her. "How 'bout that movie?" When she was out of earshot, he gave Sabovik a sour look.

Sabovik's head dropped. "Sorry, I just don't like to talk about it."

"Someday you should."

Sabovik opened the pouch. "A bunch of stuff here for you." He sniffed. "Weeeoou! You have a girlfriend?" He checked an envelope, then tossed it over. "It's from Shirley McCann. Here's another. And another. And . . ." He tossed over five more envelopes. "Geez, Nitro, all this from Shirley McCann. What would she say if she heard you talking to the good doctor like that?"

"Shirley?" Nitro grabbed the envelopes and sorted them by postmark. "Excuse me," he ripped into the first.

There were two envelopes for Sabovik. One from a bill collector, another from his mother, dated two days ago. Unusual. His mother and father were Bulgarian immigrants. Her English was poor. He ripped open the envelope, finding her scrawl on a single lined page. "My God!"

Nitro looked up. "You okay?"

"It's my dad." Sabovik quickly walked to the room across the hall. Diane was bent over a tub of metal charts. "Favor?" he asked.

She looked up. "Sure."

"I need to get a long-distance line to the San Fernando Valley."

"Anything wrong?"

"My dad. He had another heart attack."

She grabbed his hand. "In here." She walked into a small room and picked up the phone. After some strident words with the operator, she handed it to Sabovik. "Here. Give Reba the number. She can get you a line."

Sabovik stammered out the number and the switchboard operator did her magic. A distant phone rang an anemic tone. "Allo?"

The metallic voice sounded like a woman, but that was all he could tell. "Hello, hello, who's this?" demanded Sabovik.

"Allo? Allo? Is Johann?"

His heart sank. It was the voice of Stella Garret, the next-door neighbor. "Yes, this is John." He hated it when his parents called him Johann. "Stella?"

"Yes, yes," Stella said. "John, your mother not here."

"Where is she?"

Static ranged on the line. It was almost as if someone were tuning a vacuum-tube radio.

"Stella?" he demanded.

"Your mother . . . she's at . . . the funeral parlor."

Sabovik sat heavily. "What for?"

"Johann, I'm sorry," bawled Stella. "Pappa Saboviks. He no more. His heart gave out."

"No!"

Diane's hand went to his shoulder.

"You should call her there." She rattled off some numbers.

Sabovik wrote and then asked, "What happened?"

"Last week they were at the movies, he just keeled over. Then night before last . . . God has him now, Johann. I'm so sorry. First Alexander, now Constantine. Two fine Saboviks."

"Oh, God." Sabovik rested his head in his hand.

"They're together, now, little Alex and Constantine," said Stella tearfully. "They are with God."

Words didn't come. Finally Sabovik said, "Thanks, Stella. I'll call Mom at the funeral parlor."

Stella repeated the number then said, "Well, good-bye." She hung up.

"Ahh." Sabovik carefully cradled the phone and stood. "Thanks, Diane." After a moment, he let out a sob.

"John, what is it?"

"My pop . . . he's gone . . ." He snapped his fingers. "Gone."

"What happened?"

"His heart. Not the first time."

"I'm so sorry," she soothed, wrapping her arms around him. "It's okay."

Tears ran as he held her close. "First Tiny. Now Pop. What the hell's going on?" he said bitterly.

"You have your mom."

"That's about it." He gave another sob and buried his head in her shoulder.

"It's okay, John. You want me to give you something?"

"Just another minute or two."

"All the time you want."

* * *

An impatient Donovan asked a nurse and learned Diane had been headed for room 131, just around the corner. He walked to the room and looked in, seeing Nitro intently involved with a letter. Then he heard a mournful sob across the hall. The voice was familiar. Walking to the nurses' station, he leaned around and peeked in the anteroom. They were embracing, their arms wrapped around each other. Sabovik's face was buried in her shoulder. Diane's face was turned toward him, her eyes closed.

A nurse walked over, closed the door softly, and gave Donovan a *shame-on-you* look.

"Sonofabitch," he said incredulously.

The nurse walked up and said sternly, "Can I help you?"

"I don't believe it."

"Sir?"

"What a sap. I thought I knew better." Donovan walked away.

TWENTY-SEVEN

28 August 1944
USS *Matthew* (DD 548)
Mare Island Naval Shipyard
Mare Island, California

The morning dawned dim and gray on the Mare Island Naval Shipyard, where the engines of war continued their round-the-clock frenetic pitch. Switcher engines chugged alongside ships, pushing boxcars of deadly cargo; trucks rumbled, blasting their horns; angry sailors jumping out of the way; giant spidery cranes lifted everything from peloruses to new five-inch gun barrels to dry stores to medical supplies to crypto machines to pallet loads of fresh bedding. Incongruous to the mood were the strains of "America the Beautiful" as a new *Balao*-class submarine slid down the ways into the fifty-one-degree waters of San Francisco Bay, sailors, shipyard workers, and civilians cheering as she went.

Activity aboard the *Matthew* was no different. With orders to sail the coming Friday, her sailors dashed fixing last-minute disasters while others tied down gear for rough seas or tested equipment.

That was one of Donovan's concerns: making sure everything worked. That's why he'd called a department head meeting in the wardroom today and was chewing on them, one at a time. For the moment, it was gunnery officer Cliff Merryweather's turn.

"I don't know, sir, I mean I thought our shooting last week was pretty good, considering," claimed Merryweather.

Donovan shot back, "Considering what?"

Looking at Kruger, Merryweather gave a lopsided grin

and said, "Well, that's kind of obvious, sir. The fact that we haven't been operational for the past two months has taken our edge off. With time, we'll be able to—"

"That's not enough, dammit," interrupted Donovan. He jabbed a forefinger at the green baize tablecloth. "We weren't registering hits close to the sled. The interval was horrible, an average of seven seconds. And I have to think the director is out of alignment."

"But we aligned it two months ago. I mean the yardbirds—"

"Don't trust the yardbirds, Lieutenant. The Japs won't be shooting at them. They'll be shooting at us. You specifically. And with your battle station on the flybridge, you'll be the first to tell us all about what's coming our way."

Merryweather sat back and folded his arms.

Donovan sipped coffee and said, "I want a full battery alignment. And I want the computers checked as well, especially the mark 1. Also, I want to see your gun crews exercising on the loading machine each morning and each afternoon."

Merryweather's jaw dropped. "But Captain, this is our—"

"Our what?"

"Well, sir, our last week in the USA. My boys would like to spend some time ashore, if possible," pleaded Merryweather.

Donovan shook his head slowly. "Unless you can guarantee me the battery will be fully aligned by the time we shove off next Friday, I'm putting the whole ship in hack."

Corodini's cup clanked loudly in the saucer. Kruger pushed his chair back.

"No liberty before we shove off?" sputtered Hammond.

"Mr. Hammond, do you want to meet the Japs with one hand tied behind your back?"

"No, sir."

"Which reminds me, has the PRITAC[25] transmitter been repaired?"

"Uh, tubes haven't been delivered yet. And we're still waiting on—"

"Mr. Hammond. I'm not interested in excuses. Didn't you learn anything the last time we went through this?" Donovan waited until Kruger lit a cigarette and said, "Give the order."

Kruger gave a long exhale. "Sir?"

"Battery alignment. Spare parts." Donovan gave Corodini a look. "And the superheaters crap out every time we punch them up. Well, I want a stop to this. We have to train for what's out there. And we can't train with a sick ship. We must have things working. So therefore, Mr. Kruger, liberty is canceled until further notice."

There was a stunned silence in the wardroom. Kruger's eyes flicked to Al Corodini. His wife had delivered a baby girl Saturday morning and Corodini had proudly shown a picture. The chief engineer studied his coffee cup, his ears red. Merryweather looked at Donovan in shocked silence. Hammond simply glared.

"Mr. Corodini?" said Donovan.

"Yes, sir?"

"Are those superheaters working properly now?"

"Captain, we've had all four boilers up since last Saturday night. Superheaters are cutting in just fine. And we're running down vibration hazards."

"Very well. Congratulations on your baby."

"Thank you, Captain."

The morning was still cold. To Donovan it felt colder in here. And that suited him just fine. "Any more questions, gentlemen?" He made to push away.

"Yes, sir," said Howard Sloan, the supply officer.

Donovan raised his eyebrows.

"I'll take the flak, Captain for the radio parts. They've been giving us the short shrift again at the supply depot, and, well, we'll send over the goon squad again."

Hammond gave Sloan a *thank-you* look.

"See that you do." Again, Donovan made to rise.

"And Captain," said Sloan. He whipped off gold-rimmed glasses and ruffled through a bundle of supply requisitions. "There has to be a mistake on this chit." He handed it over. "It was signed by you."

Donovan examined it, nodded, and handed the chit back. "Yes, that's correct."

"I don't understand, Captain. Why do we need all those hundred-pound bags of salt?" Sloan held up the chit. "Twenty-five of them?"

"Blood, Mr. Sloan," said Donovan.

"Sir?"

"Mr. Sloan, the human body is a closed system. But when it's penetrated with something like a bullet or shrapnel, it leaks, oftentimes profusely. But we still have to fight Japs while the battle goes on. That means continuing to man our stations on bloody decks. Those decks often become very slippery and we need something to quickly absorb the blood so we can maintain our footing." He paused for a moment. "I want a bag of salt in each gun mount, one on each wing of the bridge, two in CIC, one in radio central, three of them right here, one in main-battery plot, and . . ." He looked into their shocked faces. "You get the idea.

"This is why we're staying aboard tonight, gentlemen, so that we can properly fight this ship," said Donovan. "As destroyermen, we're the ones with our necks stuck out. If you haven't thought about it, it's not just our job, it's our heritage. So make no mistake, I do intend to go in harm's way."

He stood. "That's all." Donovan walked out of the wardroom.

Donovan walked down the passageway and turned into his day cabin, closing the door. His in-basket was over the rim with official business, and he groaned, realizing he wouldn't be able to sneak a nap today.

There was a loud rap at the door. He checked his watch and then called, "Enter." Kruger walked in and closed the door.

"Have a seat, Richard."

Kruger stood at attention, his eyes fixed in the distance. "No, thank you, sir."

"Sit down, dammit," Donovan snapped.

Kruger gave him a look and took a chair saying, "I don't know how to put this, but has anything happened to you?"

"I have no idea what you mean."

"You seem on edge."

"I am."

Kruger sat back and folded his arms.

"I'm serious, Richard. These guys think this is a country club. Wait till they get out there. Hell, you know what it's like."

"Yes, I do, but that's not going to help."

"Spit it out, Richard," asked Donovan.

"They want transfers."

"Who?"

"Your four department heads, that's who."

"How about you?" Donovan began leafing through his mail. He found two envelopes from his mother. There was another flimsy letter with an APO address stamped six weeks ago. The return address read CAPT. PATRICK DONOVAN, USAAF. His younger brother Pat with the Eighth Air Force in England, flying P-51s.

"I haven't made up my mind yet," said Kruger.

"Well, you're almost out of time, Commander. We sail, in case you've forgotten, on Friday." Three more envelopes were junk mail. He pitched them in the wastebasket. "Well?"

Kruger leaned forward. "Mike . . . Captain. I'll ask again. Anything on your mind? You really seem different this week."

Donovan shook his head.

Kruger said, "What I'm trying to say is that these kids are going to war. They may not be coming back. How 'bout a break?"

There was one more envelope. A smallish one addressed in green ink and stamped SPECIAL DELIVERY. His heart jumped and he drew a breath.

"Captain? You okay?"

Donovan flipped the letter in the wastebasket.

Kruger's brow furrowed.

"Junk mail. I'm okay." Donovan said. "Like you, I realize they're going to war, Mr. Kruger. But I think you've failed to take something into account. You say they may not be coming back. Well, sir, it's our job to make sure they do come back. You and me. And the only way we're going to be able to accomplish this is to have them ready to fight. To be ready for everything the Japs can throw at us. And it's not going to be pretty, is it?"

Kruger said, "No, it's not going to be pretty. But hell, Mike, only four more nights before we shove off."

After a pause, Donovan said, "There will be an exception."

"Pardon?"

"Mr. Corodini. Let him go ashore to be with his wife and new baby."

Kruger's shoulders slumped. "I wish it were that easy."

"What?"

"He figured you would say that. He said that if his boys are in hack, then he stays in hack with them."

The corners of Donovan's mouth raised. "He said that?"

"Yes, sir."

"That's more like it."

"Sir?"

"He's backing his boys. I like that. How long to process those transfer requests?"

Kruger rubbed his chin. "Ten to fourteen days."

"Hell, we'll be halfway to Ulithi by that time. Tell 'em to go ahead and submit them."

"Aye, aye, Captain." Kruger stood and turned to go.

"How long will it take Merryweather to get the battery aligned?"

"They're on it right now. They figure a good four to six hours."

"Very well, let's see how it goes. Check with me at 1530."

Kruger was surprised. "Liberty? You mean it?"

"Maybe yes, maybe no. And Richard?"

"Sir?"

"I want you to get the ship under way on Friday."

"Aye, aye, sir."

At first, Donovan had chided himself for finally granting liberty on Monday. He did it with misgivings, but was pleasantly surprised to see the men turn to and work with determination. By Tuesday evening, the battery had been aligned—properly, he hoped—the computers tested and adjusted, magazine powder tested, the radio gear fixed, myriad spare parts boarded, and any other number of other tasks required for their deployment. Things picked up on Wednesday with a challenge from the crew for a baseball game against the officers. The officers lost fourteen–six, but they staggered back to the ship, singing and full of beer. More significant, Donovan hadn't received any requests for transfer from his department heads.

The only thing that marred the week was another letter addressed in green ink. Late in the evening, he just stared at it. An hour later, he threw it in the trash.

And now, Friday, they were ready. Instead of the usual morbid September overcast known to the Bay Area, the day dawned warm and sunny with a light wind. Quarters were held at 0700. Special sea detail was set at 0730, the officers wearing dress khakis, the crew in undress whites. After dismissal, Kruger climbed to the bridge, walked up to Donovan, and saluted. "All present and accounted for, Captain, ship ready for sea."

"No AWOLs?" Donovan asked, checking his watch: 0750.

"Seems like everybody is anxious to take this little cruise," said Kruger. "Sure you don't want another belly bomb?" He nodded to a van parked on the pier, its side panels open, young women in bright aprons serving coffee and doughnuts.

"Already had three," Donovan admitted.

"Umm, me, too." Kruger leaned over the bridge and waved. Vicky was down on the pier waving and blowing kisses from her wheelchair. She was surrounded by a number of wives, sweethearts, mothers, and fathers waving to loved ones aboard the ship that was to depart for war.

Down the way, the battleship USS *New Mexico,* looking brand new in her dazzle camouflage, was also getting under way, a larger throng of wives, sweethearts, and family standing before her. The *Matthew* and four other destroyers were assigned to escort her to Pearl Harbor. A band on the pier had been playing marches. They broke into a mournful "Now Is the Hour."

"Not making it easy, are they?" Kruger muttered.

"No, they're not," agreed Donovan.

At 0755, the boatswain's mate of the watch stepped in the pilothouse and clicked on the 1 MC. His metallic voice echoed throughout the ship: "First call, first call to colors."

Donovan turned to Hammond. "Please tell the quarterdeck to send over the gangway, Mr. Hammond. Also, tell the fo'c'sle to single up all lines." He turned to Kruger. "You ready to get us under way?"

"Yes, sir."

"Well, let's go then." Donovan headed for the ladder that led to the pilothouse. It seemed surreal when they reached the top. The crowd seemed larger. And they were arm in arm, singing with the band. Some waved handkerchiefs; a few men tipped their hats.

"It's your show, Mr. Kruger," said Donovan.

"Thank you, Captain." Kruger barked, "This is Mr. Kruger, I have the conn."

Donovan watched as Kruger went through the litany. *So far, so good.*

At 0800 the 1 MC screeched and the boatswain's mate blew a whistle. "On deck, attention to colors." All hands faced aft and saluted while the national ensign was hoisted on the fantail, the jack on the fo'c'sle, while down the pier the band played the "Star Spangled Banner."

The anthem done, the boatswain's mate called, "Ready, two."

Kruger bent over and shouted down to the pilothouse, "Take in lines one, three, four, five, and six."

Donovan relaxed with the realization that Kruger knew how to handle things. Just sit back and let him do his job.

A car barreled down the pier and drew up behind the crowd.

"Rudder amidship," called Kruger. "Port engine ahead one-third, starboard back one-third."

The order was acknowledged, and the ship vibrated as her screws bit the water, generating a clockwise twist. Kruger had opened his mouth to call for the last line when Donovan noticed a figure jump from the car's passenger side and ease through the crowd.

Just then the *New Mexico* sounded one long blast and three short. With tugs breasting her out, she was under way, meaning the *Matthew* would have to wait a moment or two until she passed. The band struck up "Auld Lang Syne." People watching the *New Mexico* began singing.

The figure who pushed through the crowd was a woman, her hands stuffed in her overcoat.

Dammit! It's Diane! Donovan thought of ducking behind

the director, but he needed to be here since they were maneuvering in tight quarters. Another glance told him the car was Walt Logan's Chevrolet. The driver stepped from the car, leaned against the fender, and lit a cigarette. He wore khakis and the bars of a lieutenant commander. ". . . my God," said Donovan. It was John Sabovik nonchalantly taking a drag.

Diane recognized Vicky Kruger and walked over. They spoke for a moment, and Vicky pointed to the flybridge. Diane picked him out and with a wave, yelled, "Mike?" A forest-green scarf was draped around her neck. Little zephyrs tugged at her hair, which glowed dark red in the sunlight. She looked gorgeous.

Kruger barked, "All stop!"

Michael T. Donovan, commander, USN, had a thorough background in ship handling, especially destroyers, and he liked to think he'd seen almost every situation. But this nonplussed him. People ashore watched Diane waving to someone on the bridge. Meantime the *Matthew,* having twisted clockwise from the pier, was more or less dead in the water, her fantail sticking out in the fairway, her bow near the pier. She was still attached to the pier by the number two dock line.

Even the fo'c'sle and bridge crews looked up at Kruger, anticipating the order to take number two aboard and back clear.

"Come on, Mr. Kruger," muttered Donovan, "We're late."

"Mike?" she called again.

Kruger's lips were pressed, his hands clasped behind his back.

"Take in two, Mr. Kruger," ordered Donovan.

"Aye, aye, Captain. Take in two." He leaned over the rail and called to Potter, "Tell the fo'c'sle to take in line two."

Potter gave the command, and sailors on the pier threw the line off the bollard. Aboard ship, the boatswain's mate of the watch again clicked his 1 MC switch and blew a whistle, saying, "Under way. Shift colors." Jack and ensign were hauled down from the fo'c'sle and fantail. A sailor at the signal bridge yanked on a halyard; a larger ensign whipped up to the top of the mast and was to-blocked.

"Sound one long blast," ordered Kruger.

The crowd on the pier shoved their fingers in their ears as the *Matthew* gave a mournful six-second blast of her horn.

The blast still echoed when Diane cupped her hands around her mouth. "Mike?" she hollered.

"Get on with it, Richard," hissed Donovan.

Kruger spat back, "Dammit, Mike, say something."

Donovan tensed. He was ready to relieve Kruger, take the conn, throw in a two-thirds backing bell, and get the hell out of here.

Another voice called from the pier. This time it was Vicky Kruger. "Mike, talk to her, you damn fool."

The crowd, sailors on the *Matthew,* yard workers, women working the doughnut and coffee van, all watched.

Shit.

He leaned out. "Hi."

She smiled, and he instantly felt sorry, and stupid, and foolish, and so very alone.

"You remember my brother Ralphie?" she called.

Donovan shrugged.

"Say yes," growled Kruger.

"Yes," Donovan called back.

"What," she called loudly.

Dammit! Donovan grabbed the megaphone and said, "Yes."

Again she cupped her hands around her mouth and called up, "That's right. Well, he came back. He joined the marines and had been on Guadalcanal and was wounded. But he's okay now. Our little Ralphie is a sergeant."

"That's mighty fine." Donovan lowered the megaphone and glanced outboard seeing that the thirty-five-thousand-ton battleship was abeam, her tugs trailing watchfully as she stood into San Francisco Bay. Time to go.

"Ralphie cleaned up his room," she said.

Donovan shrugged again. The crowd pressed in.

"Guess what he found under the bed?" she said.

It hit him. "I'll be a monkey's uncle," Donovan said.

"What was it?" an old man shouted from the pier.

"Yeah!" yelled another. "Tell us."

"Okay?" Diane yelled up to him.

"Yeah, what the hell was it, Mike?" said a grinning Kruger.

"Not what you think," Donovan retorted.

"Okay?" she yelled again.

My God, thought Donovan. She's asking me to marry her.

"What the hell, Skipper?" yelled a beefy overalled yard worker, a lunch box stuffed under his arm. "With a dame as good lookin' as that, anything's okay. So tell her yes, you dumb schmuck."

The crowd laughed and chanted, "Tell her yes. Tell her yes."

With the *New Mexico* clear, the band marched down to the *Matthew* playing the mournful strains.

"Yes. Okay!" yelled Donovan.

Diane gave a jump then pulled her left hand from her pocket and waved it at him. Carmen Rossi's engagement ring glittered from her fourth finger. She blew a kiss.

The crowd figured it out and cheered.

"I'll be damned!" Donovan grinned, waved back, and pressed the megaphone to his face.

"Okay," he shouted.

With a broad, dazzling smile, Diane stood on her tiptoes and yelled, "I love you." Sailors on the bridge and weather decks, people on the pier, swung their eyes from Diane back to Donovan.

The band drew before the *Matthew,* did a crisp left face and continued playing "Auld Lang Syne."

Donovan froze.

"Mike, now's your time to shine," said Kruger.

"Shut up," muttered Donovan. He backed away and walked around the director, returning next to Kruger. The damn *New Mexico* wasn't all the way past, so they were stuck here for a few more seconds.

"Come on, schmuck," yelled the beefy shipyard worker.

Donovan raised his hands and let them flop to his sides.

The crowd broke into a new chant with, "Say it. Say it. Say it."

Donovan raised the megaphone and called down to her. "All right. I love you, too." He grinned and pumped a fist.

Diane waved and gave another brilliant smile.

The crowd roared.

The band played and the old song swelled from the crowd:

For auld lang syne, my dear
For auld lang syne
We'll tak' a cup o' kindness yet
For auld lang syne.

More than a few sailors on the ship and people on the pier dabbed handkerchiefs at their eyes.

"Judy!" A sailor on the fo'c'sle whipped off his white hat and sailed it across. Eager hands plucked it from the air and handed it to a tearful young girl.

"Mom!" Another hat sailed across. Then another; then another. It seemed an ancient and natural custom to Donovan as white hats flew through the air. He'd never seen it done before, but he instinctively knew it was good. And if the government wouldn't pay for new white hats when they reached Pearl Harbor, Donovan vowed to pay for them out of his own pocket. The only thing that marred the exuberance was John Sabovik, leaning against the fender of Walt Logan's Chevrolet, smoking his cigarette, gazing at the hills across the way.

Donovan turned and said, "You may now order your backing bell, Mr. Kruger."

PART TWO

I hung weakly on the side of the tractor [LVT] and prayed that I would do my duty, survive, and not wet my pants.

Eugene B. Sledge, PFC, USMC
"Hitting the Beach on Peleliu"

At sea we may sink beneath the waves
On land we may lie beneath green grasses
But we have nothing to regret
So long as we die fighting for our Emperor.

Japanese Warrior's Song

TWENTY-EIGHT

2 September 1944
Grande Island
Imperial Japanese Naval Station, Subic Bay
Luzon, Philippines

Grande Island was a one-mile-long oblong island near the mouth of Subic Bay, an enormous natural harbor almost one hundred kilometers northwest of Manila. Set aside as a resort area, Grande Island usually teemed with officers, men, and sometimes their women. But on this hot and humid afternoon, the main picnic area was nearly deserted. There were just seven men scattered about, wearing cutoff trousers. Some were shirtless, and one might conclude it was a group of simple fishermen meandering about. Except three H8K2 Kawanishi four-engine flying boats were anchored in emerald-green waters one hundred meters offshore, wavelets slapping at their hulls. And Imperial marines patrolled either end of the island in plain view.

Three men wandered at the water's edge, kicking at rocks. Another pair sat in a large thatched nipa hut that was situated under the shade of a scraggly narra tree. Drinking Asahi beer, they peered at the bay where the afternoon westerly kicked up whitecaps.

Two men were at the water. One, bony and thin, stooped in shallow water near a group of rocks running his hands in the sand. The other stood patiently at the water's edge, a bucket in his hand. It was Commander Yuzura Noyama, unmindful of the patch over his left eye and horrible burn scars running the length of his right leg.

One of the men in the hut was Vice Admiral Matome Ugaki,

who yelled to the man stooped in the water, "Do you have any yet, Kurita? I'm getting hungry."

The man stooped in the water was Vice Admiral Takeo Kurita. He waved a hand over his head. "You're scaring them, my friend. All you have to do is stop yapping and we'll have plenty of fresh crab for dinner."

"At this rate, we won't see dinner until next week," yelled Vice Admiral Jisaburo Ozawa, who was seated alongside Ugaki.

"Careful one of them doesn't bite your balls off!" Ugaki yelled.

Kurita jerked something from the water and held it up. It was a hand-size black crab, its glistening claws wiggling and snapping in the sun. "Come on down here, Ugaki, and we'll see who loses his balls."

The men in the hut laughed as Kurita beckoned for Noyama to hold out the water-filled bucket.

"How many is that?" yelled Ugaki.

"Twenty-three. Now shhh." Kurita tossed the crab in the bucket and stooped to again probe rocks and sand. He found another crab, tossed it in the bucket, and said, "I think that's enough." He looked up and nodded at a group of white-coated stewards gathered behind the nipa hut. Two of them stepped out, bowed to Noyama, and accepted the bucket. As they walked away, Kurita shouted, "How 'bout a swim, Ugaki?"

Ugaki shook his head and held up his Asahi. "This is all I need for now. Besides"—he nodded to the bay—"there's sharks out there."

Kurita shouted back, "Little thing like that shouldn't bother you." Then he dove cleanly into the water.

Tominaga, the chief steward, walked out from the bush followed by the enormous bulk of third-class petty officer Minoru Onishi, clad only in a loincloth. Onishi's massive arms hung loosely at his sides. Bowing deeply, Tominaga said to Ugaki, "We can have everything ready in an hour, Admiral."

Ugaki checked his watch and looked up. "Very good. Make it so." As Tominaga walked back, Ugaki picked up his empty glass and waved it at Onishi. "Please?"

"Uhhhh." Onishi took the glass and moved off, happy for something to do.

Ugaki nodded to Ozawa and wiped sweat off his brow. "Actually, it's a good idea. Freshen up before the meal." He stood, ran to the bay, and jumped in.

"What's to lose?" grumbled Ozawa, who rose and followed Ugaki into the water.

As they ran past, Noyama noticed that Ugaki's wounds were almost as hideous as his own. One scar ran jaggedly across the man's back, another down his leg. These were wounds received when Ugaki's G4M2 twin-engine land-attack bomber was shot down by American P-38s eighteen months ago.

The other fighting admirals of the Imperial Japanese Navy turned at the ruckus and ran toward them, joining Kurita, Ugaki, and Ozawa. They were Vice Admiral Gunichi Mikawa, Vice Admiral Shoji Nishimura, and Vice Admiral Kiyohide Shima.

Noyama watched, marveling at these men who held the fate of the empire in their hands. They giggled like schoolchildren, throwing mud and splashing water. Even the withdrawn Mikawa, who had decimated the Americans at Savo Island in 1942, laughed as Ugaki reached down, scooped up dark bottom mud, and splattered him up his back.

They finished a long and relaxed dinner about six thirty and later, while the admirals smoked and drank and reminisced, Noyama slipped away and strolled across the narrow width of Grande Island to the beach on the west side, facing the ocean. Sitting on his haunches, he peered at the horizon, thinking of Hiroshi whose Shiragiku Special Attack Squadron was posted at Clark Field, a hundred kilometers to the north. Kurita had made arrangements for Noyama to be driven up there tomorrow, where he could spend a good part of the day with his little brother; in all likelihood, his last time. The deeper the sun sank in the sky, the more intense were the memories of Hiroshi, of all the antics, the stunts, the practical jokes—indeed, the two apples—and the love and understanding they'd had from two wonderful parents. Even so, Noyama had only received one letter since he'd seen his parents. It was from his father, terse and direct, almost business-like. But there was no mention of Hiroshi; it was almost as if his little brother were already dead.

The sky was mixed with a riot of reds, oranges, yellows, and pinks. Darkness had just about finished consuming the colors with its inevitable finality when something stirred behind.

"Sir?" It was Tominaga, still wearing his starched-white steward's coat. Interesting, thought Noyama. Here, high-ranking officers were dressed like peasants, while cooks and stewards in their uniforms were the only military symbols. Except for Imperial marines standing watch at either end of the island, the admirals might as well have been rice paddy farmers under the control of a benevolent white-frocked landlord.

"Yes?"

"They're ready," said Tominaga.

Noyama glanced at his watch: 2032. He'd been here for almost an hour and a half, watching the sky—letting his mind go, doing absolutely nothing. It was an art practiced over the ages by his ancestors, but something he'd been able to do only while in a hot bath—and then for only a few minutes. The modern world with all of its Western imperatives made such demands on Noyama and his fellow Japanese that at times like this, he felt as if he'd lost touch with what life was really about.

And now, watching the sunset and embraced by twilight, Noyama felt a complete relaxation. He was reluctant to let it go, knowing that, perhaps, it was the last time he'd be able to enjoy this for a long, long time. Tominaga must have sensed this because he'd approached quietly, his voice soft and tranquil.

"Tominaga?" said Noyama.

"Sir?"

"Do you have any apples in your larder?"

"Just two left, sir."

"May I have them wrapped in a silk handkerchief for my trip tomorrow?"

Tominaga hesitated for a moment, unsure. "Both, sir?"

"Please."

"I'll put them with your gear, sir." Tominaga bowed and walked into the darkness.

Noyama lingered for a few last delicious moments, watching the western horizon. Then, with a sigh, he rose and trekked in darkness across the island. A twig snapped behind him, jerking him from whatever remained of his reverie. It was a marine sergeant.

"Is this necessary?" growled Noyama.

"Sorry, sir. We've seen Igorots over here."

"On Grande Island?" gasped Noyama.

The sergeant gave a slight bow. "Just last week, they paddled over here somehow and grabbed one of our officers, a major. Just like you, he and his girlfriend went to the western beach to watch the sunset, ahh, in this case, they were skinny-dipping—excuse me, sir, this way." The sergeant gestured off to his left. Noyama was surprised to see three other marines behind the sergeant, their rifles at the ready.

Noyama had been briefed on the Igorots—natives indigenous to the Philippines. Small in stature, they were fierce warriors who were nearly impossible to dislodge from wherever they lived in the thick jungle highlands of northern Luzon. Not bothering with Philippine politics, their role in the resistance movement was unorganized and unpredictable. The Japanese had found it nearly impossible to find them and had long ago given up. "What happened?"

"The girl wandered back to camp, with no idea where the major had disappeared to. Then, a week later, just before serving the evening meal, they found the major's head in a stew pot at our garrison barracks over in Olongopo—here we are, sir."

The sergeant stepped aside, gesturing to the campfire's glow through scattered underbrush. In the east, a three-quarter moon rose, illuminating Subic Bay and the three Kawanishi flying boats bobbing obediently at anchor.

Noyama's throat felt dry. "Thank you, Sergeant."

"Not at all, sir." The sergeant and his men melted into the darkness.

Noyama walked into the nipa hut and sat behind Kurita. They were all there and had obviously been waiting. His only admonition was a grunt from Kurita, who handed a notepad over his shoulder. Noyama's job was to listen and take notes. He was there because they all had agreed he was the best. This meeting was to be uncomplicated by aides and staff and liaison officers and their pompous screaming and politics. Tonight the fighting admirals wanted to make decisions, plan strategy and tactics. After that, they would let their staffs work out the details.

Ugaki sat cross-legged in the sand before a half-finished bottle of Johnnie Walker Black Label Scotch, a leaded-glass tumbler nestled next to the bottle. A bottle of Fundatore Brandy was nestled before the Manila-based Mikawa, its color a bit lighter and not quite so threatening as the Johnnie Walker. As usual, Kurita drank tea. Deep in the shadows, one could make out the nearly fused eyes of Minoru Onishi. Still wearing a simple loincloth, Onishi's enormous arms were folded as he stood ready for whatever Vice Admiral Ugaki ordered.

With a nod to Noyama, Shima said, "Say that again for our friend here."

Mikawa cleared his throat and said, "Two weeks ago, we captured four American swimmers off Yap Island—"

"—they call them frogmen," corrected Ugaki.

"Yes, frogmen. Upon interrogation, we learned that these men were scouting the beaches of Yap for possible invasion. Moreover, one of them tipped us that they are also scouting Morotai and the Palaus."

There was a collective nod. Bracing his hands on his knees, Ozawa asked for all of them, "This means we were right? That by attacking Morotai and the Palaus, they are anchoring their southern flank, intending to attack the Philippines and not Formosa?"

"So it would seem," said Mikawa.

"Then why are they hitting the Formosan airfields?" asked Ozawa with a bit of irritation.

Ugaki gave a long belch and said to Ozawa, "You should know that. They want to clear the airspace for the Philippines." He leaned over and refilled Nishimura's glass. Then he looked to Noyama, who waved him off with, "No, thank you, sir. I have to take notes."

"Better to take notes when you're drunk," muttered Ugaki,

holding up the bottle and eyeing it. "Makes all this shit seem more believable." The bottle was empty. He pitched it over his shoulder, then reached in a wooden case and drew out a full one.

"You live in a fairyland," snapped Ozawa.

"All I'm saying is the obvious," retorted Ugaki. He poured himself a generous dollop then sipped. "Ahhhh. It's got to be the Philippines. Not Formosa. And not the Home Islands, and certainly not the Kurils. Am I right?"

"Toyoda thinks it's Formosa," said Mikawa quietly, almost reverently.

"Toyoda's afraid of his own shadow. It can't be Formosa. And this intelligence confirms it."

There was a collective gasp when Ugaki referred to their commander in chief as afraid of his own shadow. Ozawa grunted, "Stupid battleship sailor."

"Battleship, *baka*!" Ugaki sat up straight. "Okay, let's settle it, you pussies. Is it the PI or is it Formosa? Let's vote," he demanded. "Let me help you out. I say it's the Philippines. Let me help you out some more. I say it's Leyte Gulf." He looked at Kurita.

"No argument from me," replied Kurita.

"Nishimura?" demanded Ugaki.

"Bah! Formosa!" barked Nishimura.

"Ummm." Ugaki eyed Shima.

"Leyte," the diminutive Shima said. "It's the only logical place. A natural gulf with unrestricted access from the east."

"Yes? Leyte?" repeated Ugaki. "And how about you, Admiral Ozawa, our air warrior?"

Ozawa rubbed his chin and stared at each in the circle.

"Are you trying to fart?" quipped Ugaki.

"Yes, Leyte," Ozawa barked.

"Very good. And now you, Mikawa, hero of the Guadalcanal campaign. What do you think?"

Mikawa leaned toward the fire and said, "Americans are logical thinkers."

"Seems I've heard that before," said Kurita.

"They take things in moderate bites with overwhelming force." Mikawa looked around the fire. "Anyone disagree?"

When no one spoke, Mikawa continued. "Formosa would

be too big a bite. Both flanks would be exposed. Plus that egomaniac MacArthur wants to fulfill his promise to return to the Philippines. So, yes, I agree and say it's Leyte."

"How about Davao?" asked Ugaki, referring to a large gulf on Mindanao, the southernmost and largest Philippine island.

"Leyte would be relatively easy pickings. Yes." Mikawa looked up. "I agree. Leyte."

"Do you think Toyoda would go for it?" asked Ugaki.

"If we're unanimous," said Mikawa.

They all eyed Nishimura.

At length, he threw his hands in the air and said, "Leyte."

"What an intelligent choice," said Ugaki. "That means you get to drink with us." He poured a large dollop of scotch into Nishimura's glass. "Very good. We endorse SHO-1 and Mikawa can send a message to Toyoda. Now, what can we do about it?"

"Except . . . ," said Mikawa.

"Except what?" demanded Kurita.

Mikawa held his brandy glass up to the firelight and studied it. "Except Toyoda thinks, in the event of SHO-1, that it will be Davao Gulf, not Leyte."

"He's a damn fool," slurred Ugaki.

"Not to worry," said Kurita.

All eyes turned to Kurita.

"It'll be the same footprint," Kurita ventured.

"Are you speaking of the tactical plan?" asked Nishimura.

"I am."

"Well, please let us in on it," said Ozawa. "That would be very nice, I think."

Kurita looked at Ozawa. "It all depends on perfect timing. And it all depends on you."

Ugaki belched. "Are you going to keep drinking that damn tea or are you going to have a man's drink and let us in on this?"

Kurita gave Ugaki a polite smile and said, "Halsey will be in charge of their attack force—the carriers." When no one objected, he continued, "Halsey has a bigger head than MacArthur. All he wants is to sink carriers."

"Yes, yes," said Ozawa.

"And so, are you ready?" pressed Ugaki.

Ozawa's lips pressed and he slowly shook his head.

"Ozawa?" Kurita said gently.

"What a horrible choice," protested Ozawa.

Kurita said, "It's like we discussed in Yokosuka. If we sink MacArthur's amphibious forces and isolate his troops on the beaches of Leyte or Mindanao, we could buy six months, maybe a year in this war, to regroup, to train more pilots, to . . . save the homeland. Plus, think of the vast demoralizing effect it would have on MacArthur and his troops. All that effort lost. All those men—killed. All that equipment—destroyed."

All eyes turned to Ozawa, the key to the whole operation.

Almost imperceptibly, he nodded.

Ugaki burped. "This calls for another drink." He began refilling glasses.

Mikawa rubbed his chin. "So how do you bring this off?"

Kurita drew in the sand once again. "At the first sign of invasion, we go on the move. You, Shima, will bring your cruisers and destroyers down from Beppu Bay and rendezvous with Nishimura at night to transit the Surigao Strait and drive north. It's important that you keep the rendezvous—yes?" He looked at them.

When they nodded, Kurita continued, "I will take the First Striking Force, drive through the Sibuyan Sea, transit the San Bernardino Strait at night, and—"

"How will you get through?" asked Nishimura.

"Simple. Turn on the lights," said Kurita. Navigation lights through the San Bernardino Strait had been turned off since war broke out.

"Ahhh," they said.

"Now, this also is important. Once through the San Bernardino Strait, I will turn south to rendezvous with Nishimura and Shima off Leyte to destroy MacArthur and his ships. Halsey will be too far north, dallying with Ozawa's ships, to be able to return and do his job, which is to protect the fleet."

Ozawa slapped Ugaki's knee. "You've been quiet. What does the great battleship admiral think? How would you like to have MacArthur under your eighteen-inch guns?"

Ugaki fell over to his side and began snoring.

"The bastard's passed out!" snapped Shima.

Ozawa patted Ugaki's knee. "He's a warrior. He'll do what he's told." He grabbed Ugaki's bottle of Johnnie Walker and filled his leaded-glass tumbler. He toasted Ugaki, then the rest of them in turn. "Yes, gentlemen. Makes sense to me. It will buy time. And we can fight again. Yes, I say, yes if Toyoda goes for it. Mikawa?"

Mikawa said, "Very good, I'll radio Toyoda tomorrow."

Ugaki gave a long belch.

"He should be shot," snapped Shima.

"Nonsense," said Kurita with a head shake. "Ozawa is right. This man is a warrior. He'll do what he's told and he'll do a good job."

TWENTY-NINE

3 September 1944
Baguio, Benguet Province
Luzon, Philippines

Yuzura Noyama discovered his brother, Hiroshi, was stationed at Clark Field, and after some prodding by Kurita at Subic headquarters was able to raise him by telephone. They both got a day off and arranged to meet in Baguio, a resort that lies about 240 kilometers north of Manila atop the Cordillera Central mountain range in western Luzon. At 1,829 meters, Baguio had been founded in 1905 by Americans ebullient with their recent victory over Spain. Wanting a place to escape Manila's brutal summer humidity, they patterned their new city after Washington, DC.

The Manila-based Vice Admiral Mikawa pulled more strings and had a staff car assigned to Noyama. In fact, they came up with a four-door Packard convertible once belonging to General MacArthur. The Imperial marine whom Noyama had met the evening before on Grande Island was assigned as his driver. He was a short powerful sergeant named Ito who told Noyama he was in for a real treat. And he was right. While Ito wrestled the Packard's wheel, clutch, and gearshift to negotiate hairpin turns, Noyama gaped at ever-changing vistas of verdant jungle, deep fog-shrouded valleys, and vast rice paddies ingeniously terraced into hillsides. At twelve hundred meters, they ascended into a tightly packed forest of pine trees bringing a marvelous odor—something he hadn't enjoyed since home.

Sergeant Ito dropped him off at the Pompag Bar and Grille on Sessions Road. It was on the main drag festooned, with bars and comfort houses. Ito said he would pick up Noyama at six and was adamant about that: no later than six, he said. Any later and they would be driving the jungle roads in twilight or, worse, total darkness. That's when the partisans were most likely to strike, Ito warned. Terrible things happened, especially if one fell into the hands of the HUKs. Sergeant Ito waved a finger: no driving after sunset. Otherwise it's our heads in a stew pot.

Hiroshi ran up the moment Noyama walked in the door. They embraced, pumped hands, and slapped backs. A seven-piece band was imitating American jazz, and Hiroshi had to shout, "What luck. I couldn't believe it was you."

Noyama shouted back, "You look marvelous."

"As do you. How 'bout a rum and Coke?" Hiroshi waved to a table and they sat.

"They have Cokes here?"

"Well, that's what they call them."

"Okay." Noyama stifled a cough. The place was thick with cigarette smoke, and he could barely see the couples dancing American-style on the floor. On closer examination, he saw that almost everyone was military and most were officers. "You look like you've gained weight."

"A little." He tilted his hand back and forth. "They're feeding us well."

Lamb to the slaughter, thought Noyama. Hiroshi looked away, and he decided to drop it.

A middle-aged waiter of average height walked up and bent to wipe the table. He was a malado: half Filipino, half black American. He set down a wooden tray of drinks and stepped over. "Rum and Coke?" he asked Hiroshi.

"How did you know this is what we wanted?" demanded Hiroshi.

"Everyone wants rum and Coke." The waiter smiled as he stumbled through heavily accented Japanese. The smile was okay, Noyama thought. It was his eyes that disemboweled you.

Noyama nodded and Hiroshi said, "Okay."

"Hai, hai," muttered the waiter.

After the waiter moved off, Hiroshi nodded toward a Japanese civilian in the corner sitting with two Japanese colonels.

He wore a white planter's hat and a cream-colored suit. "See that man?"

"Ummm," said Noyama.

Hiroshi bent his head close. "He's *Kempetai,* the little bastard. Looking for somebody to arrest and torture."

Noyama felt a cold surge in his belly. The *Kempetai* were thought police. Special investigators with unlimited power that augmented the local garrison. Basically their mandate was to terrorize at will in order to keep the local populace in hand. "What outfit is stationed here?"

"The Nineteenth Tora."

A look passed between them, confirming they knew that the Imperial Japanese Army's Nineteenth Tora Division had become famous during the 1941–1942 campaign down the Bataan Peninsula. But now the word was that the Nineteenth was a mere shell of its former self, its real fighters siphoned off to serve elsewhere. The Nineteenth was now reduced to a polyglot of frustrated police officers, out-of-work overaged butchers, and retail clerks, capable only of garrison duty. After a moment, Noyama nodded to the drink. "So this is rum and Coke?"

"Hai, hai," grinned Hiroshi.

"I haven't tasted rum in two years. How did you manage?"

Hiroshi nodded to the row of bar girls seated across the room. "I have pull around here."

"I don't want to hear about that. Tell me about the navy. How are they treating you?"

"I'm assigned to the 215th Shiragiku Special Attack Unit." He smirked. "That's a euphemism, dear brother, for suicide body-crashing attack."

The room seemed hot, and Noyama ran a finger around his collar. "Where do you train?"

"Well, we finished up at Suzuka right after I saw you. The last week they flew us down here to Clark Field," said Hiroshi, drinking deeply.

The band struck up a loud, thumping piece and Noyama had to shout, "Why do you think your unit is posted in the Philippines?"

"I figured you'd know the answer to that. You know all the

brass. Isn't this where the Americans are supposed to strike next?"

The question seemed so innocent coming from his little brother. Yet nobody knew the answer, the intelligence about the American frogmen on Yap Island notwithstanding. It was the question on everyone's lips. "Looks like your superiors are betting on the Philippines," said Noyama.

"That's what I figure. Same reason you're here, hmmmm? So tell me, since you're close to the brass: is it the Philippines or what?"

"I wish I knew."

Hiroshi finished his rum and Coke and slammed down the glass. "How do you like this stuff?"

Noyama slammed down his own glass and said, "You say it's rum. I say it's lizard piss."

"You're not as stupid as I thought." Hiroshi's brow furrowed. "What's wrong?"

Noyama's head felt like it was closing in on him. "Smoke and this damn music."

"What?"

"Look, little brother. I can get you out of this."

Hiroshi looked away.

"Listen to me, dammit. You're right. I do know a lot of brass. Say the word and I can have you transferred out of that unit. No questions asked."

Hiroshi waved to someone across the room.

"Are you listening to me? Think of our parents. Think of—"

"Silence," Hiroshi hissed. His eyes narrowed. "There's too much at stake. I won't hear of it." A shadow crossed his face. He seemed older than his years.

"But why? Why can't you . . ."

Hiroshi stood and waved again. Through the haze, he pointed to the bar where several girls languished, combing their hair and surveying the crowd. "See that one?"

Noyama didn't feel like standing. "Hiroshi. Listen to your older brother. I'm trying to talk sense into you."

"And I to you. Now be quiet or you'll ruin everything." He pointed to a girl at the bar's end. Coyly, she returned the look, then flipped a mirror from her purse and adjusted her lipstick. "That's Nina. She's all right."

"You know her?"

"Since last night. I got here early to sample the goods and get to know the lay of the land, so to speak. She had the Cokes spiked for us."

"I hate hangovers," said Noyama. Then he sipped again and said, "Actually, it's not bad stuff."

"Are you talking about the Cokes?" asked Hiroshi.

"Both."

They laughed.

With an arched eyebrow, Nina eased off the stool, edged her way through the crowd, and stood over their table. She was very petite, with shiny straight black hair that dropped to her waist. She had a deep olive complexion and was barely five feet tall. Her lips were full and her smile would have stopped Genghis Khan at the border. Another girl followed close behind. She was a smaller version of Nina, except her hair was done in a bun wrapped behind her head. She had extremely quick eyes and wore an electric blue dress with leg slits up both sides. Perfume wafted around Noyama. He couldn't tell which one it belonged to; perhaps both.

"Nina, see? I really was telling the truth. This is my brother, Yuzura," said Hiroshi.

"You're better looking than your brother," said Nina. After they laughed, she continued, "Say hello to my cousin Maria." She nodded to the woman next to her.

"Cousins, brothers? Who's telling the truth around here?" quipped Hiroshi.

The girl in blue shot a glance at Hiroshi and stood before Noyama. "Best of the day to you," she said in faltering Japanese. She tossed another smile that could have melted the resin from the table's finish.

Noyama drew a deep breath. Her perfume found every nook in his lungs, his brain, and his stomach. His eyes seemed to bulge; and he wondered if it was perfume or mustard gas in disguise. "And to you, too," he nodded back. Maria might look intelligent and might even be intelligent. But with her Japanese, he was going to have a tough time finding out. Maybe that didn't matter.

Maria sat beside Noyama and nudged him with her hip.

Then casually, she lay a hand on his knee while laughing at something Hiroshi said.

At a nod from Nina, the malado waiter appeared, laid down new drinks, and picked up their old glasses.

Noyama's head whirled and he sipped while Hiroshi gulped. The first drink had gotten to him and he knew he wouldn't last long. What the hell was in it? And the band was playing fast and loud Filipino jazz, featuring three screeching trumpets. "I can't hear." He jammed his hands over his ears.

Hiroshi said something to Nina. She nodded, and he said, "Let's get out of here."

"To where?"

"Her place." Hiroshi and the girls stood.

Noyama stood. "Oh, no." He weaved in place. "Ito warned me about that."

Throwing down a few bills, Hiroshi shouted, "About what?"

"These people set you up for the HUKs. After they torture you, they slice off your head and throw it into the stew pot at the Subic Bay officers' club."

"Who says so?" demanded Hiroshi, wrapping his arm around Nina.

"Sergeant Ito. Don't you read your bulletins?"

Hiroshi started walking and tossed over his shoulder. "Bulletins, my foot. With where I'm going, who cares about damn bulletins?"

They had reached the middle of the dance floor and were hemmed in by the crowd as the band shifted to an American ballad. Tightly packed, the dancers moved slowly. Maria eased her arms around Noyama's neck and began swaying. He was at least a head taller than she, but somehow it all worked and they fit perfectly. He relaxed and held her close. Hiroshi shouted something.

"What?" Noyama yelled back. With the cigarette smoke, the room was closing in. And he couldn't hear the band. "What did you say?" he shouted.

Hiroshi leaned close. "Nina's father is a glassblower."

Maria's motions were all too plain and he felt himself becoming aroused. He took a deep breath. Maybe it was her perfume. "So what? Maybe you're right. We should get out of here."

"I said a glassblower, damn you," said Hiroshi.

"So what?"

"I want you to have something before I forget."

Maria clung to Noyama, moving up and down, her motions now demanding. "Let's get out of here," she rasped.

"Here," said Hiroshi. He handed over a small box.

Maria rose on her tiptoes and mouthed his ear. "Quickly, upstairs." She tugged at his coat.

"Back in a minute," said Noyama, stuffing the box in his pocket.

The corner of Hiroshi's mouth turned up. "Okay."

She led him across the room to a staircase all but obscured by cigarette smoke. "What's up there?" He instantly knew the answer and felt stupid for asking in the first place.

Even so, she looked back as they ascended with a smile that not only answered his question but helped him negotiate the stairs. His head was whirling and his stomach began to jump, a pang arising that brought a cold sweat to his brow. The question surfaced, "What the hell was in that drink?"

Another smile made it possible for Noyama to finish clumping up the stairs. He lurched down a dark hall and remembered stepping into a dark room.

Her teeth flashed in the dark. She kissed him. She grappled at his shirt buttons . . . something loud. Shouting. Thunderclaps . . .

The man in the cream-colored suit pranced up and down the main saloon of the Pompag Bar and Grille. Like a drill sergeant, he bellowed commands while kicking over chairs and tables. Noyama blinked, surprised to find himself downstairs in the main room. He lay on the floor in a corner beside a table. Someone was seated there. He looked up. "Hiroshi?"

"That's me." He seemed distant.

"What happened?"

Hiroshi handed down a cup of tea. "Drink this."

Noyama took the cup in his hands, its warmth making him feel better. He drank and the hot tea ran down his throat, invigorating him. He blinked after his second sip. The Pompag Bar and Grille looked as if the Nineteenth Tora Division had gone back to work. Tables and chairs were upended, pictures hung askew, the mirror over the bar was shattered. The cigarette smoke was gone, but the stench remained. Curtains and drapes had been pulled, windows opened, and late-afternoon sunlight cascaded into the room, revealing a truly dingy scene.

Noyama sucked in his breath. Four bodies were neatly arranged by the front door, blood running beneath them. "Hiroshi. What is this?"

Just then there was a shout at the top of the stairs. Two soldiers stood, holding a pair of arms in their hands. The man in the cream-colored suit walked to the base of the stairs and bellowed a command. The grunting soldiers picked up the man and braced him against the banister. Actually it was a bloody corpse; bullet holes ranged over the torso. With a shout, the soldiers threw the body into space. It tumbled down the stairs, falling two meters from Noyama: the malado waiter. Nonchalantly, the soldiers quick-stepped down the stairs, grabbed the waiter's heels, and dragged him over to the other bodies. One of the bodies, Noyama noticed, wore a blood-spattered electric blue dress with slits up the skirt. He gasped, "Is that—"

"Yes, you damn fool," said the man in the cream-colored suit. "Can you stand?" Noyama rose, picked up a chair, and slumped at the table beside Hiroshi.

"Papers," demanded the man.

Noyama fumbled in his pocket and handed over his papers. "Who are you?"

Hiroshi kicked him under the table. "Easy," he muttered.

"Ah, Commander Noyama. I am Major Kurishima, sir, of His Imperial Majesty's Japanese Army Nineteenth Tora Division. You're most fortunate to be alive."

"Why is that?" Noyama sipped again. His stomach began surging, and he knew he was going to be sick.

"They put something in your rum and Coke," said Hiroshi. "I should have been looking out for it."

Noyama looked up to the major. "You called me a damn fool, Major?" It was his way of pulling rank, something he wasn't used to doing.

"That car. A Packard. You were spotted before you were halfway up the mountain. You couldn't have done a better job of advertising your presence—better than an electric billboard on the Ginza. They wanted you badly."

"Why?"

Kurishima righted a chair and sat with them. "For information, of course. That car told them you were an important customer." His eyes narrowed, and he gave a tight smile. "You were a major target and were to be tortured."

Noyama nodded to the bodies at the front door and looked at Hiroshi. "Is Nina in that mess?"

Hiroshi nodded. "Six more lying outside. Dragged out and executed. They even shot two cooks."

Noyama checked his watch, "It's nearly six. I must find Sergeant Ito."

Kurishma waved a hand in the air. "Dead. We found his body in the Packard's trunk. They hadn't had time to dispose of it."

Noyama slumped for a moment. He'd liked Ito and was sorry for his loss. Then he said, "I'm due back in Subic."

"Possibly tomorrow, after we conclude our investigation."

Noyama weaved to his feet. His stomach lurched and he sat. "It has to be now. Today, Major."

Kurishima looked at Noyama, his face a blank wall.

Noyama said, "Or would you prefer to speak with Admiral Kurita about it?"

Kurishima blinked. After a moment, he said, "I'll look into it." He stood and moved off toward the front door.

There was an urgent rush in Noyama's belly. "Where's the head?"

Hiroshi nodded over his shoulder.

Noyama sprang to his feet, knocked over the chair, and ran into the lavatory, just barely making it into a stall.

He walked back ten minutes later, somewhat unsteadily but feeling a little better. He sat beside Hiroshi, sipped tea, and asked, "You all right, little brother?"

Hiroshi said nothing.

"While I was in there, I found this in my pocket." He pulled out the small box Hiroshi had stuffed there. He opened it, finding an intricate glass replica of two red apples surrounded by green leaves intertwined with a clear glass filigree. "It's beautiful. Thank you. Funny thing. I had two real apples from our larder to bring up to you, but they turned rotten."

"Doesn't matter. Please give that to Mom. But I want all of you to enjoy it."

"Okay. You said Nina's father was a glassblower? Did he do this?"

Hiroshi nodded. Tears ran down his cheeks. "You wonder why I'm in the Shiragiku. You want me to get out? To leave my friends? To embarrass my family? My country? That clapped-out major is right," he yelled, pointing. "You are a damn fool."

Silence descended as Hiroshi shouted and waved about the room. "You want your homeland to become like . . . this. A whorehouse for American occupation armies? You want them to put Mom to work in a whorehouse? Dad in the coal mines? You and me repairing their fancy cars? Is this what you want?" he yelled.

"Hiroshi—"

Again Hiroshi yelled. "I can't stand the thought of this happening back home. No, I'll not have it. I'll not have Americans raping our women. What I'm doing is the only way left."

Major Kurishima walked up.

"So bastards like this can keep torturing people," said Hiroshi, nodding at Kurishima.

"No," said Noyama. "We'll take care of Kurishima and their garbage."

"Commander Noyama . . . ," Kurishima said.

"All right, little brother," said Noyama. He reached across and grabbed his hands. "All right." They embraced. "I'll probably be right behind you."

Kurishima said softly, "Admiral Mikawa has sent specific instructions for your return. We will assign a driver and a scout car to escort you down the hill."

Noyama hugged tighter. "And thanks for those damn apples, you little fool."

THIRTY

21 September 1944
Westbound X 4293
Southern Pacific Freight Yards
Sparks, Nevada

"How are you, young man?" Milo Lattimer reached down with a beefy, callused hand.

Captain Alexander Collins, U.S. Marine Corps, accepted the hand and swung aboard the caboose's rear platform. "Thank you, sir." He grabbed a rail to steady himself. His arm was in a sling; he moved stiffly, and he had dark pouches under his eyes.

"Are you all right?" asked Lattimer.

Collins gave a thin smile. "Me? Yeah. Never better. Just a bumpy hop on a bug-smasher over the mountain this morning. And to tell the truth, this is my first outing since I was in the hospital. Besides, couldn't sleep last night. Painkillers kept me awake."

"Well, let's hope you have a comfortable ride over the hill. We'll put you on the right side." Lattimer waved through the caboose door. "Our brakeman is forward right now. He'll join us when we start up the hill." He looked at the young marine. "I hear they call you Nitro?"

"Please do that, Mr. Lattimer."

"Milo."

"Right, Milo." Nitro walked into the caboose and took a seat. Fortunately, the cupolas were located on the sides, meaning he wouldn't have to crawl up top.

There was a loud squealing noise from a walkie-talkie lying on a table. "Ach!" Lattimer reached over, clicked it, and then reached up to a cord running the length of the caboose. He yanked it twice; an air horn mounted atop the caboose bellowed in response.

Slouching in the opposite cupola, Lattimer checked his watch and said, "They're ready, so am I."

Couplings clanked down the line as Ben Soda Whiskers, opened his throttle, feeding steam to the enormous pistons powering the AC-10's drive wheels.

The consist for westbound X 4293 was relatively short today, only forty-six cars. But twenty-six were flatcars, each carrying an M4A4 Sherman tank that mounted a seventy-six-millimeter cannon. What fascinated Lattimer was that these Chrysler-built, Pacific-bound Shermans were fitted with two large air ducts. The tankers had told him that this was for fording waters up to six feet deep. Lattimer made a mental note to put that into his next dispatch for Lorena. He'd do it now, but this young marine sitting across from him had quick eyes. Even though he was tired, Collins missed nothing, Lattimer could see. Too bad he didn't die when Lattimer had shoved him out of the boxcar three weeks ago. And now Sabovik was up in the cab with Soda Whiskers and Collins was back here. He would have to be careful. What worried Lattimer was that they were here for a reason, and he racked his brain to determine whether he'd tipped them off. Lattimer leaned over. "Coffee, Captain Collins?"

"Don't forget, it's Nitro. And yes, thank you. Black, please."

The caboose lurched over a crossing as they picked up speed. Lattimer looked out the window and grinned. "Soda Whiskers is racing that damn chicken farmer again."

Nitro looked across. "Damned fool. Someone's going to get hurt."

They flashed past the road-grade crossing. All they could see was a trail of dust and chicken feathers in the wake of the stake truck. Popovits Farms had won this race.

Lattimer poured and handed over a cup. "Maybe a few chickens to get hurt, hmmmm?"

"Thanks," said Nitro. He sipped. "Ahhhh, good stuff. You railroad guys live okay. And this sure beats the hell out of riding in the engine."

"Put up your feet. Make yourself comfortable."

With a groan, Nitro lifted his legs and stretched. "Um. Swell. Thought the caboose would be rough riding."

"Some of them are," said Lattimer as he sat opposite and reached for a large black valise.

"Whatcha got there?"

"Train orders. Don't you know? This is a railroad. Worse than the navy. Paperwork never ends."

"Ummmm, we doing okay?" asked Nitro, his eyelids drooping.

"Perfect."

Three minutes later, Lattimer glanced over to see the captain's head pitched back on the cushion, eyes closed, mouth wide open. He reached over and caught Collins's coffee cup before it fell on the floor. Amazing. The young man had fallen asleep so quickly and now he was snoring, his head lolling back and forth as the train jostled.

So much the better. Lattimer looked out the window seeing the CALVEDA sign flash past; they had just crossed into California. The engines, two AC-10s in front and two more about two-thirds of the way back, were really working now, their massive steam chests chuffing almost in concert as they ground their way up the hill toward Truckee and the Donner summit. After a long and careful glance at the marine, Lattimer bent over to work at his train orders. Except he turned his back slightly to Collins; he wasn't working on train orders at all . . .

Her name was Lorena Ortiz and he'd only known her for six months. They'd sent her two weeks after Anna Thiele had the temerity to choke on a chicken bone and die. Anna, a forty-seven-year-old spinster, had clerked at the local title insurance company. Lorena, on the other hand, worked as a housekeeper and short-order cook at the Atwater Hotel over on Vermont Street, a clapboard flophouse frequented by railroaders. Where Anna was bookish and withdrawn, Lorena was outward and displayed a hot Latin temper. Anna had dressed in black muslin dresses and wrapped her hair in a tight bun. On the other hand, Lorena wore a starched-white uniform drawn tight at the waist, the effect provocative. Where Anna spoke in a low, measured tone, Lorena purposely smashed her phrases, faking an accent in a delightfully husky voice. But Milo knew Lorena was putting it all on. Her eyes sparkled when she shook her head no to a question; Lorena understood English perfectly. Even though she was regarded as the town's punchboard, he loved her and hated her at the same time. He loved her since she was such a deep, hot-blooded, tender, caring woman who made him feel extraordinarily alive, especially when they were making love. He hated her because she threw caution to the winds, didn't look for anyone following during her trips to San Francisco, and spent money faster than a Texas oilman.

Besides being females, Anna Thiele and Lorena Ortiz had only two other things in common: Both were citizens of Argentina and both worked as couriers for Milo Lattimer. At the first of each month, Milo gave them a round-trip pass to Oakland. Arriving midmorning, they would take the ferry to San Francisco and walk six blocks up Market Street to the Argentine consulate at 58 Sutter Street. An eleven o'clock arrival would ensure that Señor M. Radizar, the consul, met them in a vestibule where they exchanged pouches for Señor Lattimer. Señor Radizar also handed over an envelope containing four one-hundred-dollar bills for the courier to use as she pleased. Keeping to a strict schedule, the courier returned with the pouch by day's end and gave it to Lattimer. Running over an awkward route from Buenos Aires to Lisbon to Berlin, traffic took from thirty to forty days, when Lattimer sent messages. Most of the incoming traffic contained encryption updates and schedules for radio reports to Germany. But Lattimer had only broadcast twice in the last three years. His heart had pounded as he kept his messages to thirty seconds. It pounded even harder when, both times, a dark unmarked van with an omnidirectional, top-mounted antenna slithered through the neighborhood.

The pouches from Señor Radizar usually contained two separate envelopes. The first one held messages, code changes, and other intelligence information. The second envelope had ten one-hundred-dollar bills, which Lattimer ferreted away with his other private belongings. It was all neatly stacked in three Samsonite suitcases in his hideaway. He was just too afraid to bank it or invest it, lest someone become suspicious about how a railroad employee had become so flush.

It was in one of their tender moments that Lorena got him to talk. She discovered that his real name was Helmut Gregor Burgdorf. Born in Munich on August 14, 1914. His father, Josef Burgdorf, was a private in the kaiser's army who did well in the import–export business after the Great War to end all wars. Josef and Stella, Helmut's mother, moved in 1927 to New York City, where he continued to prosper, allowing young Helmut to stay with friends in Germany.

A dream came true when young Burgdorf was accepted to Heidelberg's medical school. But then he was kicked out in 1936. They thought he was Jewish. It was later proven a mistake, but the stigma held. Embittered, he moved to the United States to live with his parents who, by this time, had lost everything in the Depression. While Josef worked as a maître d' in the Five Palms, a five-star restaurant, young Burgdorf got a job as a brakeman for the New York Central Railroad.

German agents found him a year later. Things were grim. Stella had died, and Josef had fallen ill with pneumonia from a bitter winter. The agents treated young Burgdorf like a king, and the promise of quick cash attracted him even more. After the transfer of five thousand dollars to Banco de Buenos Aires in Argentina, Burgdorf became a sleeper agent while working full-time on the railroad.

The year 1937 was the year of the *Hindenburg* dirigible disaster. It was a disaster for Burgdorf as well, for his father, Josef, succumbed to his pneumonia. He couldn't get out of New York fast enough. Assuming the name of Milo Lattimer, Helmut Gregor Burgdorf—following the wishes of his German contacts—moved to Harrisburg, Pennsylvania, and joined the Pennsylvania Railroad as a brakeman. For the next three years, his Argentine bank account grew as he reported strategic materials and troop movements to his control. His control was particularly delighted when, in 1939, Burgdorf accepted an offer from the Southern Pacific Railroad out west. Assigned to the Sacramento Division, he settled in Roseville and became a conductor on the Sierra route, one of the most strategic routes in the nation. He kept in touch with his handlers via the courier pouch system, beginning with Anna Thiele.

He did a stupid thing right after the war's outbreak. There was a horrible troop train wreck in the Sierras. Seven men were killed and sixteen injured. Lattimer was on an eastbound freight that was stopped at the scene, the right-of-way blocked. Like everybody else, he pitched in to help the groaning injured. His Heidelberg medical training took over and before Burgdorf knew it, he was triaging patients, setting broken limbs, and working tourniquets long before medical help arrived. Lives were saved and an embarrassed Milo Lattimer was made Man of the Year by the Roseville Rotary Club.

A twenty-two-year old Cal–Berkeley graduate named Diane Logan was aboard the train that day, riding with her father. And it was a wide-eyed Diane Logan who stepped in to help Burgdorf save lives. That was one of the things that had motivated her to apply to Cal's med school. She was accepted and graduated in three years. During that time, Burgdorf made a clumsy play for her, but Stan Bartlett, a young marine dive-bomber pilot, swooped in and won her over. Lieutenant Bartlett and Burgdorf almost came to blows one night just outside the Logan home. Everybody was embarrassed, with Burgdorf vowing to concentrate on his job and forget about women.

And then Bartlett was killed over Bougainville. Good riddance. Burgdorf had given a thought about going back to Diane when Lorena came along. What a number she was, all right. It was a great convenience for Lattimer. After all, Lorena kept him contained with her favors. No longer was it necessary to chase after Diane Logan—or any other woman, for that matter. Thus, he was able to preserve his real identity . . . and concentrate on the mission.

And so today, as westbound X 4293 rumbled and clanked up the High Sierras, Milo Lattimer took out the pouch he'd received from Lorena late yesterday afternoon. After a quick glance at a snoring Captain Collins, he began decrypting his Berlin traffic using a double checkerboard code. Twenty minutes later, he sat back to read two messages. The first one said:

NEED DETAILS ON UPDATED USN TORPEDO EXPLODERS AS SOON AS POSSIBLE

Lattimer snorted. Those idiots in Berlin expected too much. Like all small ammunition items, the navy exploders were inventoried, locked, and double-locked in their containers. Then the cars were nearly impossible to get into. Trying to do something as stupid as this could cost him his life. He lit a cigar, then burned the message in a steel ashtray. Admiral Dönitz would have to figure some other way to improve his damn torpedo exploders.

The second message was a little more satisfying:

AMMUNITION SHIP SS REGINA DALMATIA DEBARKED PORT CHICAGO 29 JULY IN CONVOY TO HAWAII. BLEW UP SEA WITHOUT A TRACE. OUR CLIENTS PLEASED WITH YOUR PROGRESS. THAT MAKES TWO. CONGRATULATIONS.

Lattimer read the message again. The Japanese were pleased. So what? He couldn't care less as long as the cash kept coming. Someday, sooner than later, he suspected, both Germany and Japan would be out of the war. Then the pressure would be off and he could begin to invest his money. And he thought he knew where.

"Whatcha doin'?"

Shit! Collins! He was stretched out, yawning, and smacking his lips. For a moment, Lattimer felt a rush of anger and thought he might have to kill the young marine. "Damn schedules and maintenance reports. How do you feel?"

"Umm. Better, thanks. Say, where's my coffee?"

Lattimer handed it over. "It almost fell on the floor, my friend."

"Oh, sorry."

They watched as a noisy eastbound freight flashed past on the downslope, hauling car after car of refrigerated fruit.

Collins asked, "Where do you get such great coffee?"

While forcing a smile, Lattimer eased the pouch under his buttocks. "We work on the railroad, my friend. Anything's possible."

Collins raised an eyebrow.

Wrong thing to say. This man is good. "I mean the shippers give it to us as a favor. This blend is from a San Francisco brewer."

"Pretty fancy."

Lattimer dug in his voluminous briefcase. "They gave me three pouches this time." He tossed over a pouch of coffee. "Take this one. It's the best."

Collins held the pouch to his nose and sniffed. "Mmmmm. I can't wait to try it."

"You won't be disappointed."

"Well, thanks." Collins eyed the other pouch.

"Uh, that's for the Logan family."

"I thought Walt Logan gave up coffee after his heart attack."

"Well, that's true. So I give it to Diane and then she looks the other way while her father sneaks a cup or two."

Collins shook his head. "Damn fool."

"Damn fool," Lattimer agreed. He decided to take a chance. "Is Commander Sabovik still head over heels for her?"

Collins gave a shrug that told him *None of your business.*

Ach! Shut up and do your damn job. Lattimer had lamented that Diane Logan was more or less pledged to a navy destroyer captain now out in the Pacific; that Sabovik still hovered around her; and that he was stuck with that stupid hot tamale Lorena Ortiz for business . . . and pleasure. He sat straight and drew his best smile. "Do you play chess, Captain?"

"Call me Nitro."

"Yes. Do you play chess, Nitro?"

"Well, yes, a little."

THIRTY-ONE

29 September 1944
USS *Matthew* (DD 548)
Two miles west of Ulithi Atoll, Caroline Islands

Ulithi was discovered by the Portuguese explorer Diego da Rocha in 1526. The oblong, fifteen-mile-long lagoon remained untouched by Europeans until 1731, when Spanish priests attempted to set up an outpost there. But Micronesians drove them off and Ulithi remained in the Micronesians' hands until the Japanese set up a radio station early in the war. Believing the islets surrounding the clear, turquoise lagoon too small for an airfield and impractical for a fleet anchorage, the Japanese used it primarily for a weather station. However, Admiral Halsey's staff were well aware of the capabilities of Ulithi: the primary one was that Ulithi could safely anchor at least seven hundred ships. Plus, the atoll was strategically located just nine hundred miles east of Leyte and fourteen hundred miles southeast of Okinawa.

On 23 September 1944, American forces landed unopposed[26] at Ulithi and began turning the atoll into a massive seaport and air base. To prove the Japanese wrong, the Seabees immediately began construction of a thirty-six-hundred-foot airstrip on Falalop Islet on the lagoon's northeastern side. Asor Islet, a mile west of Falalop, became an advanced fleet base. Within days, a one-hundred-bed hospital and boat pool went up on nearby Sorlen Islet. Perhaps the most important role was served by the half-mile long Mogmog Islet, which was established as a recreation base for the fleet. Once built, the recreation center on Mogmog was one of the largest for GIs in the Pacific war, once hosting approximately twenty thousand sailors and marines.

For the present, Admiral Halsey's attack carriers were off marauding throughout the western Pacific. From Okinawa to Iwo Jima to Formosa to the Philippines, Halsey's planes hit airfields of all sizes, their intent: wipe out the Japanese air arm. Still, the lagoon bloomed with activity. The USS *Bunker Hill,* an *Essex*-class fleet carrier standing down for elevator and boiler repairs, was anchored in the lagoon's center. On either side were two light carriers, an escort carrier, and an assortment of cruisers and destroyers. Speckled throughout the rest of the lagoon were a growing number of auxiliaries, from ammunition ships to oilers, repair ships, seaplane tenders, LSTs, and attack transports. Just towed in yesterday were three barracks barges to house the Seabees shaping the islets of Ulithi Atoll.

Steaming at twelve knots, a convoy of three destroyers and three attack transports (APAs) looped around to Ulithi's western side and headed for the Rowaryu Channel—the main entrance to the atoll. The destroyers had been in a bent-line screen running interference for the fat, ponderous APAs loaded to the gunnels with Sixth Army Expeditionary troops and equipment for the Leyte campaign. All three destroyers were joining the Pacific war for the first time. The USS *Simpson* (DD 549) was screen commander and squadron flagship for the newly formed Destroyer Squadron 77, nicknamed *the Silver Bullets* after the Lone Ranger of radio fame. Just before they'd left Hawaii, the eight ships in the squadron proudly painted their DESRON 77 logo, a red-and-white-striped shield overlaid with a large gleaming silver bullet, on their number one stack. The large numerals 77 were painted in a circle in the blue field at the top third of the shield.

Matthew also wearing her brand-new DESRON 77 emblem, was second in the lineup. Third in the column was the destroyer USS *Connelly* (DD 452), also in DESRON 77 livery. The other five destroyers were a day behind, having been assigned to another convoy.

It was early morning as the APAs stood into the channel

while the destroyers scurried about outside, looking for Japanese submarines.

Donovan lay in his sea cabin[27] bunk, fidgeting. Fully dressed, he waited for Burt Hammond to call up special sea detail for entering Ulithi Atoll. He didn't want to be on the bridge too early, lest they think he didn't trust them. Actually, he didn't trust them. They were simply too young and inexperienced. But he had to let them have their head or they wouldn't grow into their jobs, and then nothing would be accomplished. Right now, Burt Hammond was officer of the deck and Ensign Kenneth Muir was the junior officer of the deck.

It was humid and Donovan's porthole was open, a clear warning for people to be discreet when nearby. At times, though, the open porthole acted as an informal channel to the captain, a suggestion box, so to speak. And he'd heard the strangest things the past few days.

"Hey, Leon," a muffled voice called. It was laced with a thick Brooklyn accent Donovan knew belonged to Estes Schumacher, an eighteen-year-old seaman striking for gunner's mate.

"Yeah?" This voice belonged to Leon Constantine, a tall, lanky seaman with a large Adam's apple, also striking for gunner's mate.

"You hear the latest horseshit?"

"Yeah?"

"We got more drills scheduled after we load ammo."

"Plan of the day sez we get to hit the beach."

"Naw, Mister Manure has screwed us again with another horseshit exercise."

"Yeah?"

This was the second time this type of disrespect had been flaunted before Donovan. Two nights ago, another sailor had referred to Ensign Kenneth W. Muir III as Mister Manure. And now Schumacher and Constantine carried on this bizarre conversation near the captain's porthole.

Donovan recalled that last evening, he had jumped on Kruger about mediocre performance in the gun mounts. Their shooting just wasn't fast enough in recent exercises: six, sometimes seven seconds between rounds for each mount on the average. Not good enough. He wanted it (gunners called this interval dead time) down to three and a half to four seconds. Especially in case of air attack, he wanted the rounds pouring out. Accordingly, Kruger ordered Ensign Muir to schedule yet another loading-machine drill for this afternoon. The loading machine was a mock-up five-inch gun mounted aft near the quarterdeck where the gun crews practiced loading dummy fifty-five-pound projectiles and twenty-seven-pound powder cases. Keeping this up for ten or twenty minutes or longer took real stamina, and the ship's loaders weren't up to that level, Donovan could tell. It was a real slave-driving business, but that's what they needed: four seconds' dead time at the most. No more. And someone had to put on the heat. Otherwise they would die. It was that simple.

Recently they'd tried to set up competition among the mounts, giving rewards to the best crew performance: cigarettes, candy, extra sack time. But so far, it hadn't worked. They needed something else to really get into it, and Donovan racked his brain to figure out what it was.

The men were almost openly grousing. Donovan had been drilling them from the Golden Gate to Diamond Head. After a week's upkeep in Pearl Harbor, he drilled them again when they stood out to sea and shaped course for the Carolines and the Western Pacific. And now they were tired; he knew they deserved a break. Kruger had announced in today's plan of the day an afternoon on Mogmog where they could guzzle 3.2 beer.

Now he had to take it from them. Upon arrival, they were supposed to top off with ammunition, an activity that could take the rest of the morning and part of the afternoon. For the rest of the day, they would be working the loading machine instead of letting off steam on Mogmog. And he had to restrict the whole crew, not just the gunners.

"Did you hear me?" asked Schumacher in a clear voice.

"Huh?"

"We ain't goin' ashore, you idiot, that's what. Say, how'd you get in the second division, anyway?"

"Got ninety-five on the third-class gunner's test. Putting on my crow[28] next week."

"Oh."

There was a moment of silence, then Schumacher continued. “You know what pisses me off about all this crap?”

“Better button your lip. Cap’n can hear you.”

“I don’t give a rat’s ass. I’m not so dumb, either. I applied to sub school right out of boot camp. And I got it.”

“You? On the level?”

Schumacher’s voice rose a notch. “A TINS[29] message.”

“Shit-hot.”

“But then they kicked me out of sub school because they said my eyes were bad.”

“Tough.”

“So I don’t get it. They send me to the fleet and assign me to a lousy tin can and what do you know? Guess why we’re up here?”

“We’re supposed to be lookouts,” said Constantine.

“A gawd-damn lookout! So here I am, a friggin’ lookout. But not qualified for submarines because of poor eyesight. How far are you supposed to see in a damn submarine, anyway?”

“Far enough to find the shitter.”

“Hey, don’t screw with me.”

“Look. Maybe you should talk to Mister Manure.”

“Screw him. And screw this ship. And screw the loading machine.”

“Look out, here he comes . . . shhhh.” The voices moved off.

Donovan yanked the phone from its bracket and punched Kruger’s number.

“XO.”

“Need you up here, Richard.”

“On my way, sir.” He hung up.

Donovan sent Kruger out to relieve Hammond and Muir and take the deck and the conn.

There was a knock at the door. “Enter.”

Hammond and Muir walked in wearing light foul-weather jackets, binoculars dangling from their necks. It was tight as the three stood in Donovan’s sea cabin.

Hammond spread his hands. “You wanted to see us, Skipper?”

Donovan leaned over and made a show of slamming and dogging the porthole shut.

Hammond and Muir exchanged glances.

"When is sea detail, Mr. Hammond?"

Hammond checked his watch. "About five more minutes, sir."

"And where are we?" demanded Donovan.

"Sir?"

Donovan let his voice rise. "Where the hell are we, in relation to Rowaryu Channel?"

Hammond said, "Ahh, we're about three miles out. I was just getting ready to call you, sir."

"Did you read my standing orders."

"Of course, sir."

Donovan turned to Muir. "And you, Mr. Muir?"

Muir gulped and then replied, "Yes, sir. I read them, Captain."

Donovan slapped the bulkhead. "Then why the hell do you have these two stupid oafs out there as lookouts, grumbling and bitching about loading-machine exercises and not doing their jobs?"

"Who?"

"Schumacher and Constantine, that's who."

After a moment, Muir replied, "They're good men, Captain. Maybe a little young. But I put them on the watch bill myself."

"Well, let me tell you what they're doing." While Muir turned red at the reference to his name, Donovan repeated the details of what he'd heard through the porthole.

With a glance at Muir, Hammond said, "Sorry, sir. I'll talk to them."

"That's it?" asked Donovan.

"Well, er, yes, sir," replied Hammond.

"Well, that's not it. I want them relieved and sent below."

An eerie silence crept into the room.

"Sir?" managed Muir.

"I said, I want them relieved right now. If you had paid any attention to my standing orders, you would have learned that Rowaryu Channel was swept of mines a week ago but there is still danger, and in case you haven't checked, the minesweepers are still out there. This means we need eyes all over the ship—everywhere, checking for mines. So far, Mr. Hammond and Mr. Muir, you have placed this ship in jeopardy by posting incompetent, careless lookouts—men who bitch and grouse instead of doing their duty—and that is looking for mines and other hazards."

Hammond tried, "I'm sorry, Captain. I didn't realize that—"

"I know you didn't realize that was going on because you two didn't read my standing orders. And you didn't realize those two were leaning against the bulkhead endangering this ship and not doing their jobs. Now get out there and take care of this before I have you relieved as well." He jabbed a thumb at the doorway.

"Yes, sir." Hammond and Muir fairly ripped the door off its hinges and scrambled out.

Steaming at seventeen knots, the *Simpson, Matthew,* and *Connelly* stood into Rowaryu Channel at five-hundred-yard intervals. A twenty-knot westerly blew as they reduced speed to twelve knots and slewed through a following sea composed of choppy gray waves topped by whitecaps. Steering was tricky and La Valle, a 210-pound quartermaster, chomped gum furiously while working his helm, keeping the destroyer on its narrow track. Donovan stood on the bridge's port wing. Kruger was on the starboard side, with Hammond and Muir hovering over the chart in the pilothouse.

It seemed anticlimactic when they popped into the lagoon. The seas moderated; the bottom was almost visible through the blue, crystalline water.

Kruger wandered over and asked, "We done?"

Donovan said, "Right. We're okay for now. We should be hearing something shortly."

As if in response, a signal lamp began blinking from the *Simpson.* Hodges, a stocky second-class signalman, stood on the signal platform and began taking the message. With a cigarette dangling from his lips, Hodges energized his signal lamp and clacked a response to the *Simpson*'s flashing light. At the same time, he dictated *Simpson*'s message to a young striker, who transcribed it on a padded form.

With a final clack of his lamp, Hodges called, "BT." He

turned off his lamp, took the pad from the striker, and entered the date/time group. Then he tore the message off the pad and handed it to Donovan.

Donovan called Kruger, Hammond, and Muir and said, "It says, 'Proceed to area Mike Mike 35 for duty assigned.' Here." He handed the message to Hammond. "Plot the coordinates and give me a course. I suspect we'll find our ammunition ship anchored at Mike Mike 35."

"Yes, sir." Hammond walked into the pilothouse.

Simpson's signal lamp blinked again. Hodges was on it before anyone yelled, a sort of demented sport around the bridge. He flashed his response, then lit another cigarette and signed off, this time with a grin. Tearing the sheet off the pad, he gave it to Donovan with a flourish.

"I'll be damned," said Donovan.

"What?" asked Kruger.

"A baseball game." He handed over the message.

YOU UP FOR A BB GAME MOGMOG, SAY 1400?

Kruger's grin was as big as Hodges's. "Hell, yes. *Simpson* verses the *Matthew.* We'll beat the hell out of those pansies."

Hodges stood close by, his face expectant.

Donovan handed the message back to Hodges and said, "Tell them affirmative, but say 1600 vice 1400."

"Skipper, that's kinda late," said Kruger. "Curfew's at 1900."

"That's the way it has to be," said Donovan, who gestured to Hodges. "Go send it to them. Sixteen hundred."

Hodges's face darkened. "Yes, sir." He walked back to his platform and began transmitting.

"Can't we make an exception, Mike?" asked Kruger.

"Mr. Kruger. We have a job to do. Number one is to reprovision this ship. Number two is to become proficient on the loading machine. We're not quite ready to meet the enemy. So we need the time."

"But—"

Donovan turned to Kruger. "The hell with baseball. I'd just as soon live out this war. How about you, Mr. Kruger?" He fixed a stare.

"Yes, sir," said Kruger.

"Very well. Sixteen hundred then." Donovan walked off.

Hammond was back with the chart. Wordlessly, he pointed to the anchorage.

"Way the hell down there?" gasped Kruger.

"What's the distance?" demanded Donovan, raising his binoculars.

"Fourteen miles," said Hammond. "Bears one-nine-two."

"Very well, make it so. One-nine-two: twenty knots," replied Donovan.

Hammond gave the order, then stepped into the pilothouse to run his plot.

Kruger turned to Donovan and said softly, "We really not getting our boys ashore today?"

"Could be. Why?" asked Donovan.

"They'll crap in their pants, that's what."

"Can't be helped, Mr. Kruger."

"We'll have to do better than that. These guys need a break."

"Welcome to the war zone, Mr. Kruger. And you know something?"

"Sir?"

Donovan pointed to the west. "Plenty of Japs that way. Just over the horizon. After we mix with them, our boys will wish we were back here, doing loading-machine drills."

THIRTY-TWO

29 September 1944
USS *Matthew* (DD 548)
Moored starboard side to USS *Mount Saint Helens* (AE 21)
Area Mike Mike 35, Ulithi Atoll, Caroline Islands

They'd moored alongside the fourteen-thousand-ton ammunition ship just before the noon meal. Wolfing their food, the crew turned to at 1245 and began passing ammunition under a searing ten-degree north latitude sun. The plan was to load ammo, shove off, and head back to their anchorage near Mogmog Islet. En route, Donovan agreed to let the gun mount crews do their damn loading-machine drills and then head ashore for baseball.

The smoking lamp was out and an eerie silence descended on the *Matthew* as they began the grim business of loading. The usual in-port jocularity was absent as it occurred to the crew that these rounds were intended for an enemy not too far away.

Using her cargo booms, the *Mount Saint Helens* landed pallet load after pallet load of ammunition on the *Matthew*'s fo'c'sle, amidships, and fantail. From there, lines of shirtless sweating men snaked into the upper handling rooms of each of the *Matthew*'s five-inch gun mounts. Vent and exhaust blowers roared at full speed in the handling rooms, yet temperatures stood well over a hundred degrees as gunners fed their rounds into ammunition hoists and struck them below to the magazines. Breaks were called every twenty minutes, with men walking among the thirsty sailors carrying water jugs and paper cups. Donovan and Kruger eased among them, encouraging, slapping men on the rump, cajoling, joking, making them feel better about what was at hand.

While the five-inch ammunition was being struck below, other crews stowed a final allotment of forty- and twenty-millimeter rounds in ready service lockers beside the guns. Another pallet was landed containing ten cases of .45-caliber ball ammunition, two cases of hand grenades, and six cases of BAR ammo.

The torpedomen worked in their own world. They started on the fantail where the bare-chested, 250-pound chief torpedoman Cecil Hammer, a veteran of World War I, roared his commands. "Come on, you lazy bastards, mule haul!" Shoving his chief's hat back on his head, Hammer bellowed as the *Mount Saint Helens*'s crane operator eased three depth charges, three hundred pounds each, on the port stern rack to replace the ones rolled in practice two days previously.

Then they turned to their main task: rounding out ship's complement of ten mark 15 torpedoes. The ten torpedo bodies were already snug in their quintuplet tube mounts: mount one located forward of number two stack, mount two aft of the stack. The torpedo director platform was mounted on the forward part of the number two stack.

Only seven torpedoes had warheads, three having been used as exercise shots, with bright yellow warheads. They had already been disconnected and now stood nose-up on a pallet on the main deck, like three yellow soldiers. It was time to switch them and connect the mark 17 mod 3 warheads, each containing 825 pounds of HBX.

Jonathan Peete stood quietly beside Hammer as he barked orders to his torpedo gang. Soon the crane operator swung the three exercise warheads high in the air and took them over to the *Mount Saint Helens* to where he dropped them into her yawning hold. Two minutes later, a pallet of three mark 17 warheads was silently hoisted out of the ammunition ship's hold.

"Mr. Peete, d'ya mind?" asked Hammer.

"Yes?" replied Peete.

Hammer pointed with a massive arm. "The only place on this here ship that I can land my tarpeders is right where you're standin'."

Peete, who had been daydreaming, jerked his head up to see the pallet load of torpedoes swaying directly above his head. "Well that's a good idea, Chief. It wouldn't do to have a squashed ensign, would it?" He stepped aside.

"Uh, sir?"

"Kind of ruin your day wouldn't it? Lots of cleaning up to do, goo all over the place, forms to fill out. You wouldn't like that, would you, Chief?"

Hammer turned his back and twirled a finger for the crane operator. But Peete saw a corner of Hammer's mouth turn up as he bellowed, "C'mon, dammit, Gus. Get them damn things down here. We ain't got all day." Hammer and the *Mount Saint Helens*'s crane operator skillfully maneuvered the load of dull-bronze warheads to a soft landing on *Matthew*'s main deck near the torpedo crane. While the torpedomen began attaching the warheads, another pallet load of six bulky wooden crates was swung aboard. These crates contained mark 6 mod 13 torpedo exploders, each weighing ninety pounds.

Donovan finally discovered first-hand the attributes Admiral Nimitz saw in Kruger. Following the sound of muted curses and screams, Donovan made his way down to the second deck just above mount 52's lower handling room and peered through the hatch. The ammunition hoist had broken down, and hydraulic fluid sprayed everywhere while perspiration-soaked men cursed and slid on the deck. Without the hoist, gunner's mates formed lines down the hatchways so projectiles and powder would continue coming down, but at a much slower pace. Donovan called for Al Corodini and Reuben Sanchez, chief engineer and electrical officer. Within minutes, they scrambled down to the lower handling room packing thick manuals. Precious minutes passed as they spread schematics on the deck and scratched their heads, impervious to men working around them, cursing, slipping, as they desperately clutched their fifty-four-pound projectiles.

"Excuse me, Captain." It was Kruger, wearing his signature grease-stained overalls. He eased past Donovan and scrambled down the hatch. Unlike the bridge or CIC, Kruger had a presence in machinery spaces. People stepped aside respectfully as he examined the hoist. Donovan smiled inwardly: Richard Kruger, a forty-eight-year-old mustang, probably wouldn't go much further in the navy. In fact, he'd be lucky to retire as a lieutenant commander. But for now, Kruger was in his element: getting dirty, working with his boys, thoroughly enjoying life.

Within minutes, Kruger diagnosed the problem and had the hoist happily clanking and cycling down ammunition.

Dudley, a dark, wiry chief gunner's mate with a thick Brooklyn accent, stepped over and shook Kruger's hand. With a voice that could rip lumber, Dudley roared, "Gawddamn good job, Mr. Kruger. You saved our bacon."

"Thanks." Kruger looked up to Donovan and gave a thin smile.

Donovan returned it with a thumbs-up.

"Aw right, XO." Corodini slapped Kruger on the back.

Pushing the three officers and their bulging technical manuals toward the ladder, Dudley said, "Now, if youse gentlemen will excuse us, we got woik to do."

Except for the ammunition hoist breakdown in mount 52, Donovan marveled at how quickly everything progressed. All due to the promise of a few hours and a couple of cheap beers on Mogmog. By 1500, the ammunition was aboard, the gunners and torpedomen securing their loads. The boatswain's mate of the watch called away groaning gun crews, who made their way to the loading machine on the quarterdeck.

On the bridge, sea detail was set with Al Corodini as OOD. The *Mount Saint Helens* pulled in the gangways and, the boatswain's mates singled up the lines without permission from the bridge. Donovan chose to overlook it.

Still wearing his engineer's overalls, Kruger walked up to Donovan and reported, "Special sea detail set, Captain. Engineering department ready for getting under way."

Donovan's eyebrows rose. *What about the other departments?*

Kruger said, "Actually, everybody is ready for getting under way. But those people on the *Saint Helens* haven't finished sorting our mail."

"Why not?"

"P5M delivered it just this morning. Our stuff is still mixed up with mail for the *Simpson* and the *Connelly*."

"Can't they send it later?"

"Yes, but there's guard mail for us in there, too."

"Meaning we have to have someone accompany it?"

"Yes, sir. Duty belt, .45 and all. So someone is going to be gypped out of our baseball game and a few beers. So I asked Ensign Muir if he wouldn't mind doing it."

"Shouldn't he be on the loading-machine drills?"

"Normally, yes, sir. But much of the guard mail is gunnery doctrine; Muir can organize it quickly. I figure we can have Cliff Merryweather supervise the drills. It's really his apple anyway."

"Okay with me."

"They figure another hour, then they'll send Muir to us in an LCM."

"Very well," said Donovan. "That it?"

"Yes, sir," said Kruger. "Other than that, we're ready in all respects."

"Right," said Donovan. He turned to Al Corodini. "You may get us under way, Mr. Corodini."

Flicking a cigarette over the side, Corodini stood on the bridge wing platform and drew to his full height. "Yes, sir." Then he shouted into the pilothouse, "This is Mr. Corodini. I have the conn." After acknowledgments, he shouted toward the fo'c'sle, "Single up all lines."

Donovan stepped over and said quietly, "Mr. Corodini, we're already singled up."

Unfazed, Corodini said, "Hell, this just ain't my day."

Donovan shrugged. Someone giggled.

Rubbing his jaw, Corodini roared at the fo'c'sle again, "Take in lines one and three."

Potter's relay was superfluous as the lines began snaking in. Corodini's voice was still echoing between the ships forward when he shouted to the fantail, a good two hundred feet away, "Take in lines four, five, and six."

Corodini was putting on a show, as if he were back on the gridiron at Ohio State. And it was catching. Portholes popped open next door. Sailors undogged hatches and walked on deck to watch the *Matthew* get under way. Kenneth Muir sauntered out on the *Mount Saint Helens*'s bridge, two decks above, and looked down upon them, a tall glass of iced tea in his hands.

In a voice worthy of a courtroom barrister, Corodini shouted, "Rudder amidships. Port engine ahead one-third, starboard engine astern, one-third." Bells clanked and men in the pilothouse acknowledged the orders with Corodini clicking off his "very wells" like a tobacco auctioneer. With one hand, he lit another cigarette, took a huge drag, looked up to Muir, and said loudly, "You play ball?"

"Not football."

"What then?" demanded Corodini as he leaned over the bridge bulwarks, watching the screws churn froth back aft.

Muir said, "Varsity third base at the University of Oklahoma."

Donovan, Kruger, and Corodini all exchanged glances. "We'll delay the game as long as possible," shouted Kruger.

Muir raised his iced tea. "That's all right, sir. I could get used to this. This ship's air-conditioned. Mighty fine in there."

Kruger shouted, "Mr. Muir. You get that damn mail sorted and report to us ASAP. That's an order."

"Doing my best, XO." Muir grinned. He took a long sip of iced tea, then sauntered to a hatch, swung the dogging lever, stepped in, and closed it behind.

Corodini shouted, "Take in two. All back two-thirds." Then he turned to Kruger, "Air-conditioning, XO? How the hell does he rate?"

"Little bastard held out on us. I'll pull his ass through a knothole," growled Kruger.

"Sound one long blast," ordered Corodini, grinning from ear to ear.

They worked up to seventeen knots and secured from sea detail five minutes later. Merryweather hovered nearby with a stopwatch as gun crews worked the loading machine. The projectile loaders were broad, beefy men who lifted their dummy fifty-four-pound rounds from the hoist and plunked them on the ramming tray. Other crews cheered or catcalled or whistled as each crew stepped in, furiously working at three-minute intervals.

Donovan and Kruger stood in shadows on the signal bridge watching the workout. Drinking coffee, they enjoyed the wind that rustled their hair and cooled their faces while beneath, the ship carved a brilliant white wake in the deep blue lagoon.

Kruger leaned on the bulwark and said, "Vicky should really see this. Maybe I can bring her back here after the war." He looked up. "You think I can do that?"

"I don't see why not." After a moment, Donovan said, "Please forgive me for prying, but how . . . how did she . . . ?"

"You mean land in a wheelchair?"

"Ummm."

"Me."

"Pardon?"

"It was my fault."

"I don't understand."

Kruger sipped and looked from side to side. Seeing nobody in earshot, he said softly, "Damn loser." He looked up. Donovan said nothing, so he went on. "I'd married and divorced twice. Both of them bad, bad deals. 'Course I was a loser, too. Then I met Vicky. What a knockout. And man oh man, she understood me. Kept me in check. Did you know she's Rocky Jennings's daughter?"

"Jennings? The two-star?" Recently retired from the navy, Rocky Jennings had worked his way up from bosun's mate as an early innovator in naval diving and salvage.

"That's him. And he stood aside and let me date her. It didn't hurt to have Chester Nimitz paving the way, either. We dated for nearly two years . . .

"But she couldn't stop me at times."

"From what?"

"Booze, that's what," Kruger fairly spat. "I would get carried away.

"Then, one night . . . I was sloshed. Really stupid. She had this neat Chevy convertible I loved." He looked up to Donovan, his fist clenched. "I drove the damn thing into a tree. She was ejected. I had minor cuts and bruises."

"My God. You don't have to . . ."

Kruger's eyes turned red. "Yes, it was horrible. She was bent up horribly; a cripple. I felt like running—maybe the Foreign Legion. But then I talked to the chaplain and he suggested the damndest thing." He paused.

"Yes?"

"Marry her. Wheelchair and all. And that's what I did, six months ago. She did me the great honor of accepting. But it wasn't easy for either of us."

It grew silent. Donovan asked, "Is there a chance of . . . ?"

"Walking again? We don't know. The docs aren't encouraging. Severe spinal cord damage, they tell us. But we keep trying. We keep—hey." Kruger pointed. "What the hell?"

Donovan looked aft into the port forty-millimeter gun tub to see Burt Hammond shove Jonathan Peete against the platform railing. Peete shoved back. Hammond took a swing, but missed.

"Sonofabitch." Donovan was down the ladder in two seconds, Kruger right behind. They were in the gun tub five seconds later, standing between the two red-faced officers. Hammond threw another punch. To Donovan's amazement, the smaller Kruger stepped in, deflected it, spun Hammond around, and slammed him against the forty-millimeter ready service locker. "Knock it off, sailor, before I put your lights out," he growled.

Donovan stepped before Peete. "What the hell's going on?"

Heaving in great gulps, Peete clenched and unclenched his fists. "Dumb shit came after me, that's what."

Hammond cursed.

Kruger grabbed his shoulders and barked, "I told you to knock it off!"

Donovan shouted, "Dammit. You two want me to slap you in chains?" He looked about. Miraculously, no one had seen—or at least they weren't letting on. The loading machine clanked merrily below as the drills went on, the mount crews awaiting their turns. "Now, what's going on?" Donovan demanded.

Hammond looked away.

Donovan said, "You better start talking, Lieutenant, or I'm stuffing you down the chain locker."

Hammond curled a lip. "He insulted my fiancée, that's what."

Donovan and Kruger looked at Hammond. "Fiancée? You?" gasped Donovan. "I didn't know you were engaged."

Hammond's shoulders slumped. "Yes, sir. About four months ago."

"To whom?"

"Velma Johnson."

"The actress?" Kruger and Donovan said simultaneously.

"Yes, sir," said Hammond.

"Well, I'll be damned," said Kruger. "But then what's all this. . . . ?"

Hammond stiffened and pointed. "Little Johnnie Hollywood here called her a whore. A punchboard."

Peete stood erect and spread his hands. "I had no idea he knew her. What are the chances of anyone out here knowing someone in Hollywood? Anyway, I might have been exaggerating a little. I only dated her twice. The first time was to—"

The afternoon sky lit up. A thundering crack threw them to the deck. That was followed by a rolling explosion of violence Donovan had never seen. He knew he'd been on the deck for four or five seconds but he couldn't get up. Nor could he hear. Only ringing in his ears. He looked over, finding Kruger trying to rise.

With a groan, Donovan got to his knees. Grabbing the bulwark, he struggled to his feet. An enormous gray-black cloud of smoke and fire roiled high overhead, blocking the sun. Metal chunks, some the size of gun turrets, fell about the ship. Something hot and metallic thumped against Donovan's left shoulder and clanged to the deck.

Someone tugged Donovan's shirt. It was Hammond, mouthing, "What happened?" Nobody could hear, he knew, but Donovan said it anyway. "The *Mount Saint Helens*. She's gone."

Kruger pointed down to the main deck. The men around the loading machine lay on the deck as if shoved over by a giant hand. A few tried to sit. One bled profusely from a cut over his eye.

A white-faced Jonathan Peete was shouting. Donovan couldn't hear, but he knew what the ensign was saying. "Muir! What about Kenny Muir?"

THIRTY-THREE

17 October 1944
IJN radar station
Suluan Island
Leyte Gulf, Philippines

Radar Operator Second Class Kozuko Tomura groaned, lifted a bamboo curtain, and peered outside. Lightning flashed and thunder shook the little four-man hut. Reluctantly he rose from his mat and pulled on shorts, shirt, and overcoat as the others snored. Slipping into split-toed sandals, he ventured outside. It was just before sunrise but still very dark as the storm raged overhead. Tomura clicked on his flashlight to find his path to the beach.

Lieutenant Hara, a fat pig of a garrison officer, wanted the lobster traps checked. Forget about the weather, Hara had screamed last night. Make sure those traps are holding. Better yet, see if they have a catch. Hara was entertaining the major tonight, and he wanted no mistakes; he only wanted lobsters.

Reveille was at 0700, and Tomura didn't have to relieve the radar watch until 0745. So he had plenty of time to find out if the trap was loaded so Hara could slop up fresh lobster at dinner tonight. The wind blew harder as he drew near the windward side of Suluan Island. It was thirty-two kilometers southeast of Leyte Gulf's wide, yawning mouth, with no protection from the storm raging from the east. Tomura shuddered when he thought about Suluan being the easternmost landfall off the islands of Leyte and Samar. After that, it was the Palau Islands, twelve hundred kilometers to the southeast. No comfort from that direction, he realized. The Palaus were now in American hands.

The storm that had been pummeling Suluan for the past two days gave him a bizarre sense of peace. They'd had the briefings. If the Americans were to invade Leyte, he'd been told, it would start right here. Also on the Americans' list would be three other outlying islands: Dinagat, Hibuson, and Homonhon. And for good reason. Each of the four islands had lookout garrisons and radar stations; they would have to be silenced also. But what about the minefields? How would the Americans take care of that?

The light was better as Tomura found the rocky path down a cliffside. Lightning flashed, thunder ripped the sky, and fist-size rocks tumbled down the cliff. He heard the ocean before he saw it; large waves rose and smashed against the rocks, vomiting their energy in great white sheets of spume. He checked his watch: 0645. It should have been much lighter, but the overcast just wasn't cooperating.

At last, he saw the ocean. Waves smacked the shore, sending foam high in the air. If that wasn't enough, the wind shrieked at more than forty knots, the sheer noise almost incomprehensible. Farther out, waves rose and crashed into each other, the ocean a confused morass of grays and anthracite blacks. He searched in vain for the buoys marking the lobster traps. No luck finding his offshore trapline. But to his left was a cove where he had laid four more traps. It looked fairly decent in there. A small banca was stowed in the rocks, and he wondered if he had time to launch, paddle out, and check for game. He looked back over his shoulder. No one was there. Nonetheless, Lieutenant Hara would kill him if he didn't at least try.

Okay. Back in fifteen minutes. The banca was where he'd left it yesterday, safely nestled among rocks. He kneeled to pick up the bow.

Something . . . something. He peered eastward, out to sea. It was getting light, but the visibility was still poor, maybe one to two thousand meters, he guessed. But something was out there. Radar Operator-Second-Class Kozuko Tomura cupped his hands around his eyes and peered again. A fifty-knot gust nearly knocked him over, and he braced himself against a wet rock. Simultaneously thunder cracked and a wave crashed a few meters away, sending salt spray high in the air.

There! It cleared and he saw a ship. No. Two ships. Big ones. Cruiser . . . maybe battleship size. Several smaller ones were there also. Destroyers? And behind them, even smaller ones. Another wave crashed and a cloud scudded past, obscuring the ships. Instinctively Tomura knew, but he wanted confirmation. Another gust of wind was followed by a loud series of crashing waves. Then the clouds parted. There they were. Closer. Radar blips were Tomura's game, and he tried to recall silhouettes he'd seen in recognition manuals. Racking his brain, he couldn't come up with Japanese silhouettes matching the ones he saw now. No . . . it can't be, he mouthed. Not in this kind of weather.

There was a flash from one of the lead ships and something whistled overhead, sounding like a freight train. The shell exploded inland near his camp. Then another, and another. Shells all around. Tomura didn't realize he was running until he slipped on the path up the cliff. He grabbed a piece of scrub brush, and that stopped his slide. Fortunate. Had he gained the crest, he would have been shredded by a shell exploding nearby.

More shells. Kozuko Tomura was pinned down as naval gunfire raged all around him. The Americans were walking the barrage from the beach to the garrison and back. Devastating. Why the hell were they out there shooting now? In such horrible weather.

Another shell crashed just meters away and lifted him. He fell among boulders with pain gnawing up his leg. His wind was knocked out and it hurt to breathe. But he braced himself among the rocks and clasped his hands over his head. His heart thumped in his chest, and he grit his teeth wondering if this was it for him. As the bombardment went on, however, Tomura wondered, of all things, about his lobster traps.

It was 0845 in Lingga Roads when Noyama tried to run up a ladder to the flag deck of the IJN *Atago.* Storm clouds roiled from the east as he stumbled his way to the bridge. But pain ranged up and down his bad leg, forcing him to wait. He was breathing hard; he was so out of shape. One deck to go.

"In a hurry, Noyama?" asked Commander Akira Nakayama, the *Atago*'s gunnery officer, a set of binoculars dangling from his neck.

Noyama waved a flimsy radio message toward the deck above. "The admiral . . ." was all he could wheeze.

"Here, let me take it."

Nakayama reached over, but Noyama waved it off. "Most secret," he gasped, leaning heavily on the rail.

Nakayama gave Noyama that look of disdain, so common to armies and navies of the world, in which the line officer accuses the staff officer of abject laziness and privilege.

"Thanks anyway." Noyama continued his climb to the flag deck, slower this time. Once there, the sentry opened the door for him. He stepped inside, headed down the passageway, and rapped sharply on the oak door.

"No." The voice was hoarse.

"Admiral, I must see you," shouted Noyama fairly clearly. "We have a signal."

"No!"

"Please, sir, it's urgent. It's from from Admiral Toyoda."

A moment passed. Then, ". . . all right. But no lights."

Noyama opened the door and walked in, finding Kurita's cabin almost pitch black. With the overcast outside, there wasn't much light to begin with.

"Sir?"

There was a gasping sound from the bunk in the corner.

"Admiral, what's wrong?" Barely able to see, Noyama rushed over and fumbled with the light switch over Kurita's bunk.

"Leave that alone," Kurita ordered. "Now tell me, what is it?"

"Dispatch from Admiral Toyoda, sir."

"You already told me that. Where is he now?"

"According to this, he's airborne heading back to Tokyo."

"And?" demanded Kurita.

"It looks like this is it."

Sheets rustled. Noyama's eyes were adjusting to the darkness, and he saw Kurita's form rise from the bed.

"Arrrrgh."

"Sir, what's wrong?" Noyama asked.

"Up all night puking. Splitting headache. Feel like my eyes are going to pop out." He clicked on the light and fumbled for his glasses.

Noyama had to admit the old man looked like a slab of bleached concrete. He also had a good idea what was wrong. He'd seen plenty of it in the Solomons. He handed over the message.

While Kurita adjusted his glasses, Noyama asked, "Anything I can get you, sir?"

"No, dammit. Koketsu was in here about half an hour ago. He gave me some pills." Captain Senjuro Koketsu was the fleet surgeon.

"What did he say?"

"Dengue fever. He took some blood and gave me aspirin."

Noyama groaned.

Kurita flashed a red-eyed look of anger. "Yes, lucky me."

"Is that why you didn't feel well last night?" Kurita had flown his staff into Singapore last night aboard his H8K2 Kawanishi flying boat. They had dined in splendor at the restaurant in the famous Raffles Hotel on Beach Road overlooking the harbor.

"I imagine."

"I'm sorry, Admiral."

"Hand me my robe."

Noyama fumbled in a pile of clothing strewn about the deck and found a silk magenta robe. Kurita wobbled to his feet and Noyama helped him poke his spindly arms through. Kurita thrust out an arm and Noyama handed over the message. He nodded. " 'Alert, SHO-1.' The Americans must be on their way."

"Yes, sir."

Someone rapped at the door. Noyama walked over and opened it, finding a flag radioman standing at attention. "I'll take it." He signed for the message, walked to Kurita's bunk, and handed it over. "Another message from CinC Combined Fleet, sir."

Kurita adjusted his glasses again and squinted at the message. "It says that a large American group of cruisers and destroyers bombarded Suluan, Dinagat, Hibuson, and Homonhon islands. Then they sent troops ashore and took the islands. Minesweepers are now working the channel into Leyte Gulf." He paused. "Toyoda is executing SHO-1, the Philippine Battle Plan."

He looked up to Noyama. "If I know anything about General MacArthur, he won't be far behind those minesweepers." Groaning, he fumbled at the sash, then finally tied it. "Call . . . call a staff meeting in half an hour"—he checked his watch—"at 1030. Lay out our contingency plans. And send a preparatory signal to all ships to raise steam, top off with fuel, and prepare to get under way."

"Yes, sir."

Kurita shuffled toward a small door. Then he stumbled and almost fell.

"Admiral!" Noyama rushed over.

Kurita waved him off. "Go. Go do what I said."

"Yes, sir."

"And Noyama." Kurita's voice sounded a bit stronger. It had some timbre.

"Sir?"

"Get that damn Koketsu back up here. And hand me my pants."

THIRTY-FOUR

18 October 1944
IJN *Atago*
Lingga Roads

The warships of the First Striking Force waited expectantly, their anchors at short stay. Steam was up, boats were griped in their davits, and loose gear was secured. It had rained earlier and the decks were still wet, but now, at just after midnight, the atmosphere was thick with the humidity that hovered at a shirt-soaking ninety-five percent. Mercifully, a light wind blew out of the northeast, carrying a promise of cooler and drier air.

A three-quarter moon shimmered over an anthracite sea, letting the night develop a character all of its own. Each man, from the lowest enlisted to the top flag-ranked officer, wondered what lay ahead. After months of waiting and planning and shouting at one another, they were poised to take action, whether it was good, bad, or indifferent. They were going to strike back, and stealth was the order of the moment. Lest prying eyes report their movement, they would wait until after moonset to get under way; all communication would be by flag hoist or flashing light. Radar and radio transmission was forbidden.

It was crowded on the *Atago*'s starboard bridge wing. Noyama was shoved between the pelorus and the bulwark. Besides the underway watch, Captain Araki, the commanding officer, the exec, and what seemed like the whole flag staff had turned out. Noyama didn't complain. Indeed, the occasion seemed historic, and he felt privileged to be up here with these men, their tired old jokes barely covering the tension.

All eyes were fixed either on the moon or the destroyer *Yukikaze*, anchored just five hundred meters off the port bow. In accordance with the SHO-1 op order, she would be first to get under way.

The unspoken question on the bridge was about the old man's condition. Dr. Koketsu, constantly at the admiral's side, was not talking. Neither was Kurita. Hard to read, he nevertheless seemed vital, the timbre in his voice near par. Just a few minutes ago, laughter ranged on the bridge as the old man hissed at someone in an exaggerated voice, "I'm fine, you damn fool. And you better be, too, because I don't want excuses from anybody." A good sign, Noyama thought, as he peered into the night.

Conversation became sporadic and stopped altogether as the moon dropped to the western horizon. When the lower limb touched Sumatra, they held their collective breath. Moments later, the yellow spherical orb descended behind sharp volcanic peaks and was gone. Noyama checked his watch: 0029. Except for a massive carpet of stars overhead, it was pitch black. And it was quiet, almost eerie.

Moonset was the signal. Rear Admiral Seiichi Abe, Kurita's chief of staff, turned aft and grunted in a hoarse voice, *"Hai!"*

The fleet signalman, a first-class petty officer, anticipated the order. He switched on his lantern and, with a red-lensed flashlight, double-checked the fleet code signal on his message pad. Satisfied, he swiveled the signal lantern toward the *Yukikaze* and clacked the lever. The bright, pencil-thin beam stabbed the darkness: Dah-dit-dit-dit-dit.

YOU HAVE PERMISSION TO RAISE ANCHOR AND GET UNDER WAY.

He did it once more. Dah-dit-dit-dit-dit.

The *Yukikaze* flashed back a single dash.

UNDERSTOOD.

Almost immediately, Noyama heard the *Yukikaze*'s anchor clanking up her hawse pipe. Soon, for there was a collective release of breath as the *Yukikaze*'s anchor housed with a hollow *thud.* Noyama caught a whiff of the ship's stack gas as her engineers cracked her throttles. She was the first destroyer of DESRON 10 to get under way. In minutes, her sisters raised anchor, cleared the log boom, and slipped out to sweep for submarines. Joining them were the destroyers of DESRON 2. After that, the cruisers raised anchor and slipped through the log boom. Following them were the battleships, all veterans of previous battles. Last to clear the log boom were the massive superbattleships *Yamato* and *Musashi,* ponderous, powerful, and sinister.

Long, rolling swells greeted the *Atago,* making her pitch easily as she steamed due east into the Natuna Sea. Kurita checked aft, waiting until they were all out. When his fleet had safely exited, he flashed the next message. It was 0127 on 18 October.

Dit-dah, dit-dit-dit. Dit-dah, dit-dit-dit.

FORM NIGHT FORMATION.

It took twenty-two nail-biting minutes for the destroyers to sort themselves into six columns. The cruisers and battleships wove in between them, taking another twenty minutes. Finally it was done. No collisions. Satisfied they were properly arranged, Kurita summoned Noyama and spoke quietly. Noyama stepped into the red-lighted pilothouse and wrote on a message blank. He signed it and handed it to the chief signalman. Two minutes later, the signal lamps blinked to all units:

COURSE 046°, SPEED 20 KNOTS.

Kurita's striking force turned left to shape course for Brunei for refueling and then resumption of the war.

THIRTY-FIVE

19 October 1944
Flag wardroom
USS *Nashville* (CL 43)
Leyte Gulf, Philippines

General MacArthur had called a staff meeting at 2000. It was a little past 2300 when, yawning and scratching, they got to the last item on the agenda: the draft of a short speech the general would deliver after stepping ashore tomorrow. The room grew silent as mimeographed pages were passed out.

Lieutenant Colonel Owen Reynolds was fidgety. So he laid the paper down to read while sitting on his hands.

At length everyone looked up.

"Well?" asked MacArthur.

Someone coughed. Finally, Dr. Roger O. Egeberg, MacArthur's physician, said, "General, with all respect, sir . . ."

"Go on, Roger."

"It stinks. It's a cliché."

MacArthur's eyes narrowed. The only sound was that of exhaust blowers. "Ummm," he murmured.

But when it became obvious MacArthur wasn't going to chew Egeberg's head off, Willoughby jumped in. "Too much Christianity," he complained.

"It's cornball," said Lieutenant General Richard Sutherland, MacArthur's aide. Everybody else went the me-too route and began clamoring to be heard. For Reynolds, the smoke was too thick, their voices too strident, and the walls were pressing in.

"Excuse me, gentlemen." No one paid attention as Reynolds scraped his chair back, stood, and walked for the door. A marine sentry opened it for him and he stepped into the night. The hatch banged shut behind and he was relieved to see the weather had moderated from the windy and choppy seas of today. Amazing, it was so dark Reynolds couldn't see one hundred feet away. And plenty of other ships were out there, nestled in their own little cocoons. Amazing, too, that no one ran into each other: the miracle of radar. *Nashville* was darkened, enveloped in a mist that gave Reynolds a sense of isolation and comfort, distancing him from the others and the living hell that was to be waged on the enemy tomorrow.

The general's flagship, a light cruiser of the *Brooklyn* class, hardly rolled as she paced lazily in a racetrack pattern around a point designated Point Fin, an arbitrary position approximately twenty miles southeast of Dinagat Island near the entrance to Leyte Gulf. Like the other Seventh Fleet ships, they were just marking time.

The invasion was on. Suluan, Dinagat, Hibuson, and Homonhon islands were now occupied, the minefields swept, and the *Nashville* waited along with 738 other ships of Admiral Kinkaid's Seventh Fleet for tomorrow, 20 October: General MacArthur's "A-Day," the day scheduled for the invasion of Leyte Gulf.

Reynolds splayed his hands before his face. Again they shook. He grabbed the rail, hard, and squeezed until his knuckles turned white. Damn hands! That hadn't happened since he'd been shot on Bougainville. It had been a vicious little firefight. They'd been ambushed, and Reynolds was trapped in the open. He was sure it was coming. And then it came. The shot hit him in the rump and flipped him on his back. He cried and prayed and played dead for twenty eternal minutes as the battle raged around him. Reynolds had almost bled to death by the time reinforcements arrived, and his hands shook for the next ten days until a crusty old army nurse walked in his room and yelled at him to knock it off.

A tear ran down Reynolds's cheek. But he was afraid to wipe at it, lest he release his death grip from the rail and his hands begin shaking again.

Those damn photographs had brought it all back! The

greatest mistake in his military career was admitting he knew something about photography. General MacArthur wanted photographs of the invasion force off Leyte, so Reynolds was stuck with the job. This morning, they'd strapped him in the rear cockpit of a low-winged Vought-Sikorsky Kingfisher, one of the *Nashville*'s catapult-launched observation floatplanes. They fired him off over whitecapped seas, and the Kingfisher clawed for altitude.

Actually, the Kingfisher wasn't that bad. It was the pilot, a thin, pop-eyed ensign, Elmer Dodd, who scared Reynolds. Fresh from amphibious flight training in Corpus Christi, Texas, the kid had just joined the fleet. Frustrated that he'd been passed over for fighters and bombers, Ensign Dodd grumbled and bitched about everything until Reynolds pulled rank and told him to shut up and just get the trembling, wheezing Kingfisher up to ten thousand feet.

When they reached their altitude, Reynolds leaned out of the Kingfisher's rear cockpit and clicked his pictures. As he did, it seemed these ships not only stretched from horizon to horizon, but over several horizons. He marveled at the men-of-war lying down there; engines of death populated with young men and boys who, just a year ago, were baling hay or jerking sodas or chasing girls. Among the 738 ships maneuvering below were eighty combatants. Six of these were old battleships, five of which had been raised from the muck of Pearl Harbor, now poised to deliver vengeance. Screening the battleships were three heavy cruisers, five light cruisers, and forty-eight destroyers.

There were also eighteen "escort carriers," divided into three groups of six each along with their destroyer screens. The carriers' decks were built on ponderous, single-screw merchant ship hulls, capable of no more than eighteen knots. But these "baby flattops," as they were known, were crucial to the invasion. The fighters were to provide combat air patrol for the Seventh Fleet while the bombers were to do bombardment and other ground support work for the troops ashore. Reynolds clicked away, realizing Mike Donovan was down in that mess. He made a note to look him up to see if he were close by when he returned to the *Nashville*. Close to the Leyte coast were the hundreds of amphibious and service ships supporting the 160,000 ground troops of General J. R. Hodges's XXIV Corps and Major General F. C. Silbert's X Corps who would storm ashore over the next two days.

And this wasn't the end of it. One hundred miles farther out, Halsey's Third Fleet paced back and forth. Responsible for overall protection of Kinkaid's Seventh Fleet and the disembarked troops, Halsey had eighty-five of the U.S. Navy's newest warships. This included eight *Essex*-class carriers, eight light carriers, six fast battleships,[30] six heavy cruisers, nine light cruisers, and forty-eight destroyers.

Time to go home; he'd shot two rolls. Reynolds had just picked up the intercom mike when something jarred the little Kingfisher. Smoke poured from her Pratt & Whitney R-985 radial engine. The canopy glass shattered around him and his instrument panel disintegrated. Something flashed overhead and swooped into a climbing turn. Reynolds was sure his heart stopped when he focused on the sleek airplane's pale green wings and fuselage. There were bright red orbs near the wing tips. *Meatball! A Zero. That was a Jap!*

Reynolds shouted into his mike, "Elmer! Elmer! Did you see that?"

Silence. Reynolds looked up and to his left. The Zero was halfway through its turn. He'd be back on them in thirty seconds. *Thirty seconds to live. Oh, dear God.* "Elmer! Do we bail out?" Reynolds shouted, his eyes fixed on the Zero.

"Shut up, dammit," Dodd shouted back. He flipped the Kingfisher into a hard right bank and soon they were in one of the white puffy clouds that dominated the skies.

That was when Reynolds's hands began to shake. Just like on Bougainville, he'd known it was coming. Just like on Bougainville, he'd been exposed and there was nothing he could do about it. Just like on Bougainville, he'd wanted to crap in his pants. Tears ran from his eyes; bitter frustration and anger was lodged in his heart. "Ensign Dodd, what is going on?" yelled Reynolds.

"Losing oil, sir," came the response. "Think the sonofabitch hit our oil reserve tank and—" They burst from the cloud. The Zero shot past, smoking heavily, its pilot slumped over the instrument panel. Two F6F Hellcats followed, squeezing off rounds from their .50-caliber machine guns. With a gloved hand, the pilot of the second Hellcat waved casually as he flashed past.

But Reynolds couldn't wave back. His hands still shook.

"Damn," muttered Dodd. "They told us they'd wiped out the Jap air force." The Kingfisher's engine backfired and caught.

"Looks like they forgot to check with Tojo," said Reynolds. "We gonna make it?"

"Yes, sir. This thing will glide forever. That is, if there's no more Japs out there."

"If one comes again, I'll get his picture," said Reynolds drily.

Reynolds was still clutching the rail when someone moved beside him. He looked up. "Evening, General."

MacArthur nodded. "You okay, Owen?"

"Of course, sir."

"Thanks for getting those pictures. They turned out just fine. Glad to hear they bagged that Jap."

"Thank you, General," lied Reynolds.

The mist had cleared, and they watched as a destroyer overtook them steaming regally along their starboard side. She was close enough to hear her exhaust vent howling. But it was strange. Reynolds couldn't see a sign of anyone on her weather decks, or bridge, not even the glint of binoculars: a ghost ship.

"You didn't offer any thoughts about my statement tomorrow," asked MacArthur.

Statement. Strange word. Reynolds said, "Wasn't trying to duck the issue, General. The smoke just got too thick in there for me. I needed fresh air."

"Can you believe Egeberg?" asked MacArthur.

"There was a lot coming from every direction," hedged Reynolds.

MacArthur turned to Reynolds. "I repeat. You didn't give your opinion in there. You're the only holdout."

"General, I don't think that I'm qualified to—"

"That's an order, Colonel," MacArthur said gently.

Doing his best to steady his hands, Reynolds said, "I'd play it the way you have it. It's not meant for people back home.

It's meant for the Philippine people. Yes, it may sound cornball to the Average American Joe, but these aren't average Josés out here. They're Hectors and Pablos and Carmellas. And their tastes are different. They're more simple. They don't need a lot of politics and whoop-de-do." Reynolds looked aside for a moment, then added, "No, sir. I don't go along with those in there. I wouldn't change a word."

MacArthur looked out to sea. "I love it here. And soon I'll again walk on Philippine soil. You know, this message is from the heart. That's what I really feel right now. That's what I want to say."

"I'd go with that, General."

"Thank you, Owen."

"Yes, sir."

"Everything lined up for tomorrow?"

Reynolds's task in the morning was to land with the third wave on "Red Beach," near Tacloban, and make sure the quartermasters properly set up a mobile broadcasting connection to the Armed Forces Radio Network. Later, when it was safe, the general, his staff, Philippine president Sergio Osmeña,[31] and Resident Commissioner Carlos Romulo were to come ashore and gather around to listen as MacArthur delivered his speech. "All set, General."

MacArthur waved a finger under Reynolds's nose. "Don't forget to wear your helmet and to pack plenty of Atabrine tablets[32]." MacArthur's tone was like that of a drill instructor admonishing recruits to use condoms when going into town on furlough.

"On my bunk, General."

"Very good, Owen. See you tomorrow at Red Beach." The general turned and walked back inside.

THIRTY-SIX

20 October 1944
USS *Nashville* (CL 43)
Northern Transport Area
San Pedro Bay, Leyte Gulf, Philippines

Admiral Thomas Kinkaid, Commander of the Seventh Fleet, wrestled with the decision of when to enter the gulf. Finally he picked 0200 and so, by the hundreds, ships began slipping into Leyte Gulf. Hours later, they were in the green waters of San Pedro Bay, the gulf's northern extremity, where they anchored according to a masterfully choreographed plan. The amphibious ships inshore, combatants farther out; the latter included three old battleships, *Mississippi, Maryland,* and *West Virginia,* along with countless cruisers and destroyers.

The landing force consisted of two groups. The Northern Transport Group was ready to land at an area designated Red Beach and White Beach just two miles south of Tacloban City. Seven miles south, troops of the Southern Transport Group were poised to assault Orange, Blue, Violet, and Yellow beaches.

The navy crews had been up all night at battle stations. For the troops, reveille was at 0430; chow was served at 0500.

A-Day dawned hazy and muggy, the sun's first rays heralding a massive shore bombardment. The battleships, cruisers, and destroyers opened up as navy TBFs and SB2Cs swooped down with engines screaming, bombing enemy positions. Several columns of smoke soon rose along the beach, the coastal plain, and around Tacloban, Leyte's capital. Dozens of assault boats swarmed about, crammed with troops, their diesel engines growling: LCVPs, LCMs, and the bigger LCIs. At 0800, the bombardment was walked five hundred yards inland, and the first of sixteen waves swarmed ashore. Resistance was light, and by 1000, when the second wave came in, the first wave had fought their way three hundred yards inland.

A group of ponderous, flat-bottomed LSTs followed the second wave and drove themselves up on White Beach. Expecting a Japanese counterattack from the sea, they frantically disgorged their cargoes, trying to get away before sunset.

Peering through binoculars, Owen Reynolds was perched on the gunnery officer's platform, two decks above the bridge of the *Nashville*. He was scheduled to go ashore with the third wave, which consisted of thirty-five LCVPs and six LCMs, each containing a Sherman M4 tank. They were forming up in a circle five hundred yards off their starboard side. It was almost time for Reynolds to board a lone LCM that stood waiting near the quarterdeck, rocking in the chop, its twin diesels idling. It was loaded with the mobile communications truck and sound engineers who would set up General MacArthur's radio network.

Beside Reynolds was the ship's gunnery officer, Lieutenant Commander Charles T. Corbett. "King Charles," as he was known, was five-six when he wasn't hunched over studying gunnery manuals. A former gunner's mate, Corbett was balding, with thick bushy eyebrows and intense blue eyes. He continually chomped lighted cigars, the captain's standing orders against smoking during general quarters notwithstanding. Smoking in the gun turrets was, of course, forbidden, but the gun director crews followed Corbett's example and blue cigarette smoke gushed from the director's portals as if it had been hit by an antitank round.

The only reason Corbett and his director crews got away with smoking is that they were excellent shots. Corbett, especially, had an uncanny eye for spotting his gunfire. He'd already proven it several times this morning. The man loved his six-inch rifles and gladly boasted about them to anyone within earshot.

They looked to the skies as the cacophony of the ship's

gunfire was again broken by a high-pitched engine noise. Another Japanese Val dive-bomber pulled out of its dive and screamed overhead.

Reynolds watched it go, thinking, *Talk about bum poop.* They had been told Halsey's Third Fleet had wiped out the Japanese air force on Formosa and in the Philippine Islands. Reynolds wished Halsey were here now, watching the Japanese bomb and strafe. As least the ships were safe for the time being—it was apparent the Vals were targeting the troops ashore. To Halsey's credit, his own Hellcats and Corsairs followed the Vals in, shooting them down, in most cases, before the Japs got to their targets. For that reason, the *Nashville* and other ships in Leyte Gulf checked fire lest they hit their own planes.

The *Nashville* had taken a fifteen-minute break, and now her main battery of five gun turrets, each containing three six-inch rifles, trained out to port. Reynolds slapped his palms over his ears. *Crack!* The light cruiser fired another full salvo, making his eardrums ring. A full head shorter, Corbett stood beside him, legs planted, teeth gritted, binoculars poised, ready to spot the fall of shot. How the hell does he stand it? Reynolds wondered.

Pressing his binoculars to his eyes, Reynolds scanned their landing zone. He knew combat when he saw it. And there was plenty of it on Red Beach, right where they were going. Japs were dying in there. So were Americans. His butt started throbbing, and he tried to put it out of his mind. Maybe I'll get lucky and fall down a ladder and break a leg or something.

The *Nashville*'s six-inch guns roared again. Their target was Hill 522, a humpback-shaped mountain, so called because it was 522 feet high. The assault troops ashore were taking artillery fire, and there was strong suspicion that a Japanese observation post was situated on the hill, if not the guns themselves. Also, Hill 522 overlooked the area where the general planned to land. So it had to be neutralized quickly.

With raised binoculars, Corbett chomped his cigar and watched as the *Nashville*'s shells exploded on the north side of Hill 522. Suddenly he roared, "Shit, counterbattery! Mount 65!"

A shell plopped in the water two hundred yards off the port bow. Water hissed as a large frothy-white column rose fifty feet in the air.

A wide-eyed Caldwell, his third-class yeoman phone talker, shouted into his phone, "Counterbattery, mount 65!"

Within seconds the after six-inch gun mount erupted with a salvo from all three of its six-inch cannons.

"Where are they?" asked Reynolds.

Corbett stuffed his cigar in his mouth and waved in the direction of Hill 522. "See that puff of black smoke near those trees?"

Reynolds raised his binoculars. "Not sure, I think—"

The three rounds from mount 65 landed near the trees.

"Up one hundred, left seventy-five," roared Corbett into his mouthpiece.

The spot was applied, and five seconds later the guns of mount 65 again belched their defiance.

Reynolds laid his binoculars on the spot and saw three more explosions. Then there were more explosions. Dirt, rocks, and tree limbs soared into the air. Flame and smoke billowed up five hundred feet.

"Looks like we got an ammo dump," muttered Corbett, his binoculars jammed to his eyes.

Caldwell grinned and said, "Gunnery, aye."

"What?" demanded Corbett.

Caldwell said, "Captain and the general send their compliments, sir. Good shooting."

They looked down at the bridge. The *Nashville*'s captain and General MacArthur both looked up, grins on their faces, giving a thumbs-up.

Reynolds grinned back at them, trying to look lighthearted. But inwardly, his stomach churned. He hadn't slept well. And a nightmare had awakened him a little before one in the morning. After that, any attempt at sleeping was useless. And from the groans in his stateroom, the other three officers were having trouble sleeping as well. "Looks like you just made full commander, Charlie," he said.

"Bullshit."

Caldwell keyed his mike. "Quarterdeck says your mike boat is making the starboard side, Colonel."

Reynolds glanced aft, seeing it was true. He said to Corbett, "Time to head over to the soft sands of Paradise Island, Charlie. Keep your powder dry." They shook.

"Don't worry about that. You just watch your ass."

"Don't I know it." Reynolds reached for a ladder.

Corbett nodded to the M1 carbine slung over Reynolds's shoulder. "You know how to use that?"

"I've been around, Charlie."

"How 'bout the general, I hear he's going ashore?"

"Pretty soon."

"Will he carry a carbine, too?"

"No."

"Guy is crazy. There's tons of Japs over there."

Reynolds's head was almost down to deck level. He looked up and spoke sotto voce. "Keep a secret?"

"Sure." Corbett kneeled to hear.

Reynolds nodded toward MacArthur. "See that bulge in his rear pocket?"

"Yeah."

"That's all he carries. A single-shot derringer."

"Fer chrissake. What's he expect to do with that?"

"In case the enemy captures him alive."

"Oh."

From the beginning, things went wrong. The security detail of twelve soldiers wasn't aboard the LCM. An intermittent rain began to fall, and the LCM ran aground thirty yards offshore. By this time the radio broadcast engineers, who had never seen combat, were pop-eyed, their Adam's apples bouncing. And it was obvious they didn't know a damn thing about the M1 rifles slung over their shoulders. So far, the only good thing was that Owen Reynolds made it ashore in one piece, and that he was alive.

Reynolds ordered the bow ramp down and had the truck, a Studebaker ten-wheeler, driven off in three feet of water. The driver, a curly-haired Texan named Corporal Stoddart, slapped the door and yelled "Yippee-yi-yay" as he jazzed the throttle. Ten feet from shore, the engine died. Bullets whizzed about; Reynolds couldn't tell if they were American or Japanese. A mortar round landed thirty yards away with a loud *Whap*. Definitely Japanese.

His radio engineers fell face-forward in ankle-deep water and clamped their hands over their heads. Reynolds walked among them, shouting and kicking them to rise. They struggled to their feet, their eyes darting about, mud and sand running down their faces. He got them together again, and they pushed, and groaned, and grunted, and cursed, trying to get the recalcitrant Studebaker ashore. Reynolds spotted a D4 Caterpillar off-loading from an LST fifty yards down the beach. He ran down and talked the bulldozer driver into helping them. Quickly they connected the tow wire, and soon the Studebaker was high and dry, with Stoddart working on his engine.

At the same time, Reynolds had the engineers unlimber their equipment. In charge of the group was Oris Gillespie, a staff sergeant who, only months before, was one of the top broadcast radio technicians at NBC radio studios in Hollywood. On the way in, he'd told Reynolds that he could have sat out the war on deferment, watching girls strut down Sunset Boulevard. But instead, Gillespie wanted to serve. By the expression on his face now, Gillespie didn't look so sure.

The Studebaker's engine caught with a roar. "Yaaaahoo," shouted Stoddart. "Where to, Colonel?"

Reynolds thought about that while the others jumped in back. A security squad was supposed to have picked out a place for broadcasting and set up a perimeter. But they hadn't shown up.

"Sir?" Stoddart asked again.

Reynolds hopped in beside Stoddart. "See that?" He pointed to a dry culvert about two hundred yards inland. "Looks safe enough. Take us in there."

"Good enough for me, Colonel." Stoddart ground his gears into compound low, and five minutes later the Studebaker jiggled and bounced its way into the culvert. Actually it was a rather picturesque place. Lush trees and vines surrounded it on both sides. Bougainvillea grew down to the edge; aside from a few smoking bomb craters, the clearing would have been perfect for a South Seas cruise line poster.

Stoddart said, "This should just about do it. Lemme get that generator going and I'll—ahh!" The driver's windshield shattered and a bullet tore a hole in the side of his helmet. He fell over the wheel with a groan.

"Everybody out!" yelled Reynolds. He kicked open the door and fell to the ground with a thud.

Gillespie crawled up alongside, dragging his rifle in mud. "Wha—wha the hell is it?" Stoddart groaned up in the cab.

Reynolds yelled, "Stoddart, you all right?"

". . . can't see," was the weak reply.

"Keep still!" Reynolds checked around, seeing the rest of the engineers alive, but shaky.

Then he unlimbered his carbine and peeked over the truck's fender. *Ping!* A bullet punched a hole in the fender six inches from his face.

Reynolds saw the smoke puff. "Sonofabitch," he growled. He rose up and emptied all eight rounds of his carbine into the trees across the culvert.

Just then a squad of soldiers rounded a boulder and fell on their bellies. A sergeant crawled up to Reynolds and said, "Obermann, Colonel. What the hell are you doing in here, if you don't mind my asking?"

Reynolds shrugged. "Seemed like a good place to set up our equipment. You our security?"

"Yes, sir."

"How'd we miss you?"

"Someone fouled up. They stuck us in another boat that landed us on White Beach. We had to fight our way back up here. Plenty of snipers."

The rain trickled to a drizzle. "Well then, welcome to the sunny Philippines."

"Sheeyaat."

Reynolds rose above the fender and said, "See the taller of those two trees over to the left?"

"Sir."

"That's where the little bastard is."

"I see." Water dripped off Obermann's nose as he yelled over his shoulder, "Hey, Louie."

"Yup," came a voice from behind the truck.

"See that tall stand of trees over there?"

"Yup."

Obermann growled, "The one to the left. He's up there."

"Yup," said Louie. A long, stringy kid about nineteen years old crawled around the Studebaker, hoisted a BAR onto the fender, and began squeezing off rounds. After Louie's fourth round, someone screamed from across the culvert. Obermann yelled, "Hodgkins and Somerville, it's all yours."

Two soldiers rose and zigzagged across the culvert. After a while, two shots were fired and they emerged from the overgrowth. One holstered a .45 and said, "Dead, all right, Sarge. Looks like Louie blew his heart out."

"Okay." They stood and Obermann turned to Reynolds. "Colonel, we'll set up a perimeter and make sure everything is secure. You can start setting up."

"Thanks, Sergeant."

"And sir?"

"Yes?"

"These Nips like to hide in foxholes covered with branches, so watch your ass."

Reynolds's butt ached. "Never occurred to me."

A medic worked on Stoddart, finding that the bullet had creased his forehead. Blood had gushed down, temporarily blinding him. The medic cleaned the wound, dumped in sulfa powder, and wrapped an ungainly bandage around Stoddart's head. The medic said, "I put a couple of staples in there, but it needs sutures. Report to the debarkation center." He wrote on a large red cardboard placard and hung it around Stoddart's neck by a string. "Now skedaddle." He jabbed a thumb toward the beach then dashed off in another direction.

Stoddart climbed into the truck bed and began tinkering with the generator.

Reynolds called up, "You're supposed to evacuate, Stoddart."

"When pigs fly, sir, with all respect, that is." Stoddart grabbed a wrench and began tinkering.

"Stoddart, I want you to—"

" 'Scuse me, sir, but it makes sense that we should all work to get this damn thing going before the general shows up. And I feel good enough." He lay down his wrench. "If this generator don't work, it's curtains for us. And I don't think the general wants that, does he, sir?"

Reynolds couldn't argue with the logic. "All right, but keep your damn head down. And you're gone when that thing starts. Hell, Stoddart, you've got an R&R ticket at least, maybe a trip home."

"I know, sir." He thumbed a button on the generator panel. The engine cranked and roared to life, dark blue smoke gushing out of the exhaust stack. Stoddart grinned and adjusted the idle.

"Nice job. Now get going," yelled Reynolds.

"In a minute, sir. Gotta make sure it's running okay."

In the back of his mind, Reynolds knew Stoddart was not going to evacuate until he was pushed out. But there was no time to argue. He walked over to a small, fidgety private with a walkie-talkie. "What's the word, Kramer?"

"They're on their way in, Colonel."

"When?"

Kramer asked the question and then looked up. "Cox'n says they're five hundred yards off the beach, sir."

"Okay." Reynolds looked up, seeing the skies darken with the promise of more rain. Crossing his fingers, he hoped their equipment would survive and that Stoddart's generator would keep going.

"And sir?" said Kramer.

"Yes?"

"Cox'n says the piers are all blown up. He's gonna have to unload them right on the beach"—Kramer pointed—"right over by that LST, he says."

"That'll be a neat trick." Reynolds turned to Gillespie. "Sergeant! Showtime. You're on." With a shrug, Gillespie spun dials on a tall radio console.

"Can you make me feel more confident, Sergeant?" Reynolds demanded.

"Just about got it, Colonel. I'll know in another five minutes," said Gillespie. He moved to another console and flipped switches.

"Well, that's good, because that's about when General MacArthur will be here."

Gillespie said, "I'll get it, sir. You just bring the general."

"Okay, be right back." Reynolds walked toward the beach. The rain had stopped, and after living in his own microcosm for the last three hours, he'd forgotten about the frantic activity back here. If anything, it was even more intense as men stormed ashore, formed up, and trudged inland. Still more LSTs squeezed in, their crews forming human chains to unload supplies. Occasionally a Japanese dive-bomber buzzed overhead, chased by navy fighters. Billowing smoke was trapped beneath the cloud layer, turning the windless day into a sickening pall.

Then he saw it. An LCM, flying a small red flag with four gold stars, maneuvered toward shore. Several helmeted heads peeked over the gunnels; one wore an officer's cap. *Brass! The general.* If he was lucky, the cox'n would be able to drive his LCM all the way up on the beach. If not, they'd have to walk in knee-deep water like Reynolds.

Sure enough, the general's LCM grounded about forty yards off the beach. Waves slapped at the transom. The engines roared, and muddy prop wash frothed as the cox'n tried to twist it in closer.

Reynolds walked up to the navy beachmaster, a full commander, and heard him say, "Screw 'em. Let 'em walk ashore, just like everybody else. And tell 'em to do it quick because I need that spot."

A man stood beside the beachmaster with a walkie-talkie. "You want me to say it just like that, Commander?"

The beachmaster sighed. "Just tell them there's no alternative."

The talker relayed the word. Moments later, the LCM's bow ramp splashed down. Along with the beachmaster, his talker, and hundreds of others, Reynolds watched as General of the Army Douglas A. MacArthur strode out on the bow ramp and jumped into knee-deep water. Looking straight ahead, he slogged forty yards to the beach as men gaped. His entourage followed. Among them were generals George C. Kenney and Richard K. Sutherland, Dr. Roger O. Egeberg, Philippine president Sergio Osmeña, and Resident Commissioner Carlos Romulo. All wore steel helmets, except for MacArthur, who wore his signature Philippine marshal's hat, dark aviator glasses, corncob pipe, and khakis, which moments before had been crisp and starched. Emerging from the water, MacArthur stopped next to a burned-out jeep, jammed his hands in his rear pockets, and looked about, waiting for the others to catch up.

A first lieutenant with a heavy five o'clock shadow ran up to MacArthur, followed by a platoon of men. He said, "Excuse me, General, but we're not quite secure here. Plenty of Jap snipers. You and your party better get down."

"Who are you?" demanded MacArthur.

"Er . . . Lieutenant Peoples, sir."

A bullet ricocheted off the jeep's fender as if to italicize what First Lieutenant Peoples had just said.

A high-pitched voice screeched from the jungle just fifty yards away, "You all die! FDR eat shit!"

Peoples dropped to his knees behind the jeep. "See what I mean, sir? You gotta be careful."

The others crouched behind the jeep, but MacArthur remained standing. He pointed toward the jungle. "Looks like you have a job to do, son."

"But we're detailed to protect you, sir."

MacArthur again pointed. "Then I repeat, Lieutenant Peoples, the enemy is that way. Now go do your job."

"Y . . . yes, sir." With a whistle, Peoples ran in a crouch toward the jungle, his men following, their equipment clanking.

Reynolds walked up and saluted. "Ready, General."

MacArthur returned the salute as rifles popped near the jungle. Then machine guns rattled. Grenades exploded. A flamethrower roared into the grove. The whole stand of coco palms lighted up in a bizarre orange-red as black smoke billowed overhead.

"Looks like Mr. Peoples is on it," said MacArthur. He looked at Reynolds, "Lead on, Owen."

A half-track drove up. A captain stood and offered MacArthur a ride. But the general waved it off as he slogged inland with his entourage. Owen Reynolds led the way, as a light mist became a drizzle. It was a downpour by the time they reached the culvert. While Gillespie briefed MacArthur on the microphone, Obermann walked around the truck and whispered, "Little bastards tried a banzai raid while you were gone." He pointed to some bodies splayed about thirty yards away.

Reynolds's eyebrows shot up. "Everybody all right?"

"Everybody except him." Obermann pointed to a wet tarp. A pair of army boots stuck out from the bottom.

"Who?"

"Your driver, Stoddart."

Reynolds swallowed hard to keep down the nausea. "Stoddart."

"Guy was pretty good with an M1," said Obermann. "He took a bullet meant for me."

Reynolds leaned against the truck. Stoddart had a million-dollar wound. He could have been on an LCVP right now headed for a hospital ship and a back area for two weeks of R&R, maybe even better. "Stoddart," he said slowly. He looked up. "What else?"

"We're okay for now. And I have my men posted. But I can't guarantee anything. You better tell your general to watch his keister. The Japs are out for him."

"You tell him, Sergeant."

"Sheeyaat." He waved a hand at Stoddart's corpse and hissed, "Are you sure all this bullshit PR for Dug-Out Doug is worth it, sir?"

An enraged Reynolds went to grab Obermann's collar. But just then the men around MacArthur surged into a tight group. All eyes fell on the general as he said, "Okay, this is it." He nodded up to Gillespie, who threw a switch.

MacArthur started out with, "People of the Philippines: I have returned." His voice shook a bit, and he paused for a moment to compose himself. "By the grace of Almighty God, our forces stand again on Philippine soil—soil consecrated by the blood of our two peoples. At my side is your president, Sergio Osmeña, a worthy successor of that great patriot, Manuel Quezon. The seat of your government is now, therefore, firmly reestablished on Philippine soil. The hour of your redemption is here."

The roaring rain became a fitting backdrop as MacArthur's voice grew strong and deeply resonant. "Rally to me. Let the indomitable spirit of Bataan and Corregidor lead on. As the lines of battle roll forward to bring you within the zone of operations, rise and strike. Strike at every favorable opportunity. For your homes and hearths, strike! For future generations of your sons and daughters, strike! In the name of your sacred dead, strike! Let no heart be faint. Let every arm be steeled. The divine guidance of God points the way. Follow in His name to the Holy Grail of righteous victory."

MacArthur stepped back and handed the mike to Osmeña, who had removed his helmet, letting the rain mix with the tears on his face. Then he spoke in his native Tagalog, wiping at his eyes.

They were ankle-deep in mud, but they were riveted to the scene. Osmeña handed the mike to Romulo, who removed his helmet and spoke haltingly, also in Tagalog.

Gillespie rose to his feet in the truck and caught Reynolds's eye.

Reynolds raised his eyebrows. *Are we broadcasting okay?*

Gillespie nodded and flashed a thumbs-up.

Obermann saw Gillespie, too. "I take it back, Colonel," he said softly.

"Pardon?"

"It is worth it."

THIRTY-SEVEN

20 October 1944
IJN *Atago*
Brunei Bay, Borneo

The First Striking Force pulled into Brunei Bay, just before sunset. Waiting at anchor was Vice Admiral Nishimura and his Southern Force of two battleships, two heavy cruisers, and four destroyers. While fuel barges dashed about in a breezy seaway.

Nishimura's barge cast off from his flagship, the 29,223-ton battleship *Yamashiro.* Pitching and slewing in the chop, the barge took a full thirty minutes to make the starboard side of the *Atago.* At 1930, Nishimura and an entourage of five officers stepped onto the *Atago*'s quarterdeck. Captain Araki; Rear Admiral Abe, the chief of staff; Noyama and other staff officers were there to greet him.

After bows and handshakes, Nishimura's party headed for Kurita's cabin. Deep in conversation, they split off in twos and threes. An anxious Nishimura quickly moved ahead, followed by a puffing Noyama, shuffling his fastest to keep pace. The admiral grandly dashed up ladders, ducked through hatches, and threw perfunctory salutes as he passed guards in flag country. With a final burst of energy, Noyama caught up just as they reached Kurita's cabin.

"There is something you should know, Admiral," wheezed Noyama. He edged between Nishimura and Kurita's door.

"Well, yes, you damn fool. I'm here to see Kurita." He elbowed Noyama aside.

"Please listen, Admiral." Noyama explained Kurita's condition and that he hadn't improved much. He finished by explaining that Dr. Koketsu had ordered complete bed rest.

"Rest, nonsense," replied Nishimura. "He can rest when he's dead. Right now I need him. The whole damn fleet needs him." He waved a sheaf of papers at Noyama. "Have you seen this?"

"Sir?"

"That damn MacArthur has landed. Leyte Gulf. Right where we thought he would. Eight o'clock this morning."

"Yes, sir. We've read the dispatches."

"Did you hear about his broadcast?"

"I hadn't heard that, Admiral," Noyama admitted.

Nishimura went on, "The damn fool is so predictable. He walked ashore and broadcast a radio message to the Filipinos." Nishimura wagged his elbows against his rib cage and puffed up his cheeks. "People of the Philippines, I have returned," he mimicked in a deep falsetto. "You can unlock your doors now. Your wives and daughters are safe with me. Please send them to the town square for processing along with all their jewelry." He grunted, "Hah!"

Noyama grinned. "He was really there?"

Nishimura turned serious. "Apparently it is true. He landed and did make that broadcast from Tacloban Beach. Had I known that, I would have ordered a detachment of marines in there to shoot the bastard."

"That would have been nice."

"We've got to get moving." Again, Nishimura raised his hand to knock.

"The admiral really does feel horrible—"

Nishimura clamped Noyama on the shoulder and said with a pixie grin, "Noyama, I've known Takeo Kurita for a long, long time. He is one of the hardiest people I know. I'll cheer him up and hand him back to you in fine shape."

Twenty minutes later Nishimura stepped out, looked at Noyama, and shook his head. "Take good care of him, Commander." Without another word, he left the ship.

THIRTY-EIGHT

23 October 1944
IJN *Atago*
Palawan Passage, Philippine Islands

After refueling the First Striking Force sortied from Brunei at 0800 on 22 October and now, at daybreak on the twenty-third, began to transit the Palawan Passage, the western approaches to the Philippine archipelago. The evening before, Kurita had dictated the setup for a night formation from his bed. The strike force was to sort itself into five columns. Cruisers and battleships were set in columns two and four. Destroyers formed a protective screen in columns one, three, and five. *Atago* was designated formation guide at the head of the second column; the cruiser *Myoko* was also a guide at the head of the fourth column. With that done, they steamed on a course of 045°, speed twenty-five. Battle condition III was ordered at 0000 and they were to go to full battle stations at 0700.

Noyama rose early. His stateroom was aft, two decks below the main deck near the seaplane hangar. Keeping the lights off, he dressed quietly, since many of the flag staff were still asleep—they'd worked late last night. Shuffling fast, he checked into the flag bridge, signed dispatches, spoke with Admiral Takata for a minute, then walked down three flights to the wardroom for breakfast.

Noyama had just taken his place at the table with twenty other officers when the Chelsea clock, a gift from the British at the *Atago*'s launching in 1932, chimed five bells.[33] Three seconds later, Captain Araki stepped in and walked to the head of the table. As always, Araki scanned the officers, now standing at attention, then, with a nod, waved them down. Araki had always seemed stiff and distant to Noyama. They never spoke, except on official business. He never seemed to relax; on the bridge or anywhere else on the ship, Araki was always in formal tunic, never in fatigues. And yet Noyama saw him laughing and slapping his knee when off duty with his sanctum sanctorum, his inner circle of officers consisting of the executive officer and department heads. But with Kurita's flag staff, Araki was precise, exacting, always by the book.

Today was no different. A forever correct Araki poured tea and began passing a silver platter of *umeboshi,* dried plums.

The platter reached Noyama, and he sensed that Araki's gaze had followed it down the table directly to him. "Sir?" asked Noyama.

"Are we going to ring formation anytime today, Commander?" asked Araki, with evident sarcasm. The ring formation was an air-defense formation usually set up for daylight hours.

Noyama said, "I believe the signal is on the flag bridge, now, Captain. We should be executing momentarily."

"I see. And where are your colleagues this morning?" He waved at empty chairs with the back of his hand.

"Still asleep, Captain. They were up late last night. Admiral Takata is on the flag bridge if you'd care to—"

"No, no. That won't be necessary. And how is the *Chujo*?" Another silver platter was passed. This one was loaded with *mochitsuki*—rice cakes.

Noyama dropped one on his plate and said, "Better, I think, Captain. His temperature is down." Noyama bit into a *mochitsuki* and chased it with water. "Dr. Koketsu says he will be able to—"

An explosion shook the ship. Plates jumped on the table. Someone cried out in the pantry.

"What?" shouted Araki. He turned to the chief engineer. "Get the—"

Another explosion, far worse than the first, made the *Atago* jump and vibrate horribly. She seemed to twist from end to end and then rolled drunkenly to port. Noyama's chair fell over. He found himself on his hands and knees looking eye to eye with the chalk-faced chief engineer. The lights blinked on and off as crockery, teacups, fine china plates, silverware, and water glasses crashed to the deck. Amid the mess was the remnants of a fruit bowl. Two apples rolled among the debris, making Noyama think of his brother.

Captain Araki yelled at the chief engineer, "Get going. Damage report, quickly!" The chief engineer scrambled to his feet and dashed out before the others could stand.

"Get moving all of you!" Araki shouted to the rest. Then he bolted out the door and up three flights to the bridge.

Stumbling along, Noyama was thirty seconds behind Araki. Usually quiet, the bridge was in chaos, a number of men shouting at once.

Araki barked, "Silence!" He yanked a phone from its bracket and held a finger in his other ear. "Very well," he roared. "Secure boilers one and two. What? All right. Secure those, too. How many casualties?"

Just then something between an explosion and a volcano erupting, rumbled beneath their feet. Noyama pitched to the deck and swore he felt it grow warm. He rose to his feet, slipped and slid his way to the pilothouse hatch, and yanked it open. To his surprise, Kurita stood there. "Admiral, I—"

Kurita, wearing fatigues, brushed him aside, walked in, and barked. "Araki, how serious is it?"

Araki clutched the phone in his hand. "Bad enough, Admiral. Torpedo hit in the forward fireroom. Another forward, under turret two. Everything's gone in the fireroom. We just had to secure boilers one and two. Three and four were caught in the initial explosion and were goners. The after fireroom isn't much better off. Packing glands from shafts three and four have ruptured and it's flooding massively. From what I can tell, the fire mains are useless and we can't control fires headed for the forward magazine. We're flooding those now but I can't—"

Something rumbled and exploded deep inside the *Atago.* She gathered a list of ten degrees to port. Noyama checked his watch. Five minutes couldn't have passed, yet incredibly the *Atago*'s bow was almost awash. And she was nearly dead in the water, the other ships pulling away. Ships aft of the *Atago* hove out of column to avoid her and began passing, while destroyers dashed back and forth dropping depth charges.

Suddenly four explosions ripped the cruiser in second column. Raising his glasses, Noyama watched an enormous tower of smoke billow from the *Maya,* a sister ship to the *Atago.*

There were three more ripping explosions from another cruiser. This time it was the *Takao,* another sister to the graceful *Atago* and *Maya.*

"How many submarines do they have out there?" gasped Araki as the *Atago* leaned farther to port, creaking and groaning.

The faces of Kurita, once the *Atago*'s skipper, and Araki, her current skipper, flashed with the same horrible thought: the *Atago* was going down—fast. Araki held the phone away from his ear: "Chief engineer reports all power lost, Admiral. No chance of lighting boilers."

"Can you counterflood?" asked Kurita.

"If we can get power to the pumps. Right now there's a serious fire forward. We're trying to flood the forward magazine." He paused. "Actually, I think we're beyond counterflooding."

Kurita nodded.

An astounded Noyama checked the pilothouse inclinometer. The list had increased to eighteen degrees. Worse, the *Atago* was dead in the water. Aft, screams echoed as fires shot up the boiler room hatches.

Captain Araki calmly turned to his officer of the deck. "Call for abandon ship, Mr. Hitsuke. Make sure all classified material is destroyed." He turned to Kurita and asked, "Shall I have the *Kishinami*[34] come alongside and take you off?"

Kurita looked at the deck and finally nodded. "We'd better, if only to transfer off the wounded. We'll go later if . . . if . . ."

"Better do it now, Admiral, I think we're about out of time." Araki gave the order to the signalman. Then he turned to Kurita and offered a hand. "Good-bye."

Kurita seemed at a loss for words. "You . . . you're . . ."

"Yes, good-bye." Araki reached for Noyama. "You're a good

staff officer, Noyama. Probably better than you were a pilot. Good luck to you."

An astounded Noyama took Araki's hand. "Sir, I don't know what to—"

"Go, you two. Now. I have work to do." Turning his back, Araki grabbed the phone and began yelling at the engineers to get out. At the same time, he grabbed a length of line and began tying himself to the chart table.

Kurita turned to Noyama. "Where's our people?"

Noyama sputtered for a moment. "Their bunks, sir. They worked late last night, and Captain Takata gave the second and third section permission to sleep in until seven."

Kurita looked aft for a moment. "I hope they're not stuck back there. If so, they're goners. Come on. There are some things I want to pack."

"Yes, sir."

Kurita grabbed a life jacket from a rack and handed it over. "Here. Why didn't you have one on?"

There was no time to argue. Noyama wrestled into the life jacket while Kurita took a last look around his bridge. Books, papers, manuals, and charts were scattered on the deck. Officers and men dashed about, oblivious to the detritus beneath their feet. The ship was now listing a good twenty-five degrees. More loose gear crashed to the deck and slid to the port bulkhead: pencils, ashtrays, a sailor's hat, magazines, helmets, chalk.

The ship gave an awful screech and rolled farther to port. Kurita slipped. Noyama grabbed his collar and dragged him upright, one foot braced on the port bulkhead, the other on the deck. Men screamed. Steam shot out the uptakes. Boats, ammunition, portable pumps sailed across her decks, some equipment striking men and catapulting them into the water.

Fifteen minutes after the first torpedo hit, the once mighty *Atago* capsized with a great lurch, smoke and steam billowing high in the air. Noyama found himself in the water, his eye patch hanging around his neck. Quickly adjusting it, he found Kurita three meters away, treading water. But he didn't have a life jacket and his face was blue, his teeth chattering even though the water was at least twenty degrees Celsius.

A sailor drifted by in a life jacket. He was dead, half his

face gone. Quickly Noyama untied the jacket and pushed the corpse away. Then he swam over to Kurita. "Admiral!"

Kurita spat water. "Wh . . . what?"

"Here, put this on."

Kurita nodded and let Noyama manhandle him into the life jacket.

Noyama had just tied the last lines when the *Atago* gave a great screech. Her stern rose high in the air, her ensign waving in the morning breeze.

"Araki," gurgled Kurita.

"Yes, sir," said Noyama.

With a final vindictive blast of putrid air, the *Atago* slid into the depths, pulling with her dozens of screaming sailors. Around them floated what was left of a proud ship that only twenty minutes before had been steaming at twenty-five knots.

The destroyer *Kishinami* picked up the *Atago*'s survivors. The heavy cruiser had gone down in eighteen minutes. For many, there just wasn't time to get out. Lost was Kurita's chief of staff, Rear Admiral Seiichi Abe, along with a large number of flag staff trapped belowdecks in their staterooms. But the overweight Rear Admiral Satomi Takata got out, puffing and gasping, with ten others, including second-class petty officer Kurusu, Kurita's valet. Dr. Koketsu also survived and, once aboard the destroyer, immediately had the admiral rushed to the captain's day cabin, where he rubbed Kurita's feet and arms, drying him out, getting him warm.

Later that day, they again transferred, this time to the comfort of the giant battleship *Yamato*. Ugaki and Captain Ishima, the ship's commanding officer, waited in flag headquarters as Kurita, Noyama, Dr. Koketsu, and the bewildered staff shuffled in.

The normally ebullient Ugaki planted his hands on his hips. "Round one didn't go well."

"What can you tell me?" rasped Kurita.

"That you need to go to bed, dammit," shot back Ugaki.

"No, no. Our ships. Where do we stand?" protested Kurita.

"Submarine got your ship."

"I know that, you fool."

Ugaki went on, "They got the *Maya,* too. She sank faster than the *Atago.*"

The compartment fell into a shocked silence.

"And the *Takao* took four torpedoes," added Ugaki. All eyes were fixed on him as he went on. "Fortunately, her damage control crews were able to control the fires and flooding. She'll survive, but she's a wreck and is headed back to Brunei with the *Isokaze*[35] as escort." He looked at Kurita. "What do you think?"

Kurita's eyes glistened. "Think? Think? We damn well will go on. That's what I think. And it's almost certain we'll see action tomorrow. Not much time to get ready." Kurita turned to Dr. Koketsu. "What do you have in your kit to keep us awake?"

THIRTY-NINE

24 October 1944
USS *Matthew* (DD 548)
50 miles east of Samar
Philippine Sea

Six destroyers of DESRON 77 had left the light carrier *San Cristobal* (CVL 32) at 2030 the previous evening and run east to a point one hundred miles off the east coast of Samar. It was a calm, flat sea and the *Simpson, Connelly, Thompson, Kumm, Toohey,* and *Matthew,* easily joined up with the tanker *Caliente* (AO 53) at 2345, topped off with fuel oil, and broke away two hours later to head back to the *San Cristobal.*

Donovan and Al Corodini, the *Matthew*'s chief engineer, were especially relieved. They were almost down to 5 percent remaining fuel, and the options were grim. That was the thing about the destroyer navy, Donovan reflected. Run here, run there; always at twenty-five or thirty knots, chasing carriers for flight ops or frantically steaming to another station, getting ready for more flight ops. And that sucked up fuel oil, by the ton. Ever since they'd left Ulithi, they'd been running at twenty or more knots—which, among other things, was a strain on the engineering plant, especially the fragile superheaters. It was beginning to show the stress. Number two evaporator, one of the *Matthew*'s two water-generating evaporators had given out. Fortunately, it was a repair job they could do under way, and the engineers were down there now, frantically working to get it ready for tomorrow morning, when they rejoined the *San Cristobal*. The challenge was simple. Not having a second evaporator meant they wouldn't have enough freshwater to feed the boilers at over thirty knots, which meant they couldn't keep up with the *San Cristobal* during flight operations. Not good.

A godsend was that the *Caliente* had sent over fresh milk, meat, produce, eggs, and mail. Everything had tasted like cardboard lately, which was just about what they were eating. But now, with something fresh in the larders, everyone looked forward to good hot chow tomorrow morning. Another godsend was the weather. The sea had been unusually calm, giving them a fine passage out to the *Caliente,* an easy time alongside taking on oil and goods, and a smooth run back to the *San Cristobal*. Larry Fox, commodore of Destroyer Squadron 77, had them in a bent-line screen, steering a sinuous course with the *Simpson,* Fox's ship, as the guide. The only thing betraying their presence as they steamed at twenty-two knots over a black, glossy sea were six brilliant white foaming wakes stretching far behind the destroyers.

And now, at 0300, the *Matthew* hardly rolled under a cloud cover that pressed down to five hundred feet. A three-quarter moon cast a little light loom, but not enough to silhouette an enemy submarine. It was hard to sense they were under way inside the pilothouse. Their only illumination was from red lights and a muted white binnacle light. Donovan sat in the captain's chair, one of three deck-mounted overstuffed chairs on the bridge. There was one on either bridge wing; this one was inside the pilothouse against the starboard bulkhead. He stretched and yawned, knowing he should be in his rack getting shut-eye. But until a few minutes ago, there had been just too much to do.

Now things were settled down and it was strangely quiet as the ship dashed through the night. He felt completely detached from the six other watch standers in the pilothouse, now only dark, faceless shadows.

With a surreptitious glance over his shoulder, Donovan eased the envelope out from under his foul-weather jacket. It had come over from the *Caliente* with the rest of the mail and had found its way to him an hour later. It was addressed in her signature green ink, and he'd been waiting three tooth-gnashing hours to read it in peace. Slowly he turned the envelope over in his hands. He held it to his nose. No perfume. No roses. Not even a whiff of ink. But a faint odor of ether or alcohol seeped through. She must have written this while at work. How could that happen? Alcohol and ether evaporate in seconds. Somehow she'd pulled it off. Either that or she was deliberately tormenting him.

"Coffee, Captain?" Al Corodini, the officer of the deck held out a chipped mug.

"Thanks, Al." Donovan accepted the mug and asked, "What's the latest on number two evaporator?"

"Back on the line in two hours, Captain, three, tops."

"Keep on it, Al."

"Will do, Captain." Corodini backed away, stepping through the hatch to the starboard bridge wing.

The others kept their eyes ahead, ignoring him.

Now. He ran a finger under the envelope flap and pulled out three crisp onionskin pages, also done in green ink.

My Dearest Mike,

Would you believe? As of today, I've been an intern for one year and they have yet to throw me out of town. I always worried about interning in the place where I grew up, but so far people seem to accept me as Dr. Logan rather than that skinny freckle-faced kid, once known for throwing a rock through Mr. Stippenfelt's front window (that's the dark green two-story across the street). Stippenfelt called the police, they had to drag my dad home from work—it was awful. Truth is, I was aiming for his cat, the damn thing was keeping everyone awake. I mean everyone. Actually, Ralph put me up to it. *Dared me* is a better term. Bet me fifty cents that I couldn't hit the cat. Well, I missed the damn cat, Fritz was his name, and sailed a boulder through that window with a resounding crash. Old Stippenfelt was inside listening to Jack Benny on his Philco. But it only took two seconds for him to come roaring outside. Ralph ran. I was so scared I was rooted to the spot, a stupid grin on my face.

The cops came and they couldn't find my dad right

away, he was out somewhere sorting freight cars. So they dragged in Milo Lattimer, a family surrogate, to make peace. I had to wash cars and mow lawns for two months to pay for that window.

And now it's come full circle. Old Mr. Stippenfelt was rolled into emergency today with a coronary. I was on duty and I have to say, we did a pretty good job stabilizing him. Don't know if he recognized me, though. Maybe it's just as well. He probably would have died of shock.

Speaking of Milo Lattimer, John Sabovik seems very interested in him. Can you figure out why? John keeps asking Dad and me questions. Right now he's over at the dispatch office looking through records. Despite what happened between you two, John has always been proper with me, oftentimes funny, especially when that damn Nitro is around. Those two deadpan each other and it's hilarious. But when Milo's name comes up, John becomes hollow-eyed and distant.

Saw a great movie the other night: *Arsenic and Old Lace* with Cary Grant, Raymond Massey, and Peter Lorre. Speaking of deadpan, those guys really are masters of the art. I saw the play once when I was at Berkeley, but those three executed this seamlessly. Hope you get to see it soon. Or maybe you already have.

Enough of that. How are you doing? Maybe not a Pacific pleasure cruise, but one I hope that's comfortable and safe for you. Especially safe.

I miss the hell out of you and think of you almost every minute. Almost gave a patient the wrong medicine yesterday because you were on my mind. So please, please, do me a favor and come home before I really hurt somebody. Just kidding. But just come home soon. Now. I miss you.

Much, Much Love,

Diane

With a smile, Donovan rearranged the pages and began to read again.

"Excuse me, Captain?" It was Lieutenant Sloan, the supply officer.

"What?"

Sloan handed over a clipboard. "The manifest for stores taken aboard, sir."

"Thank you, Howard." Donovan ran a finger down the list. "You think the eggs are really fresh?"

"Look okay, Captain. About a four-day supply, though, that's all."

"Better than nothing. What's this? They sent over movies, two of them?"

"Well, yes, sir. We exchanged actually. Two of ours for two of theirs." It was a common practice in the fleet. That way, everyone had a chance to see something new.

Donovan signed the clipboard and handed it back. "What'd we get?"

"Claudette Colbert."

Donovan groaned. "*Since You Went Away*?" They'd seen the tearjerker so many times on the way out from Ulithi everyone knew the lines by heart. They'd only gotten rid of it last week.

Sloan nodded. "Sorry, sir."

"What's the other one?"

Sloan said, "*Arsenic and Old Lace,* sir."

Someone tugged at Donovan's sleeve. "Sir?"

He'd fallen asleep. Through sandpaper eyes, he made out Burt Hammond's face. "Yes?"

"It's 0400, sir. I've relieved Mr. Corodini as officer of the deck. Mr. Peete is junior officer of the deck. Boilers one and three are on the line, as are generators one and two. All systems in the operations and gunnery departments are functional, the engineering department is likewise functional except for work continuing on evap number two. ETR is 0600. We're on course two-six-five, speed twenty-two, in a bent-line formation. Steering a sinuous course, *Simpson* is still the guide. The whaleboat is gripped out for plane guard duty, sir." Hammond stepped back. "Uh . . . Mr. Peete has the conn, sir."

"Very well, thank you, Burt."

Donovan closed his eyes to drift off. Then he snapped wide awake. "Who?" he muttered. There, on the starboard bridge wing, he saw them through the porthole, laughing and talking. Hammond and Peete, the bitter enemies he and Kruger had pried apart at Ulithi. Before the horror of the *Mount Saint Helens* explosion and the loss of Ensign Muir, it was all they could to keep the two from trying to kill each other. That included keeping them off the same watch bill. But the recent events had been sobering. Not just for Hammond and Peete, but for the whole ship. It was a *Welcome to the war zone* wake-up call that instilled a grim determination the crew hadn't felt before. Fortunately, CinCPac sent along Ensign Steve Flannigan, a quiet, self-reliant journalism major from the University of Washington, to replace Muir. He'd been delivered by the *San Cristobal* via highline a few nights before; he'd previously been the second division officer aboard the destroyer *Kingsbury,* which had been sunk last month by a mine. Flannigan worked in almost right away, but Hammond and Peete still antagonized one another, almost openly, military courtesy notwithstanding. Donovan and Kruger decided to have one of them transferred as soon as they reached Pearl Harbor. But there they were, out on the starboard bridge wing, gabbing like two old men in the local hardware store eating soda crackers and talking politics.

Donovan grabbed the telephone from the bracket and pushed the button marked XO.

A raspy voice answered, "Kruger."

Donovan covered the mouthpiece. "Richard, for crying out loud, what are you doing?"

"Sir?"

Donovan hissed, "Hammond and Peete, dammit. Why are they standing the same watch up here together?"

"Oh, sorry, Captain. I didn't have a chance to tell you."

"Tell me what?"

"Mr. Flannigan sprained his arm during uprep so the doc took him off the watch bill for twenty-four hours." Flannigan had become a regular JOOD under Hammond.

"Richard, don't try my patience, dammit."

"So Burt Hammond specifically requested Jonathan Peete as Flannigan's replacement."

"You're kidding!"

"Honest injun."

"I thought those guys hated each other." Donovan glanced out the porthole. Peete was facing Hammond now, his hands moving in open gestures.

"Well, Captain, quite a bit happened since mail call, and after all, you've been on the bridge for almost twenty hours."

"So that makes me the last to know?" Donovan said drily.

"Dammit, Mike, listen to me."

It was Richard Kruger, the grizzled chief petty officer, talking to a boot ensign.

Donovan knew when to shut up.

Kruger continued. "We had mail call in the wardroom. Good news and bad news." He paused. "Okay, the good news first. Johnnie Hollywood's father sent him a letter apologizing. Now he wants to welcome his son back a hero."

"What's Mr. Peete say?"

"That his father is doing this because it's good for business."

"What a sick world," said Donovan.

"I'll say, but that's Hollywood. Peete says he's going to do it, though. He likes the idea that it's good for business and that he'll have a job when he gets back."

"I get it," said Donovan. "Now the bad news."

"More news from Hollywood. Hammond got a DJ."[36]

"From the movie star? Velma Johnson?"

"One and the same. We were sitting there reading our mail when, all of a sudden, Hammond goes berserk, screaming that Velma has run off to Brazil with her chiropractor. Peete starts laughing and says that's part of her gig. Before Brazil, she ran off to Mexico with her dance instructor. He said she disappears for about three months and then sneaks back into town.

"Well, it was quiet for a moment and I expected the two to reach across the table and rip each other's throats out. Then, I'll be damned, Hammond starts laughing and says, 'Good riddance. Dame was costing me a fortune, anyway.'

"So Merryweather starts laughing, then Jack Kelso. We're all laughing, Jonathan Peete included. So much so there's tears running down our faces. Pretty soon, Hammond and Peete are talking. Seems like Hammond was paying for her apartment on Sunset Boulevard. He had bought her a bunch of clothes and loaned her at least three grand. And then there was an engagement ring—a two-carat rock. Peete is telling him how to get it all back without having to go to some schlock Hollywood attorney."

"How can he do that?"

"Well, remember who his father is?"

Donovan did. Michael Thomas Peete was best known for playing opposite Gwendolyn Long in the 1934 smash hit *A Lonely Night in Paris,* winning the Academy Award as best actor. "You mean his father's connections?"

"Exactly. Apparently they're long and far-reaching. Michael Thomas Peete knows everybody and has influence everywhere. So Velma Johnson will be removed from the scene, and Mr. Hammond will recover his rock and his money. Either that, or she'll never work in Hollywood again."

"How about the clothes?"

"She gets to keep the brassieres."

"I'll be damned." Again Donovan glanced through the porthole out to the starboard bridge wing. No, they hadn't stabbed each other. Instead Ensign Jonathan Peete held up a stadimeter, checking the range to the *Simpson.* Now it was Hammond doing the talking. By his gestures, it looked as if he was explaining how to keep station in the formation. Donovan leaned over and checked the radar repeater. Range was off by about twenty yards: bearing was smack on. "Okay, Richard. Your social experiment seems to be working. Everybody is still alive up here."

"One more thing."

"Shoot."

"Your crew and your ship need an alert captain tomorrow, not some clapped-out caffeine addict who talks to himself and drools from the side of his mouth. So climb out of that damn chair, go to your sea cabin, and get some sleep."

"Okay."

"Good night, Captain."

Donovan hung up and walked to the starboard hatch. He called to Hammond: "I'll be in my sea cabin, Burt. Please wake me when we close to within five thousand yards of the *San Cristobal*."

"Yes, sir," said Hammond.

Donovan fairly stumbled the ten steps to his sea cabin. The last thing he remembered was wondering about Cary Grant, Raymond Massey, and Peter Lorre.

FORTY

24 October 1944
USS *Matthew* (DD 548)
Twenty miles east of Leyte, Philippines

At 0445, the *Thompson* and *Kumm* split off and ran fifty miles south to rejoin DESDIV 77.1, where they joined the screen for the carrier *Alliance* (CV 35). *Matthew* and the three other destroyers in DESDIV 77.2 rendezvoused with the *San Cristobal* at first light under a two-thousand-foot overcast. They set up a diamond formation around her with the *Simpson* two thousand yards directly ahead. *Connelly* and *Toohey* were stationed two thousand yards on either wing. The *Matthew* was tucked in plane guard position, two thousand yards astern, where she could pick up survivors from ditching planes.

Running at twenty-four knots, the *San Cristobal* launched her CAP[37] of four F4F Wildcat fighters at 0600. There was no breeze, and the sea was quiet; ten minutes later, they cranked formation speed up to thirty-two knots to give eight lumbering TBFs plenty of wind over the deck for the first strike of the day. Fortunately, Corodini's engineers had just finished with the evaporators, and the *Matthew* had no trouble making fresh water to feed her thirsty boilers. With the TBFs gone, they settled down to wait . . . and to have their first real eggs, toast, and orange juice in two weeks.

After that, Donovan tumbled into his bunk and slept soundly. Two hours later, the buzzer over his bunk ripped him from his sleep. He grabbed the handset. "Captain."

It was Cliff Merryweather, the OOD. "Sorry, Captain. You

asked to be called when the first strike returned. They're inbound about five minutes out."

"Very well, I'll be there in a minute." Donovan bracketed the phone and lay there blinking, his eyes feeling as if they were coated with sandpaper. *Dammit. Go do your job.* He stood, stretched, brushed his teeth, ran a razor over his face, put on a clean shirt, and pronounced himself ready to rejoin World War II.

Two minutes later, he was on the open bridge wing, comfortably settled in the captain's chair, drinking coffee.

"Morning, Skipper." Richard Kruger walked up and stood beside him.

"Morning, Richard," replied Donovan. Then he leaned forward and called to a thin, redheaded ensign wearing headphones. "And how are you this morning, Mr. Flannigan?"

"Fine, Captain," said Flannigan, dabbing at his mouth with a handkerchief. They'd assigned the new ensign as junior officer of the deck at general quarters but quickly discovered how easily Flannigan was taken seasick, often heaving over the side, his face turning a putrid green. Aviator glasses couldn't hide dark circles under his eyes. Still, Donovan and Kruger agreed the kid had heart; he wouldn't quit. So for the time being, they'd decided to keep him there to see if he could conquer it.

Hearing the rumble of R-2600 engines, they looked up to see two groups of TBFs drop through the overcast and wallow overhead. Tired, and low on fuel, they formed into single file and lowered their wheels, flaps, and tail hooks, looking as ungainly as ducks with their feet spread for a landing.

Donovan jabbed a finger at the two formations.

"What?" asked Kruger.

"One missing. Probably lost over the battle zone. See? The first group has four planes, the next group only three." Donovan called over to Merryweather, "Cliff, check with combat to see if they have anything on a missing TBF. Maybe we'll have a straggler."

"Yes, sir," replied Merryweather.

Donovan turned to Kruger. "And how are the Bickersons this morning?"

A corner of Kruger's mouth turned up. "Hammond and

Peete? So far, so good. I gave them a bit of extra sack time. Figure they might need it later. How did it look to you?"

"Like a couple of old fraternity pals."

With straining engines, the first group of TBFs were lined up for their final approach.

"So maybe we don't have to send off that transfer request?" asked Kruger.

"I hope not. But I want to talk with them, because—whoa." The second group of TBFs flew over. Now, there were four, not three planes in the group, their wheels all down.

"Take a look at that," said Donovan, jumping to his feet. "Why would a—dammit," he growled.

They watched in horror as the last plane in the group opened fire on the third TBF in line.

Smoke poured from the Avenger's engine. It rolled into a shallow dive to its left.

"Shit," yelled Kruger. The last plane in the formation was a Zero, its round red insignias clearly obvious as it eased into the number three position.

Donovan barked, "Meatball! Mr. Merryweather. Sound general quarters. Take that damn plane under fire immediately!" He dashed inside the pilothouse, yanked the TBS from its bracket, and shouted, "Flower Pot! Flower Pot. This is Monkey Wrench. Be advised last plane in the group now over me is a Jap. We're opening fire!" He ran back to the bridge wing as the Zero began shooting at the next unsuspecting TBF. Donovan yelled at Merryweather, "What's taking you so—"

Wham! Mount 55 cranked out a round. Another round blasted from mount 53. The engine of the second TBF sputtered as the Zero fired into it. "Get him, get the sonofabitch," yelled Donovan. The second TBF drunkenly rolled on its back and plunged straight down into the ocean. "My God," yelled Kruger, shaking his fist at the sky.

Until now, Donovan hadn't really felt hatred for the enemy. Not even when Tiny or Mario was killed. Before, he'd felt a deep sense of gloom and loss. In a way, he'd felt that he had something to do with it; that it was partly his fault. And with that came the lingering sense of guilt and the nightmares and sleepless nights. Now, suddenly, an abject hatred for this enemy consumed him, turning his entire being into white-hot outrage. How can somebody do such a horrible thing to another human being? How can anyone tolerate leaders who drive their people into such a frenzy, throwing away their lives for a sick, criminal society? His mind snapped to the matter at hand. "Richard, you belong in combat."

"On my way!" Kruger dashed off.

Mount 52 roared. Its muzzle was no more than twenty feet from their ears; the blast nearly knocked them over. The other ships began firing. Suddenly the Zero disappeared in a greasy, black puff of smoke, pieces spinning off in all directions.

"Skipper, look." Burt Hammond, the general quarters OOD, jabbed a finger toward the *San Cristobal.* The first TBF that had been shot up was still airborne. Smoking and trailing fire, it wallowed in for a landing aboard the carrier. By a miracle, it struggled to the aft end of the flight deck, the tail hook caught the first wire, and the plane stopped. "Amazing," said Hammond.

Donovan called to the sailors atop the pilothouse, "You lookouts. Vigilance. Look for Japs."

He grabbed Flannigan's shirt. "What are you doing, son?"

"GQ communications, sir," was the immediate reply.

"Well, dammit, while you're communicating, look for Japs." Donovan spun away.

As if on cue, one of the lookouts pointed off the starboard bow. "Aircraft, sir, fifty feet off the deck. Looks like a torpedo bomber."

"Dammit," muttered Donovan. He looked up to Merryweather and shouted, "Cliff, you got that Kate[38] at zero-three-zero?"

Merryweather shouted back, "On target and tracking, sir."

The guns roared in unison as the Kate turned directly for the carrier's starboard beam. The rounds missed, the gunners frantically reloading. One second, two seconds, three seconds, four—

Mount 54 got it off first, quicky followed by the others. A shell hit the ocean right in front of the Kate, spewing up a tall column of shrapnel and water. The water column faded to mist, to a white opacity. The Kate didn't appear on the other side.

Donovan looked up to a grinning Merryweather and gave a thumbs-up.

Another Kate punched through the overcast, a five-hundred-kilogram bomb clutched to its belly. A Wildcat followed close behind, smoke puffing from its wings as it fired its six .50-caliber machine guns. Fire burst from the Kate and it continued right into the ocean, hitting with a mighty splash.

Donovan grabbed a sound-powered telephone and punched CIC.

"XO."

"Richard. We had no warning of this, for crying out loud. What's going on with the IFF?"

Kruger cleared his throat. "Best I can tell, Captain, is that they mixed in with cloud cover and the returning TBFs. Nobody figured it out."

"Can't your people count?" demanded Donovan.

Hammond pointed almost straight up.

Kruger shot back, "Captain, dammit. We're tracking them and—"

"Hold on," Donovan said.

"What is it, Mike?"

Donovan sucked in his breath as a Kate plunged almost straight down through the overcast, its engine screaming, a bomb slung under its belly. Instinctively he knew what the pilot intended. In seconds, the Kate dove straight for the *San Cristobal*'s flight deck and crashed where the stricken TBF had come to a stop. A black-red greasy ball of flame erupted from the flight deck.

"Oh, God."

"Mike, what the hell is it?" shouted Kruger.

"That man wanted to die."

"Who?"

Donovan said, "I wouldn't have believed it if I hadn't seen it. A Jap deliberately dove straight down out of the overcast and crashed right onto the *San Cristobal*."

"You're kidding!"

"No, and I—"

A loud explosion erupted from the carrier. Smoke poured from her flight deck. Flame boiled out of the hangar deck and up toward the deck-edge gun tubs and the island. There was another explosion, louder than the first two. Flaming airplane parts spun across the deck and into the water.

Donovan forced himself to breathe. Then again. "We've got a bad one, Richard. Call over there if you can, and ask if we can render assistance."

"Combat, aye." Kruger hung up.

The carrier seemed to have slowed. "What's our speed, Burt?" he asked Hammond.

"Fifteen knots, Captain," came the reply. Then Hammond pointed. "Is that what I think it is?"

Donovan raised his binoculars. "Those poor bastards." Men were trapped by the fire in the starboard gun tubs. Some jumped over the side, their clothes smoking. Donovan clamped Hammond on the shoulder, "Burt, call away the boat crew and have the bosun's roll the boarding net over the port side."

He leaned in the pilothouse and said to the lee helmsman, "Tell main control to stand by for maneuvering bells. We may be going alongside the *San Cristobal* to render aid."

Calling to Potter, Donovan said, "Tell Chief Casey to stand by to treat burn victims."

"Yes, sir."

"One more thing."

"Sir," said Potter.

"Have Chief Casey break out the salt bags. We're going to need them."

"Salt bags, yes, sir." Potter gulped and gave the order.

Yet another explosion roared from the *San Cristobal*. Smoke billowed through what was once the forward elevator. The whole forward part of the ship was afire. More men jumped over the side, the sea dotted with them.

Donovan checked the sky. Two Wildcats zipped overhead. The TBFs were gone; hopefully they'd found another place to roost. He grabbed the phone and punched combat again.

"XO."

"Richard, what's the story on the air threat?"

"Looks clear for the time being, Captain. The CAP was overwhelmed. Japs came from every direction."

"But we're okay for now?"

"Looks like it. Radar is clear."

"Good enough for me." He hung up and grabbed Hammond's elbow. "Burt, I'll take the conn. I want you to direct the rescue operations, but don't leave the bridge. I've sent word to the doc and he's ready."

Hammond's face was chalk white.

"You okay, Burt?"

"Never better, Captain." Hammond stumbled and braced a palm against the bulkhead.

"Here." Donovan shoved Hammond's head toward his knees for a moment. "That better?"

The color returned to his face. "Never better, Captain."

Donovan slapped him on the rump. "Get going."

The *Matthew* pulled eleven *San Cristobal* sailors from the water, two burned seriously. The *Toohey* picked out another seventeen. Then they stood close by the carrier for three intense hours, spraying water into her hangar decks, dousing fire after fire. At last, the largest fires were extinguished on the carrier. Although she still looked like a smoldering volcano, her skipper declared her out of immediate danger, saying her engineering plant was in reasonable shape and she could sustain fifteen knots. But men were still trapped by the fires and the *Matthew* was ordered alongside for rescue. Ten jumped safely; another fell between the ships. There wasn't time to think, as Donovan kept his destroyer in close to *San Cristobal* as screaming, desperate men leaped onto her fo'c'sle.

Hammond pointed off to starboard just as the last man had jumped.

"Dammit," muttered Donovan. It was a wind line bringing a series of long rolling groundswells toward the *Matthew.* "All back two-thirds," he shouted.

The screws bit the water too late. The first swell rolled under the *Matthew,* lifting her bow up into the *San Cristobal*'s overhanging catwalk. There was a terrible screeching and ripping of metal as the destroyer's stanchions, cleats, bits, and port anchor chewed up through the *San Cristobal*'s catwalk and gun tubs.

Finally gathering sternway, the *Matthew* backed clear, pulling a thirty-foot section of twisted smoldering wreckage onto her foredeck, some of it draping over the side. A small section burst into flame but a repair party was called, the fire put out in minutes. Soon they were chopping and cutting at the wreckage, throwing pieces over the side.

By three that afternoon, the overcast had burned off, and the seas remained calm. The carrier's skipper ordered the *Toohey* and *Matthew* alongside, where the two destroyers set up a highline and transferred the grateful *San Cristobal* sailors back to their ship. Last to return were the burn victims, who were sent over in stokes litters.

An hour later, the radar was still clear. They were about a hundred miles east of the Leyte coast on course one-two-zero, speed now up to twenty knots. The seas were still calm, and all fires on the *San Cristobal* were out. But she looked ugly, especially her blackened and wrecked forward section.

Donovan stood the crew down to a condition III watch and took a tour of the ship. His first stop was CIC, a space of perhaps twelve by eighteen feet on the main deck just aft of the wardroom. Always dark, CIC was crammed with radar repeaters, target-tracking and communications equipment, and backlighted tote boards. The executive officer, four officers, and ten sailors manned the area during general quarters. But now they were down to a condition III watch of just five men.

Donovan walked into CIC to find Kruger leaning on the DRT,[39] reading a report. His hair was rustled when he passed beneath a whining blower outlet. He stopped and raised his head, letting the blast of cool air dry the sweat on his brow. "Ummm." He turned his face higher, letting air wash over his face. "Not bad. Where you guys hiding the beer?"

Kruger said, "In the fridge under the DRT."

"Well, I'm going to guess it's—"

Ensign Kubichek, the communications officer, thumped in and edged among sailors. "Priority, Captain," he announced, passing a clipboard over to Donovan.

All fell silent as Donovan signed for the message. It was classified secret, but everyone in here was cleared for at least that, so he read it aloud. "Message from COMDESRON 77, info *San Cristobal,*" he announced.

"Uh-oh," said Kruger.

"Right. He's ordering the *Toohey* to accompany the *San Cristobal* to Ulithi."

"Soft duty."

"I'll say."

"Is that it?"

"No," said Donovan. "Larry is attaching us TAD to Taffy 3, where we're supposed to await orders for further assignment."

"Who the hell is Taffy 3?" demanded Kruger.

Donovan gave a thin smile. "Perhaps you can look it up, Mr. Kruger."

Kruger retorted, "I think that's a great idea."

Whitman, a first-class radarman, plopped a thick manual on the DRT and wordlessly thumbed pages. He finally found what he wanted and pushed the manual toward Kruger. "Here sir."

Donovan looked over Kruger's shoulder as he read. "Taffy 3 is a carrier group, just like ours."

"And where are they?" asked Donovan.

"According to this, they should be stationed about forty miles off Samar."

Donovan turned to Kubichek. "Okay, Rudy, thanks. Please draft two messages. The first one is a roger to COMDESRON 77 saying we're on our way to rendezvous with Taffy 3. The next message is a flashing-light message to the *San Cristobal,* requesting permission to proceed on duty assigned."

"Yes, sir." Kubichek walked out.

Donovan said, "I'm going to check up forward."

Donovan was amazed at the huge pile of junk on the foredeck. Cliff Merryweather and his first lieutenant, Jack Kelso, moved about, watching over the shipfitters who bent with acetylene torches, cutting up the heavier pieces of wreckage. Jonathan Peete and chief torpedoman Hammer moved among the sailors, helping to throw loose pieces of junk over the side. Donovan walked up to Hammer. "How goes it, Chief?"

"Seen worse, Skipper. Gotta tell ya, though, that was a

pretty chickenshit thing that Jap did." Wearing heavy asbestos gloves, he grabbed an indistinguishable piece of twisted, smoking metal and heaved it over the side.

"They're getting desperate, Chief. They know the end is near."

"Gimme a .45 and ten of them Japs and I'll show 'em how close they really are to the end."

"You'll get your chance, Chief." He walked over to Jonathan Peete, finding him stooped over, yanking on a long section of I-beam. "How you doing, Mr. Peete?"

Peete lifted the I-beam high over his head and, with a growl, tossed it over the side.

"Fine, Captain."

"What's that?" Donovan pointed to a thick, smoldering lump of wreckage jammed next to mount 51.

"Looks like what's left of an engine, sir," said Peete. "It's part of jumbled wreckage that fell on us from the *San Cristobal* when we pulled clear."

"Oh." Donovan recognized a section of propeller blade bent around the engine.

Merryweather walked up. "Kind of bizarre, isn't it?"

"Wonder if it belonged to a Wildcat or a TBF?" asked Donovan.

Merryweather said quietly, "I don't think either one, sir."

"Pardon?"

"Right there." Merryweather pointed. "Part of the cowling. It's painted black."

There was a sinking feeling in Donovan's stomach.

"That's right, Captain. This is what's left of the Jap's engine. And look here, on the cowling, some Nip writing and an insignia of some kind." Merryweather pointed to the cowling, a still-recognizable section of about two by three feet. Japanese characters were written in yellow on one edge. Prominent in the middle was a meticulously drawn picture of two red apples on a square white field bordered by gold filigree.

He noticed a welder cutting the crumpled cowl in sections. "What are you doing?"

Merryweather gestured. "Well, the marines and army guys

are always taking Jap flags and samurai swords. Why can't we grab a souvenir for a change?"

"Why not?" Donovan replied sarcastically.

"You want a section, Skipper?" asked Merryweather.

"Sure, why not?" said Donovan.

FORTY-ONE

24 October 1944
IJN *Yamato*
Sibuyan Sea, Philippines

The dive-bomber roared overhead. Added to the crack of antiaircraft guns, the noise was incredible. Sixteen men braced themselves in the armored flag bridge. Noyama had been briefed that the main deck armor plate aboard the 65,000-ton battleship *Yamato* was 198 millimeters thick. It was designed to survive a direct hit from a five-hundred-kilogram bomb dropped from three thousand meters. During the months swinging at anchor in Lingga Roads, Noyama had walked the decks of the *Yamato* and *Musashi* many times. On occasion, he'd dug a heel at the deck, finding no resounding thud, just the sound of his heel hitting something very, very solid. Yes, the *Yamato*'s main deck did feel 198 millimeters thick.

But this bomb burst with a terrible roar. Everyone was knocked over by the concussion, including Kurita, Ugaki, and Takata, their arms and legs tangled and jumbled together. Groaning and cursing, Ugaki was first to his feet, brushing off his tunic. With both hands, Kurita grabbed the chart table and hauled himself to his feet, blinking. Then he grabbed his head, cried out, and fell to his knees.

Noyama's leg had given way with the blast, and he had trouble getting up. Finally he limped around the chart table. "Admiral?"

Kurita muttered something. But the ack-ack, and the screaming engines outside, and the screaming men inside, obliterated the answer. Finally Kurita rose and began moaning and pounding his head on the chart table.

"Admiral!" gasped Noyama.

"Headache. Ahhh," murmured Kurita.

Noyama grabbed the talker. "Dr. Koketsu. Where is he?"

The talker spoke on the sound-powered phone for a moment, then said, "Sick bay, sir."

"Get him up here," said Noyama, rushing back to Kurita.

Kurita's eyes opened and he blinked again. "Any damage?"

Noyama checked a tote board. "Bomb hit forward near the anchor chain. Damage superficial." Those decks really are thick, he thought to himself. "Are you all right?"

Kurita grabbed his head again, "Shit, this hurts. And my knees feel like they're going to break in half. Even hurts to bend my damn arms."

Noyama grabbed a rolling high stool. "Here, try this."

Kurita nodded and sat. "Koketsu?"

"On his way."

Smoke gushed through an exhaust vent, filling the flag bridge. A rating rushed over and cranked a valve shut, but the damage was already done. Everyone was coughing and hacking and waving their hands at the smoke.

"Open that damn hatch," sputtered Kurita.

"But sir . . . ," said the rating.

"We must breathe. Open it, you fool," barked Kurita.

The rating undogged the hatch. Fans were turned on, and soon the space was clear of smoke. Noyama ducked outside to see a fire on the fo'c'sle, the smoke enveloping the forward part of the ship. But no, the bomb hadn't penetrated the deck.

The noise outside was deafening, as if all of the *Yamato*'s twenty-five-millimeter antiaircraft guns were firing at once. All around them, the First Striking Force unleashed its fury at Halsey's planes, the sky dotted with innumerable flak puffs. From all quarters, Halsey's dive-bombers and torpedo planes buzzed like hornets in coordinated attacks. Noyama was amazed at the sheer size of the attacking force.

Worse, Kurita's mighty fleet steamed circles in the Sibuyan Sea, totally confused, some ships nearly ramming each other as they frantically maneuvered to avoid U.S. Navy bombs and torpedoes. Since 1030, death had been raining from the sky. Now at four in the afternoon, they'd staggered through at least five devastating air raids. Just fifteen minutes ago, they'd heard that the heavy cruiser *Myoko* had taken at least one torpedo and dropped out of formation. Worse, the super-battleship *Musashi* trailed thirty-two kilometers behind, billowing smoke and listing. Recent reports said she was dead in the water, with at least fifteen torpedo hits and as many bomb hits. And the planes kept coming down on the *Musashi,* singling her out.

Someone flashed past Noyama and ducked through the hatch: Dr. Koketsu. Noyama turned to follow and was nearly shoved inside by the concussion of clattering antiaircraft guns. He found Koketsu standing beside Kurita, jamming a thermometer in the admiral's mouth, his hand atop the admiral's shoulder.

Kurita, his voice hoarser than ever, leaned around Koketsu and yelled at Lieutenant Commander Seiji Takahashi, his communications officer. "Where's our air cover? What about Fukudome?[40]"

"I'm trying, sir. Reception is poor." Takahashi was rattled. He was a replacement for the fleet communications officer Commander Yonishi Matsuda, who had been lost on the *Atago.* And gone with the *Atago* were the fleet air codes, so Takahashi had very little to work with. Still he gamely kept at it, speaking into the handset while Kurita shouted in his other ear.

Kurita jumped to his feet. "Get that silly bastard to—"

With both hands, Dr. Koketsu pushed the admiral back onto his stool.

"Let go!" shouted Kurita, the thermometer nearly falling out.

"Fine," said Dr. Koketsu, catching the thermometer. "If you wish to die, then I'll be glad to get out of here."

Noyama walked up. "Admiral, please."

Glaring at both, Kurita sat.

"That's better." Dr. Koketsu reinserted the thermometer and said, "Your fleet needs you, Admiral, and you need me. We can get this done."

"What the hell's wrong with me?" grumbled Kurita. "I felt fine this morning."

"It's your dengue fever. I told you it's going to take two or three weeks. Remember?"

"I don't have two or three weeks," bellowed Kurita, clasping his hands over his ears. "Close that damn hatch!" he shouted to a rating.

The hatch was closed and dogged again. At length Koketsu pulled out the thermometer. "Hmmmm. It's only 38.9." He thumbed Kurita's upper and lower eyelids. "How much sleep did you get last night?"

"Enough," Kurita shot back.

Imperceptibly, Noyama stood a bit behind Kurita, shook his head, and waved two fingers: *two hours*.

Glancing at Noyama, Dr. Koketsu asked Kurita, "Were you unconscious just now?"

Kurita barked, "No."

Noyama nodded. *Yes*.

Koketsu looked across the flag bridge to where Ugaki and his staff were clustered. He cast a hand at a silver carafe. "What's that?"

"Water, sir," replied one of Ugaki's lieutenant commanders. "It's Admiral Ugaki's personal carafe. He won it in a shooting contest four years ago at the Emperor's Aviary."

"Pass it over, please," asked Dr. Koketsu.

Ugaki slowly looked up, his face saying, *What the hell's going on?*

Dr. Koketsu beckoned with fingers on an upraised palm. He looked at Noyama and said, "Your job is to make sure he drinks plenty of water." He pulled a bottle from his pocket and slammed it on the table. "Aspirin. He can have two every four hours. If he needs more, call me."

"Yes, sir," said Noyama.

With a look at Kurita, he said, "Most importantly, he must sleep. If he doesn't, then the dengue will simply be prolonged." He looked Kurita in the eyes. "Do you understand, Admiral?"

"Don't you have anything better than aspirin?" rasped Kurita.

"That's all I have for now. And I want you to go to bed," said Dr. Koketsu.

Kurita cast a hand toward the sound of screaming engines overhead. "Hear that? There's a war on."

"Very well," said Dr. Koketsu. "I'll have a cot sent up. Use it when you can." He stood and looked Noyama in the eye. "Keep me informed. Make sure he gets some sleep. And make sure he drinks water." Then he dashed out the hatch.

"Yes, sir," Noyama called after him.

Kurita rolled bloodshot eyes across the room to Ugaki, whose hands were full dealing with the *Musashi* situation. It was looking worse. And it wasn't just the *Musashi* that Noyama saw as he looked up to the BATDIV 1 status board. The battleship *Nagato* had received two bomb hits; the *Haruna* had been straddled by five near misses.

"Tell *Musashi* to make for the nearest beach," Ugaki ordered his communications officer, a completely bald lieutenant commander named Boshiro Hirota. "She can become an AA platform."

"Admiral Inoguchi reports *Musashi* has lost all power," Hirota reported. "She's listing thirty degrees and her bow is almost awash."

The rattle of cannons and machine guns told the story of the living hell outside as bombs and torpedoes continued to be launched from enemy planes. The sudden silence in the room told of the *Musashi*'s own living hell as they realized she could be lost.

Ugaki pounded his fist, "Can she make a beach?"

Hirota relayed the request.

They heard a buzz as the message came back. Refusing to raise his eyes, Hirota said, "No, sir. Admiral Inoguchi reports the list is almost thirty-five degrees now. He is going to give the order to abandon."

"No!" shouted Ugaki. He reached for the phone.

"Leave it alone!" Kurita rasped from across the room. "Inoguchi is a good man. He knows what he's doing."

Ugaki stiffened, turned his back, and jammed his hands on his hips.

Kurita added, "What destroyers are available to pick up survivors?"

Hitching his pants, Rear Admiral Takata checked a tote board and said, "Right now, the *Tone*[41] is standing by *Musashi*.

Destroyers *Kiyoshimo* and *Hamakaze* are to the farthest rear of our formation and should be available, sir."

Kurita said, "Right, send *Kiyoshimo* and *Hamakaze* for the survivors. Recall *Tone* to us. We're going to need her."

"Yes, sir." Takata grabbed a message pad and began scribbling.

"Ugaki," shouted Kurita.

Ugaki turned and hissed, "How can I help you, Admiral?"

"Listen to me, all of you." Kurita wobbled to his feet and braced a hand on the chart table. "We're sailors of the Imperial Japanese Navy. So let's act like it. Let's get organized. Look outside. We're all a jumble. Ugaki, get your battleships in order. Takata. Same with the cruisers and destroyers: get them organized. As soon as possible, I want to turn west and get out of range of Halsey's damn airplanes. They're pecking at us one by one, and at this rate we'll never make it through the San Bernardino Strait."

As if on cue, it became quiet outside. Takahashi covered his earphone with a hand and reported, "Cease fire. The enemy is retiring."

Ugaki turned to a petty officer. "Damage reports?"

"Just the two bomb hits, sir."

Takahashi held up his hand. "*Myoko*[42] took a hit in the after engine room. Two shafts out of order. Ten degree port list. Best speed is fifteen knots."

Kurita snapped, "Dammit. Another one gone. Send her back to Brunei." Then he shouted, "Well, what are you all waiting for? Lets get all these portholes and hatches open and get some real air in here. After our minds have cleared, let's figure out how far west we have to go before we turn again for the San Bernardino Strait." His voice crackled as he pointed through a newly opened porthole. "Look at that idiotic fleet out there, pride of the Imperial Japanese Navy. All turning in circles, doing their best to ram each other. You'd think we were the damn Chinese navy!" He pointed a bony finger. "Get those ships organized! I want us in a proper ring formation on base course two-nine-zero in five minutes."

He beckoned to Noyama.

"Yes, sir?"

Kurita's face looked jaundiced and pallid. But his eyes were afire as he hissed, "Get a message off to Fukudome. Where is the air cover you promised? Be blunt about it. I repeat, Where is the air cover you promised? A copy of that goes to Toyoda, Nishimura, Shima, and Ozawa."

"Yes, sir."

"Good. Get on it."

It was 1710 when Dr. Koketsu popped through the hatch. Kurita sat on his stool at the chart table. He was fast asleep, his head cradled on his arms. Dr. Koketsu growled when he saw a form on the cot, its face to the bulkhead. He strode over and kicked him in the rump.

"Ahhh." Rear Admiral Takata turned over and sat up. "I'll have your balls!" He rose.

"That's Admiral Kurita's cot, you fool," shot back Dr. Koketsu, a captain, a rank lower than Takata. "He should be—"

"I gave it to him," said Kurita.

"Sir, how do you feel?" asked Dr. Koketsu, walking over.

"Like the zookeeper's heels have marched through my mouth."

"Are you drinking water?"

"And pissing it away just as quickly."

"Good. I want you to—"

"Takata. We're ten minutes late." Kurita looked up to the clock. "Order formation course change for the San Bernardino Strait."

"Yes, sir." Takata rose, hitched his pants, and threw an ugly look at Dr. Koketsu. Then he grabbed a message pad and went to work.

Noyama was surprised. Kurita's voice sounded fairly strong. "Here, Admiral," he said, pushing over Ugaki's carafe, "It's full."

Takahashi walked in with a clipboard. "For you, sir."

Kurita signed for the message and then read it. "Well, we have our orders." He lay down the clipboard and called across the room. "Where's Admiral Ugaki?"

"On the bridge with Admiral Morishita, sir," replied Hirota.

The place came to life as they went back to work. Kurita looked again at the message and asked Noyama, "Where's your little brother?"

"Second Air Fleet Group at Clark, sir," replied Noyama.

Kurita leaned on the chart table and said quietly, "I wonder who will die first."

"Sir?"

For the first time in days, Kurita looked positively rested and at peace. "We're headed for the San Bernardino Strait. Even if we make it through, I doubt if we'll live to see the sunset tomorrow." With a nod, he walked to a status board.

He'd left the clipboard in plain sight. Noyama spun it around. It was from Admiral Toyoda, CinC of the entire Combined Fleet, to all commands:

ALL FORCES WILL DASH TO THE ATTACK, TRUSTING IN DIVINE GUIDANCE.

FORTY-TWO

24 October 1944
Price House
MacArthur command post
Tacloban City, Leyte Island, Philippines

"*Verdammit,* no!" Major General Charles Willoughby shouted in his thick German accent. His cold was decidedly worse, making his demeanor nearly intolerable. He sneezed once again and carefully dabbed at his nose. Intelligence chief to Douglas MacArthur, Willoughby was six-three, wiry, with thin lips, sharp features, and straight black hair meticulously parted down the middle. His "summer cold" had been dogging him for days. He'd picked it up while at sea on the *Nashville* and hadn't been able to shake it. Worse, it made him irritable to those working around him.

Although they got along well, Owen Reynolds didn't want to risk another outburst from his boss. It was 2300 and everyone else was asleep upstairs, getting their first solid rest in weeks: MacArthur, Kenney, Huff, Eichelberger, and Sutherland. Anxious to get off the *Nashville* and see the action close-up, MacArthur secured the Price house in Tacloban City, capital of Leyte, for a command post. Perfectly suited, the Price house was a two-story stucco-and-concrete mansion on the corner of Santo Niño and Justice Romualdez streets right in the center of town. The home's original owner was an American businessman, Walter Price, now a captive of the Japanese in Santo Tomás prison on Luzon. Price's Filipina wife had been tortured by the Japanese and lived in the jungle while the Japanese turned her home into an officers' club. Even now she was too frightened to return.

MacArthur had received more than he'd bargained for earlier this evening. A fully active Japanese fifth column promptly broadcast the news of MacArthur's new headquarters to Manila. During a lull in the rain, Japanese fighters attacked the Tacloban airfield and fired a fuel dump, the flames roiling a thousand feet into the overcast and lighting up the surrounding area, including Tacloban City. Mercifully, the rain put it out an hour later—but not before the planes found the prominent Price house and raked it with cannon and machinegun fire. There were no injuries and now, two hours later, General of the Army Douglas A. MacArthur slept within six feet of where two twenty-millimeter cannonshells had punched holes in his bedroom's thick concrete walls.

Lightning flashed. Thunder rumbled, bringing more of the rain that had been pounding Leyte for the past four days. Not only did the rain slow MacArthur's advance across the island, but it also kept Tacloban's only airfield bogged, making flight operations impossible. The Tacloban airfield had been key to their advance. They'd expected to have P-38s and P-47s supporting their troops by now. Instead the fighter-bombers sat mired in mud while engineers sat out the storm, waiting for the earth to dry. The navy continued to fly air cover, but they were overextended, running low on fuel and ammunition. And the planes were getting tired.

Born in 1892, Adolf Tscheppe Weidenbach was the son of Baron von Tscheppe Weidenbach of Baden, Germany. After attending the University of Heidelberg, he migrated to the United States in 1910 and changed his name to Charles Willoughby. He joined the army in 1914, reached the rank of major, and served on the western front in World War I. Willoughby went into the intelligence business in 1924 and served abroad as a military attaché in South American embassies. MacArthur found Willoughby in 1939 and appointed him his intelligence chief. He'd served well ever since, often colliding with the erudite, Yale-educated politico Lieutenant General Richard K. Sutherland, MacArthur's chief of staff. Owen Reynolds often wondered if MacArthur kept those two around just for the fun of watching them fight. Both were born to the purple, but their two cultures couldn't have been more diverse: Willoughby, the Prussian son of a German baron, versus Sutherland, the son of a senator from West Virginia, later a Supreme Court justice.

For now the blue-blooded chief of staff was asleep, while the red-eyed blockheaded German was reading copies of radio traffic from Halsey's Third and Kinkaid's Seventh fleets. Reynolds decided to try one more time. Pointing out one message, he said, "General Willoughby, I don't think General MacArthur realizes the Japs have reversed course in the Sibuyan Sea and are once again headed for the San Bernardino Strait. Worse, I don't think Admiral Halsey realizes it, either."

"*Ja!*" Willoughby sat heavily in a chair and sniffed. He was a great pouter and, with his regimented Germanic background, was hard-pressed to give up on his own conclusions. He waved at another message. "But then how do you explain this contact report of another fleet of Jap ships up north"—he squinted at a map—"about four hundred miles north? Four carriers, it says the Japs are throwing at us. Now, that's what I call a major threat, and that's where Halsey is going. The other ships you speak of in the Sibuyan Sea were wiped out today. All that's left are stragglers." He checked a thick operation order. "Besides, look at this. We have carrier groups off Leyte."

"But those are escort carriers, sir, not fleet carriers," protested Reynolds.

"But they have airplanes, don't they, with torpedoes and bombs?"

"Yes, sir, but—"

"Here, for example." Willoughby slapped his hands over his face and sneezed loudly. After wiping with a handkerchief, he continued. "This group"—he thumbed a page—"Taffy 3, now posted farthest north. Hmmm, let's see, six aircraft carriers—"

"Slow targets on merchant hulls. Hell, they're so slow they can't get out of their own way, General. Eighteen knots maximum. And they only have . . ."

Willoughby turned a baleful eye: his right one.

"Sorry, sir."

Willoughby continued, "Six aircraft carriers, three destroyers, and four destroyer escorts. Now, don't you think that should be enough to handle a few stragglers?"

Reynolds scratched his head. "Well . . ."

"And here. See this? There are two more Taffy groups south of Taffy 3. Taffy 1 and Taffy 2, all about the same size. I'll be damned. Taffy 3 is commanded by that rear admiral. Clifton Sprague? Remember him? They call him Ziggy. We sat beside him during the Manus pre-sailing conference last month."

"Yes, sir, I do." Reynolds recalled a two-star aviator whose face had creased and wrinkled long before its time. And it wasn't from lack of sleep. Reynolds had seen too many faces like that out here. Even his own.

"They should be able to take care of whatever fools come out of the San Bernardino Strait, don't you think?"

"But that's just it, General," protested Reynolds. "The Japs are in the Sibuyan Sea now and are heading east. What if they come in force? We should—"

"We don't know how many."

"What if there's thirty or forty of them, General? Maybe more. Here, look at this PBY report. The navigation lights are on in the San Bernardino Strait for the first time in three years."

"That was probably part of their plan, don't you see? Whoever was supposed to turn on the lights did it anyway." Willoughby snorted. "He didn't know about Halsey's great victory today. All those ships we sank. We even got that big superbattleship they keep talking about. Those damn lights don't mean a thing."

Reynolds sighed and pointed to another message. "And more Japs are approaching from the south, through the Surigao Strait. That'll be a night battle."

Willoughby pulled out a dark medicinal bottle of terpin hydrate and took a swig. He squeezed his eyes shut for a moment and let it burn in his throat. "Ahhh. That stuff is lethal. Better than cognac." He capped the bottle and shoved it in his back pocket. With a wink at Reynolds, he asked, "Ever try this?"

"No, sir."

"Get Doc Egeberg to fix you up when you have a bad cough or cold. It's got codeine."

"Really?"

"Yes. Tastes great, but it constipates you. I won't be shitting for months." After wiping his mouth, he burped and said, "As I was saying, the Surigao Strait is Admiral Kinkaid's responsibility. He has waiting six battleships plus eight cruisers, thirty-seven destroyers, eleven escorts . . . even . . ." He coughed. ". . . PT boats. Impossible for the Japs to get through."

Reynolds said, "I agree with that, sir. But it's the San Bernardino situation that worries me. Look, I'm not a master of naval strategy, but leaving the strait unguarded looks like poor policy to me. And the navigation lights *are* on."

Willoughby rose to his feet, wobbling somewhat. Dabbing at his nose with a handkerchief, he said, "You are a good officer, Owen. Always, your work has been near perfect if not so. And you have combat experience, just like I have—a quality that's critical for an intelligence officer." He tried a smile. "*Ja*. You're right. You have no naval experience. Leave it up to them."

"Yes, sir." *But the San Bernardino Strait is unguarded and the damn lights are on,* he wanted to shout. He checked his watch: 0030, half after midnight. Probably too late anyway. Halsey is too far along in his dash north intercepting those Jap carriers.

Willoughby raised his little dark bottle of terpin hydrate and gulped. "Ahhh. Now I'm doing something I should have done hours ago. Good night, Owen." He walked out.

"Good night, sir."

FORTY-THREE

25 October 1944*
IJN *Yamato*
San Bernardino Strait
Philippine Islands

Noyama's headphones were connected to the *Yamato*'s main radio room, signal bridge, battle center, main-battery plot, and pilothouse; others gathered in flag plot were connected to the screen commanders, tactical commander, group commander, and intelligence commander. The seven staff officers of Ugaki's Battleship Division One intermingled around the chart table with Kurita's beleaguered staff of fifteen, their phone cords often tangled.

Miraculously, the noise level was low as their eyes darted to tote boards or examined the master chart or paged through thick operating manuals. Occasionally someone would glance over the radar operator's shoulder to see the disposition of the First Striking Force. For now the picture was all too evident. They were at battle stations and steamed in single file through the San Bernardino Strait at twenty-two knots. Samar Island lay to their right, the southernmost extremity of Luzon to their left. *Yamato* was the last ship in a column twelve kilometers long consisting of four battleships, six heavy cruisers, two light cruisers, and seven destroyers. *Yamato* was now at the narrowest part of the strait, where it closed down to within three and a half kilometers.

There were treacherous whirlpools out there, and the current, racing from the Philippine Sea to the Sibuyan, often

---

*Time stated in local time, H time + 8, for the Philippines.

gushed through at eight knots—which meant the navigation team on the bridge had their hands full. Rear Admiral Morishita, *Yamato*'s commanding officer, dashed with his men from bridge wing to bridge wing, taking sightings on buoys or dark promontories, shouting orders at the helmsman. Minutes ago, the Matnog Bay buoy had popped up on their starboard side exactly where it should have been. So far, there'd been no groundings or close calls.

With everyone else, Noyama wondered what lay on the other end. What if Halsey was there, stretched across the strait? He could "cap the T[43]" and wipe them out, one by one, as they steamed through. Reversing course would be extremely difficult. With a darkened ship and all the mayhem, there were sure to be collisions. That's why Kurita had ordered life jackets to be worn. The admiral was sure death lay on the other side. Worse, when they'd all exited, they'd be even more vulnerable as they changed from transit formation to air-defense ring formation. With a twelve-kilometer-long column, it would take an hour for all ships to exit and get sorted out. And given all his fast battleships, Halsey could have them for breakfast.

Something cracked. Rear Admiral Takata had snapped a pencil in half. Nervously, he hitched up his pants and then tossed both pencil halves into a metal wastebasket, two meters distant. "Bull's-eye," he claimed, rearranging his belt. "Maybe someday I'll play baseball." He grabbed another pencil and bent over the chart.

Kurita ignored him and turned his back.

"Lose weight," snorted Ugaki. "Otherwise, you'll never make it around the bases." Snickers ranged around the table. The navigation lights beckoned in silent invitation.

Noyama clamped his hands over his earphones just as the Matnog Bay beacon passed down their starboard side. They looked at him. He tried to keep his voice level as he reported, "Flashing-light message from *Kishinami*. They're passing Bingay Point to starboard. The lighthouse is operating. No radar contact. It looks clear, so far." He checked the clock, 0035, made an entry in his log, and looked up. Their faces said the same thing. The destroyer *Kishinami* had safely exited the San Bernardino Strait and was in the Philippine Sea. Now what?

"I know this," said Kurita. "Halsey is out there somewhere. Tell *Kishinami* to steam ahead thirty kilometers and report again. We must be sure."

"Yes, sir." Noyama relayed the message to the signal bridge with a copy to the pilothouse.

The signal bridge came right back with another message. Noyama reported, "Bingay Point lighthouse in sight."

They looked at the radar screen. "Nine kilometers ahead," muttered Kurita. "Where the hell is Halsey?" He looked up to Ugaki.

Ugaki shook his head.

"All right, then," said Kurita, "if Halsey is playing cat and mouse, let's not make it too easy for him."

"No, we don't want to do that," said Ugaki.

"What if we go to twenty-seven knots?" said Kurita.

"Tougher firing solution for him, tougher fuel consumption for us," said Ugaki.

The two admirals locked glances and imperceptibly nodded.

Noyama asked, "Increase formation speed to twenty-seven knots?"

"Affirmative, execute immediately," said Kurita.

"Yes, sir." Noyama gave the order to the signal bridge.

Half an hour later, they were out of the strait and steaming east along the northern coast of Samar. To the relief of everyone in flag plot, they had safely changed to an air-defense ring formation. In the center were the four battleships *Yamato, Nagato, Kongo,* and *Haruna*. The next ring contained their four heavy cruisers; the third ring held two light cruisers and two heavy cruisers; the outside ring had the seven destroyers.

Noyama checked the chart. Bacan Island, on the northeast extremity of Samar, lay about eighty kilometers ahead. Then they would turn south and dash the 160 kilometers to Leyte Gulf.

He glanced at their faces. To a man, their expression was one of incredulity. They had all expected to be dead by this time.

Kurita eased next to him and muttered.

"Sir?"

"When was the last time we heard from Nishimura?"

Noyama checked a log. "About five minutes ago. The Southern Force is well into Surigao. They will pass Panaon Island in fifteen minutes. Admiral Shima is about fifty kilometers astern. Nishimura expects to transit into Leyte Gulf right after that. So far he's seen a few PT boats, but otherwise the enemy situation is unknown."

"He's too early, dammit," said Kurita. "So is Shima. They won't be able to select targets at night. They need daylight." He raised bloodshot eyes to the overhead. "We're two days late and this has turned into a mess." He spoke loudly so that Ugaki, half asleep in a chair across the room, could hear. "Fuel is precious. I'm reducing speed. Besides, I'd rather see Leyte Gulf in the morning than in darkness."

Ugaki waved a hand and nodded off.

Kurita snorted. "A warrior. Doesn't anything bother him?"

Noyama raised his eyebrows.

"Yes, give the order. Formation speed, twenty knots."

"Yes, sir." Noyama called the signal bridge and relayed the order.

Kurita bent over the radar operator's shoulder for a moment. "Expand your range to the maximum. Let me see the northeast quadrant."

"Yes, sir."

Trailing his phone cord, Noyama walked over and looked over their shoulders. Nothing. The radar was clear.

They looked at each other. "Where is he?" said Kurita.

"Could he be going after Admiral Ozawa?" asked Noyama. Steaming about five hundred kilometers to the north, Ozawa had reported he'd finally been detected by U.S. Navy reconnaissance planes.

"No, he's not that stupid." Kurita shuffled over to the cot Dr. Koketsu had rigged. He fell heavily into it but lay on his back, his hands folded behind his head, eyes wide open. "Where is that damn Halsey?" he muttered.

PART THREE

Attack immediately with all weapons, closing to point blank ranges, while Convoy and Carrier get clear. This would be a "Captain's battle," where the task of each Captain is to get a maximum number of shells and torpedoes into the enemy as quickly as possible.

COMTASKGRP 14.3-A, Annex B
23 October 1941
Rear Admiral H. K. Hewitt
(On dealing with German surface raiders in the North Atlantic)

Despair not an enemy because he is weak,
Fear him not because he is strong.

Japanese Imperial mandate

FORTY-FOUR

24 October 1944*
Eastbound X 4236
Southern Pacific Railway staging yard
Truckee, California

Fred Droesch, the brakeman, muttered, then rolled over in his bunk.

"Go back to sleep, Fred. I'll get it." Milo Lattimer jumped from the caboose and walked toward Ida's coffee shop across the yard, an empty thermos swinging from his hand.

They'd just passed the High Sierras' 6,899-foot summit and pulled into the Truckee station; here they had cut out two helper engines, now deadheading back to Roseville. A muted sunrise brought dark clouds that tumbled overhead in a confused array. A cold zephyr ruffled his hair and swept over his bald pate. It was the seasonal warning that winter was about to descend on the mountain, bringing rain and snow and miserable short days and long cold nights. Looking both ways, he stepped over the eastbound line and ducked behind a quietly hissing switcher engine, waiting for orders to spot logging cars on the number three track.

"Hey, Milo." A red-faced Charlie Hester, the maintenance foreman, caught up to him, puffing.

"Slow down, Charlie. You'll have a heart attack."

"You know you had a phone call?" Hester wheezed in the summit's thin air.

"What the hell?"

Hester flicked his eyebrows up and down a couple of times.

---

*Time stated in local time, U time − 8, for the U.S. West Coast.

"You know who." He twirled a finger in the air and grinned. "Henry said to give you this." He handed over an obsolete train order. A number was written on the back. Lattimer's heart skipped a beat when he saw "the indians are coming" written beside the number. It was a code phrase: *Emergency—contact me immediately.*

"That number's in Roseville, ain't it?" Hester pointed.

"It is." Lattimer swore under his breath. He'd been trying to keep his liaison with Lorena quiet, if not a secret. But things get around in a small town, especially among railroaders. And particularly when Lorena grew short of money. That's when she began putting out in earnest.

And that happened all the time. God! Lorena could burn it fast. During her courier missions in San Francisco, she would go into Gump's or Saks Fifth Avenue and blow whatever Radizar gave her: nylon stockings, near-black-market silk dresses, patent-leather shoes with impossibly high heels, flimsy lingerie that she immediately put to good use. Then there was that damn expensive perfume she insisted on wearing: Arpège. Everybody turned their heads at that. Or that tight skirt and damn fox-fur coat she got last month, the combination devastating. She'd worn it last Saturday night when they went to the movies. Her hand had rested lightly on Lattimer's arm as she strutted down Vernon Street, her perfume flooding all of downtown. Heads turned, traffic stopped, servicemen gawked, some whistling and shouting "Hubba-hubba" while wives threw sharp elbows into husbands who had the temerity to glance. Lattimer didn't give a damn if she wanted to blow her wad on such nonsense except that it drew attention to him. When he tried to warn her of it, she only raised an eyebrow and gave a coquettish smile. Now the good citizens of Roseville were abuzz about Lorena Ortiz's nocturnal habits and how a housemaid working at the Atwater Hotel could afford such a snazzy wardrobe. Lattimer vowed to do something about it. Quick.

The indians are coming. Call immediately. They'd joked about it often and had never had to use it. Until now. And the number on the slip of paper wasn't her studio apartment with the squeaky Murphy bed. Where then?

The nearest phone was in the dispatch office a quarter mile

down the track. No wonder Hester was out of breath. He'd had to run with the message. Worse, there wasn't enough time to reach the dispatch station and then double back to Ida's to fill his coffee thermos. He was out of coffee in the caboose. And the stove was low on fuel; it was getting cold in there. "Dammit," he said again.

"Ain't my fault," said Hester. "See you at Ida's." He moved off.

"Thank you, Charlie." Lattimer stood for a moment, rubbing his jaw. *The indians are coming.* Lattimer bent into a bitter wind and began his trek to the dispatch office.

He tromped in five minutes later and strode up to Skinner's desk. Skinner, a mousy little man with rimless glasses, sat behind a rolltop desk piled high with manuals, padded forms, and loose documents. Skinner didn't look up as he bent over filling in a legal-size form.

"Henry, can I use your phone, please?"

Skinner dipped his pen in the inkwell and kept scratching.

"Henry!" demanded Lattimer. "I'm out of time."

Without looking up, Skinner said, "Personal business or company business?"

"Henry, dammit!"

Skinner nodded across the room to a wall-mounted phone.

"Thanks." Lattimer walked over, dialed the operator, and gave the number on the slip.

She picked it up on the second ring. "Allo." It was vintage Lorena, murdering her English.

"*Schatze,* it's me."

"Where have you been?"

"Honey, we just got into Truckee. I called as soon as I got your message. Where are you?"

"Public phone, the train station."

Sure enough, he heard a steam whistle hoot in the background. He checked his pocket watch: six fourteen. "Why so damn early?"

Ignoring the question, she asked, "Do you remember that man I spoke of the other day?" Her voice was level, businesslike. Lorena Ortiz was not a hot Latin lover today.

He felt an odd, forbidding stirring deep in his bowel. "The one you thought was following you?" he asked quietly.

"Yes. I got a close look at him today from the alley. He is following me. And he set up a camera across the street from me in an apartment house."

"You're not imagining things?"

"No, and I'll tell you something else. He's that fellow with the tall butch haircut who rides your train. That marine."

"Shit!" Lattimer's stomach felt like it had turned to concrete. He glanced over, seeing Henry Skinner still bent over his report. But his pen was idle, his head cocked toward Lattimer.

"That's not all," Lorena continued. "This morning I found out he and his navy friend have set up a twenty-four-hour surveillance on your room. There are three teams, two people in eight-hour shifts, across from your house right now."

"Gott." That slipped out. "How do you know?"

"What else? A client."

"And you verified it?"

She gave a short laugh. "Do I need to? This guy is a sergeant on the police force."

"Oh."

"As soon as the sergeant pulled up his pants and got out, I went looking for myself.

"They're watching you, all right. And next to their room is a small bathroom with an open window."

"Yes?"

"If you look closely, you'll see a camera with a telephoto lens mounted on a tripod."

Lattimer turned and glanced across the room. Henry Skinner was now sitting back, fingers laced behind his head, watching intently.

He turned to the wall and said softly, "We better scram." Lattimer was surprised at what he'd just said. He never believed he would say it. He never expected to have to lam out. It occurred to him how much he liked it here in Roseville. The trains, the farms, the hot dry summers. All the oranges he could eat. The people, especially the people. Fine, solid people whose parents and grandparents had fought their way to California over the Sierras. He glanced out the window.

Even now, as a thunderstorm built, he longed for the raw majesty of the High Sierras, the Donner Pass, tall redwoods, snow, and breathtaking vistas stretching fifty miles to the horizon.

"Yes, I'm leaving to visit Mr. Radizar"—the Argentine consul in San Francisco.

"Have you called him?"

"Yes."

"Will there be room for two?"

She paused. Then, "Yes."

Lattimer exhaled loudly. "Thank you."

"De nada."

"What line is it?"

"Pan American Fruit Lines."

"Can you wait for me? I lay over in Sparks tonight and will be back tomorrow morning."

"I'll be gone by then."

"Lorena—"

"I'll wait for you until six PM tomorrow."

"Six PM? Where?"

"With Mr. Radizar until we walk over to the ship. He has arranged passage for two. The SS *Pan-American Trader* leaves at six PM tomorrow."

"What pier?"

"I don't know yet." Her tone changed. "I . . . I think I better go."

"What's wrong?"

She hung up.

Lattimer cradled the receiver and leaned against the wall, rubbing his chin. Something didn't add up. He caught Skinner's eye as the little man looked away. "Henry, do you have today's *Chronicle*?"

Skinner nodded to his desk. "Came in an hour ago." He put his feet up on the desk, grabbed the paper, and leaned back. "About time for my break and to see how things are going." He made a show of reading the front page.

Lattimer walked over and snatched it out of his hands.

"Hey! You can't—"

"Try and stop me, you little turd. Besides, I'm only borrowing it." Lattimer nodded to a thermos in an open drawer. "That yours?"

Skinner started to rise. Lattimer shoved him back in the chair. "Stay," he barked. He grabbed the thermos and unscrewed the top. "Tomato soup?" He looked down to Skinner. His glasses were askew on his face, and he tried to adjust them. But his hands shook. Finally he gave up and managed, "Y . . . yes."

"Thanks." Lattimer checked the *San Francisco Chronicle*'s table of contents then flipped to page sixteen. Steamship movements were posted in the lower left-hand corner. Running his finger down a column, he found the listing for the *Pan-American Trader.* She was moored at Pier 42. Departure was posted for eleven o'clock tonight.

Verdammit! She'd said six tomorrow.

It hit him. Lorena had a good idea where he kept everything. The money, the fuses, the tools, the explosives, the radio. He hadn't told her directly, but she knew enough to be dangerous. God, what a fool he'd been. He should have seen this coming a long time ago.

Skinner tried to rise again. "I need that thermos."

Lattimer pitched him into the chair and shoved with his foot, making it roll across the room and crash into the opposite wall. As it went, he eyed Henry Skinner's meticulously chalked tote board. The next train for Roseville was due to leave in five minutes. It was supposed to be spotted on track four. He leaned over and glanced out the window. Sure enough, she waited there. Two AC-10 engines in front, and two more in the middle, pulled a mixed consist of eighty-five cars. The board said the conductor was Adrian Khastor, the brakeman was Stan Tilden. Khastor was a six-five giant who loved beating up hobos. Tilden, a brakeman's brakeman, had lost two fingers of his left hand and one in his right, all in the performance of his duty. If it were not for the war, he'd be retired. Most likely, Khastor would have coffee to spare, but Skinner's tomato soup sounded good. Besides, it would be the last time he'd be riding the Southern Pacific. It didn't matter what Skinner did.

"I need it more than you do."

"The soup is for my ulcer. I can't have anything else."

Lattimer actually felt sorry for the little bastard. Aside from being a snide, impudent little gnome, Henry Skinner was a good dispatcher, one of Southern Pacific's best. Except he had ulcers.

He pulled out his wallet and tossed over a five-dollar bill. "Send Charlie over to Ida's."

"I can have you fired for this," Skinner sputtered.

"Fix up your stomach first. Ida makes great tomato soup." Lattimer walked out.

FORTY-FIVE

24 October 1944
Southern Pacific staging yards
Roseville, California

Walt Logan jammed the receiver to his ear and shouted into the mouthpiece, “Are you okay, Henry?”

Sabovik sat on the edge of Logan’s desk, listening to metallic muttering on the line’s other end.

Logan spoke louder: “Is that all, Henry? Your damn tomato soup? What are you bitching about? Get your dead butt over to Ida’s for a refill. What’s the big deal?”

The receiver growled again.

Logan said, “All right, all right, Henry. Keep your shirt on. We’ll get someone up there right away.” He jiggled the receiver hook. “Ruby, put me through to the bunkhouse.” Walt looked up to Sabovik and whispered, “You’re not going to believe this.”

Logan leaned down to the mouthpiece. “Frank, it’s Walt. I need a conductor right away. Who’s on standby? What? Milo Lattimer jumped ship up in Truckee. Who can you get . . . Taylor, Jeb Taylor . . . ?”

With a blast of its whistle, a Big Boy locomotive thundered past on track two hauling a long consist of refrigeration cars. But that didn’t deter Walt Logan. Sabovik couldn’t hear a word, but Logan’s lips kept moving in a world of chuffing steam engines and clanking, grinding railroad stock.

Finally the caboose trailed past. Logan was saying, “. . . is he sober? No, I’m not kidding. Everyone knows about Jeb . . . okay, he’ll do. Get him over here and we’ll deadhead him to Sparks. Yeah, right away.”

Logan hung up. His wooden armchair protested loudly as he tilted back and eyed Sabovik.

"Believe what?" asked Sabovik.

Logan slowly shook his head. "I've known Milo Lattimer for a good—" He shook his head again. "—a good five years now. He came for dinner all the time, especially after Ralphie lit out. We . . . we played chess at least twice a month. Hell, you've been over. You've seen us. For a while there, I thought he and Diane might end up together. Even at that he's been like family. Now . . ."

"Walt, what is it?"

Logan looked up. "He jumped his train up in Truckee. Slapped Henry Skinner around, our dispatcher. All over a stupid thermos of tomato soup."

Sabovik felt a surge of adrenaline. Somehow the case was beginning to unravel. Following the *Mount Saint Helens* explosion in Ulithi Atoll, they'd traced explosion commonalities back to Roseville and the route over the Donner Pass. Rear Admiral Cactus Jack Egan had moved mountains and delivered to Sabovik top-secret West Coast freight manifests for the past twelve months along with a complete load-out list of specific ammunition ships, and where the ammunition was off-loaded.

After exhaustive examination of these manifests and eyewitness accounts of the explosions, they'd detected a pattern. The grisly data pointed toward torpedoes. But that seemed impossible, since torpedoes were shipped without exploders. Only when the torpedoes reached their launch platforms were the exploders inserted and made ready. Just ten days ago, Cactus Jack had again convened his committee on Yerba Buena Island. What could be making torpedoes go off? they wondered. It was a dead end. Yet after examining all the other data, there seemed to be no other conclusion.

The tempo picked up when navy CID picked up something interesting on a records check. It concerned Milo Lattimer's date of birth. Lattimer claimed he was born in Queens Hospital, New York, on 11 July 1918. However, the records check indicated Queens Hospital had had a terrible fire on 23 June 1917, and had to be completely closed for renovation. It didn't reopen until New Year's Day 1920. Something didn't add up. Sabovik reckoned it was a mistake a spy could have made if he hadn't lived in the area. That's when they began watching Lattimer. "Where is he now?" asked Sabovik.

"I have no idea. He could have jumped on any number of trains. Hell, they're grinding through Truckee every five minutes. East or west. I can't say which way he went."

The phone rang and Logan picked it up. "Hold on, he's right here." Logan handed over the phone. "It's Nitro."

Sabovik grabbed the phone set. "Fire away."

"It's Lorena. She fell, or was pushed, I don't know."

"Fell— What?"

"Over here at the Atwater. I got a couple of photos of it. She came flying through the fire escape doorway, crashed through the rail, and went down."

"How far?"

"Three stories."

"Jesus. What's the coroner say?"

"John, she's still alive."

"What?"

"I don't know how she survived, but she landed in a Victory Garden: radishes. Ambulance attendants are getting ready to pack her up."

"Wait a minute." Sabovik leaned back, biting his thumbnail. He covered the mouthpiece and asked Logan, "What time did Lattimer go missing?"

Logan checked his notes. "A little after sunrise. The X 4236 was supposed to leave Truckee at six twenty. He didn't make it back aboard."

"Could he have hopped a train and made it back here since then?"

"Yes."

Sabovik said into the phone, "Nitro."

"I'm here."

"Has the ambulance left yet?"

"Not yet, but any moment. I don't see how she lived through that. Looks like everything's broken. And she rattles when she breathes. It's like—"

"Get in the ambulance. Stay with her."

"You want me to—"

"Do you have a sidearm?"

"Only this little .32 automatic shoved in my back belt."

"That'll do. It could be Lattimer. He's on the loose."

"Well, how do you like that? What happened?"

Sabovik explained. "Could Lattimer have gotten into her apartment without you seeing?"

"I suppose so, if he went around the side— Look, they're closing the ambulance doors. I better scram."

"Go, then. Stay with her." Sabovik hung up.

The door opened and a large man tromped in, wearing a fur cap. "Hi, Adrian," said Logan. "Whatcha got there?"

Adrian Khastor held up a thermos. "Milo left this on my rig. Could you put it in his box?"

Logan and Sabovik exchanged glances. "Did he ride down the hill with you?"

"Yep."

"When did you get in?" asked Sabovik.

Khastor pulled out a pocket watch and raised the lid. "About an hour ago." His face darkened. "Anything wrong?"

"What was he like on the way down?" asked Sabovik.

Khastor looked at Logan, who nodded: *Yes, it's okay to answer this man's questions.* He replied, "Funny that you ask; Milo was moody. Not like him. Wouldn't talk. Just looked out the window with his arms folded."

"Is that all?" asked Logan.

"He didn't want to play chess. Not that I could beat him."

"Okay, thanks." Sabovik dashed out.

Harry Turner was in a hurry for one simple reason. He'd been gambling at a truck stop just outside Reno. Now he was four hours late hauling his truckload of aircraft engine parts over the Sierras. He'd simply lost track of time. And that's not all he lost. He'd lost seventy-five dollars at the crap table, and he knew Sylvia would be furious when he returned home to Oakland this evening. But for now, he was pushing "Big Mo"—that's what he called his Mack truck—for all he was worth. Big Mo's six-cylinder engine purred like a kitten as he fed in more gas. Fifty-five . . . sixty . . . sixty-five. He was passing almost everybody on the downgrade. But it was still early. The highway was empty, and Harry was making good time. He sat back and tried to relax. Time for another cigarette. Coordinating thumb and forefinger with the matchbook cover, he expertly flicked up a light as Big Mo rumbled around a shallow curve. Gently, he laid the Chesterfield on his lip and bent slightly to touch it to the flame.

Harry Turner didn't see the yellow school bus pull out. When he looked up, it was just one hundred feet away. The image of the shocked bus driver filled his mind as he jammed on the brakes. As Big Mo flashed closer he saw a startled seven-year-old boy. He had crystal-clear blue eyes. A red-and-black-checkered cap covered most of his straight blond hair. His mouth opened in incredulity to the shape of an O. Harry Turner hit the brakes hard, whipped the wheel to the right, and prayed.

Big Mo hit the school bus in the engine compartment with a terrible crash. The bus flipped on its left side and spun wildly, as if a three-hundred-foot drooling giant were playing spin the bottle. It made one and a half clockwise turns before the crumpled engine compartment slammed into a redwood tree. On the other side of Highway 80, Big Mo also rolled onto the driver's side. The big Mack truck caromed forward 227 feet before it crashed into a drainage ditch.

Big Mo's gasoline tank exploded.

Screams were heard as far as Strockmeyer Farms, nearly a quarter mile away . . .

Sabovik pulled up in Walt Logan's dark blue Chevy two-door coupe and stepped out. He'd been to Roseville Community Hospital many times, but he'd never seen it like this. At least four ambulances choked the emergency room entrance. Another ambulance caromed around the corner, its siren screeching. He heard at least one other, blocks away, getting closer.

Quickly he walked over to one of the ambulances, a gleaming red Cadillac. It was empty; the driver sat at the wheel, making notes. "What happened?" asked Sabovik.

The driver, with slicked-back, pomaded hair, had a blood-spattered white coat. He looked up, took in Sabovik's navy uniform, and said, "Damn truck hit a school bus out on the main highway."

"How bad was it?"

"Bad enough. Two kids dead. Truck driver dead. At least twelve injured kids. Some pretty awful." He nodded back at the emergency room. "Hey, I'm sorry, maybe one of them's yours?"

"No, that's okay," said Sabovik.

"Good. Look, here comes another. Gotta scram." He started the Cadillac, dropped the shift lever into low gear and pulled away with a screech. Another ambulance drew to a halt and expertly backed into the space, its siren mournfully winding down.

The rear door blasted open and the attendants quickly wheeled out a gurney carrying a young boy. He was unconscious, a black-and-red-checkered cap jammed under his belt. Blood ran from under a bandage on his head. The ambulance attendants were joined by two nurses at the doorway, the four of them wheeling the gurney through the door and into the emergency room.

Sabovik walked through the doors of what surely captured the essence of Bedlam Hospital. White-coated figures rushed about, trays and instruments scattered on the floor. A boy was being given a transfusion, the blood bag suspended high over the gurney as physicians worked on his chest. A girl, no more than seven years old, whimpered as a nurse tried to console her. Her face was red and she'd almost bitten through her lower lip. A bone protruded from her arm with a greenstick fracture; the nurse was trying to immobilize it as the girl spasmed in pain.

Their whimpering, and shock, and incredulity, seized him like a giant steel claw. He was surprised there was no out-and-out screaming. But each groan, each tear, each blink of the eye conveyed pain, abject distress, and hopelessness in its rawest form. It reminded him too much of that horrible night aboard the *Tampa*. And Tiny.

Wait until the parents show up, he figured. That's when the screaming begins.

Get out.

Quickly he strode for the double doors and walked through. Diane Logan ran the opposite direction, her brow knit.

"Hey." She almost ran past. He had to grab her arm. She hadn't recognized him.

She drew up. "John. Oh, I'm sorry. Listen, I've got to—"

"This is important. Do you know of a patient named Lorena Ortiz?"

She hadn't heard. She tried to pull away.

"Dammit, listen to me," he shouted. "Lorena. Lorena Ortiz."

She looked up, recognition flowing over her face. "Yes . . . Lorena. We had her in surgery. Punctured lung. Multiple fractures, including her skull. Massive internal bleeding. Lacerations . . . I don't know, about everything that could go wrong when you fall three stories. Why?"

"Will she make it?"

A nurse punched open one of the double doors and shouted at Diane, "Doctor, please!" Then the nurse spun and went back in. Beyond the doors, the children's groans beckoned in concert, as if a macabre chorus rehearsed a slow, morbid song.

Diane jerked her arm. "John, dammit."

Sabovik yelled, "Will she make it? Tell me."

Her face froze in a cold expression. "Of course not. We . . . we have all this. I have to . . . triage . . . which means I don't have time to try to save her. All we can do is keep her out of pain." She pulled away and took a step then turned, her eyes narrowed. "Nitro is with her. That sick sonofabitch is trying to make her talk. What did Lorena Ortiz ever do to you? Bomb the Washington Monument or something?"

"Is she talking?"

"Sadist!" Diane Logan turned and dashed through the double doors.

Sabovik ran the other way to the nearest desk and barked at the nurse. "Your patient, Lorena Ortiz, where is she?"

Looking to the emergency room doors, the nurse stammered.

"Lorena Ortiz, dammit!" shouted Sabovik.

She pointed down the hall, "R . . . room 226. Through those doors. The old section."

Sabovik dashed through the doors, nearly knocking over two nurses and a doctor running the opposite direction. He turned the corner, finding the lights dimmer in this section. He had trouble reading the doorway numbers but eventually found the door to 226. It was nearly closed. Softly he pushed it open and walked in. It was dark. But he saw a form bent over the bed. A man said in an accented voice, "*Schatze?* Can you hear me?" He was dressed in a white surgical gown, a mask over his face.

Sabovik looked around. *Where is Nitro?* He stepped to the opposite side of the bed and asked softly, "How is she doing, Doctor?"

"Shhh." The doctor glanced at Sabovik then shook his head and gently laid a stethoscope on her chest.

Lorena Ortiz went, "Ahhhgghhh."

"Schatze," whispered the doctor. He bent closer. "Listen, she's trying to say something. Hear?"

Lorena Ortiz's mouth opened wide, and she gave another death rattle. Sabovik bent close to hear.

Schatze! I get it! He straightened up. Almost not in time. The doctor's fist swiped past where his neck had just been, a cold, gleaming scalpel in his hand.

"Scheiss!"

Sabovik stumbled backward and fell against an armchair. The chair spun on the floor and he fell over an inert form. It was too dark but he recognized Nitro's crew-cut silhouette. And a dark sticky substance pooled under his head.

The doctor began moving around the bed toward Sabovik.

"You haven't a chance, Lattimer. Give yourself up," said Sabovik. Madly, he fumbled over Nitro's body, running his hands down the marine's back. Where the hell did he keep it?

"I think she just died, Commander Sabovik. And I also think you will, too." Taking his steps carefully, Lattimer eased around the bed, his hand raised, the scalpel gleaming.

"The place is surrounded," Lattimer said throatily, realizing his voice lacked conviction. "Why did you push her?"

"She knew too much. Just like you." Lattimer stepped closer. No more than five feet away.

Sabovik ran his hands around Nitro's back and around his belt line. Nothing, dammit. He looked up. Lattimer was poised to jump. The railroad conductor was at least six-three and weighed 220, far too much for Sabovik. He scooted away.

"Ahhh." Nitro's left hand. It moved! God! The finger pointed to the corner. Quickly, Sabovik glanced over there.

Something gleamed dully under the radiator. He slid over and reached.

Lattimer must have seen it, too, for he pounced.

Dear God, let the safety be off. Sabovik grabbed the pistol, raised it, and pulled the trigger. The gun bucked in his hand, the report crashing in the room. The round ripped through Milo Lattimer's heart, killing him instantly. But John Sabovik didn't know this. He pumped another round into Lattimer's corpse just before it crashed on top of him.

FORTY-SIX

24 October 1944
Lattimer home, 224 Poplar Lane
Roseville, California

Milo Lattimer's home was a two-bedroom bungalow on Poplar Lane. No more than a thousand square feet, it was a little Craftsman-style building set well back from the street. Two enormous oak trees flanking the walkway shaded the house with somber tones over an unkept yard enclosed by a rusty, hip-level chain-link fence. Built by Harry Ferguson in 1922, the little house had been part of a two-acre chicken ranch with a gully running in back. Ferguson's Chicken Ranch thrived until 1937 when a furious rainstorm hit; the gully's banks overflowed, washing away most of Harry Ferguson's chicken coops, livestock, a small barn, and the single-car garage containing a 1933 Plymouth coupe, now a rusted hulk in the gully. Ferguson boarded up the three remaining chicken coops and rented the house to Milo Lattimer for seventy-five dollars per month. With that, he and his wife, Alice, moved south to Canoga Park in the San Fernando Valley, where he rebuilt his chicken business and fared much better.

Walt Logan's Chevy rattled to a stop in front of the house. Inside were John Sabovik and Diane Logan, still in her lab coat. Wedged between them was Nitro, his face ashen white and his head wrapped in bandages.

Sabovik flipped off the key, but the engine was hot and began to diesel over. The car bucked as he hit the brake and popped the clutch, killing the engine.

"Does that all the time," said Diane, surveying the house.

"Try tuning the engine," said Nitro.

"Try getting parts," said Diane.

Nitro waved the back of his hand. "Details."

Sabovik opened his door. "Let's go."

Diane lay a hand on his arm. "John, is this necessary?"

"Of course it is," said Sabovik. But then he saw her eyes well up. "Hon, what's wrong?"

"I just can't believe this. Invading Milo Lattimer's house. You don't realize how kind he was. He helped cure people. He brough . . . he brought"—she rubbed a hand over her face—"Mike Donovan to me. Carried him right into the emergency room. Knew exactly what was wrong." She grabbed Sabovik's sleeve. "Couldn't it be someone else? Maybe some other fiend set all this up. Maybe—" She paused. "—you killed the wrong man."

"Hon," Sabovik replied. "He damn near killed Nitro and he was for sure going to kill me. You should have seen him swing that scalpel. He knew how to use it."

"All these years we've known Milo Lattimer. It's because of him that I became a doctor. He's . . . he is . . . was part of the family."

Sabovik offered, "Well, I'm sure glad you became a doctor." He stepped out.

She nodded at the bungalow. "Shouldn't we wait for next of kin or something?"

"I doubt if Milo Lattimer, or whatever his name was, had any next of kin." Sabovik was having second thoughts about bringing Diane. There were plenty of doctors now at the hospital taking care of the schoolchildren. But she'd finished her shift long ago, was getting punchy, and needed to get away from it. Sabovik agreed to let her come since she might know something that could help their investigation.

"Wait up," said Nitro.

Diane lay a hand over Nitro's forehead. "You still have a fever." Lattimer had hit Nitro over the head, opening a terrible scalp wound. Diane had taken sixteen sutures and she thought he was in shock, but the marine wouldn't slow down. "You've lost blood," she continued. She grabbed his wrist. "See this? Your pulse is still ragged."

Nitro gulped down a small carton of orange juice and

tossed it on the floor. "Not that I'm ungrateful, Doctor, but I have to go."

"It's your funeral," she said.

Nitro sighed, "I have work to do, Doctor."

She called out the window to Sabovik. "Can you talk sense to him, John? He should be in bed."

"Don't worry. He's just a dumb jarhead." Sabovik turned and walked toward the house.

Nitro gave a lopsided grin. "Hear that? I think he likes marines."

There was no outdoor furniture or flowerpots on the front porch, just a dusty doormat.

Sabovik tried the front door, finding it locked.

Diane asked, "Shouldn't we wait for cops?"

Sabovik said, "We don't want the local police right now. But the FBI is sending a forensics team from the San Francisco field office."

"Why don't we wait? I mean, do we have the authority to do this?" she asked.

Sabovik said, "This is a highly classified matter—a matter of national security, actually. And I'm the lead in this investigation. We have all the authority we want."

"But this is Milo's house. His private residence," she said.

Sabovik nodded toward the Chevy. "Maybe you'd like to leave." He held up keys and jiggled them.

She drew herself up straight. "No. Please, go ahead."

"Ever been inside?" asked Sabovik.

"No."

"Okay." Sabovik looked under the mat, finding nothing. Then he felt the eaves all the way to each of the porch's corners. He looked at Nitro and shook his head.

With a shrug, Nitro nodded at the front door. "Might as well."

"Right." Sabovik stepped over and threw a shoulder at the door. The lock gave way with a soft *crunch.* The door squeaked in protest as he pushed it all the way open. They walked into a plainly furnished living room. There was an armchair in one corner beside a gas stove, a plain wooden chair in the opposite corner. On the other side of the armchair was a mahogany cabinet, its finish done in high gloss.

Nitro stepped over and raised a lid. "Looky here. RCA console phonograph and radio. Nice, looks brand new." He stooped and looked inside. "Automatic record changer. What'll they think of next?"

Sabovik picked up some record albums off of a stack. "Let's see. Toscanini plays Beethoven. Okay. Furtwängler plays Wagner. Right. Lauritz Melchior sings Verdi. Check. Hello?" He held up another album: "Spike Jones. Mr. Lattimer had a sense of humor," Sabovik said without conviction. He could still feel Lattimer's corpse collapsing on top of him. Only seconds before, the enraged man, alive and full of the devil's own fury, had been intent on slicing John Sabovik to pieces with a surgeon's scalpel.

"Nitro, I'd like you to sit." Diane pointed to the armchair.

"In a minute." Nitro stumbled toward the kitchen.

Sabovik barked, "She's right, Captain Collins. I want you to sit and be quiet. That's an order."

Nitro stopped.

"Right now, Captain."

"Right." Nitro stepped back, sat heavily in the armchair, and idly shuffled through record albums.

"Okay." Sabovik looked around, finding a small desk with the usual bills, flyers, and bank statements, the highest balance: $477.23. After a cursory look at the floor, ceiling, and walls, he moved to the kitchen. Everything was in order, washed dishes neatly racked up on the drainboard. The bedroom was simple with a twin-size bed, dresser, end table, and chair. In the closet were boots, shoes, working shirts and trousers, one dark blue suit, foul-weather gear. Nothing out of order. Same for the bathroom. The other bedroom, simply furnished, yielded nothing. He walked into the living room and shook his head. "Damn. There has to be something."

"You'd think so," said Nitro.

"You missed this." Diane walked in from the bedroom and threw a bathrobe in Nitro's lap. "Take a whiff."

Nitro held it to his nose. "Wheeeow! This has got to be Lorena."

Sabovik tried it, finding it heavily laced with perfume. "Not cheap stuff, do you think?" he asked Diane.

"Arpège," she replied. "No, not cheap."

"Home sweet home," said Nitro.

"What else?" Sabovik peered behind the gas stove. He began tapping on the floors and walls.

"Mind if I take a nap?" asked Nitro.

Sabovik looked at Diane, who nodded.

"Use the bedroom," said Sabovik.

"I do believe I will," said Nitro, rising. With a yawn, he said, "I have a question for you."

Sabovik dropped to his knees and peered beneath the record player. "Shoot."

"The sixty-four-dollar question is, what is not here?" asked Nitro.

"What?" Sabovik straightened up.

"I'm asking, is there something that should be here that is not?"

"Like a case of dynamite," Sabovik said with sarcasm.

"You're not listening, John."

"Try me."

"See over there?" Nitro pointed to the opposite corner to a pile of newspapers. "Half of them turned to the weekly chess puzzle."

"So what?" said Sabovik, looking around the room. Come to think of it, he hadn't seen a chess set. "Yeah . . ."

"So where is it?" asked Nitro.

Sabovik sat back and snapped his fingers. "I'll be a monkey's uncle. Where the hell would it be?"

"A place large enough for him to sit back and work his chess puzzles. Also, you might take a whiff of some of these record albums. They smell like shit. I mean the real stuff." He paused for a moment. "Now this stupid jarhead is going to take a nap." He shuffled off.

A team of three overalled FBI forensics specialists pulled up thirty minutes later in a panel truck. Neighbors gathered in front as the investigators opened the back door, grabbed satchels, and walked into the house. Soon great screeching noises echoed from the living room as they pried up floorboards and broke into walls.

Sabovik was in the kitchen on his back under the sink, shining a flashlight up into rusty plumbing. Diane stood nearby, her hip braced against the drainboard. "Find anything?"

"Three copies of *Mein Kampf.*"

"Very funny."

Nitro walked in, smacking his lips and scratching his belly. Nodding toward the living room, he said, "Those guys could wake the dead."

"How do you feel?" asked Diane, reaching for a glass and nearly knocking it over.

"Like I fell off the roller coaster at the Long Beach Pike. But on balance, not bad." Nitro took the only kitchen chair and said, "Look, I got to thinking. What'd I say about the record albums?"

Sabovik bumped his head on the hot-water valve and cursed. "You said they smelled like shit. Maybe it's just mildew."

Nitro said, "Nope, I got to thinking. They smell like shit. Specifically, chickenshit. That's what they smell like."

"Come on."

"But then don't pay any attention to this old farm boy, who grew up shoveling horseshit, cowshit, hogshit, chickenshit, batshit, dogshit, all kinds of shit."

"You have discriminating tastes," said Diane drily.

"Have you looked in the chicken coops?" asked Nitro.

Sabovik scooted from under the sink. "Dammit." He looked up to Nitro. "Stupid jarhead."

"Right," said Nitro.

They started on the first of Harry Ferguson's three remaining chicken coops. Boards squeaked in protest as the FBI trio pried at them with crowbars. They entered and poked around. At length they walked out, shrugged, and went to work on the second coop.

"Here we go," one of them called. He walked over carrying a board. Bulky and with dark curly hair, his name tag read: HASKELL. Sabovik bent to see shiny common box nails protruding from the board's four corners. "Looks like Milo Lattimer made a mistake," he said. "Keep at it."

"Right." Haskell walked back into the coop.

Moments later, a board squeaked in protest. Someone shouted, "Hold everything."

"Let's go," said Sabovik. They walked into a dark, musty space, perhaps ten by fifteen feet. The chicken cages were still in place, but boards were missing from the back wall. One could see blue sky, vegetation, and a creek running down the gully.

Haskell pointed. "Here." He pushed a chicken coop aside. Beneath was a dirt-covered trapdoor. He bent to pry it up with a crowbar.

"Better not," said Nitro. He walked over and stooped alongside Haskell. "This is my department."

Haskell looked at Sabovik. "What the—"

"He's EOD," said Sabovik.

With an exaggerated bow, Haskell said, "Please, be my guest." He rose and stepped away.

Nitro studied the trapdoor for perhaps two minutes. Then he carefully felt along the door's edges. Rubbing his chin, he looked up to Diane. "You carrying your stethoscope?"

"Of course." She pulled it from her lab coat pocket and handed it over.

Nitro listened for a good thirty seconds and turned to Haskell, "You, sir. Can I use your flashlight and crowbar?"

Haskell handed them over.

Nitro said, "You all should know that in this business, I keep my last will and testament updated at all times. How about you?" He eyed them. When there was no response, he continued, "I thought so. That means you must leave this room and stand at least fifty feet away. I'll call if I need anything."

Sabovik said, "Nitro, don't you think that—"

"Come on, John, we're wasting time."

Moments passed. Finally Haskell said, "Okay, it's your neck." He beckoned to his partners and eased out.

Sabovik took Diane's elbow and gave her a gentle push toward the door. "Nitro, what if I—"

"It's only a precaution. Now get going. I'll be done in a minute. Please." He waved toward the door.

"Call if you need anything," said Sabovik.

"Right."

Outside, they made small talk for ten minutes. Then, the conversation ran out. Birds chirped and locomotives hooted in the distance. Sabovik checked his watch. "He's been in there twelve minutes, dammit."

Diane tensed. "Maybe he's passed out."

"What's wrong with him?" asked Haskell.

Sabovik said, "Yeah, he could have passed out or something. I'm going to—"

Nitro walked out, flipping something in his palm. "Sorry, took a little longer than I thought."

"What is it?" asked Sabovik.

"Neat little deal. Simple pressure switch hidden under the trapdoor. Almost didn't see the little bugger. He had it set to go off if the timer wasn't deactivated in sixty seconds."

"And?"

"Took me forty-two seconds to find it."

"For crying out loud," said Sabovik.

"Find what?" asked Diane.

"About five pounds of plastic explosive," said Nitro.

She gasped. "Good God!"

"And you should see what else is down there," said Nitro.

"What?" asked Sabovik.

"His chess set."

FORTY-SEVEN

24 October 1944
Lattimer home, 224 Poplar Lane
Roseville, California

Nitro led a wide-eyed Sabovik, Diane, and Agent Haskell down a steep ladder into a neat but cramped room perhaps ten by twelve. The walls and floor were finished in concrete; a long hip-level workbench, its plywood top varnished to a high gloss, ran along one side. Above the bench was a wooden bookcase stuffed with journals, manuals, and a number of manila folders. Surrounding the bookcase was a large selection of Peg-Board-mounted tools. Beneath the bench was an electric heater and two stools. A small portable record player sat on one end. Milo Lattimer's chess set was perched at the other end. Its intricately carved alabaster pieces were perfectly spotted on a mahogany board inlaid with ebony and ivory. A sink with hot and cold running water was at one end of the bench. On the opposite wall were an electric drill press and lathe. Floor-to-ceiling cabinets were built against the other wall. An overhead fluorescent light fixture cast good light.

Nitro waved an arm. "Everything a grown man could want. Take a look at that." He stepped over to the portable player and shuffled through records.

"Do you mind?" asked Agent Haskell.

"What?" said Nitro.

"We'd like to dust for fingerprints. Do you mind?" Haskell reached in his pocket, pulled out rubber gloves, and passed them around.

"Good idea," said Sabovik, snapping on his gloves.

Nitro did the same and resumed examining the record albums. "Hmmm. Here's 'Moon Over Monakura.' " He flipped through. " 'In the Mood' and 'Stardust.' " He looked around. "No Wagner or Beethoven down here. What's this?" He picked up a handkerchief and sniffed. Then he handed it over to Diane. "Same stuff?"

She took a whiff and murmured, "Arpège. He brought her down here?" Sabovik pointed to the two stools under the workbench.

"Oh."

Nitro coughed politely and said, "The guy dug out the room and pitched the dirt into the gully. Neat." He pointed to a package on the workbench. It was wrapped in shiny waterproofed paper, red and green wires trailing from within. "And here's his little bundle of joy." Nitro flipped it in the air. "About five pounds of plastic bonded explosive. It was taped under the workbench and connected to the pressure switch."

"Geez! Take it easy," said Haskell.

"It's safe, don't worry," said Nitro.

"Just the same," cautioned Haskell.

Nitro slid open one of the cupboards. "This guy wasn't fooling around." He waved to a number of neatly stacked bundles. "Here's his stash of plastic explosive." He slid open another cupboard and looked inside, finding four Samsonite suitcases. He lifted one out and undid the snaps. "Wheeeow. Take a look at this."

They walked over. "Holy smokes," said Sabovik. The suitcase was stuffed with neatly bundled twenty-dollar bills. "Must be thousands."

Nitro peeked in the other three suitcases. "Wow. Enough for some really good times. What do you say, Diane? Hubba-hubba, baby. You and me down Havana way?" He snapped his fingers over his head and twirled a circle.

"Pig." Diane turned her back.

Sabovik closed the first case and yelled up at the trapdoor. "Hey, guys."

Two faces appeared.

"Here you go, fellas," Sabovik said. "Count and tag it." Puffing mightily, Sabovik and Haskell hoisted the four suitcases up to waiting hands.

"What else?" Sabovik stepped to the bookcase and pulled out a journal.

Nitro opened another cupboard. "Here, John, take a look."

Sabovik's attention was riveted to the journal. "Holy smokes," he said.

"John?" asked Nitro.

"Wait one." Sabovik waved him away.

"Okay then," muttered Nitro. "Mr. Haskell, give me a hand?"

"Call me Larry."

"Larry it is. Over here, please." Haskell walked over, and together they hoisted a bulky crate and carried it to the workbench, laying it down with a thud.

Sabovik looked up from his journal. "What do you have?"

Nitro pried the lid off the crate. Inside was a complex shiny device. "Yeah. A full, in-the-raw mark 6 exploder."

"A what?" asked Diane, adjusting her glasses.

"Exploder," said Nitro. "A trigger, basically. Makes the torpedo blow up."

"Oh."

"Now take a gander. Here, gimme a hand, Larry." Carefully, Nitro and Agent Haskell lifted the exploder out of the crate.

"Good God," grunted Larry as they set it on the bench. "Weighs a ton."

"Ninety pounds," grunted Nitro. Carefully they rolled the exploder to its side, revealing a rectangular stainless-steel baseplate formed to fit the front curvature of a torpedo warhead. A sinister array of gears and shiny steel parts greeted them. A wire coil encircled part of the mechanism. The baseplate was twelve by fourteen inches, the circumference ringed by twenty-four countersunk screw holes. Yellow letters were stenciled on the plate:

DUMMY—EXPLODER COVER
USE CAUTION WHEN REMOVING
DO NOT LEAVE CAVITY OPEN
RE-INSTALL MARK 6, MOD 13 EXPLODER IMMEDIATELY
REF: BUORD INST 24–15 (A) 1905.1

Nitro said, "This is supposed to be a dummy baseplate. Fits in the bottom of a mark 15 torpedo warhead. All a dummy plate does is protect the exploder cavity while the warhead is in shipment. Keeps out dust and corrosive material. There's nothing else to it." He looked up. "Okay so far?"

They nodded.

Nitro said, "But here's the trick. Somebody just looking at it thinks it's a dummy baseplate as labeled, but it's a real exploder."

Sabovik whistled.

Nitro continued, "Milo Lattimer was a railroad conductor. He had access to manifests and figured a way to defeat the locks on cars carrying ammunition. So he sneaks into a car with torpedo warheads and inserts these exploders with phony cover plates.

"He must have been trying to insert one of these that night I surprised him at Jasper Flats. Come to think of it, that's the first time he bopped me over the head. I should have learned my lesson.

"Here's how it works." He pointed. "This component here is the detonator. And this one is the booster charge. Putting it simply, the detonator fires the booster charge, which detonates the torpedo warhead. Now, the detonator is triggered by a contact fuse or a magnetic fuse, which should be in this area here. But look. He's removed the arming impeller mechanism and in it's place—geez, look at the workmanship—he's installed a timer and a battery. Like a Swiss watch, except this one is German." He waved to the machinery behind him. "He used that equipment to build the timers. Must have been a master craftsman."

"He was that," agreed Diane. "Fixed everything around the house, even our grandfather clock."

"Okay," Nitro continued. "So he sets this timer for, say, ten days, or ten weeks, or ten months. When it counts down to zero, it closes this switch here—see . . . see this?"

They nodded.

"The circuit is complete," he went on. "The electricity hits this detonator, which kicks off the booster charge, which zaps all of the 825 pounds of HBX in the torpedo warhead.

Now, that packs a hell of a wallop and can sink a good-size ship—say, a destroyer or, worse, an ammo ship or dump."

"Dirty bastard," said Haskell.

"Hey, look at that." Nitro pointed to another crate under the workbench. "Strange, that box is labeled differently. Maybe we should take a look. Larry . . . ?"

"I dunno. Think I blew out a hernia with the last one," said Haskell.

"Come on, girls," said Sabovik, pitching in. Huffing and puffing, they uncrated another exploder.

They watched as Nitro poked around. Finally he unscrewed the cover from one of the components. "Holy shit!"

"What," said Sabovik.

"This guy really had it in for us," said Nitro. "What if the exploders are booby-trapped as well? That means an unsuspecting torpedoman on a destroyer or cruiser can install a booby-trapped exploder into a warhead, thinking it's okay. He doesn't know that Lattimer has this thing rigged to go off in his face when he launches the torpedo."

"Sonofabitch!" said Haskell.

"We have two versions of this thing?" asked Sabovik.

Nitro said, "Looks like it." He continued. "Here, look at this. Once aboard ship, dummy plates are removed and the torpedoman installs the exploder, no more the wiser."

"What do you mean?" asked Sabovik, leaning in for a closer look.

"Well, to the average torpedoman, this looks like a real exploder. See here? Impeller, everything in place. But right here"—Nitro tapped the magnetic sensor case—"this device is a factory-sealed unit. Torpedomen in the fleet are not supposed to open it." Quickly he unscrewed eight screws from the cover, lifted it off, and pointed to a little spring-actuated mechanism inside. "See these pawls? He's rigged it so that once they flip over, the charge goes off if you try to remove the exploder. Also, it's set to go off when it engages the firing lug in the tube. The beauty here is that the whole thing utilizes this one timer—see it here?—so either way, you're screwed."

Sabovik sat back and rubbed his chin. "But this thing is so damn heavy."

"I grant you that, but then Milo Lattimer was a very strong man. After all, he carried Mike Donovan into town. He could handle something like this."

Diane sat back, her face white. "My God. This is so hard to believe."

"Believe it," said Nitro.

She said, "You don't understand. He damn near raised me, especially after Mom died. Did you ever consider that maybe someone framed him?"

"I know, hon," said Sabovik. He nodded to Haskell. "After they dust for fingerprints, you'll know one way or the other."

She ignored him. "He and Daddy are best friends. They work on the railroad. They play . . ."

Nitro slid over the mahogany board.

". . . chess," she said softly. Her shoulders sagged.

With a sigh, Sabovik opened the journal and flipped pages. "This is his log of the ships the torpedoes were loaded on. Here's an entry for the *E. A. Bryan* in Port Chicago. Here's another entry for *Regina Dalmatia,* which blew up on her way to Hawaii. He has check marks by both." He said to Diane, "What more proof do you need, hon?"

Diane turned away.

"Commander?" said Nitro.

"What?"

"Sometimes you can really be a boor."

"I only . . ." It dawned on Sabovik and he said, "Diane, I'm sorry. I really am."

She nodded, moved to the far side of the workbench, and reached for a record album, instead knocking over a jar of machine screws. "Sorry," she said softly, adjusting her glasses. Then she picked up a record album: Gene Krupa.

Sabovik said, "Look at this last entry. It's for the *Mount Saint Helens.*"

Nitro said to Agent Haskell, "That's the ammo ship that went up in the Ulithi Atoll three weeks ago."

"Oh," Haskell said.

Checking back in the log, Sabovik said, "Oh, God."

"What?" the others said.

"We may not be done with this guy. According to this, he

got a version one—a warhead with a dummy booby-trapped cover plate—and a version two, a booby-trapped exploder, aboard the *Mount Saint Helens.*"

"What type of ships use those exploders?" asked Agent Haskell.

"These are for mark 15 torpedoes: cruisers and destroyers."

"We should consider," Nitro offered, "that both versions could have been aboard the *Mount Saint Helens* when she blew up. Therefore we may not have anything to worry about."

Sabovik said, "Do you want to take that chance?"

Nitro sighed. "Not on your life."

"I don't, either," agreed Sabovik. "And I'm saving the worst for last. See this column?" He pointed to a series of numbers in the page's last column.

"Date/time group?" said Nitro.

"Exactly," said Sabovik. "Get a load of this. Here is the time that version two exploder is set to blow up." He pointed to an entry.

"Yikes!" said Nitro. "Today: 1800."

"Geez," said Haskell. He checked his watch: 1:22 PM. "Less than five hours."

Sabovik said, "Right. Not a moment to lose. We have to find out which ship received that version two exploder and let them know."

Haskell said, "Hell, that thing could be anywhere in the world. How you going to get a message to her?"

"Things get easier when you have Admiral Cactus Jack Egan pulling strings," said Nitro.

"Who?" asked Haskell.

Sabovik quickly explained, then said, "Nitro. Let's get over to my office. Maybe ask Admiral Egan to call in a message to SERVRON 10."

"What's that?" asked Haskell.

"Service squadron ten. They're responsible for ammo ships in the Pacific, specifically Ulithi. If they've kept good records, we should get a match on lot numbers so they can tell us which ship has the rigged exploder."

"You can do that? You have priorities for that kind of radio traffic?"

Sabovik replied, "Like I said, Cactus Jack Egan speaks with the authority of Admiral Ernest J. King. We can radio anywhere in the world with the highest priority and get answers almost immediately. Let's hope he's in." He turned for the ladder and said to Nitro, "Bring that log."

"I'm sorry, that's evidence," protested Haskell. He moved next to the ladder, barring their exit.

"What?" said an incredulous Sabovik.

Nitro said, "Agent Haskell, you're a nice guy, but we have an explosion to stop before it happens."

Haskell shook his head. "Fine, just leave the log."

"Come on, Larry, people are gonna die," urged Sabovik.

Again, Haskell shook his head.

Nitro said, "Look at it this way, Larry. There are two of us and if you don't let us pass, we're going to beat the shit out of you."

Haskell stood straight. "Not without a fight."

"Boys, boys," said Diane.

Sabovik silenced her with a dark glance.

"Maybe so." Nitro reached behind his back and whipped out his .32 automatic. "I hope you don't mind eating a little lead in the meantime." He snapped the action.

"Boys!" shouted Diane.

"Easy, hon," said Sabovik, keeping his eyes on Haskell.

Haskell spread his arms and said, "What will the director say?"

"Screw Hoover," said Sabovik.

Haskell sighed "All right, screw him." He stepped aside. "Godspeed."

Leaving Diane to help Haskell and the FBI, they jumped in Walt Logan's Chevrolet and raced for town, the dark blue coupe popping and backfiring as they went. They pulled up before Sabovik's office, unlocked the door, and dashed inside. Sabovik grabbed the phone and was relieved to hear Admiral Egan pick up the line almost immediately. Sabovik explained what had happened; Egan soon agreed to send the message to SERVRON 10 in Ulithi. "Then we wait," Cactus

Jack Egan said. "I'll get back, shouldn't take long. Maybe half an hour or so."

Sabovik looked at his watch. "Sir, it's nearly 1400. That thing's due to go off in a little more than four hours."

"Well, if you keep sniveling, I won't be able to send the message, will I?" Egan said drily.

"No, sir. Sorry, sir. Good-bye, sir." But Egan had already smashed his phone down. Sabovik glanced at Nitro, who judiciously kept his face averted.

Nitro went for coffee, and they waited and walked and grunted at one another for the next twenty minutes. Then Sabovik sat and wadded-up paper, shooting baskets from ten feet away.

Nitro joined in. They began betting, with Sabovik getting the better: thirty-five minutes.

"Do you suppose we should call him?" asked Nitro.

"He'd rip our heads off," said Sabovik, tossing a paper wad. Miss: "Dammit."

The phone rang. He ripped it off the hook before the second ring. "Sabovik."

"Okay, Egan here. Sorry this took so long. Everyone in Ulithi is still spooked about what happened. But they're eager to help. They had a lot-number match for us within ten minutes. Now, I've been trying to get a top-priority message off to the ship, which is out in the war zone. But shit! You wouldn't believe the red tape around here. The weasels here in COMTWELVE wouldn't budge an inch until I threatened to call Ernie King. 'Are you sure you're cleared?' the sniveling bastards kept asking. Hell, they've got radio equipment gathering dust here that can reach Buck Rogers on Pluto, but they were afraid to spin the dials for me."

"We should have sent some marines," said Sabovik.

"I'll say. Luckily, these bastards don't realize Ernie King is in London at a Joint Chiefs of Staff conference. Otherwise it would have been a no-go. Anyway, I got the message off to her. I signed it with your name because I'd just as soon stay in the background with this."

"Why is that, Admiral?"

"I have my reasons."

Sabovik wasn't sure whether or not to thank Egan, so he said, "Well, yes, sir. Is the ship still in Ulithi?"

"Not at all. She's right in the middle of it off Leyte, dishing it out to the Japs."

"Who is she, sir?"

"A tin can: USS *Matthew.*"

FORTY-EIGHT

24 October 1944
USS *Lexington* (CV 16)
Philippine Sea

Commodore Arleigh[44] Albert Burke was a forty-three-year-old blond, blue-eyed Swede who'd grown up on a farm in Colorado. He was the oldest of five siblings; his mother, Clara, was a schoolteacher who soundly developed her son's intellectual appetite. On the other hand, Burke's father taught his boys the physical rigors of farm life, especially surviving cold winters. Burke wanted to attend West Point as he neared high school graduation. The family applied to their local congressman but he was turned down because all the West Point appointments had been issued. The Burkes asked again, this time for the naval academy. The answer was yes, and after attending Columbia Prep School, Burke entered the naval academy in June 1919, one of 709 midshipmen.

As a farmer's son, Burke flourished under the academy's physical demands, even joining the wrestling team. His mother's rigorous training gave him the academic wherewithal to pass his courses and graduate in 1923 with a decent class standing of seventy-first out of 413.

A surface warfare officer through and through, Burke first served in battleships, then cruisers, and later his beloved destroyers, constantly studying gunnery and torpedo tactics. By 1939, he'd risen to command the destroyer USS *Mugford* (DD 389).

Burke's World War II action began in the Solomon Islands campaign when he was appointed commodore of Destroyer Squadron 23—eight *Fletcher*-class destroyers nicknamed the Little Beavers. In November 1943, Burke performed brilliantly in the battle of Empress Augusta Bay in Bougainville, where his Little Beavers torpedoed several Japanese warships. A month later, he repeated his performance at the battle of Cape St. George, New Ireland, and thus obtained the sobriquet of Arleigh "31-Knot" Burke as his Little Beavers dashed from action to action. By the time he was relieved, Burke's destroyers had sunk: one enemy cruiser, nine destroyers, one submarine, and several small vessels. Additionally, they had shot down more than thirty enemy planes.

Burke was shocked at his next assignment. Instead of further rising in the surface navy as he'd expected, he was sent to the carrier navy, a whole new world. He was appointed chief of staff to Vice Admiral Marc A. Mitscher's Task Force 38, the main carrier striking force in the Pacific. Burke wanted no part of the carrier navy and did everything he could to get out of it. Mitscher, slight of stature and a craggy-faced quiet man who could have as easily passed for a tire salesman, didn't want Burke, either. An acerbic pioneer of naval aviation, he had no use for a nonflying "black-shoe"—as they were called. Mitscher, who had flown planes from the navy's first carrier, the USS *Langley,* wanted a seasoned combat pilot as his chief of staff. No finer example of oil mixing with water ever existed: both ignored each other for the first two weeks.

But the two were soon forced to put aside their differences and plan the June assault on the Marianas. Mitscher's keen strategy and Burke's planning skills resulted in their pilots shooting down 395 Japanese planes, accounting for about 92 percent of the enemy's pilots, a deathblow to their air arm.

Mitscher was so impressed with Burke's performance as his chief of staff that he put him in for promotion to rear admiral, jumping him over several other captains. But Burke, believing himself unworthy and afraid of negative notoriety, asked Admiral Nimitz not to endorse the recommendation. Like a jilted lover, Mitscher resented Burke's refusal to accept the promotion, and the two went back to war, glaring and hissing at each other. A compromise was reached with Burke elevated to the wartime rank of commodore, which required neither congressional approval nor an increase in pay.

Thus Commodore Arleigh A. Burke was chief of staff of the most powerful naval force in the history of mankind. Mitscher's Task Force 38 consisted of four task groups of about four carriers each. In all, the four groups totaled eight fleet carriers, eight light carriers, six fast battleships,[45] six heavy cruisers, nine light cruisers, and forty-eight destroyers, with Mitscher flying his flag in the attack carrier *Lexington* (CV16).

Another reason the Mitscher/Burke team worked so well is that Burke had a strong physical constitution and could back up the admiral when he became physically exhausted. Mitscher, the brilliant strategist, often became weak and frail in the tropics. A year before, he'd become very ill, his weight dropping to 115 pounds. Nimitz took him off the line for six months to recuperate. Restored to a semblance of health, the old man maintained it by eating well and getting plenty of rest, which meant early to bed and reading himself to sleep with his favorite form of fiction, seedy detective stories.

The weather was ugly as Task Force 38[46] pounded its way north at sixteen knots. Battleships and cruisers buried their finely crafted noses into enormous waves with white water billowing all the way back to their bridges. The cumbersome carries simply plowed through the waves while the little destroyers pitched and bucked in troughs, struggling to keep station.

Wind howled as the *Lexington* drove herself into a great rolling wave. Green water flooded the forty-millimeter gun tubs on the bow, and vicious stinging spray whipped across the flight deck.

But it had been a humid day, and now, at 2200, everyone sweated in the flag bridge. Admiral Mitscher leaned on the conference table, talking to Commodore Burke and Commander James H. Flatley, a short dark Irishman who was the task force operations officer. They had just received a radio dispatch from the carrier *Independence* that one of her search planes reported the Japanese Center Force was once again on an easterly course through the Sibuyan Sea, headed toward the San Bernardino Strait. More alarming was that the navigation lights had been turned on in the strait, something that hadn't happened since the Japanese conquered the Philippines in 1942.

Mitscher yawned, reread the dispatch, and patted his mouth.

"What about this?" asked Burke.

"What about it?" retorted Mitscher.

Burke held up the dispatch. "Should we ask Admiral Halsey for orders, sir?"

"He knows what to do. Call me at 0600. Good night, fellas." With that, Mitscher walked though the door and to his stateroom, where he would don his dressing gown, climb into bed, grab the latest Dashiell Hammett, and fall asleep within five minutes.

With Mitscher asleep, Commodore Arleigh A. Burke was, in effect, commander of Task Force 38.

And he felt uneasy.

Not uneasy about the weight of command on his shoulders; Burke was uneasy about what the Japanese were up to. Something was missing.

That afternoon, Task Force 38 was putting the finishing touches on mauling the Japanese Center Force in the Sibuyan Sea, a performance that included sinking one of those two monster battleships. The ships were last seen retiring in a confused mess west toward Borneo. Halsey believed his bomber and torpedo plane pilots when, exuberant after a victorious day, mauling the Japanese, reported the Japanese Center Force was finished and no longer a threat. Halsey, infected with their enthusiasm, sent a message to General MacArthur and Admiral Nimitz saying so.

The victory in the Sibuyan Sea was overshadowed at 1540 when the third piece of the puzzle fell into place. Elements of a Japanese northern attack force were sighted by a reconnaissance plane about three hundred miles north; four carriers were sighted an hour later. At 2022 Admiral William F. Halsey Jr. ordered Mitscher's entire Task Force 38 north to launch an attack early the next morning. As a backup plan, Halsey formed a group on paper called Task Force 34. It was supposed to be composed of four fast battleships, two heavy and three light cruisers, and sixteen destroyers, and was intended to defend the San Bernardino Strait. But Halsey never executed the plan, and now all of the fast battleships and cruisers were going north to engage the Japanese northern fleet.

Except for a few seagulls, the San Bernardino Strait lay unguarded.

The Japanese were steaming east again, hell-bent-for-leather toward the San Bernardino Strait. And Arleigh Burke had a queasy feeling.

Flatley brought the carafe over and poured coffee for both. "What do you think, boss?"

Burke snapped from his reverie and said, "Those boys up north don't have enough planes to hit us or they would have done it by now."

"Makes sense. So where do we go?"

"Well, I'm wondering what they're doing up there to begin with?"

"Yes?"

"I'm wondering if the northern fleet is a decoy?" said Burke.

Flatley rubbed his Irish jaw, liberally covered with five o'clock shadow. "Jeepers, now wouldn't that be something?"

"If the Center Force gets through the strait, they'll have everybody in Leyte Gulf for lunch."

"Do you think we should ask the admiral?" asked Flatley.

"No." Burke knew Mitscher would skewer him if he awakened him so soon. "Better wait."

Burke filled his pipe and smoked while Flatley ran a dead reckoning plot. Later they drank more coffee and talked of the Japanese Southern Force now headed for the Surigao Strait. Burke was confident admirals Kinkaid and Oldendorf had that situation in hand. It was the Center Force that worried him. He dithered until 2305 when a messenger from radio central walked in and held out a message board. Burke signed, detached a copy, and read it. "Holy cow," he said.

"What?" said Flatley.

"Another *Independence* search plane reports the Japs are now heading east through the San Bernardino Strait. The navigation lights are still on." He looked up. "It's happening."

"Shall we awaken the admiral?" asked Flatley.

"Not yet, hold on." Burke yanked a TBS handset from the

bracket and called, "Pickle Barrel, this is Bald Eagle, over." *Pickle Barrel* was the call sign for Halsey; *Bald Eagle,* for Mitscher.

"Pickle Barrel, over."

Burke took a deep breath. "This is Bald Eagle. Interrogative if you have Running Bear's 242330. Over." Running Bear's 242330 was the *Independence*'s reconnaissance report on the Japanese Center Force in the San Bernardino Strait.

"That is affirmative. Pickle Barrel, over."

Burke's fist clenched as he asked, "Do you have any instructions for Bald Eagle? Over."

"Bald Eagle, this is Pickle Barrel. Negative. Out." The radio clicked loudly.

"Dammit," said Burke. He twirled a pencil for a moment, then looked up. "Better go in there." He nodded toward Mitscher's stateroom.

"Shit to pay," said Flatley.

Burke nodded. "Either way there is." They eased past the marine guard in the passageway and knocked. There was no answer so after the third knock, Burke opened the door. "Admiral," he called softly.

"I hear you," Mitscher croaked. Covers rustled, and his bunk light clicked on. He wore his favorite dressing gown. "Go ahead," he said, raised on an elbow.

"I'm sorry to waken you, sir," Burke began.

"Hell, you've already done that. Now what is it?" growled Mitscher.

Burke replied, "We have a report from the *Independence.* One of her planes spotted the Jap Center Force. They're going through the San Bernardino Strait. The navigation lights are on and they're steaming east."

Mitscher blinked. "Navigation lights still on?"

"Yes, sir."

"Does Admiral Halsey have that report?"

Burke replied, "Yes, sir."

Mitscher looked up to Flatley then leveled his gaze on Burke. "If he wants my advice, he'll ask for it." He reached up, fumbled at his light, and clicked it off.

"Good night, Admiral," said Burke, walking out of the stateroom.

They didn't speak until they reached flag plot. A tote board showed the Japanese Southern Force about to enter the Surigao Strait. Flatley turned to a radarman: "Can you get their TBS broadcasts?"

"Sometimes." The radarman turned up the speaker.

Burke leaned against the plotting table while the speaker screeched and growled. "What if the Jap Center Force is for real? At last count, they still had four, maybe five battleships, including another one of those big bastards. What then, Jimmy?"

"I'd say those guys in Leyte Gulf better hunker down, sir."

"I'd say you're right."

While he was thinking this over, the TBS loudspeaker squealed and screeched with news of the fight developing down in the Surigao Strait with the Japanese Southern Force. The radarman, a skinny dark-haired second class named Kupps, reached over and twirled a knob just as the speaker barked, "Ipana, this is Horse Trader. SITREP. Over." *Horse Trader* was the call sign for Admiral Thomas Kinkaid's Seventh Fleet Command Center aboard the command ship USS *Wasatch* (AGC 9), anchored in San Pedro Bay. He was asking for a situation report from Ipana, the call sign for Rear Admiral Jesse Oldendorf's main battle line of six battleships defending the Surigao Strait.

The speaker squealed for a moment then said, ". . . my peter tares now engaging enemy. So far, so good."

Burke and Flatley exchanged glances. They'd seen the Oldendorf's op plan for defense of the Surigao Strait. Right now the Japanese force was trying to push its way through a line of thirty-nine PT boats. There were three battle lines after that. The first two consisted of twenty-eight destroyers; next were four heavy and four light cruisers. Topping it off was the main battle line of six battleships, five of them veterans of Pearl Harbor.[47]

Kupps twirled the squelch dial again. Beads of perspiration stood on his brow. He locked his intense blue eyes onto Burke in a near-death grip. "What do you think, sir? Do we have enough firepower down there to handle the Japs?" It was no secret that Kupps had a brother, a radarman aboard the battleship *Pennsylvania.*

Burke puffed his pipe and clapped the boy on the shoulder. "Plenty of firepower down there, son. Your brother's going to do fine. You just listen." He was glad Kupps hadn't asked the sixty-four-dollar question. Where was the firepower to oppose the Center Force now transiting the San Bernardino Strait?

FORTY-NINE

25 October 1944
IJN *Nachi*
Mindanao Sea, Philippines

Vice Admiral Kiyohide Shima's Second Striking Force dashed through the night at twenty-five knots. The sea was lumpy and it was overcast, making the outlying islands guarding the Surigao Strait invisible. Rain occasionally pelted the heavy cruiser *Nachi* as thunderstorms roiled, lighting bolts flashing in the night. Luckily, they'd just had radar installed, making station keeping and navigation easier, especially on a dirty night like this. Steaming over a period of three days from Beppu Bay, Shima's force of three cruisers and seven destroyers was trying to rendezvous with Vice Admiral Shoji Nishimura's Southern Force of two battleships, one cruiser, and seven destroyers. And so far, there was no radar contact up ahead. Just myriad small islands, so characteristic of the Philippine archipelago.

Shima paced nervously in the *Nachi*'s flag plot. "Dammit." He turned to Rear Admiral Yatsuki Ishii, his chief of staff. "What does radio say now?"

Ishii had been trying to hide in the gloom. Shima was livid over the fact that they hadn't rendezvoused with Nishimura as planned. Worse, Nishimura hadn't bothered to wait for him. The crazy man had jumped the gun and was forty kilometers ahead—eager for a nighttime showdown in Leyte Gulf—something frowned upon by the SHO-1 planners in Tokyo.

Also, it was ominous that there had been no radio contact with Nishimura's force for the past half hour. They were, most likely, well into the Surigao Strait and, explosion after cataclysmic explosion had lit up the skies in that direction. The radar showed no blips. Prospects looked grim.

"Ishii!" shouted Shima.

Ishii snatched a phone from its bracket. "I'm checking now, sir." Like Ishii, the rest of the staff kept quiet and looked away, not wanting to bear the wrath of Vice Admiral Shima.

A voice announced, "Radio central."

Ishii recognized the voice of Captain Wakita, the battle station watch commander. "Wakita. Anything from the *Yamashiro* yet?" The battleship *Yamashiro* was Nishimura's flagship.

"No, sir. Sorry, sir."

Shima was watching, so Ishii, afraid to hang up, held the phone to his ear.

"Is there anything else, sir?" asked Wakita.

"No, I guess that's it." Expecting a blast of invective, liberally sprinkled with spittle, Ishii hung up and turned to face the old man. Instead he saw a blinking light through the porthole.

Shima whipped around. "Target?" he demanded.

Mikuma, the flag warrant officer, poked his head into flag plot. "It's the *Shigure,* sir."

"Shigure," shouted Shima, a bit of hope creeping into his voice. Shigure, a thirty-four-knot destroyer of fourteen hundred tons, was part of Nishimura's southern attack group. Ishii checked the radar, seeing that the ship had separated from the greenish blob landmass of Camiguin Island. Maybe others were out there as well.

Shima walked over and likewise checked the radar. Nothing. They waited a minute. Then another. Nothing. Shima's jaw worked. His face grew dark. He ripped open the door and loosed his vitriol into the night: "What the hell's the *Shigure* telling us, Mikuma?"

Mikuma was right there. "Sorry, sir. He forgot to use an authenticator. We have it now." He read, " 'Two hits aft. One serious. Am having rudder trouble. Many casualties. Difficult to maintain station.' "

They could see the *Shigure* now. Her silhouette was vaguely outlined against a storm cloud. She was steaming in the opposite direction and would pass to port by about a thousand meters. With a closing rate of about fifty knots she would be lost to the storm clouds in a moment.

"Dammit," hissed Shima. "Quickly, man. Ask about the rest of the Southern Force." He slapped Mikuma on the rump.

"Sir!" Mikuma dashed out to his signal platform and blinked his message.

Now abeam and rapidly drawing down their port quarter, *Shigure*'s signal light stabbed the darkness with her reply.

Mikuma muttered and clacked off.

"Well?" demanded Shima.

With a pencil stub, Mikuma filled in the date/time group and then recited: "All ships gone."

"Gone!" Shima gasped.

"Yes, sir," said Mikuma, stepping backward into the safety of his little signal bridge.

"Gone," Shima whispered.

To Ishii, it seemed he and Shima were the only ones on the *Nachi.*

"Gone," Shima repeated. At length, he straightened up and rubbed his chin. "Come." He walked into the flag bridge and yelled at the flag operations officer, "Reverse course, reorient the formation." Then he grabbed a message pad and wrote for a moment. He tore it off, checked it, and made a few corrections. He handed the message over to Ishii. "See that it goes right away." Then he walked through the hatch and stood alone, watching as the helm orders were shouted below to the bridge. The cruiser's luminescent wake curved into the night as she reversed course toward Borneo.

Ishii grabbed a phone and punched a button.

"Radio central," said Wakita.

"This is Admiral Ishii," he said stiffly. "I have a message to be sent to Admiral Toyoda, CinC."

"I understand. Please go ahead."

"It's from Admiral Shima." He read off the text:

THIS FORCE HAS CONCLUDED ITS ATTACK AND IS RETIRING FROM THE BATTLE AREA TO PLAN SUBSEQUENT ACTION.

FIFTY

25 October 1944
MacArthur command post
Tacloban, Leyte, Philippines

Lightning flashed. Thunder rattled outside from yet another interminable storm. At four in the morning the humidity was sponge-squeezing thick with condensation running down the basement's concrete walls. Converted from a wine cellar to a radio room, the twenty-by-thirty-foot space was jammed with tall transmitting and receiving equipment. Aside from the regular watch section, the radio room was crowded with ranks and ratings ranging from three-star general to buck private, their billowing cigar and cigarette smoke so thick, it was almost impossible to see across the room.

The off-watch people were down here for two reasons. The radio room was the safest place from marauding Japanese Zeros that had been shooting up the Price house since MacArthur took up quarters here. No doubt, the U.S. Navy owned the sky, but that didn't stop Luzon-based Zeros from racing over, taking a potshot or two, and then running for home at deck level, literally weaving among trees in the jungle. It was like something from a cheap western movie. A bounty had been put on MacArthur's head, and the Zero pilots were trying their damndest to collect.

The other reason everybody was down here was to listen to fragmented radio broadcasts coming from Kinkaid's Seventh Fleet battleships, now locked in battle with a Japanese surface force 120 miles south in the Surigao Strait. It was like listening to a football game on the Armed Forces Radio: Network screeches and squealing interspersed with loud, impassioned play calling from Bill Stern, followed by frustrating moments of silence, the process repeating itself all over again. Sometimes men cheered, shook hands, slapped backs, or thrust fists in the air. Other times they shrugged and stared at the floor. Everyone in the room had a stake in what happened down there. If Oldendorf's battleships didn't hold the line, the fox would be in the henhouse.

Owen Reynolds was jammed in a corner with his boss, Major General Charles Willoughby. The coffee had long since turned cold, but Reynolds kept gulping. He'd not eaten since late yesterday afternoon, and his stomach rumbled in protest at his fourth cup.

In a thick accent, Willoughby said, "How can you drink that shit, Owen? It'll burn a hole in your gut." He raised a water jug and drank. Wiping his mouth with his sleeve, he confirmed, "Besides, that damn caffeine keeps you awake."

Reynolds nodded. "Worse than the swill aboard the *Nashville.*"

Willoughby said, "Now navy coffee . . . hmmm. It's not really that bad, is it? Yes, it is designed to keep you awake, but not as dangerous as this stuff. My God." He pointed to Reynolds's cup. "That looks like it was strained through the kaiser's socks. Why are your hands shaking?"

Reynolds gave the obligatory smile. "Tastes like it, too. Maybe I'll shift to water." What he really wanted was a bottle of scotch. . . .

Early in the morning, Major General George C. Kenney, MacArthur's chief of staff for air operations, had gone scouring for new airfields, a top priority. MacArthur decided to go along. When Kenney protested, MacArthur said that it was good to find out how the other half of the world lived. They shanghaied Owen Reynolds because of his combat experience, and because he knew his way around an M1 carbine. Kenney found an old Japanese airfield all right, but one end was still owned by the Japanese. They pulled up just after an artillery barrage, the smoke clearing. Reynolds strapped on his helmet and hunkered down behind the command car as a vicious firefight broke out at the airfield's other end, explosions thundering down the runway. The driver, two heavily armed sergeants, and a wide-eyed Kenney took cover with Reynolds. But not MacArthur. With his hands nonchalantly shoved in his back pockets, the general walked around a burning Japanese tank that had been knocked out only moments before, its dead three-man crew scattered about.

"What do you think, Owen?" Kenney asked, his .45 pistol drawn. "Maybe we should pull back?"

"They'll do all right, General," replied Reynolds, surprised the words got out. Had Kenney looked closely at his knuckles around the trigger guard, he would have known Reynolds could not have fired a shot, his hands were so locked up. His mouth was dry and he constantly swallowed. His stomach felt as if it had turned to a lead slab. Beyond his stomach, he'd lost touch with his bowels, making him wonder if he'd lost everything down there. At the same time, he felt like wetting his pants, but so far he'd kept that under control. And then there was that damn MacArthur walking around out there as if he were on a sightseeing tour. "I just don't know how long it'll take them."

"That's what I'm afraid of," said Kenney.

Twaannng! A bullet ricocheted off the command car's fender and zipped into the distance. Reynolds rose to find that the bullet had hit just six inches above his head. *Dammit. I've already given up half of my ass. Lemme out of here.*

Two more bullets dug holes in the dirt near where MacArthur walked; another slammed into the tank. "General!" called Kenney. "Maybe you should get over here?"

"It's okay, George," called MacArthur. "They're about done."

A machine gun opened up to Reynolds's left, making everyone jump. But then he recognized the resonant bark of a .30-caliber air-cooled machine gun. He relaxed a bit and forced himself to breathe. Then again. But like on Bougainville, just before he was shot, his hands shook.

Kenney nodded toward MacArthur and said, "I don't understand it."

Reynolds took a drink from his canteen and handed it over to Kenney. "I don't, either. How can he just walk around in front of the Japs like that? It's almost like he's giving them the finger . . . uh, sir."

Kenney gulped at the canteen and then handed it back. "Suicidal. That's all. Just plain suicidal."

Reynolds's hands were shaking even now as he cocked an ear toward the receiver.

It bleated, making the room grow quiet. Then it blared. "Ipana, this is Horse Trader. Interrogative targets. Over."

The receiver squealed until a radioman, wearing sunglasses and a sleeveless khaki shirt, reached up and twirled a fine adjustment. ". . . Horse Trader, this is Ipana. That last Jap just blew up. Lit up the whole sky. Plenty of fires all around but negative. We have no more targets. Over."

Once again, the crowd cheered and burst into applause.

"Ipana, this is Horse Trader. How many targets is that so far? Over."

"Horse Trader, this is Ipana. Wait one . . ."

Willoughby muttered, "PT boats, destroyers, cruisers, and now these damn battleships." The fragmented reports, although not at all negative, didn't tell them what was going on in Surigao. Nobody would know at least until daybreak.

"Horse Trader, this is Ipana. Best estimate is seven to ten. Over."

"Horse Trader. Roger. Please confirm, over."

"Seven to ten what?" muttered Willoughby. "Sampans, bathtubs, what the hell are they shooting at?"

The loudspeaker squealed again. "Horse Trader, this is Ipana."

"Horse Trader, over."

"This is Ipana. Seven to ten targets destroyed. A few casualties from friendly fire. There is no more enemy. We're picking up survivors. Ipana, out."

Pandemonium broke out until a beefy major stood on a stool and shouted, "Quiet! My men can't do their jobs. This is a restricted space, and by God, I'm going to throw you out of here. I don't give a rat's ass what your rank is."

Quickly it became very quiet. Some began to walk out.

"Look at your damn hands, Owen." Willoughby walked over to a watercooler and returned with a glass of water. "Here. Drink this. No more coffee."

"Thank you, sir," said Reynolds. He raised the glass and

swallowed half. It was lukewarm but tasted good. He put it down, his hands still shaking.

"Get some sleep, Owen," said Willoughby. "I need you fresh and alert tomorrow."

"Sir?" Reynolds pointed.

"What?"

"The tote board."

Imperiously, Willoughby cranked his head around. "Is there something wrong?"

Reynolds's hands shook when he was under fire on Bougainville. They shook today at the airfield. And they shook tonight while the navy was fighting the enemy down in Surigao Strait. But that should have been it. Apparently, the enemy had been turned away. Why were his hands still shaking? "Halsey, sir. What if he's not guarding the San Bernardino Strait? We'd be left wide open."

Willoughby snorted. "Halsey demolished them yesterday in the Sibuyan Sea. Anything left over can be handled by Task Force 34." He yawned and pat his mouth. "I'm going for some shut-eye, Owen. I advise you to do the same." He started off.

"But sir." Reynolds pointed again. "That last message at sunset had the Japs going east again, toward the San Bernardino Strait." It hit him. That's why his hands were shaking.

"Don't worry, Owen. Kinkaid knows what he's doing. So does Halsey." He held up three fingers of one hand and four of the other. "Remember? Task Force Three-Four. All those new damned battleships. Not to worry. Now, good night." General Willoughby walked toward the door.

"Good night, sir," said Reynolds, looking at the tote board.

"No, Colonel Reynolds. You're to go to your quarters."

"But—"

"And get some rest. That's an order."

"Yes, sir." After a moment, Reynolds followed Willoughby up two flights of stairs. He walked into his room, finding that his roommate, a quartermaster corps bird colonel, wasn't there. Sitting heavily on his bunk, he held out his hands. Lightning flashed, thunder rumbled, rain pounded. His hands still shook, and he didn't think he could stop it until he figured out what was going on.

He lay back on his bed, scrunching covers, wondering if Task Force 34 was really guarding the strait. He'd always admired General Willoughby's cool intellect and his ability to think under duress, especially when MacArthur ranted and demanded answers.

But this time? *General, I think you're full of it.* Reynolds tossed again but he couldn't sleep as lightning threw Kafkaesque shadows across the room.

FIFTY-ONE

25 October 1944
USS *Matthew* (DD 548)
Forty miles east of Paninihian Point
Samar Island, Philippine Sea

She has the greenest eyes. And her hair; it's auburn with a wonderful sheen that's positively spectacular when the sun catches it just so. A good-looking woman all right, and he'd told her that the night before he'd walked out on her in the hospital. "Green eyes, auburn hair, dynamite legs. That makes you an intelligent woman," he'd said to her.

"Legs?" She'd ripped off her thick glasses and knit her brow. "Is that all you care about?"

Donovan smiled down at her. "Well, yes. What else is there?"

"Damn you." She reached up and threw her arms around his neck, kissing him deeply. Her lab coat had a starchy odor, but her hair more than made up for it. It had its own unique scent. She folded into him. He reached down and—

The buzzer rang, once, then two more times.

Diane vanished, gone with some ghoul's push of a button. He was ready to kill whoever was on the other end. She was replaced by stark reality as he blinked himself awake. Pressing in on him were the dull, rust-coated bulkheads of the captain's sea cabin.

Dead tired, he'd turned in early last night about 2130. He made a big mistake in asking Chief Casey to give him a mild sedative. Now a glance at the bulkhead clock told him: 0653. He'd been out—ye gods—nine hours or so. What the hell was that, a mickey? Donovan fumbled above his bunk for the phone. He ripped it from its bracket and shouted, "Captain," almost adding, *dammit.*

Someone babbled on the other end. It sounded like Kruger.

"Captain!" Donovan shouted again.

"Mike!" Kruger's tone was high-pitched. "We got shit to pay out here."

"Out where? Richard, where the hell are you?"

"Oh, sorry. On the bridge trying to get a morning fix. You better get out here and we should go to GQ."

"Very well, make it so. I'll be right out." If Kruger wanted GQ, then let him have GQ, Donovan figured as he hung up. The general quarters alarm sounded as he splashed water on his face. Feet thumped. Men raced up and down ladders, manning their battle stations.

Outside his sea cabin, the six-man main-battery director crew yelled at each other as they stomped into the barbette room and, one by one, scrambled up the ladder into the director. Donovan quickly buttoned his shirt, tied his shoes, jammed on his helmet, and grabbed his binoculars. Throwing on his life jacket, he yanked open the door, stepped through the barbette room and onto the starboard bridge wing to find . . . rain. It was pouring, the water gushing from the sky in large globs, the noise incredible. The storm was so thick, it was hard to believe sunrise was nearly twenty minutes ago.

The pilothouse was abnormally quiet. Usually chatter was going on, but now, nothing. Maybe they don't like wearing life jackets and helmets so early in the morning, Donovan reckoned. Kruger and Hammond were bent over the radar repeater in the corner. He checked the compass: course was two-five-zero, as it had been all night. The pitlog reported their speed at fifteen knots. He had to shout against the downpour's roar. "We manned and ready, Mr. Hammond?"

"Yes, sir," reported Hammond.

"Then what do you have?" asked Donovan.

Kruger's face was pressed to the hood on the radar repeater. "Take a look." He stepped away.

Donovan cast a baleful eye at Kruger, then bent to the repeater. He ran the curser all the way out. West of them, at perhaps twenty-five miles, was a tight concentration of blips steaming in what looked like three columns—about twenty ships as near as he could tell. To the south was another concentration of ships. Six large blips were in a circular formation surrounded by seven smaller blips. "What's going on here?" asked Donovan.

Kruger said, "The ones to the west popped up about three minutes ago. Course one-seven-zero, speed twenty."

"Interesting." Donovan ran the cursor on the southern group and asked, "The group to the south is Taffy 3?"

"Right."

"And what do you think about the group to the west?"

"I gotta think Japs," said Kruger.

"Why not Halsey?"

"We've tried to raise them with Task Force 34's call sign on the R/T. Nothing. And look at that formation. Columns. Halsey would be in a circular formation."

"Report it."

"We're trying, but we haven't been able to raise them yet." Kruger waved a hand at the storm. "Interference."

"Well, hell, keep trying," said Donovan. "What if—"

The 29 MC[48] blared over the chart table. "Bridge, combat." It was Ken Talbert, the CIC officer.

Hammond reached up and flipped the lever, "Bridge, aye."

"We just copied a strange message from a TBF calling Derby Base."

"Who's Derby Base?" asked Hammond.

"*St. Lo*[49], sir. The TBF says they're over a large concentration of Jap combatants: four battleships, eight cruisers, twelve destroyers. It's got to be those ships ahead of us, sir."

Donovan's stomach churned as he again checked the radar repeater. This seemed all too real. But why couldn't it be Halsey?

The 29 MC squawked again. "Now Derby Base is asking the TBF to authenticate, sir."

"Well, let's see what happens," said Hammond. "In the meantime, keep trying to contact them." Hammond switched off.

"Combat, aye—wait one."

"What?" barked Hammond.

"The TBF reports flak and AA fire. He sees lots of pagoda masts and says he's going in for an attack."

"Bridge, aye," muttered Hammond.

The 29 MC blared again. "Bridge, radio central." It was Rudy Kubichek, the radio officer.

"Bridge, aye," barked Hammond.

"Japs."

"What?"

"Japs were jabbering all over the secondary tactical circuit before it faded."

"No kidding?" said Hammond.

"What do you want me to do?" said Kubichek.

"Here," muttered Kruger. He reached up. "If they come up again, Mr. Kubichek, tell them to kiss my ass. In the meantime, fix the damn circuit. Bridge out." He flipped the 29 MC lever and looked at Donovan. "Japs."

"Too bad it's not Halsey," said Hammond. "Looks like it's going to be a nice, pleasant day."

Donovan took a mental inventory of all the things he had to do. Then he said, "Okay, Richard. You better head down below."

"On my way." Kruger dashed out.

Donovan turned to Hammond. "Where's Mr. Flannigan?"

"Out on the starboard bridge wing. Unless he floated away." A corner of Hammond's mouth turned up. "I figured the rain would keep his mind off puking."

"What do you think? We're going to need him."

"Fingers crossed, Skipper."

"Very well. I need him on the TBS. We have to know what Taffy 3 is doing."

"Yes, sir, he's on that."

"Who's the screen commander?"

"Commander Thomas in the *Hoel,* sir."

"And we haven't reported in to him yet?"

"Not yet, Captain. As soon as the TBS is up."

"Okay. Now, what's the status of the plant?"

"Boilers one and three on the line cross-connected, saturated steam; generator one on the line," reported Hammond.

"What else?"

"Everything else works except for the damn radios."

"Very well. Potter!"

"Huh?" Yeoman first class Lucian B. Potter leaned against the bulkhead on the opposite side of the pilothouse. He looked over at Donovan with red, puffy eyes. Long straw-colored hair stuck out from under his hat.

"Potter, dammit! Do you know I can have you shot for sleeping on watch?"

"Sir!" Potter gulped, his eyes growing wide. Then he gasped and clutched his throat.

"What the hell's wrong, Potter?" shouted Donovan.

Potter wheezed, "Swallowed my gum, sir."

"Are you all right?"

"Yes, sir."

"Are you ready to go to war?"

Potter stood straight and rasped, "Why, yes, sir."

"Why isn't your hair combed? Didn't I tell you to keep your hair combed?"

"Yes, sir." Potter whipped off his hat, ran his fingers through his hair, and jammed his hat on at the correct angle.

Sailors snickered.

"That's better, Potter. Now get over here and listen up, dammit."

Potter walked over, trailing his telephone cord. "Sir!"

"Okay, Potter. Tell main control to light all boilers and superheaters and split the plant. Tell them I want generator number two on the line as well."

"Yes, sir." Potter bent to give the orders, his tones remarkably authoritative.

Donovan returned to the radar repeater, finding that two of Taffy 3's screening ships had peeled off and were moving directly north, toward the enemy. My God, he thought. Those people are attacking independently. "Mr. Flannigan?" he called.

". . . sir?" came the weak reply.

"Where the hell are you?"

As if from a bizarre puppet show, the redheaded ensign popped up before a porthole. He'd been kneeling, working on something on the open bridge. "Right here, Captain."

"How do you feel?"

"It's okay . . . if I don't think about it." He tilted his hand from side to side. "I was working on the TBS socket. Looks like it's fouled with moisture. I'll have it fixed in a moment."

"Very well, keep at it." He turned to Hammond. "How about CW?"

Hammond rubbed his chin. "Rudy's been up all night trying to calibrate our transmitters. But the tubes keep blowing. It's all this damn humidity." He waved an arm toward the sky. "It has them arcing. Right now, there's so much ozone in radio central the place smells like Frankenstein's jockstrap."

Donovan waved a hand at the phone. "Give me Mr. Kubichek."

"Yes, sir." Hammond yanked the phone from its bracket and punched radio central. "Rudy? What . . . whoa. Who? No shit? Here, the captain wants to talk to you." Hammond handed over the phone.

Donovan began, "Mr. Kubichek, I want those transmitters—"

"Captain, we got the SECTAC[50] circuit back up. And the Japs are still on it, like they're in the next room."

"Shift frequencies, Mr. Kubichek."

"We're trying, Captain."

"In the meantime, tell the Japs to kindly go screw themselves."

"Glad to do that, Captain. Don't know if I would recommend using the word *kindly*."

Donovan grinned. "What's the story on the CW equipment?"

"We're working on it. ETs have stuff spread all over the deck."

"Well, get with it, Mr. Kubichek. We're in the midst of a war."

"There's something else, Captain."

"What?"

"We've copied a plain-language message from Vice Admiral Kinkaid to Admiral Halsey."

"What? Plain language? Impossible." It seemed inexplicable that admirals would communicate with one anther in uncoded language, especially in the presence of the enemy.

"That's what I thought, too, sir."

"Well, what did it say?"

"Admiral Kinkaid reports Jap battleships and cruisers are

approaching and requests Admiral Halsey to send fast battleships and an immediate air strike by fast carriers."

"Good God."

"Amen to that, sir."

Donovan hung up and returned to the radar repeater. "Now our escorts are all on the formation's port side, interposed between the carriers and the Japs. And those other two escorts are still charging north by themselves."

The PRITAC speaker boomed, "Bookbinder, this is Hot Rod. Little Wolves form up to execute William, out." Rear Admiral Sprague in the flagship *Fanshaw Bay* was telling his escorts to get ready for a torpedo attack.

Flannigan called through the porthole, "TBS is back up, sir."

Donovan said, "I heard it. Okay, tell Hot Rod and Bookbinder we're reporting in for duty assigned and ask for instructions."

"Yes, sir," said Flannigan.

The clouds broke, the rain gone as quickly as if some ghoul in the clouds had twisted shut a gigantic valve. Sunlight streamed in the porthole. Suddenly it became quiet as pink daylight trickled into the pilothouse and lighted the bulkheads. The ocean was a deep blue, and steam rose off the *Matthew*'s wet, glistening decks.

"So much for hiding under cloud cover," said Hammond.

Donovan stepped out to the starboard bridge wing, finding a drenched Ensign Flannigan bracing his arms against the bulwark and scanning the western horizon with binoculars. Following suit, Donovan found the horizon clearly etched against the morning sky. Just above, he made out several dark specks flying in a large circle.

"See anything, Mr. Flannigan?" asked Donovan.

"Not yet, Captain. I—"

"—Target zero-four-five. Shit, oh dear. Several targets zero-four-five. Sonofabitch." It was a lookout on the pilothouse pointing west.

Again Donovan raised his binoculars and adjusted the focus. *Oh, my God.* Ten seconds passed before he caught himself and forced himself to count. There were six sets of upperworks on the horizon. One set flashed. Moments later, four red-colored splashes rose a thousand yards ahead.

"Oh, shit," someone groaned from the pilothouse.

"That's heavy-duty stuff they're sending our way," said another.

"Lemme out of here," said a third.

Donovan yelled over his shoulder, "Mind your tasks."

"What the hell is that?" asked Hammond, pointing at the fading columns of red water.

"Dyeloads," said Donovan.

Flanningan's binoculars were jammed into his eye sockets. His Adam's apple bounced up and down as he rasped, "Wha . . . wha . . . what are dyeloads?"

Donovan said, "Ship A fires red, ship B fires green dyeloads, ship C fires yellow, and so on. Therefore, each gunnery officer can spot his own shot and adjust accordingly."

"Oh. Just one ship wasting all that stuff on us?" squeaked Flannigan.

"Right. See that?" Donovan pointed to multiple gun flashes. "They've opened fire. We're small potatoes so it looks like somebody is using us for target practice."

"If we're so damn small, then why don't they shoot at us with BB guns? That stuff looks like eight-inch. Maybe bigger."

Another group of shells fell closer, perhaps five hundred yards off to their right, the columns of red hissing water rising fifty feet in the air.

Donovan called to Hammond, "Burt, see those shells? Head straight for them." Chasing the splashes was something Donovan had learned in the Solomon Islands campaign, the theory being that the enemy gunner would adjust his aim, his next shells not falling where he'd shot before.

"Yes, sir." Hammond gave the rudder order.

Flannigan grabbed his headphones, then said, "Monkey Wrench, roger out."

"What?" asked Donovan.

Flannigan gulped and said, "The screen has executed William, Captain." *William* was the code word for a torpedo attack. "Tabby Cat and Cherokee have attacked independently. And"—Flannigan's Adam's apple worked up and down—

"they've ordered us to make smoke and also attack independently."

Donovan checked the radar, seeing that the two attacking destroyers had closed to within ten thousand yards of the Japanese group. They're really mixing it up. Donovan reached up and keyed the 29 MC. "Combat, bridge. Who are Tabby Cat and Cherokee?"

Kruger came right back. "*Tabby Cat* is call sign for the screen commander, Captain, who's riding in the *Hoel. Cherokee* is the *Johnston.* Looks like they're hell-bent-for-leather."

"Roger." The *Johnson,* Donovan recalled, was nicknamed "GQ Johnnie" because her skipper, Commander Ernest E. Evans, often exercised his crew at general quarters. The call sign was interesting because Evans was a Cherokee. "What other ships are in the screen?"

"DD *Heermann,* then the DEs *Dennis, Raymond, John C. Butler,* and *Samuel B. Roberts.*"

"Bridge, aye." Donovan released the talk button and glanced to the south. Lazy black smoke rose above the horizon, looking as if a series of buildings were on fire. It was the smoke from the destroyers screening Taffy 3. And the Airedales were busy, too. He counted at least ten American TBFs, diving on the enemy ships.

Things to do. *Get going*. "Mr. Hammond."

"Sir?" Hammond ran from the pilothouse.

"We're going to attack with torpedoes now. Prepare to come right to two-six-five, speed thirty-three knots."

"Thirty-three?" Hammond was incredulous. It was drilled into watch officers that the *Fletcher*-class destroyers, originally rated at thirty-five knots, could barely make thirty-three knots due to the addition of equipment. But that was only if they had a clean bottom and light load. Moreover, the ships' superheaters were notorious for breaking down. A call for thirty-three knots was something one usually didn't do.

"That's correct, Mr. Hammond. Two-six-five will do for now, please." He grabbed Potter by his life jacket straps and yanked him over. "Okay, son, pass the word to Mr. Corodini that I'll soon want turns for thirty-three knots. And tell him to make as much smoke as possible."

"Yes, sir." Potter keyed his mike and began talking.

Twenty seconds later, the bridge phone buzzed. Hammond answered, then held out the phone. "Captain, it's Al Corodini."

Donovan grabbed the phone. "Good morning, Mr. Corodini. How can I help you?"

When it came to his engines, Corodini didn't waste words. "Thirty-three knots, Captain? We'll tear up the plant."

"How long do you think the plant will last at that speed, Al?"

"Sir?"

"You heard me."

"I wouldn't give it half an hour. Any more than that and she'll blow a gasket somewhere. A bearing, a feed pump. Who knows?"

"That's good enough for me, Mr. Corodini, because there's a good chance we'll be dead by then."

It was silent on the other end.

Donovan said, "I'm sorry, Al. I know you love your damn engines, but right now, I need everything you and your feed pumps and bearings can give. So crack the throttles wide open, tie down the safety valves, and hang your hat on the damn steam gauge."

"Jesus."

"And make smoke, son. Plenty of it."

"Jesus."

"You're a good engineer, Al. You and your boys keep at it and we'll do just fine."

"Yes, sir."

FIFTY-TWO

25 October 1944
USS *Matthew* (DD 548)
Thirty miles east of Paninihian Point
Samar Island, Philippine Sea

"Lieutenant Hammond, execute, please," barked Donovan.

Hammond's eyes glistened. Perhaps it was from the wind, but then Donovan saw something in his face that said, *I know we have to do this but God, I'm scared.*

Me, too, Burt. He clutched the bulwarks tightly with both hands to make sure nobody could see they were shaking.

Hammond swallowed twice and hollered, "Right ten degrees rudder. Steady up on course two-six-five. All engines ahead flank. Make three hundred thirty-three revolutions for thirty-three knots."

Helmsman and lee helmsman acknowledged his orders almost simultaneously; the engine room telegraph clanged as the lee helmsman shoved the handles all the way down.

Ensign Flannigan handed Donovan the phone. "XO, sir."

Donovan jammed it to his ear and said, "Richard?"

"You're the captain, right?" asked Kruger's metallic voice.

"Last time I checked."

"Well then, shouldn't you say something?" said Kruger.

"I've been thinking about it. I guess now is the time."

"We don't have much of it left."

"And what's left is not going to be pretty."

"I know, but they have a right to know what we're in for."

"I'll say. Thanks for reminding me." He hung up and walked around the full circumference of the bridge, ignoring the faces of signalmen, boatswain's mates, and gunners. Just a few short months before they had been torn from their wives and sweethearts while going to high school and college or working for a living.

What do I tell them? That their chances of dying are certain? That we're sailing into the jaws of hell at thirty-three knots? A phrase from the "Navy Hymn" popped into his mind.

Oh hear us when we cry to thee
for those in peril on the sea.

He leaned on the bulwark and stared into the ocean. *Yes, dear God, please let me do a good job and keep my men and this ship safe. Amen.*

He stepped into the pilothouse and keyed the 1 MC. "This is the captain speaking." His voice echoed metallically from speakers throughout the ship. "You should know that we are now making a torpedo attack on a major portion of the Japanese fleet. I wish I could tell you that our chances are good, but they're not. But if we don't do our jobs, a lot of men will die and our carriers will be sunk, therefore prolonging this war. So we've got to do what we can to slow these bastards down. I know every man will do his job. And I'm proud to serve with you. That is all." He clicked off, staring at the mouthpiece, wondering how they would take it. From the corner of his eye, he noticed that men in the pilothouse glanced at him and then looked away. Their faces were not looks of disdain or cowardice. Nor did they show fear or anguish. That was put aside as their training took over, and they bent to their tasks, ready to do what they had to do. The fear would come later. After the battle, if they lived. There would be sleepless nights, with excruciating nightmares; vivid recollections of severed limbs and decapitated heads, bloodied comrades, and burning flesh. Donovan swore the stench of the *Tampa* was still with him. But then the thought of the *Tampa* brought back images of Tiny and his big, oafish, smiling face. Tiny, dammit! And John. They'd been such good friends. Then no longer good friends. But as he looked ahead at his last few minutes, Donovan realized that didn't matter. Worse, he felt shame and anguish with the thought that his damn ego had gotten in the way and kept him from trying to reconcile with John Sabovik.

I should have tried harder. And didn't John Sabovik drive Diane all the way to Mare Island to see me off? He was trying, why didn't I? Dear God, you gave me a wonderful woman to marry. And I refused to do anything about John Sabovik. I haven't even written him. Oh, God, what have I done? Please let me do a good job, protect my crew, and go home to Diane. Then I'll call John. And Tiny, this one's for you.

"Hodges," he called.

"Sir," replied the signalman.

"You have a battle flag?"

"A lollapalooza, Captain."

"Then run it up."

"Aye, aye, Captain." In moments, Hodges and two of his signalmen pulled a flag from the flag bag and snapped on the hanks. His two apprentices fairly jumped the halyard, running the flag up and to-blocking it in three seconds. The ten-by-twenty-foot national ensign broke and crackled with the wind.

Donovan shouted, "Mr. Hammond?"

"Sir?"

"I have the conn."

"Yes, sir." Hammond leaned into the pilothouse. "Captain has the conn."

The *Matthew* came alive as she built speed; her uptakes squealed as she sucked in massive loads of air to feed the boilers. Leaping through the waves, she accelerated into her turn to meet the enemy. Standing high on the starboard platform, Donovan checked the gun crews on the weather decks. Their stance told him what he wanted to know. They were crouched behind their guns, eyes on sights, hands ready with ammo, fingers poised on sound-powered phones. Down in the forward engine room, Al Corodini and his machinist's mates, enginemen, and boiler tenders were throwing all the steam they could to the turbines. Yes, they were ready.

They were soon up to thirty-three knots with the *Matthew* dipping and rolling in the waves. For sure, Donovan was scared to death, and he hoped it didn't show. What he hadn't told them on the 1 MC was that it was going to happen soon, most likely in the next ten minutes. He just hoped there would be time to fire all their torpedoes. With guns ranging from six- to eighteen-inch, the enemy fleet was far superior to the *Matthew*'s five five-inch popguns; worse, each of the Taffy 3 carriers had just one stern-mounted five-inch gun. If there was any chance, it would be from the Taffy 3 and 2 and 1 Avengers and Wildcats, now furiously buzzing above the Japanese.

"Range?" Donovan shouted up to Merryweather.

"About twenty-one thousand yards, Captain." Ten and a half nautical miles.

The *Matthew* plunged ahead, steaming against the enemy at almost a perpendicular course.

Where the hell are the red shell splashes? Donovan fine-tweaked the focus knob, bringing into view the upperworks of four gigantic warships—one a *Kongo*-class battleship.

On the other side of the Kongo was a bigger battleship—a monster. A battleship so large, he'd never seen anything like it in the recognition manuals. Two Avengers dove on her, slinging sticks of bombs across her path. All but one of the bombs missed as the giant swung though a turn and headed the other way. The last bomb bounced off her forward turret and exploded harmlessly just before it plunged into the ocean.

Closer, two columns of heavy *Tone*-class cruisers rose above the horizon. Great sheets of water peeled off their bows; smoke erupted from their eight-inch guns as they fired at the carriers of Taffy 3.

Donovan hailed atop the pilothouse: "What's the range now, Mr. Merryweather?"

"Nineteen thousand yards, sir."

"See that *Tone*-class cruiser at the head of the column closest to us?"

"Sure do, Captain," called Merryweather.

"Take her under fire when the range reaches eighteen thousand yards." Eighteen thousand yards or nine nautical miles was the maximum range for the five-inch/38 dual-purpose gun.

"On target and tracking, Captain. Computer has solution."

"Very well."

The cruiser at the head of the column must have sensed

what was coming, for her entire main battery of nine eight-inch guns slowly trained around and pointed directly at the *Matthew.*

"Now we get to find out how good these guys are," muttered Merryweather.

Smoke belched. Three red water columns rose off the port bow, about three hundred yards away.

"Good enough," said Merryweather with professional admiration. "A tight twenty-five-yard grouping." Merryweather might as well have been judging a skeet-shooting competition at the local hunt club on a balmy Sunday afternoon.

Suddenly three shells whistled over and landed two hundred yards behind them.

"Bracketed!" screeched Hammond.

Do something. Donovan yelled to the helmsman, "Head for those splashes, now." He pointed to the still-churning waters where the first three shells had hit.

"Yes, sir." La Valle eased in a bit of left rudder, and soon the destroyer sliced through the foaming red pools where the shells had landed moments before.

Two red splashes smacked the water, exactly where their track would have been.

The third shell was close, just twenty-five yards to starboard. Hot shell fragments rattled against the ship. The water column rose and hissed and tumbled upon them, drenching the forward section of the destroyer.

Donovan was soaking wet. And there was something else.

"Good God," shouted Hammond. He rushed to Donovan, yelling, "Call a medic!"

"What the hell are you doing?" said Donovan, pushing him away.

"Captain, shit, what is it?" said Hammond.

"I dunno, wha—" He looked down. Red, everything was a glistening red. The deck, bulkheads, portholes, the main-battery director, everything. "It's the dye, Burt. Take it easy."

Hammond's mouth worked. "Shit, you look like some monster from a Bela Lugosi movie."

Even Merryweather was red. Donovan called, "Cliff."

An incredulous Merryweather tried to wipe himself off.

But there were large globs and it smeared into his life jacket and trousers. "What is it?" he screeched.

"Cliff, dammit, Lieutenant Merryweather, you're okay. Do you hear me?"

Merryweather froze for a moment, then looked down at Donovan. His eyes refocused and he said, "Sorry, Captain. Shit. Do I look like an ad for the Red Cross or what?"

"Most beautiful, Mr. Merryweather. Now listen up. I want you to call Mr. Peete in the torpedo director, okay?" As torpedo officer, Jonathan Peete's battle station was in the torpedo director platform mounted on number two stack.

"Yes, sir."

"Tell him I want a ten-shot set up on that *Tone*-class cruiser, the one in the lead. Got it?"

"Yes, sir. The one in the lead."

"I repeat, tell Ensign Peete to shoot all ten torpedoes." Donovan didn't explain to Merryweather the reason was that their chances were less than 50 percent to get close enough to launch torpedoes. And that their chances were less than 10 percent to be able to come around for another torpedo attack. By that time they were sure to be dead. He continued. "Tell him I want a one-degree spread, intermediate speed, six-foot depth. Shoot at ten thousand yards."

"Ten thousand yards, yes, sir," said Merryweather.

Hammond yelled up, "Cliff. Tell the little bastard he better not miss, or I'm gonna go back there and kick his ass."

Merryweather said, "He'll appreciate that, Burt." Then he bent to his sound-powered phone to relay the command.

Wham! Wham! Mounts one and two barked from the foredeck. Cordite smoke momentarily swirled around the bridge, giving Donovan that centuries-old scent of war at sea. A quick, horrible image flashed through his mind of what a shell does to man's flesh when it rips through a ship's interior at twenty-seven hundred feet per second. Far better that the shell detonate. It would mean instant, merciful death and a good deal of obliteration of what happened to the hapless men in that millisecond. Without exploding, it would be up to the medics to rush into a compartment, most likely afire, and—while slipping and sliding on bloody decks—work through the body parts and human goo to see if anyone was still alive.

Opening fire meant the range had closed to eighteen thousand yards. *Not long now*. They sailed through a trail of smoke, the Japanese column momentarily lost from sight. Donavan pulled a handkerchief from his pocket to wipe off his binoculars, but it soon turned red.

"Here." Hammond leaned into the pilothouse and handed Donovan a clean pair of binoculars.

They emerged from the smoke as the forward five-inch guns again barked. Donovan trained on the lead *Tone*-class cruiser. Her guns had trained around and she was again firing at the carriers. "Range?"

"Sixteen thousand," yelled Merryweather.

Something exploded on the cruiser's foredeck. Pieces twirled in the air; smoke poured and flames jumped, engulfing the forward eight-inch gun mount. "A hit, Cliff. Good going!"

Merryweather grinned. "We sure got something."

Someone yanked at Donovan's sleeve.

"Look at her burn," shouted Donovan. "Pour it to them."

Matthew's five-inch guns roared with Donovan feeling a surge of pride as his gunners worked into an easy rhythm. The dead time was phenomenal—between three and four seconds—as the *Matthew*'s five-inch guns cranked out round after vicious round. The loading-machine drills, as morale crushing as they had been, were paying off.

To the southeast, Donovan saw the other two *Fletcher*-class destroyers were in range, their guns barking in rapid succession. Amazing, thought Donovan. We're close enough to shoot back and the Japs haven't touched us yet. Just wait.

Potter keyed his sound-powered phone. "Bridge, aye." He looked up to Donovan: "Our last salvo knocked out the surface search radar. ETs are on it. Exec advises it'll be up in ten minutes."

"Very well," said Donovan. Dammit! Now the radar. What else?

Again someone tugged at his sleeve. "Captain."

"What the hell?" Donovan looked down. It was Ensign Kubichek, the radio officer.

"Captain, you've got to read this." He held up a clipboard.

A red-coated Donovan yelled, "Get below, son. I've got a battle on my hands."

"Please, Captain," said Kubichek.

"Who's it from?"

"COMTWELVE, sir."

"COMTWELVE? Dammit, sailor, you want me to sign for some damn spare parts list in the middle of a battle? Get the hell off my bridge!"

Six shots whistled overhead and fell four hundred yards astern. Quickly he searched, finding a squall off to his right. "That's enough of that. Come right to three-zero-zero," called Donovan. "Head for that squall."

"Three-zero-zero, aye, sir," replied La Valle.

"Captain, you must," shrieked Kubichek.

Donovan growled, "Lay below, mister, or I'll have you thrown in the chain locker."

Hammond dashed over. "Rudy. Fer chrissake, get below to your station."

Kubichek planted both feet on the deck, ripped off the message, and jammed it in Donovan's hands. "If you don't read that message in the next five minutes, Captain, I'm not going to have any station to lay below to."

Donovan turned the message over in his hands, smearing it with red dye. Mounts 51 and 52 roared again, making him blink each time. And this time, the forward-facing mount 53 joined in, her field of fire unmasked. Then they were into the squall, a strange, thin mist swirling around them.

"Captain!" It was Kubichek again, shrieking, tears running down his face.

Donovan said, "What the hell's gotten into you, son?"

FIFTY-THREE

25 October 1944
IJN *Yamato*
Thirty-two kilometers east of Paninihian Point
Samar Island, Philippine Sea

Wearing a starched-white waiter's jacket, third-class gunner's mate Minoru Onishi palmed a tray over his head and elbowed his way through officers crowded around the plotting table. Perched on the tray was a frosted glass and bottle of Asahi beer for Onishi's master. And he wasn't going to let anyone get in his way. He cared not about the strident babble of admirals or captains or commanders around the table. Nor did he consider the path to his master a challenge. Nor did the roar of the *Yamato*'s guns detract from his mission, nor even the fact that a major battle was under way. Onishi had been ordered to bring beer to Vice Admiral Ugaki, and nothing would stop him.

Noyama watched Onishi with an odd detachment; it was an isolated vignette, the only thing happening in this world: a stupid oaf delivering beer to his master.

He was torn from his daydream when a blast roared outside. The *Yamato* vibrated as she loosed a nine-gun salvo from her 18.1-inch guns. Air seemed to vanish from the compartment. Seconds later, Noyama felt he could talk and breathe and live. He tried to edge his way through the crowd toward Kurita who, with Ugaki, was dictating a situation report to CinC Toyoda in Tokyo. Worse, they hadn't heard from Ozawa and his Northern Force. Without that information, they couldn't solve the Halsey equation. Where was he?

Noyama turned, finding Onishi looking down at him as if

he were a peasant in a rice paddy. Long ago, Noyama had learned to step aside when Onishi was on one of his Ugaki assignments. The beast didn't care if he ran over an officer or enlisted, and it was too much trouble to bring charges against him. Ugaki would just have them waived. Noyama stepped away and Onishi passed with an "Uhhhh."

Noyama swore under his breath; flag plot wasn't big enough for everyone. The five-by-five-meter area was filled with Ugaki's Battleship Division One staff. Added to that were the remnants of Vice Admiral Kurita's First Striking Force staff. Crammed on the aft bulkhead was a wide variety of radio equipment and the assorted operators and supervisors to manage communications of the First Striking Force and Battleship Division One. Men cursed as they tripped over phone cords, spilled cigarette ashes, or knocked papers on the deck. Moreover, it was hot and humid with this damn Philippine tropical weather. Half the radio operators and a few of the junior officers were shirtless and wore hachimaki, the warrior's traditional headband. The rest had their shirt-sleeves rolled up. Many were crowded around the damn plotting table, their babbling and sweat mingling with the cannon fire.

Lieutenant Commander Boshiro Hirota, Battleship Division One's communications officer, was one of the officers competing for Ugaki's attention. Running a handkerchief over his bald head, he yelled across the table, "*Nagato* reports the six carriers are *Independence* class." *Nagato* was one of the battleships in his Battleship Division One.

But Ugaki picked it up and turned to Kurita. "There, you hear? That's Halsey out there. What more proof do you want?"

"Yes, but those are thirty-three-knot ships. We'll have a hard time catching them," complained Kurita.

Noyama edged through in time to hear Ugaki lower his voice and say, "We'll never have an opportunity like this again."

"I know, I know, that's why I ordered a general attack instead of a ring formation. But now, with all these damn airplanes buzzing around, I'm not so sure. I don't want a repeat of yesterday."

"Well, I say pour it on. Run the fleet speed up to twenty-five knots, dammit."

The ship vibrated as she leaned to port, again turning to avoid a bomb. They didn't hear the airplane, but the bomb exploded close aboard with a loud *bang* that vibrated throughout the ship.

Undeterred, men shouted, each with his own strident message.

Ignoring them, Kurita hissed, "We have fuel oil to think about, you damn fool. And I don't want to be the one on record who lost two of our finest battleships in as many days."

Ugaki rubbed his chin, thinking about the *Musashi* and how she'd been sunk yesterday by Halsey's incessant air attacks. The same could happen today to *Yamato,* he admitted to himself.

Onishi leaned over and, with an enormous barnyard reach, carefully placed the tray before his admiral.

"Thank, you, thank you, Onishi," said Ugaki, pouring his beer.

"Uhhhh." Onishi bowed, grunted, and backed away, captains and commanders bouncing off his enormous frame.

Ugaki's eyebrows went up. "Want one?"

Kurita shook his head. "I'd pass out."

Ugaki made a show of pouring the beer and letting the foam build. "How much sleep have you had, Takeo?"

"Enough."

"How much, dammit?"

"Nothing since the *Atago* went down."

Ugaki leaned close. "And you were up most of the night before. That's nearly fifty hours you've gone without sleep." He hissed under his breath, "How the hell do you expect to survive the mission? How do you expect to serve your men? Your ships? Your Emperor, if you continue on like this?"

Kurita shrugged.

"Your dengue fever is not getting better."

"Quiet, they'll hear."

Ugaki said sotto voce, "The hell with the others. And the hell with your clouded judgment. And the hell with the fuel oil. I say go after Halsey's carriers, now. If we do that, we'll have more than accomplished our mission. The Emperor will be proud."

"But are you sure it's Halsey?" Kurita pounded his fist. "We have yet to hear from Ozawa. What's he doing? Did Halsey go after him? And the *Nagato*'s report? I need confirmation that they are *Essex* class. And we'd have it if our damn reconnaissance planes would return. But they've been shot down. So who do I count on?" he yelled.

Ugaki stepped back.

Men babbled, waving papers in the air.

"Silence!" yelled Kurita.

When they quieted, he said, "Most of you are veterans of previous battles. Please conduct yourselves accordingly." He turned to Noyama. "Commander, get this message off to CinC immediately."

Loudly, Noyama said, "Yes, sir." He limped around the table and took the message.

"Top priority. It must go out immediately."

"Yes, sir."

"And Noyama." Kurita pulled Noyama close and said softly, "Find Dr. Koketsu and get something to take care of this splitting headache. Damn, I can hardly see."

Noyama said, "Maybe, Admiral, you should—"

"Dammit, not you, too," growled Kurita. "No more sniveling. Get Koketsu up here, now."

"Yes, sir." Noyama grabbed the message blank and walked over to the long-range radio operator.

Just then Hirota called, "*Suzuya* reports two *Baltimore*-class[51] cruisers attacking with torpedoes. One has already launched and seriously damaged the *Kumano.*" He clamped his hands to his headphones and yelled into the mouthpiece, "Yes, it's confirmed. The other *Baltimore* cruiser has launched ten torpedoes, which are headed directly for us."

"A spread of ten?" gasped Ugaki.

"Yes, sir."

"We must avoid." Ugaki received a confirming glance from Kurita, then spaced two fingers over battleship icons on the plotting table. "With a spread that wide, two of us are in danger," he muttered. "Signal *Haruna* and *Yamato,*" he said to Hirota, "to reverse course to comb the torpedoes' course and make maximum speed to evade." Again he glanced at Kurita, the two deathly afraid of losing another *Musashi*-class battleship. He snapped his fingers at three junior officers at the opposite end of the plotting table. "You there. Make yourselves useful. Work out a course to evade, quickly now." Then he called to Hirota, "Tell them to make their course zero-zero-zero, speed twenty-seven until we come up with something better."

"Yes, sir." Hirota relayed the order by radio to the *Haruna* and by sound-powered phone to the *Yamato*'s captain, Rear Admiral Morishita, down on the heavily armored bridge.

Men began plotting evasion courses at the table's end. One of them, a junior officer, muttered a little too loudly, "Strange, there's plenty of targets out there, but now our main battery's out of range. I'll bet our boys in the turrets are getting itchy fingers."

"You." Hirota pointed a finger. "Silence."

"Sorry, sir."

Rear Admiral Takata took advantage of the moment and pushed his way through the crowd.

"Admiral, you must see this." He pushed a flimsy in Kurita's hand.

"Just read it," said Kurita.

Takata hitched up his pants and rasped, "*Takao*[52] reports intercepting a plain-language appeal for help from Admiral Kinkaid to Admiral Halsey to send fast battleships and carriers."

"Plain language?" said Kurita as the *Yamato* leaned into her turn to port.

"Yessir."

The ship heeled at least ten degrees as she powered through her turn. At the same time she reached twenty-seven knots. Kurita rested a hand on the bulkhead and asked, "What's gotten into Kinkaid?"

"He's desperate, that's for sure," said Ugaki.

"Do you suppose that's not Halsey out there?"

"Who else could it be?"

"Kinkaid's escort carriers."

"Impossible," said Ugaki.

With a grimace, Kurita grabbed his head. "Where the hell is Koketsu?" he shouted to the overhead.

"I'll get him, Admiral," said Noyama, handing the message to the coding officer. He grabbed the port hatch lever, undogged it, and pushed the door open. Wind blasted in. Papers scattered and the flag officers cursed as he began to step outside. They were in a rain squall, the visibility down to two hundred meters. But the rain felt good on his face, and fresh air filled his lungs.

Kurita barked, "Noyama, get back here."

"Sir?" He stepped back in, redogging the hatch.

"I can't recall, did we inquire about Ozawa in that message?"

"Yes, sir, we did."

The admiral's eyes were bloodshot, and he was having trouble standing. "And?"

"It's being encoded, now, sir. Should go out in the next few minutes."

"Very well. I just want to—"

"Yeeeeeeee!" screeched one of the junior officers. He pointed at a porthole in the forward bulkhead.

Ugaki rushed up, pushed the man aside, and shouted, "You have him, Morishita; run the bastard down!"

Noyama rushed outside, finding they had cleared the storm cell and were steaming into clear weather again. Directly ahead, no more than two hundred meters away, was an American destroyer, running at great speed, sheets of water peeling high off her bow.

Hunching down, he grabbed the rail and yelled, "*Bakayaro!* We've got you."

Inside, Ugaki described the impending collision with the glee of an announcer calling a steeplechase. Before him, the American destroyer was square in his sights, the great battleship's bow aimed directly at the American's bridge. They were so close he saw faces of the men in the open gun mounts look up in surprise at the horrible apparition that had suddenly pounced upon them from out of the rain.

Closer.

It would be impossible not to hit. As the distance closed,

Kurita's hoarse voice mingled with the others as they yelled and shouted.

And yet this destroyer, or this cruiser, or whatever it was, was as beautiful as a white dove just before a cat leaps to snatch it from the air. With raked stacks and mast, her lines were lean. She had mottled blue paint, and an American red-and-white-striped shield was painted on her forward stack; a gleaming silver bullet standing upright over the figures 77. An enormous battle flag streamed from her mast.

At great speed, she squatted by the stern, a great rooster tail shooting out a white foaming wake. Noyama would be sorry to see the ship go down.

Maybe not.

The nearer they drew, the more he noticed the enemy ship leaning to starboard. Heavily. Yes, her rudder is hard over. Will she make it? He couldn't help himself as he began urging, routing for the little ship to draw clear.

Her stern moved quickly away as her rudder's advance and transfer took effect.

Something else. Men on the American's bridge, looking up, their mouths open. One of them was perched high on a platform. He was bareheaded, a megaphone in his hand. Red. He was red from head to toe. In fact, much of the bridge glistened in a reddish tinge. So did the other people. *Why are they red?* And that man must be the captain. No matter, he stood proud and tall, glaring up at the seventy-thousand-ton battleship rushing to cut him in half. What the hell have these people done to themselves? War paint? Are these American Indians?

FIFTY-FOUR

25 October 1944
USS *Matthew* (DD 548)
Twenty-nine miles east of Paninihian Point
Samar Island, Philippine Sea

Donovan screeched, "Where the hell did that thing come from?" They'd just popped out of a squall and were about to be T-boned by a seagoing behemoth. The enormous bow—the *Kiku,* the Emperor's gilded chrysanthemum symbol, on her nose—barreled straight for them at a horrendous rate. He grabbed a megaphone and yelled at La Valle in the pilothouse, "Left full rudder!"

A cold lump formed in La Valle's belly; sweat stood on his bow as he spun his wheel furiously. Checking the rudder angle indicator, he yelled, "My rudder is left full, Captain." He looked over to Woodruff, the lee helmsman. "Put on your face mask, Nick, it's deep shit."

Woodruff's eyes were like saucers; he gulped a couple of times. "Maybe we should jump."

"No, better to stay aboard. That thing's screws would chop you to shark bait."

Donovan bellowed into the pilothouse, "Increase your rudder to hard left."

"Hard left?" answered La Valle.

"That's what I said, sailor. Put it in the stops, dammit."

La Valle spun the rudder all the way over. "My rudder is hard left, sir."

"Very well." Donovan realized those may have been the last words he would ever utter.

The *Matthew* heeled farther to twenty degrees. Looking

aft, he took heart. The fantail rapidly slid to starboard, out of the battleship's way.

Details stood out as the battleship's bow loomed over him. The starboard anchor pitted with rust; the port anchor, newly painted. That damn gilded flower on the nose, and, yes, clear blue water peeling off those tremendous bows.

"Go, go, go," urged Merryweather from the pilothouse.

She was clear! The giant ship's bow ran past the fantail with no more than twenty yards to spare. Three Japanese sailors stared down at them from the main deck. One of them shook his fist. Potter shouted up to them, his voice echoing between the hulls, "Hey Tojo! Go take a flyin' leap in a rolling doughnut."

The Japanese shouted back. One flipped the finger.

"Meet her!" yelled Donovan. "La Valle, don't let our nose get into her."

"Meet her, aye," replied La Valle. With all his strength, he whipped the wheel to zero degrees rudder angle. "Wouldn't do that, Captain," he gasped. La Valle knew what Donovan meant: too much rudder and they would keeping turning and nose into this monster's port side. Too little and the *Matthew*'s fantail could get clipped. Easy, easy. He fed in a little right rudder. There! The bullnose steadied up on a course about two degrees to the right of the battleship's track. La Valle shouted, "Got it, Captain, steady on course one-eight-seven."

"Well done," said Donovan.

"Where . . . where the hell did that thing come from, Captain?" said Flannigan, his face a pasty white. Without radar, he was as exasperated as everyone else. The thing had just pounced upon them without warning.

"Better yet," said Donovan, "what the hell is it?" The gigantic ship raced down their port side at a relative speed of nearly sixty knots. Guns. All he saw were guns sticking in the sky like a porcupine. Everywhere. Mostly antiaircraft guns. But he did get a glimpse of an enormous superfiring number two turret that mounted three enormous rifles, their muzzles larger, he thought, than even the *Iowa*-class battleships he'd seen. Then came a heavily armored superstructure. He spotted the bridge. Above that was a signal platform and then another deck housing, maybe a flag bridge, he reckoned. A man stood at an open hatchway, an officer. Then the man did the damndest thing. He drew to attention and saluted.

Donovan yanked his garrison cap from his pocket, jammed it on, and faced the rapidly disappearing Japanese officer. For whatever reason, he snapped a salute. The man was soon out of sight. The battleship's after turret swooped past, followed by her counter, drawing a churning, foamy wake.

Donovan muttered, "Why the hell did I do that?"

His answer was a salvo from the after turret: three enormous shells screeched overhead like three freight trains. He was surprised to find himself on the deck; his back had slammed against the pilothouse bulkhead, smearing it with red goo. The blast's overpressure had taken them all by surprise and had thrown them down before they knew it.

He shouted up to Merryweather, "Open fire, dammit."

"Aye, aye, sir." A cloud of smoke shrouded the ship's aft section as the after two five-inch mounts opened up, the forty- and twenty-millimeters guns chattering right after.

"Captain?" It was Kubichek, the radio officer.

Good God. That damn message. He'd just finished reading it when that damn Jap's bow came at them as they shot out of a squall. Mired in red goo and rainwater, he held it up again.

SECRET

TO: C/O USS MATTHEW (DD 548)
FROM: COMNAVDIST12
SUBJ: MK 6 TORPEDO EXPLODER—LOT NO. ALX24 114 UP
INFO: 1. CNO
2. CINCPAC
3. BUORD
4. COM 3
5. COM 38
6. COM 7
7. COM TG 77.4.3
8. COMDESPAC
9. COMDESRON 77
10. ONI 24.4
REF: A. BUORD INST. 25.27.36(A)
B. BUORD INST. 2731.1.3(B)

1. BE ADVISED MARK 6 EXPLODER LOT NUMBER ALX24 114 UP IS BOOBY TRAPPED.
2. SUBJECT EXPLODER BELIEVED ISSUED TO YOU VIA USS MT. ST. HELENS IN ULITHI.
3. MT. ST. HELENS LATER BLEW UP VIA ANOTHER BOOBY TRAPPED EXPLODER.
3. SUBJECT EXPLODER RIGGED TO DETONATE 10250900H.
4. BE ADVISED SUBJECT EXPLODER WILL PREMATURELY DETONATE ON ATTEMPT TO FIRE FROM TUBE.
5. FURTHER, EXPLODER WILL DETONATE IF WITHDRAWN FROM TORPEDO.
6. RECOMMEND USE OF ORDNANCE EXPERT ABOARD NEAREST AD.
7. GOOD LUCK.
SABOVIK BY DIRECTION

BT

Wham! Wham! Wham! Three enormous shell splashes walked up their wake.

"La Valle, left standard rudder." To Flannigan he shouted, "Tell the exec and Mr. Peete to lay to the bridge, please."

"To the bridge?" Flannigan gulped.

"That doesn't mean tomorrow, Mr. Flannigan. I mean now." Donovan checked his watch: 0842. If that message is right, the thing will go off in eighteen minutes.

"Yes, sir."

Four six-inch gun shells walked across their bow no more than one hundred yards away.

"All engines ahead full," called Donovan. "Make turns for twenty-five knots." The bell was no sooner answered than two six-inch shells landed directly ahead of where they would have been. Then the battleship's aft turret roared again; three giant green water columns rose five hundred yards to starboard.

The *Matthew* was still in a left turn, almost parallel the battleship's course. "Rudder amidships," called Donovan. They were bracketing him, and it was only a matter of time. All he could do was chase the splashes, run for cover, and hope for the best. His heart jumped as he spotted another squall line about a mile ahead. He sighted it over the pelorus and said, "Come right to zero-two-four, all ahead flank, make turns for thirty-three knots."

Not enough time.

Two TBFs popped out of the clouds, dove down on the water, and steadied up for a run on the battleship, their wings about five hundred yards apart. Except for her main battery, all the battleship's guns shifted fire to the Avengers, which lumbered along at fifty feet off the deck.

"Thank you, thank you," Donovan whispered as the Avengers drew closer, their torpedo doors springing open. The two released at the same time, their mark 13 torpedoes cleanly diving into the water with a small splash. Then they peeled away in opposite directions, the AA fire following but not at all effective.

The battleship turned ninety degrees to the left, waited a bit until the torpedoes passed harmlessly by, then turned ninety degrees to the right, resuming her northerly course.

A thousand yards to the squall line.

One of the TBFs flew right overhead, wagging its wings. The pilot clasped his hands over his head and waved. A spontaneous cheer rose topside from the men on the weather decks. Donovan was still shouting when Kruger and Peete dashed up, nearly out of breath.

"Skipper?" said Kruger.

"Read this," said Donovan in a hoarse voice. He handed the water-soaked flimsy to Kruger.

The battleship's main guns belched again; three freight-train-sounding shells rattled over their heads and exploded five hundred yards behind, raising large green water columns.

"Good God," said Kruger. He looked at his watch, then absently noticed the red stain that had transferred to his hand. Wiping it on his trousers, he asked, "If this is right, we've got about fifteen minutes or so."

"Bridge, aye," Flannigan said. "*Johnston* reports ten torpedoes in the water, fired at that battleship. So we have our own incoming."

"Shit, what else?" groaned Hammond.

Donovan said to Potter, "Tell the people on the fantail to

keep a sharp lookout for overtaking torpedoes." He turned to Peete. "Okay, Johnnie, any ideas?"

The ship ducked into the squall line, this one only a misty drizzle. Donovan muttered, "Let's see if we can park in here for a little bit." He called into the pilothouse, "All engines ahead standard, make turns for twenty knots." He looked down. "We're waiting, Mr. Peete."

Peete took the message from Kruger, red stains running down his hands. ". . . not sure."

A number of six-inch shells ripped into the mist, landing short. Nevertheless, for three seconds, their world was dominated by ripping, thundering explosions. Their ears still rang when Kruger said, "He's firing blind."

"He'll try again. That's a pretty tight pattern. He must have a fire control radar of some kind," said Donovan.

"Wonderful," said Kruger.

Donovan raised an eyebrow. "Mr. Peete?"

Peete ran a hand over his face. "Jesus, I don't know. I have a couple of ideas, but this? It could be a real kiss-off."

"What are you thinking of?"

"I'd like to look at the firing lug, first."

Donovan checked his watch. "This squall isn't going to last forever. Also, there's a great big Jap battleship out there just waiting for us, so . . ." He straightened up. "Here's what's going to happen. I'm going to duck out of this squall and fire nine of our torpedoes at that sonofabitch. You, Mr. Peete, have little more than ten minutes to verify that this so-named torpedo exploder is indeed aboard and to somehow get rid of it before 825 pounds of HBX vaporizes us, in which case we'll be meeting our honorable ancestors long before those Japs over there."

"Bridge, aye." Potter leaned over and said, "Combat reports surface search radar back on the line, sir."

Hammond said, "I'll check." He ran into the pilothouse and called, "Battleship bears two-eight-two, range four miles, Captain."

A salvo flew over them, the explosions ear shattering. Fragments rained among them.

"He's bracketing," said Donovan. "Come left to three-zero-zero. All ahead flank, indicate three-three-three turns for thirty-three knots. Woodruff, tell main control to make black smoke and plenty of it. Combat, give me a course to launch torpedoes at five thousand yards."

"Coming left to three-zero-zero," shouted La Valle as three shells erupted to port. The blasts were still echoing when Woodruff called, "All engines ahead flank, three-three-three turns for thirty-three knots, fireroom's making black smoke."

"Very well."

Kruger's expression said, *Let's get rid of those damn torpedoes now and haul ass.*

Donovan smacked his lips, the red dye running into his teeth. "Stay up here much longer, Mr. Kruger, and you're going to look like a snow cone, just like me."

"Let's just shoot, Captain."

Donovan said, "I'm for that. We'll unload those nine torpedoes now. Ensign Peete, what happens after that is up to you, Chief Hammer, and your torpedomen. If this message is right, and I have no reason to doubt John Sabovik, my advice is not to remove the exploder. There's just no time to fiddle with the thing no matter how good Chief Hammer thinks he is. Besides, they say not to do it, and they have an EOD guy to back it up. A marine, I've met him. So I'd try to figure a way to launch it from the tube. Get going." He offered his hand. "Godspeed, son."

Peete shook with Donovan, his face saying, *Do I have a choice?* "Do my best, Captain." Hammond punched Peete on the arm, "Go get 'em, Johnnie."

Kruger said, "Maybe I better go back with him. There's not a lot of time to explain to the torpedomen."

Donovan rubbed his chin. "I need you in combat."

"Mike, fer chrissakes."

Donovan asked, "Aren't you second in command? Who takes over if a Jap shell hits the bridge?"

"I'll just be a minute."

Peete said, "I don't have time to argue, gentlemen." He took off.

"Look, Mike, I know what has to be done," shouted Kruger.

"So do I, and so does Mr. Peete. And so will Chief Hammer."

"I beg to differ and there's no time for Hammer. Come on, Mike!"

"All right. It's against my better judgment, but all right," said Donovan.

"Thanks." Kruger followed Peete around the corner and down the aft ladder to the 01 level and the torpedo mounts.

Two minutes later, the *Matthew* popped from the squall into sparkling blue waters, the brilliant sunshine making them blink. Almost dead ahead, the battleship stood out in clear and horrible abundance. Black smoke gushed from her funnels; water peeled magnificently off her bow while aft, white foam spewed from her fantail.

Trailed by Potter, Donovan dashed to the port bridge wing. "Open fire," he shouted.

"Gun control, aye," shouted Merryweather. Within seconds, the two forward-facing five-inch guns barked at the battleship. The forty- and twenty-millimeters chipped in as well.

"The battleship is still on course zero-zero-zero, speed two-seven," reported Flannigan.

Hacking and coughing with the smell of cordite, Donovan said, "Very well."

"Captain." Merryweather listened to his phones for a moment, then said, "The XO and Mr. Peete confirm the torpedo in tube ten is loaded with a mark 6 exploder lot number ALX24 114 UP. Sir, do you mind telling me what's going on?"

"In a minute," Donovan shouted back, checking his watch: 0852. *Hurry.*

Donovan looked aft, seeing the torpedo mounts trained to port. "Does Mr. Peete have a firing solution, Mr. Merryweather?"

Smoke puffed from the battleship's main battery. Shells raced over and were lost in the fog they'd just left. Now the battleship's six-inch cannons opened up, pumping steadily.

"Affirmative, sir. Two-degree spread. Zero gyro angle. Medium speed. She's such a big bastard, I told them to set depth to ten feet."

"Very well. Commence firing tubes one through nine," barked Donovan. Again he checked his watch: 0855.

"Shoot—tubes one through nine!" shouted Merryweather.

The five tubes of mount one coughed at one-second intervals, each kicking out a mark 15 torpedo armed with a mark 17 warhead, carrying 825 pounds of HBX. Next, torpedo mount two fired tubes six though nine, also at one-second intervals. The fish leaped into space, their counter-rotating propellers spinning as they dove cleanly into the water.

Donovan mulled over the fact that the torpedo speed was only thirty-three knots. That was only a six-knot advantage over the battleship's. "Time to target?" he yelled to Merryweather.

Holding up crossed fingers, Merryweather replied, "Four minutes, fifty-four seconds, Captain."

Time: 0856. Damn, we may not live long enough to see if the torpedoes hit. He thought about getting on the PA system and addressing the crew. But somehow he didn't think it would help right now. Plus, that damn Jap was still shooting and getting closer. Worse, he was overcome with the urge to scream and vomit at the same time. To raise his head to heaven and rage to God about how unfair this was. About how little time he had to live. About the girl he loved and how much he wanted to be with her. To hold her, kiss her, nuzzle his face in her rich auburn hair.

Mario Rossi's face popped into his mind. He was grinning, shouting something, throwing his fist in the air. *What the hell is it, Mario*?

The man seemed to be saying, *You stupid mik! Go get those bastards*.

Sailors ran forward on the 01 level. Donovan stepped to the signal bridge, seeing it was the entire torpedo gang, Chief Hammer included. He hollered down, "Chief, what's going on?"

World War I veteran torpedoman chief Cecil Hammer torpedoman stood beneath him red-faced, his fists planted on his hips. "Them sonsabitches kicked me offa my tarpeder mount," he shouted.

Donovan checked his watch: 0858.

Hammer was still talking. "And get a load of this. Johnnie Hollywood and that damn snipe are wrecking my mount. And they won't tell me why they ain't firing tube ten. They ain't talking about nothing. Bastards just ordered me to clear the mount with everyone else. Me." He thumped his chest. "Kicking me offa my mount."

A shell raced over and exploded two hundred yards to port. "Snipe?" demanded Donovan.

"Mr. Kruger. Once a snipe, always a snipe. The bastard's telling me to get offa my tarpeder mount when there's Japs out there," Hammer bellowed. "And guess what?"

"What?"

"Them pissants are knocking off my firing lug with a chipping hammer and chisel." His face flushed even redder. "Can you believe that shit? My tarpeder mount. In the middle of a battle? What the hell is this navy coming to, Captain?"

Time: 0859. No matter. Grabbing the rail, Donovan yelled at the top of his lungs, "Shoot it, now!"

Tube ten coughed. The deadly pencil-thin torpedo flashed from the tube and hit the water with a splash. Three seconds later, the torpedo exploded, almost knocking Donovan off his feet.

Chief torpedoman Hammer raged up to Donovan, "What the hell? Them dumb bastards can't even shoot straight. Look what they did to my tarpeder. Sheyaat. A premature. That's downright embarrassing, I'll tell you."

Merryweather yelled, "Dammit, she's coming left to comb wakes." He pointed to the battleship, now heeled in a turn to the left.

Donovan yelled down to Chief Hammer, "Chief, grab your crews and lay back to your battle stations. I'm sure Mr. Kruger and Mr. Peete will explain."

"What's there to explain? Them bastards wrecked my firing lug. It's a tender job." Chief Hammer whipped his cap off his head, slapped it on his thigh, and started aft, motioning the others to follow.

The battleship was stern-on to them now, a target angle of one-eight-zero. Unless they were extremely accurate, all torpedoes would miss.

Overhead, a flight of four F4F Wildcats swooped past. Then they lined up two on each side of the ship and began their firing runs. "Yeaaaah. Go get 'em," yelled Potter.

Everyone cheered as the Wildcats shot past—the first two

not firing, the second ones pouring .50-caliber rounds into the battleship's bridge.

Just then another round blasted from the after main mount. The shells landed in a tight pack just one hundred yards to port.

Getting close. Donovan gave the order to steer for the splashes. La Valle was right with him, and soon they steered though the turbulent water just as the Wildcats lined up for another strafing run. This time, neither fired. But the battleship's AA battery filled the sky with flak as the planes zipped past.

"Out of ammo," said Donovan to Hammond. "Can you believe that? They're making sacrificial runs for us."

As if in confirmation, a TBF Avenger flew low on the water across the *Matthew*'s bow, its torpedo doors open. But no torpedo was dropped. All the torpedo bomber did was hose down the bridge with its puny single forward-firing .30-caliber machine gun.

The battleship twisted farther to port in a frantic attempt to avoid what the TBF appeared to be launching.

The flyboys are doing a great job. And we've done our job. We've pushed this monster out of the fight. Unmask the battery and get the hell out. The saving grace of another squall beckoned about a thousand yards off the starboard bow. Donovan stepped to the pilothouse and shouted, "Come right to zero-four-five."

They were almost to the squall when Mario Rossi suddenly popped up before him. Like Donovan, he wore battle dress, even down to the same life jacket and helmet, the letters C/O stenciled in white right above the brim. And he was chewing gum as he always had. The wad so big it clacked in his teeth.

"What the hell?" gasped Donovan.

Mike! You stupid or something? What the hell are we paying you for? Stay on that battleship's ass. Keep him out of the damn fight.

Donovan forced himself to take a deep breath. Then another. Mario was right. It wouldn't do to run now. The carriers and men of Taffy 3 were depending on the tin cans, on the *Matthew*—and those brave airmen up there.

Dammit! *Diane, I love you. Good-bye.* "Belay that," he shouted into the pilothouse. "Come left to three-four-zero." He yelled up to Merryweather, "Give him all you've got, Cliff."

"We're on it, Skipper," called Merryweather.

Hammond jumped from the pilothouse. "What the hell?"

The battleship's after battery blasted again, the rounds whistling overhead and smacking the water two hundred yards to starboard, raising tall green water columns that hissed like a locomotive pulling into a station.

"Button your helmet strap, Mr. Hammond, we're going after Japs."

The Wildcats zipped past again on simulated runs. But that didn't deter the battleship's six-inch battery from firing furiously at the *Matthew*.

But the shots were wild. Merryweather yelled, "You bastards can't hit the broad side of a barn."

"Geez, lookit that," said Potter, pointing.

A squall line seemed to jump up right before the battleship. Already her forward part was swallowed up.

"Sayonara, Tojo," whispered Hammond.

A foggy mist swirled around the battleship. Again, Donovan forced himself to breathe as she disappeared like an evil apparition in a horror movie. "I can't believe it."

The battleship was almost gone. But then her after main battery belched just as she was completely enveloped.

Three armor-piercing shells raced toward them. The first ripped the air search radar antenna off the tip of the mast, smacked the water, and ricocheted for another mile and a half.

The second shell penetrated the after engine room plating six feet below the main deck and smashed the port turbine, releasing scalding steam. Impact wasn't sufficient to detonate the armor-piercing fuse on the giant projectile. Thus it exited to starboard ten feet below the waterline, tearing a jagged nine-by-five-foot hole. A two-foot section of the high-pressure turbine spun out of the wrecked casing and ripped through the forward bulkhead into the after fireroom, gouging a four-by-six-foot hole in number three boiler. Killed outright in the engine room were the M division officer,

Lieutenant (jg) Henry M. Lonigan, and eleven of his enginemen. A chief and three of his boiler tenders lost their lives in the after fireroom. The after engine room was completely flooded in five minutes. The rest of the engine room crew got out and secured the hatches. The after fireroom was saved, and number four boiler continued to function.

The third shell passed through the 01 deck just abaft number one stack. It continued through the ship's office, exited through the starboard bulwarks at the main deck, and plunged into the water, also without exploding. Killed were Lieutenant Commander Richard (n) Kruger, Ensign Jonathan M. Peete, and chief torpedoman Cecil P. Hammer as they stood arguing forward of number one torpedo mount.

FIFTY-FIVE

26 October 1944
IJN *Yamato*
Cuyo East Passage
Sulu Sea, Philippines

The First Striking Force sailed through calm, flat waters in five long columns, on course 207 degrees, speed twenty knots. To port was Panay Island, the irregular humpback mountains silhouetted by a rising moon. Cuyo Island lay in darkness to starboard. They had just entered the Sulu Sea and were shaping course for the Balabac Strait and Brunei for refueling.

The three days of incessant air attacks were done, the evening cool. With the danger past, Vice Admiral Matamo Ugaki had convinced Kurita it would be good exercise to simply go down two decks to his day cabin and dig up an overcoat.

Kurita walked into his anteroom to find Dr. Koketsu sitting casually, his hands folded. Beside Koketsu on the green baize-topped conference table was his opened black bag.

"What do you want?" demanded Kurita.

"Admiral, you need to sleep," said Koketsu.

"Nonsense, I feel fine," Kurita rasped. His skin was a blotchy pale yellow, and dark circles had formed under droopy eyelids.

"Listen to you. Here, do you mind if I take your temperature?" He reached into his bag.

"Leave me alone and get out." Kurita walked to an ornate cabinet trimmed in mahogany, opened the door, and reached in.

The bedroom door squeaked open. Kurita spun. "Ugaki. What the hell are you doing here?"

Noyama and Onishi followed Ugaki through the bedroom door.

"What are you doing? Get out, all of you," Kurita shrieked.

Ugaki said, "I'm sorry, Takeo. Dr. Koketsu has me convinced something bad is going to happen if you don't sleep."

"You are not authorized," Kurita gasped. "I'll have you on charges." He looked around Ugaki and pointed to Noyama and the gigantic Onishi. "You, too," he shouted. "Traitors!"

Ugaki said, "You may have us on charges, but then how can you prefer charges if you're dead? I believe the Americans call it a Hobson's choice."

Something clanked. Kurita looked over to see Dr. Koketsu lift a syringe and vial from his bag. He raised the syringe to the light and tested the plunger; thin clear liquid squirted out.

"No!" Kurita ran for the door.

Noyama stepped between Kurita and the door. "Please, Admiral, you're killing yourself. You're no good to us dead."

"Aaaaieee." Kurita reached to dig for Noyama's eyes. Ugaki stepped in and grabbed one of Kurita's arms. Noyama grabbed the other, but his gimpy leg gave way and the threesome fell awkwardly to the plush carpeted deck. Kurita struggled mightily and with a growl, flipped over and rose to his knees.

"Ahhh," growled Ugaki. "Help! The sonofabitch bit me!"

"Uhhhh." Onishi was there in two steps. Pushing Ugaki and Noyama aside, he encircled the struggling Kurita with a thick left arm and effortlessly raised the kicking and screaming admiral off the deck. Onishi looked at Dr. Koketsu.

"The bedroom, quick," ordered Koketsu.

"Uhhhh." Onishi walked to Kurita's stateroom, the admiral roaring as he remained locked under Onishi's arm. At the door, Kurita grabbed the jamb with both hands, but Onishi easily peeled Vice Admiral Takeo Kurita's fingers away and carried him over to his bed, the perfumed sheet turned down and ready. Onishi eased Kurita onto the bed and pinned his hands to his chest with one gigantic paw, using his other to keep the admiral from kicking too much.

"Perfect, just perfect. Hold that," said Koketsu. He walked

through the door, bag in hand, followed by a rather frazzled Ugaki and Noyama.

"Uhhhhh."

"A few moments longer. Keep him there," said Koketsu.

"I'll have you all shot!" screamed Kurita.

For a moment, Noyama was afraid Kurita was going to get loose. But Onishi's strength was overpowering.

"Ach!" Kurita yelled as Koketsu jabbed the needle into his arm and pushed the plunger.

Having regained his composure, Ugaki leaned over Koketsu's shoulder, his hands behind his back. "What is that stuff?"

"Morphine. It'll put him away for a good ten to twelve hours."

Kurita growled and fought as Onishi held him down. But after a minute, his eyes grew dull. ". . . shot," was his last word. His eyes closed, and he was gone.

Silently they removed Kurita's clothes, gave him a sponge bath, and dressed him in silk pajamas. Ugaki snapped off the light over Kurita's bunk, followed the others out, and softly closed the door.

They stood awkwardly in the anteroom until Ugaki asked, "Should we do anything?"

Koketsu said, "Just let him sleep. He'll feel much better tomorrow, although he may be a bit weak and giddy. Make sure he has a good breakfast."

"Very well. Thank you, Doctor," said Ugaki.

"You look like you need sleep, too, Admiral. I suggest you hit your bunk as well. In fact, all of you should turn in." He eyed them. "I don't think the Americans are through with us yet."

"Thank you, Doctor," repeated Ugaki.

"Soon, I trust?" Koketsu backed away.

"Soon," said Ugaki.

"Good night, then." He walked out.

"He's right. That's where I'm headed," said Ugaki. "But first—" He walked to a cupboard and pulled out a bottle of his signature Johnnie Walker Black Label Scotch. "Care to join me, Noyama?"

Noyama said, "Thank you, Admiral, but one taste of that

and I'd fall flat on my face. And I still have to finish the admiral's endorsement to the action report."

"That's okay. I'll have Onishi carry you to your stateroom." Ugaki retrieved three glasses and said to Onishi, "You, too, old friend?"

"Uhhhhh."

"Good." Ugaki poured two fingers each in the three glasses and handed them over. He raised his glass. "The Emperor." They clinked.

"The Emperor," said Noyama, carefully sipping.

"Uhhhh." Onishi downed his in two mouth-dripping gulps.

Ugaki rolled his eyes at Noyama as if to say, *Pity.* Then he asked, "I think we're out of this one, Noyama, don't you?"

Noyama realized what he was getting at. Japan once had the world's third largest navy, and certainly the best in number of new ships. Also, they didn't have to fight a two-ocean war as did the British and the United States. But now, the Imperial Japanese Navy was reduced to rubble.

He nodded, "The navy? Yes, sir. I don't see how we can do any more." Earlier in the day, they'd learned that Vice Admiral Ozawa's sacrificial plan for the Northern Force had worked perfectly. He'd diverted Halsey, all right. But he'd lost Japan's two remaining aircraft carriers and five cruisers in the bargain.

After sinking just one American aircraft carrier, Kurita had broken off the action and pulled away from the battle at 0927. They later received word that another aircraft carrier in the grouping was sunk in a body-crashing attack by the Shiragiku. But they didn't see it. For the next two hours Kurita steamed back and forth, regrouping his forces into a ring formation so he could march into Leyte Gulf. But the U.S. Navy air attacks grew thicker and thicker. Kurita lost two heavy cruisers; another was seriously damaged. So at 1236, he decided to retire from battle and ordered a formation course change to 000 degrees, heading north for the San Bernardino Strait. Noyama helped draft the message he sent to Toyoda:

FIRST STRIKING FORCE HAS ABANDONED PENETRATION OF LEYTE ANCHORAGE. IS PROCEEDING NORTH SEARCHING

FOR ENEMY TASK FORCE. WILL ENGAGE DECISIVELY, THEN PASS THROUGH SAN BERNARDINO STRAIT.

They'd passed through the San Bernardino Strait all right, but today had been hell as the U.S. Navy threw wave after wave of airplanes at them while they frantically drove west and then south, attempting to steam out of range. The attacks had been ferocious. But absent the distraction of surface targets, their gunnery had been much better. They'd lost only the light cruiser *Noshiro*. The heavy cruiser *Kumano* had been hit and was now en route to Manila for repairs. Even at that, they'd done all right, Noyama admitted to himself. By tomorrow morning, he was sure they would be clear. They would almost be to the Balabac Strait, the only worry there being submarine attack. Horrible visions of the *Atago* came back to him, and he hoped the destroyers would do a better job screening the strait.

Onishi began to nod, his eyelids closing. Finally he lowered his head on his arms.

"He's been on the go, too, poor fellow." Ugaki reached over just as Onishi's empty glass fell from his massive paw onto the green baize and rolled toward the edge. Ugaki caught it, saying, "Do you know who this man is?"

"Your valet."

"Yes, and he's my nephew. His IQ is low and they were going to shove him into the coal mines. But I promised his father something better: so I pulled strings and got him into the navy." Ugaki reached over and patted Onishi on the shoulder. "You've done well, old friend." He looked up. "His father made me promise to not let Onishi dishonor his Emperor. Do you think he's accomplished that, Noyama?"

"He serves admirably, Admiral." Now it was Noyama's turn. His eyelids were so heavy, he was sure it would take bamboo sticks to hold them up.

Ugaki downed his scotch and then waved the bottle at Noyama, his eyebrows raised.

"No, thank you, sir."

Ugaki poured and asked clearly, "What do you plan to do now?"

The vice admiral's tone snapped him awake. "I must admit

I've been thinking about that, Admiral. Um . . . for quite a while, in fact."

"And?"

". . . my brother. He joined the Shiragiku. I've been thinking of joining him."

"Amazing. Body-crashing attacks. Me, too. That's where I plan to go." Ugaki thumped a fist and grinned. "Give it one last shot for the Emperor." He began humming a tune. "Ever hear it?"

"Yes, sir."

Ugaki hummed again and then sang softly,

At sea we may sink beneath the waves
On land we may lie beneath green grasses.
But we have nothing to regret
So long as we die fighting for our Emperor.

"You in the Shiragiku?" asked Noyama.

"Yes, of course. I'm a tired has-been. A battleship admiral with no battleships." He waved around the room. "These things are useless as teats on a boar, Noyama. The *Yamato* was obsolete the day she was launched. Airpower. That's where my money goes. Look what the Americans did to the *Musashi* two days ago." He smiled and asked, "So where is your brother now?"

"I believe he's gone, Admiral. His was one of the first squadrons to finish training. They were assigned to the Philippines, Clark Field, actually. I spent time with him the day after our Grande Island conference, and he told me they were assigned on the front line."

"Yes," said Ugaki. "I heard about your little Baguio soirée."

Noyama sat straight. "You did?"

"Those girls gave you a run for your money, no?" Ugaki laughed and downed his glass in a final gulp. "Ahhh. That stuff's good. Look, see here, Noyama. You don't really plan to follow your brother into the Shiragiku, do you?"

"Well, yes, sir. I'm a pilot. And I know my way around a fighter better than most."

Onishi moaned and turned his face sideways, his massive

lower lip falling open and resting on the green baize. He smacked his lips and began snoring.

"Well, you're not going to do it, you idiot."

"Sir?"

Ugaki leaned forward. "I said, you're not going to do it. Look. It's over for me and fools like me who embodied the Bushido Code and all that it stood for. Is your father a samurai?"

"No, sir. He's an assistant trainmaster at the Yamashina station in Kyoto City."

"Perfect. You come from good working stock. You see, there's nothing left here for me. When the opportunity presents itself, I'm going to commandeer a land-attack bomber, a pilot, and dive into an American carrier with a full bomb load. That's what I'm going to do before all this is over."

"But then why can't—"

Ugaki grabbed Noyama's arm. "Allow me to beat some sense into you." He waved to the overhead. "How many air attacks did we have today?"

Noyama shrugged. "Several. Five, maybe six. A couple of hundred planes at a crack."

Ugaki waved again. "Yes, hundreds of navy planes. And then those damn B-24 bombers this morning. Where in the hell did they come from?"

Again Noyama shrugged.

"Oh, how I wish our planners were smart enough to build four-engine strategic bombers like that. Too bad the Americans can't hit a mirrored shithouse at high noon."

"Ummm." Ugaki was right. They'd counted more than forty B-24 bombers dropping in excess of 150 half-ton bombs. All had fallen wide; not a ship was touched.

"Can you imagine crashing into a carrier with one of those?" He cackled. "Wake up!"

Noyama's eyes had nearly closed. "Sir." He sat staring, and tried to arrange himself.

"Here's what I'm trying to say." Ugaki thumped his chest and went on, "This old has-been will go out trailing a white scarf, dying for his Emperor as he tries to take out a carrier. There's nothing else left for me." He pointed. "But for you, there's *Dai Nippon* and her future."

"What?"

"Shut up and listen." Ugaki favored himself with another dollop of scotch. "Those B-24s. All those F6Fs and TBFs and SB2Cs and F4Fs. Where did they come from, I ask you? No, don't answer. I'll tell you. Those planes come from a culture and society that's smart enough to develop the technology and produce it on a massive basis. Those planes up there today. They're not only better than what we have, they have far greater numbers.

"You're a good officer, Noyama, and here's what I want you to do. I want you to survive this war. I want you to go to work for *Dai Nippon* and give her what she deserves in the proper way. We don't need to kill all these people down here. We can buy our way if we do it right. Through hard work, we can build an empire that will be equaled by none. And it's going to take men like you to get it started. So you, my friend, are not going to join the Shiragiku. While you leave that little detail to me, you are going to survive and take our country to new heights. You will be part of the new Japan."

Noyama looked into Ugaki's eyes, finding him dead serious. "I'm not sure . . ."

"Look, I can say this because I'm so damn old and I can see this clearly. Somebody has to do it. And it might as well be you. And I want you to find a nice woman and raise a good family in the process. Name one of your sons after your brother and another after me." He sat back and grinned.

"This . . . this . . . is impossible," muttered Noyama.

Ugaki quaffed the last of his scotch. "Ahhh. Great stuff. Of course this is possible. All you have to do is survive this war. Kurita and I have talked it over and we'll make it possible. We're going to post you to counting paper clips in the Niigata prefecture, something challenging like that. After the war, you get busy."

"Admiral, I'm not sure."

"I assure you, Noyama, you can do it. Now." Ugaki reached over and slapped him on the arm. "Now, how about another scotch?"

FIFTY-SIX

29 November 1944
CinCPac headquarters
Makalapa, Territory of Hawaii

Donovan walked into the outer office, finding Lieutenant Arthur Lamar on the phone. The flag secretary stood, excused himself, and rang off. "Commander Donovan, it's great to see you again. Welcome back." They shook.

"Good to be back, Lieutenant." He looked around. "Looks the same but . . ."

"A little bare, maybe?"

"Yes, that's it. Where is everything?"

Lamar grinned. "We're packing. We're moving CinCPac headquarters soon."

"Where are you going, or is that a military secret?"

"It's okay, sir. Guam. We're going out to be closer to the action."

"Thank God things have moved along so well."

"Amen to that, Commander. Er, excuse me, sir." Lamar walked to Nimitz's door, knocked, and poked in his head. Then he waved with, "Please, come in, Commander. Zero Zero is all set now."

"Thanks." Donovan walked in.

Admiral Chester Nimitz stepped around his desk, his hand extended. "Welcome back, Commander. Welcome back." They shook, and he waved to a group of rattan chairs arranged before a window looking out on Pearl Harbor. "Please."

As they sat, a soft groan echoed from under the desk. Nimitz's schnauzer got up, waddled over, and plopped down within his master's reach.

Nimitz scratched the dog's ears. "You remember . . ."

"Yes, sir. Makalapa."

"Can't get rid of him. Follows me everywhere."

"Best kind of watchdog, Admiral," said Donovan.

Nimitz snorted.

Lamar said, "Commander, you have a choice: there is regular coffee; or you can have tea; perhaps some of Admiral Spruance's coffee; and then there is papaya juice."

Donovan asked, "Admiral Spruance's coffee?"

Nimitz said, "It's Ray's hobby. He buys his beans from God knows where. Some from Mexico, some from South America, some as far away as the Solomon Islands. All over. Today, we have . . ." He looked at Lamar.

"Kona coffee, sir," answered Lamar. "Grown right here in the islands."

Donovan smacked his lips. "I'll try it."

Nimitz nodded. "Me, too."

"Coming right up." Lamar walked out.

It grew silent for a moment. Nimitz said, "Seems like years ago when you sat in here. You were on your way to take command of the *Matthew*."

"Five months ago, sir."

"A lot has happened all right."

"Yes, sir."

"First of all, you didn't have malaria, did you?" Nimitz skewered him with a blue-eyed glance.

Donovan suppressed the impulse to jump to attention. "Well, no, sir. Turns out I had a little trouble with my belly."

"Appendicitis is a little trouble?"

How the hell does he know that? "Well, sir, I recovered quickly and was able to take command on time."

"Some vacation. A civilian doctor, I'm told," Nimitz snapped.

Donovan didn't want to get into the business about Dr. Duberman, so he said, "Well, sir, maybe that was meant to be, because I'm going to marry her."

"The doctor?"

"Yes, sir. Seems only fair. She saved my life, so I figure maybe I should return the favor."

Nimitz's eyes crinkled for a moment, then he said, "Congratulations. When will you tie the knot?"

"We haven't figured that out, yet, sir. We just got engaged." He told the admiral about how Diane flashed Carmen Rossi's ring before the crowd just as the *Matthew* was shoving off for the war zone.

This time Nimitz smiled. "She chased you all the way to Mare Island?"

"I couldn't believe it. Now that I think of it, I didn't have a choice, did I?"

"Yes, you did, and you made the right one, all right. She sounds like a fine lady. I'd like to meet her someday."

"It will be my pleasure, Admiral."

Nimitz gazed out the window for a moment. "Tell me, how's your ship? Can I do anything?"

"We got in late yesterday and have been well taken care of, Admiral. Snug as a bug," said Donovan. With just one engine, they'd cleared the antisubmarine net and limped into Pearl Harbor at 1900 yesterday. They dropped anchor in the West Basin and had chow. Donovan posted an anchor watch and, too exhausted to go ashore, turned in at 2000, sleeping the sleep of the dead. Most of the crew did, too, just a few going on liberty. But two, Donovan discovered, got in a fight late that night and landed in the brig.

This morning, he was paying his respects to CinCPac while temporary executive officer Al Corodini took a pilot aboard to maneuver the destroyer into a floating dry dock. Tomorrow they would begin strengthening the temporary patch in her after engine room. After provisioning, the *Matthew* was scheduled stateside for repairs at Mare Island Naval Shipyard.

"How was the ice cream?" asked Nimitz.

"Admiral, I can't tell you what the simple things in life mean, especially after you've been away for a while. Chocolate and vanilla ice cream, fresh milk, and bread and meat. And a turkey with all the trimmings for tomorrow. We'll eat like kings. I didn't realize it was you who did it. Thank you very much."

Nimitz nodded toward the door. "Art takes care of that. He

has a real knack for it. At any rate, I'm glad you'll be able to enjoy a peaceful Thanksgiving with your crew."

Donovan said, "I'll make sure to thank him, too. What a swell treat."

"There's more on the way, Commander."

"Hula girls?"

Nimitz guffawed. "We'll leave that up to your sailors." Then he said, "I've read your action report and, with that torpedo business and all, it's nothing short of amazing. I have to say, you boys did a marvelous thing out there. But tell me, how was your trip back?"

"We almost lost her twice getting to Ulithi. Then we spent ten days alongside the *Vulcan*[53] patching our hull, which looked like Swiss cheese. But forgive me for asking, what happened after that battleship put out our lights? My boys would like to know, too. I owe it to them."

Nimitz asked, "You really don't know?"

"No, sir, I don't."

Lamar walked in, carrying a silver coffee service. He set it down and then glanced at the admiral, who nodded. Lamar poured and passed around the coffee, then sat across from them and pulled out a pen and pad.

Donovan sipped. "Wow."

"What do you think?" asked Nimitz.

"Compared to this, the stuff we have aboard ship tastes like metal shavings. This is heaven." He sipped again.

"Glad you like it. I'll send a pound back with you."

"Thank you, sir."

Nimitz clasped his hands over a knee. "Let me give it to you straight. The tin cans and aviators saved Taffy 3. Most likely, you also saved Taffy 2 and Taffy 1, as well."

Donovan whistled. "How can that be? We were a Johnny-come-lately."

"You, the *Johnston,* the *Hoel,* the *Heermann,* and the DE *Samuel B. Roberts* charged in there and confused them so much, they couldn't coordinate their operations. Along with the flyboys you kept the Japs from entering Leyte Gulf and having General MacArthur for breakfast." Then he quickly summarized Oldendorf's victory over Nishimura in Surigao

Strait the night before, and Halsey's victory over Ozawa's decoy force.

"Did you say the *Johnston*? The last I heard from her is that she was launching a full salvo of torpedoes," said Donovan.

"When the *Yamato* saw *Johnston*'s torpedoes, she reversed course and sailed north right into your lap. And then, while Taffy 3 ran southeast, you stalled the *Yamato*, taking her out of the fight."

"*Yamato*?"

Nimitz explained what intelligence had learned about Japan's superbattleships and finished with, "And we got her sister ship the day before."

Donovan repeated the name softly. "*Yamato.* So that's what we were jousting with. Eighteen-inch guns." He whistled. "Admiral, you should see the hole that thing put in the engine room."

Lamar's pencil was poised. "None of the shells detonated, right?"

"That's correct," said Donovan. "But the damn things tore right through us like a hot knife through butter."

Lamar cleared his throat and said, "Japs were firing armor-piercing shells. Not enough to do real damage."

"That may be, but we took some hits that got our attention," said Donovan.

"I didn't mean it that way, sir," said Lamar.

Donovan waved a hand. "No. What I meant is that, yes, we were lucky, but there's nothing you can do when those things tear into you. It was a real slaughterhouse."

He paused. "I lost twenty-three men."

"I know," said Nimitz.

"And I'm sorry to report, Admiral, Richard Kruger was one of them."

Nimitz's right eye blinked. "I didn't realize that."

"There were twenty-two others. We buried . . . we . . ." Donovan picked up his cup and drank.

"Maybe we can take this up later," said Nimitz. "After all—"

"—buried them at sea. Two more guys died en route to Ulithi and we had to do it again the next day. Can you believe that? Two funeral services in two days? We got pretty good at it."

The clock ticked.

"I'm sorry. That came out wrong," said Donovan.

Nimitz said, "That's okay. We have three of your boys at Aiea and they seem to be doing okay." Once the *Matthew* had pulled into Ulithi, they flew out another three seriously wounded to the Aiea Naval Hospital at Pearl Harbor.

"That's good to hear, Admiral. I plan to go over there this afternoon."

"Good," said Nimitz. "The tough part about your job is writing the letters."

"Yes, sir. I did that on the way from Ulithi, and it wasn't easy. They were mailed this morning."

"Never is."

Donovan leaned forward. "Can I ask a question?"

"Shoot."

"What were we up against out there, Admiral? I mean, do we know how many Japs there were?"

"Best we can tell, the flyboys counted four battleships, six cruisers, and about ten destroyers."

"Holy smokes. And so what happened?"

"The Japs turned tail and headed back to the San Bernardino Strait. That's what happened," said Nimitz.

"Good God," said Donovan. "Pardon me for being the devil's advocate, but what in the hell for? They had us by the you-know-whats." He downed his coffee.

"More?" asked Lamar.

Donovan looked at the cup, realizing that he'd drunk it all. "You bet. Thanks. Thanks also for the Thanksgiving turkey, Lieutenant. Nothing like a taste of home."

Lamar nodded. "No, sir, nothing like it."

Nimitz continued, "The battle off Samar will be one of the great unanswered mysteries of all time. I'm sure naval warfare schools will study this one well into the next century."

"Amazing," said Donovan.

"Best as we could tell, the action of the tin cans and the aviators confused them and essentially drove them off. And then Bill Halsey was coming back hell-bent-for-leather. So we figure they wanted to get back through the San Bernardino Strait before Halsey showed up and shut the door."

"I'll be damned," said Donovan.

Nimitz nodded. "In war, can you ever find a situation where all is in place yet nothing goes exactly as predicted?"

"I haven't seen it yet, Admiral," said Donovan.

"Neither have I," said Nimitz. "But what astounds me is the way you all reacted. When the order came to attack, nobody flinched. Nor did you bitch or scream or protest or write your congressmen. You just did it. You charged into the face of overwhelming odds. I'll repeat what you just said. *Amazing.*"

"Yes, sir."

"Did you know we lost the *Johnston*?"

"No, sir."

"Or the *Hoel* and the *Samuel B. Roberts*?"

"No, sir."

"Did you know the Japs sank the *Princeton*[54], the *Gambier Bay*?"

"I heard about the *Gambier Bay.*"

"Later that day, a kamikaze got the *St. Lo.*"

"Kamikaze?"

"It's what the Japs call a suicide attack. They intentionally crash their planes into ships. All of a sudden, they're doing it in an organized manner."

Donovan nodded. "I've seen that, Admiral. We were plane guarding for the *San Cristobal* when she got hit." He explained what had happened. But he didn't mention the souvenir he recovered from the wreckage of the Japanese plane.

"I'm afraid we're going to see a lot more of it. They've lost all their trained pilots, so this is the best they can do."

"Hideous."

"Yes, it's a dirty business. But so far, we've given far more than what we got." Nimitz ticked the Japanese losses off on his fingers and finished with, "The Jap fleet is done for, thanks to you."

"That's nice, sir. But the men deserving the thanks are still out there."

"You know, I hear that all the time and I appreciate what you're trying to say. But dammit, you do deserve our thanks and you damn well better be prepared to accept it, especially when you get back to the mainland and mingle with civilians."

Donovan sat straight. "Yes, sir."

Nimitz continued, "For example, we're awarding Ernest Evans the Congressional Medal of Honor. I'm proud to say I endorsed that recommendation this morning."

"That's great, Admiral. From what I know, he deserves it," said Donovan.

Nimitz stared at the rattan carpet.

Lamar said softly, "Posthumously, sir. Commander Evans didn't make it."

"Oh," said Donovan. "I'm sorry."

"Did you know him?" asked Nimitz.

"Met him a couple of times at skipper conferences. We nested with the *Johnston* once. They were a great bunch."

Nimitz continued, "There'll be Navy Crosses for Rear Admiral Sprague, commanders Copeland of the *Samuel B. Roberts,* Kintberger of the *Hoel,* Hathaway of the *Heermann,* and a whole slew of those brave pilots. Some of them had run out of ammo and were making dummy runs to draw the fire from planes attacking with real ordnance."

"Yes, sir. They did that right over us. Never seen anything like it. Saved our bacon two or three times."

"Right." Nimitz downed his coffee and sat forward.

Time to go.

"Can I put my two cents' worth in, Admiral?"

Nimitz stood. "Certainly."

"I'd like to recommend two of my boys for the Silver Star," said Donovan.

With Makalapa in tow, Nimitz walked to his desk and fussed with papers. "Who?"

"Ensign Jonathan Peete and Lieutenant Commander Richard Kruger."

Nimitz threw a steely glance, then said to Lamar, "Art, will you please excuse us?"

"Yes, sir." Lamar walked out.

What the hell have I done? Donovan remembered the last time he was alone in Admiral Nimitz's office. He'd almost passed out. Suddenly he felt like that now. Except this time, he didn't have a leaking appendix. He wondered if he should start faking malaria again.

When the door closed, Nimitz asked, "Have you forwarded your recommendations to COMDESRON 77?"

"Yes, sir. Larry Fox approved them, and they're back on the *Matthew.* You should have it in tomorrow's pouch."

"I want to ask you a question, Commander Donovan. But you don't have to answer it."

"Do my best, Admiral."

"You've recommended Lieutenant Commander Kruger for the Silver Star."

"Yes, sir."

Nimitz folded his hands and asked, "Would you also recommend him for command?"

Donovan felt like a brand-new salvo of three gigantic shells from a Jap battleship crashed into him. He ran his hand through his hair.

"Commander?" prodded Nimitz.

Donovan looked up. "Admiral. There's no doubt he and Ensign Peete saved the ship. Had he not gone back there and acted quickly, it's likely we all would have been killed. But . . ."

"But what?"

"But my dilemma is just that. I told Richard not to go back there. I told him to stay at his GQ station—CIC. I told him we needed someone to back me up in case I was incapacitated or killed. He wouldn't do that. Like many times before, he had to go hands-on and do it himself. And like a damn fool, I let him go." Donovan slowly shook his head. "Chances are, that torpedo would have gone up if he hadn't gone back there with Peete. And then we'd all be dead." He looked up. "But if you put it like that, Admiral, no, I'm sorry. I know you were friends, and I'm probably scuttling his memory when I say, no sir, I wouldn't have endorsed Richard Kruger for command. I'd put it like this. You can take Richard out of the engine room but—"

Nimitz finished it for him, "—but you can't take the engine room out of Richard." He nodded. "I agree. What a horrible thing to say about one who's dead.

"Yes, Richard was a great engineer. He saved me many

a time aboard the *Augusta,* just like you." He looked up. "You're going to see Vicky?"

Donovan exhaled. "First chance I get, sir. Actually, there are two letters I have to deliver in person. One to Vicky Kruger, the other to Ensign Peete's father. He should know how brave his son was."

Nimitz stood and extended his hand. "Give them both my best and please ask if I can do anything. And of course I'll endorse the Silver Star recommendations for both of them. Please forward them on to me as soon as possible. Perhaps you'll be able to deliver the medals in person."

"Yes, sir. I'll be glad to do that. Thanks again for the ice cream and the turkey. My boys will sure love it." Donovan bent to grab his cap.

"Oh, one more thing, Commander."

"Yes, sir?"

"You're being recommended for the Navy Cross, too."

"Good God."

Nimitz laughed. "No, it's just me, Chester Nimitz. Now go on out there and fix your ship. And go home and get married. Just make sure you bring her by when all this is over."

Donovan met Al Corodini at the officers' club for lunch. After dessert and coffee, Corodini stubbed out a cigarette and heaved his massive bulk from his chair. "I bailed our lads out of the brig."

Donovan rose beside him and raised his eyebrows.

Corodini grabbed his hat. "The Hollywood Club in Pearl City. Bunch of cruiser sailors fresh from Mare Island singled out two of our boys. Yelled at them as being from *Matthew* the Motionless."

"Who were our guys?"

"Would you believe it? La Valle and Potter?"

"Potter!" With difficulty, Donovan suppressed a smile.

Corodini laughed, too. "They fought back-to-back. Took six MPs to take 'em down. Damn near wrecked the place. Mirrors busted, the whole shebang."

Donovan looked the other way, his grin growing wider.

"Lotta damage, skipper."

"Do tell."

"Gonna cost the welfare fund about twenty-five hundred bucks."

"Worth every penny," said Donovan.

Corodini gave an exaggerated, "I beg your pardon, sir?"

"Go on Al, get out of here."

"Can I drop you somewhere?"

"No thanks, I have a jeep from the admiral's car pool."

"Well, la-di-da." Corodini rolled his eyes. "See you later, Skipper." He walked out.

At the desk, Donovan exchanged a ten-dollar bill for nickels and dimes. Then he waited for one of the three phone booths in the lobby. He couldn't help but watch a young ensign through the glass of one of the booths. The towheaded man pulled a handkerchief, dabbed his eyes, and blew his nose several times. Finally the accordion door sprang open and the ensign walked out, stuffing a handkerchief in his pocket. There's a man who's going out to the war zone. *Godspeed, sailor.*

He slipped in, dialed the operator, and drummed his fingers for two minutes while the operator made connections. His heart jumped when he heard, "Roseville Community Hospital."

The operator said, "Commander Michael Donovan calling person to person for Dr. Diane Logan, please."

The receptionist put the call through and someone answered, "East Wing." The operator repeated, "Commander Michael Donovan calling person to person for Dr. Diane Logan, please."

"Oh! Commander Donovan. Yes, please, oh, yes, hold on." Her hand covered the phone. Then she said, "I'm sorry, Dr. Logan is just finishing surgery, she'll be available in ten minutes."

Donovan said, "Tell her we'll call back."

The operator relayed the message and then asked, "Is there anything else I can do for you?"

"Donovan thought for a moment and then said, "Yes." He pulled out a black address book and gave a phone number and extension at the Twelfth Naval District in San Francisco.

"Also person to person?"

"Yes. To Commander John Sabovik. S-A-B-O-V-I-K. Do you have that?"

"Yes, sir, I do." Static ranged on the line as she dialed the number.

Tomorrow is Thanksgiving, Donovan mused. Never a better time to put things right. He sat back waiting, sorry he hadn't done this a long time ago.

The phone began ringing.

Something caught his eye through the glass outside the booth. "Good God!"

It was Mario Rossi wearing dress khakis, shiny commander shoulder boards, full campaign ribbons, and combination cap. With folded arms, he grinned and chewed gum. *I stand relieved, sailor. Great job.*

Donovan jumped to his feet and gaped out the window. "Mario!"

Rossi stood right on the other side of the glass. *I'm done holding your hand, you crazy mik. Good-bye*. Mario walked off.

The phone picked up. "Lieutenant Commander Sabovik."

Donovan cleared his throat. "John, it's Mike."

EPILOGUE

There are no fifes and drums up at the front. You beseech alternately God and the Devil to help you. But they don't. In a war, both are so busy. Why does God let it happen? You ask. You want to reproach Him for it. But it was not God [who] let it happen. He gave man freewill, the liberty even to wage war. A thief or a murderer cannot reproach the police because he is a thief, or a murderer. Nor can you reproach God because there is a war.

Sven Hassel, *The Beast Regiment*

In anguish, we uplift
A new unhallowed song:
The race is to the swift:
The battle is to the strong.

John Davidson

EPILOGUE

25 October 1994
Highway 78
Two miles west of Julian, California

The black Mercedes E300 drifted easily through curves on the two-lane road, Walt Donovan confidently letting the car's suspension do the work. Apple orchards, gurgling streams, and sun-drenched meadows flashed by as the sedan accelerated down a straightaway.

In the backseat, Diane Donovan stomped her right foot to the floor and shouted, "Walter, dammit. I'd like to live a few years longer, if you don't mind."

Sitting beside his wife, Mike Donovan glanced at his son's eye roll in the rearview mirror. "He's doing it on purpose, honey," he whispered.

"Shhh," she said.

Walter said, "Sorry, Ma. This thing gets away from me from time to time."

Bullshit, figured Donovan. Walt loves his toys. He has a Ferrari at home in Pacific Palisades and he probably wishes he were driving it now on this fine backcountry road. But the usually cavalier Walter A. Donovan was edgy today. The reason was the thin, sharp-featured woman sitting beside him wearing impossibly dark sunglasses. She was Martha Mays, his latest live-in. Martha Mays, with stretched youthful looks and a finely coiffed silver-blond ponytail, was a movie producer like Walt. It was a symbiotic relationship. Each needed something from the other, and it seemed to be more about business rather than love or even sex. They had been together for the past two years, producing, between them, three top hits. It turned out Walt had better contacts with the studio executives and A-list stars while Martha, an ex–Beverly Hills entertainment banker, knew more about digging up money, especially overseas, where the markets were lucrative.

Martha Mays, to the surprise of all, had said she would be glad to join them today. Then it turned out she really wanted to drop off a spec screenplay to a director in Rancho Santa Fe on their way to Julian. And now, after lunch, a cell phone was again jammed to her ear.

"What's so special about today, Pop?" asked Walt from the front seat.

"Today is the fiftieth anniversary and there's somebody who has to know something."

"Who is it?"

"Yuzura Noyama."

"Whoosat?"

"I'll let you know when I meet him."

"Where did you find this guy, Pop?"

"Slow down!" yelled Diane.

"Sorry." The speedometer drifted from eighty-five down to forty as Walt smoothly guided the Mercedes through a curve.

"I found him in *Fortune* magazine." He waved a copy of the latest issue.

"I don't get— Hold on." Walt picked up his cell phone and began talking loudly.

"The Hollywood two-step," Donovan said to his wife, who responded with her own eye roll.

Just then Martha Mays squealed and tugged Walt's sleeve.

He whipped aside his cell phone. "What, dammit!"

Martha said breathlessly, "It's Jerry Kingsley. Marty Savedra is attached!"

"What are his reading fees?"

"A million five. Plus twenty percent of the gross."

"He's screwing us."

"Walt! Marty needs an answer."

"Let me think about it." He resumed his conversation.

They had lunched in the Driftwood Lodge Hotel located high in the mountains in Julian, in northeast San Diego County. Later they'd strolled through the quaint town buying trinkets, with Mike, Diane, and Walt enjoying a marvelous apple pie à la mode at George's Confectionaries. Martha Mays waved off her piece saying, "Sorry. I'm up half a pound this morning. Too much rich Japanese food."

"Up half a pound," Donovan had snorted to his wife on their way out of George's. "She couldn't weigh more than one hundred. Hell, the wind's going to blow her away."

"Shhhh," said Diane. "She was nice enough to come."

The truth was, Martha had jet lag and, unable to sleep, was bored. She'd flown in from Tokyo two nights after gluing together, with masking tape and chewing gum, a deal for financing a Soviet-era movie about identical twins separated at birth—one American, the other Soviet. The Russians, desperate for money, had given them clearance to shoot it at their supersecret submarine base in Petropavlosk on the Kamchatka Peninsula. The Japanese bankers inked the deal almost right away, and she returned early. But there was a problem, Donovan had heard. Something happened and Walt couldn't deliver Brad Pitt. And then Chris Cooper fell out. A scramble for other actors was on with Walt rapidly digging through his bag of leading men. The deal was in jeopardy, and the Japanese bankers were sure to withdraw if they got wind of it. It was as if a three-hundred-pound block of ice rested between son and girlfriend in the front seat as they haggled on their cell phones.

But not in the backseat. Donovan took his wife's hand, now covered with age spots. To him, she was still beautiful. Unlike the temperamental toothpick in the front seat, Diane had kept her weight and figure. Yes, the years had taken their toll; her auburn hair was now gray and she moved slowly, especially after a stroke last year that had partially paralyzed her left side. But she'd recovered and almost regained full use. What hadn't changed were her eyes. Quick and green, they skewered you. Or in Donovan's case, they took him in and then gave it all back plus a lot more.

The reason Walt was driving today was that the Department of Motor Vehicles had restricted his father's license. Donovan had passed out with a minor heart attack just three months ago, and the cardiologist still hadn't cleared him. Soon, he hoped. The motorcycle trip to Cabo San Lucas, Mexico, this time last year was still fresh in his mind, and he wanted to do it again. The three tired has-beens, as they called themselves, John Sabovik, Owen Reynolds, and Mike Donovan, had bought Harley-Davidsons. Wearing black headbands and leather jackets, they rattled their way down Baja California's sometimes wild peninsula, drinking beer, telling rotten jokes, and laughing themselves silly. Their wives met them in Cabo, where they sold their Harleys and returned to more civilized ways. They flew home after four marvelous days of just sitting on the beach and eating bananas. Then Mike had the heart attack last spring, postponing their much-vaunted return trip to Cabo.

Another reason Walt was driving was that Donovan had fallen and sprained his leg the previous week. Now he walked with a heavy limp. Lucky you didn't break it, the doctor said, clicking his teeth as if Donovan belonged in a rest home. So now, he and Diane had to put up with his bickering son and stormtrooping girlfriend. The specter of the return trip hung heavy over them, much of it on crowded freeways as the pair in front squabbled and punched cell phone numbers.

Donovan snapped his fingers.

"What's that?" Diane asked.

"Life. It's all gone by so damn fast."

"Thirty-five years in the navy can do that to you."

"Maybe so, but it seems like yesterday when I first met you."

She smiled and squeezed his hand. "Not for me; you're a handful."

"What?" That surprised him. There was more buried in that retort than he could work out at the moment. "Want to go back and try again?"

She smiled, "Come on, just kidding."

"Glad to hear it." They couldn't have done any better as far as children were concerned. Their daughter, Jennifer, was a schoolteacher and had presented them with two fine grandchildren. Their younger son, John, was a commercial real estate appraiser and had given them five marvelous grandchildren. It was their older son, the Harvard-educated Walt, named after Diane's father, who was the handful. After Stanford Law School, he had immediately gone into entertainment law and made a bundle. Now, as he rolled the dice again in movie production, it looked as if Walt Donovan was on the cusp of something really big. Thank God his previous two marriages had been childless; he lived his life so quick. Often glib with a strong Irish sense of humor, Walt was usually the life of the party. But many times, he just went too far.

"Hey, throttle-jockey, slow down," said Donovan.

"What?"

"Here, turn here," Donovan pointed to the sign saying HIGHWAY 79.

"Pop, for crying out loud. That goes to Palm Springs."

"Please, do it."

Miraculously, Martha Mays was off her cell phone. She turned in her seat and gave Donovan a thin smile. "We are on a schedule, you know."

"You'll be home in time for your protein drink, honey." Donovan smiled back and winked.

Martha whipped her head around, her silver-blond ponytail rustling over the soft tanned leather headrest. Donovan could have sworn the three-hundred-pound ice block in the front seat had grown to five hundred pounds.

Diane pinched him. "What are you doing?" she hissed in his ear. "Can't you see they're close to finishing an important deal?"

Donovan pursed his lips and imitated a loud Clark Gable. "Frankly, my dear, I don't give a damn."

Diane folded her arms and looked out the window.

Walt turned right onto Highway 79 and punched the accelerator, the Mercedes roaring down a straightaway. Diane again jabbed the floor with her right foot on an imaginary brake pedal.

"Slow down. It's only another half mile," said Donovan.

"You have something in mind?" asked Walt.

"Actually, I do. I was trying to tell you back there when the cell phone rudely interrupted us. And please slow down. You're scaring the crap out of your mother."

"Sorry." The speedometer backed off to sixty.

"Here, turn in here, please."

Walt slowed. "What's this? An apple orchard? Wow! Snazzy

place." He turned into a large driveway which led under a sign that read:

TWO APPLE RANCH
PRIVATE PROPERTY

A logo depicting two red apples on a square white field bordered by gold filigree was painted on either side of the sign.

Martha Mays leaned over and whispered to Walt.

"Is that right?" he whispered back.

She nodded.

Walt called to the rearview mirror, "Did you know that this place is owned by a rich Jap? The apple orchard is just a front for his U.S. real estate holdings."

"No, it's owned by the founder of Kyoto Bank, Yuzura Noyama. He's retired and lives here with his daughter."

"How do you know?"

He waved the *Fortune* magazine. "I found him in this. That's what I was trying to tell you."

"So what's he to you?"

After a moment, Donovan said, "I'm not sure yet. But if he's who I think he is, it will mean a lot to both of us."

"Gotta do better than that, Pop. You're talking in riddles."

"That's the best I can do for now," said Donovan.

"Well, then, we'll just have to go with that. So what do we have here? No country store. No apples or apple pies or trinkets or gizmos for sale. Just that beautiful Spanish-style—geez—mansion. Get a load of that."

"Yes, pull up there."

Walt did so and then switched off the engine. It was a rambling two-story home with a lush green lawn extending toward a meticulously kept apple orchard. A swimming pool and outbuildings were on one side. A bricked pathway led to a large interior courtyard where, visible through a filigreed wrought-iron fence, several children played around a fountain. The courtyard was cloistered on one side and festooned with potted geraniums and azaleas, English ivy growing up the opposite walls.

"Nice," said Walt. He rolled down his window, letting in a soft breeze.

Diane took a deep breath. "This is for me." She turned to her husband. "Is this it?"

"Pretty sure," said Donovan.

Walt turned around. "What aren't you letting me know, Pop?"

"Never mind."

An Asian with a full white mane of hair sat in a wheelchair near the fountain watching the children. It wasn't cold, but he wore a dark gray Windbreaker. A black patch covered his left eye, and a blanket covered his lap. Beside him was a beagle, which he petted occasionally.

Walt turned in his seat and asked, "Pop, is this about willie willie twice?"

Donovan leaned forward. "Look, kid. I think it's about time you showed some respect. It sure as hell isn't called willie willie twice."

Walt fixed his father with a barrister's stare. "I mean no disrespect, Pop. But maybe someday you could let us in on what the hell happened out there. You never talk about it, so we don't know."

Donovan felt as if he'd been run through by a sword. It was true. He'd been closemouthed about the war ever since he'd returned, hardly even sharing it with Diane. Only when John Sabovik or Owen Reynolds or another World War II vet was around would he talk, and then, only with them. On occasion he still awakened sweating with nightmares of Tiny or the shattered, ripped-open bodies of Richard Kruger and Jonathan Peete that he'd helped pull from the *Matthew*'s wreckage. To this day, he couldn't look at a rack of lamb or spareribs, the similarities so vivid.

He glanced at Diane, her face saying, *He's right, you can't hold it in forever.*

Donovan gave a loud exhale. "Okay, someday soon, son." He patted Walt on the shoulder and winked.

"Okay."

"Whew! Getting hot in here," said Martha Mays, raising her eyebrows and fanning herself with great exaggeration. "Think I'll cool off." She opened the door, walked over to a bench under a tall eucalyptus, and sat, where she flipped open her cell phone and punched numbers.

Walt nodded toward the house and asked softly, "Is this part of it?"

"I hope so."

"You're talking in riddles again, Pop."

"I know. Here, this won't take a minute," said Donovan. He grabbed a large paper bag.

"What's that?" asked Walt.

Donovan slid a large curved section of metal from the bag. Jagged around the edges, it was deeply smudged with a faded caricature of two apples on a white field with gold filigree.

"The same damn apples. Where'd you get it?"

"Would you believe me if I said willie willie twice?"

"Here we go again," said Walt, throwing his hands in the air.

"Walter," said Diane. "Give him some slack."

"Okay, okay," said Walt.

Donovan got out of the car and hobbled up five steps to the front porch. After knocking, he stood back, the bag grasped behind.

The door opened. An Asian woman with pulled-back hair stood in the doorway, bowed, and folded her hands. Donovan introduced himself and began speaking. Three times she shook her head. She began closing the door when Donovan brought out the bag and pulled out the metal section.

The woman's hand went to her mouth. She seemed to think for a moment, then accepted the metal and closed the door, leaving Donovan alone on the doorstep. He turned and faced the car, spreading his hands.

"What the hell is he doing?" asked Walt.

"You're watching your next film project," said Diane.

"Look!" Walt pointed. The Asian woman had stepped into the courtyard and walked up to the white-haired man. With a deep bow, she handed over the metal section. The man held it up to the light and examined it for a minute or so, then waved his hand, resting the metal in his lap.

Martha Mays walked over from the eucalyptus tree and got in, pocketing her cell phone. "Jerry Kingsley wants to see both of us."

"When?"

She said, "Today, if possible. He says he can get Matt Damon."

"Cool. Lemme go find out what the deal is with Pop." He opened the door to get out.

"Right." She sighed and turned to Diane. "We really should get going."

Diane looked away.

"Only be a minute." Walt walked toward the steps.

Just then the door opened and the woman reappeared. She said something and opened the door for Donovan to walk in. Then she gently closed it behind them.

Walt walked back and got in. "Dammit. I don't know."

"Knock on the door," said Martha. "Insist that they admit you."

"What?" said Walt.

"Pound on the damn thing," hissed Martha Mays. "I'm not letting you bungle this deal."

"Martha," said Diane.

Martha Mays's five-hundred-dollar ponytail again grazed the headrest as she turned her head. She lifted her dark glasses so Diane could see for certain she was raising an eyebrow.

"I want you to shut up," said Diane Donovan.

Martha Mays whipped forward. "Walt!"

"Shhh, check this," said Walt. He pointed to his father, who walked up to the white-haired man in the courtyard. After a moment, they shook, and the white-haired man held up the metal section. Donovan spoke for at least three minutes, all the times gesturing with his hands as a pilot might describe a dogfight.

Gradually the white-haired man's mouth fell open.

Suddenly he threw his hands to his face and leaned forward. Donovan dragged over a chair and sat beside him, laying a hand on his arm. Then his arm went around the old man's shoulder. The white-haired man was crying. So was Mike Donovan. They hugged and began talking and smiling, sometimes babbling and talking and smiling at the same time.

Walt gasped, "What the hell? Now they're saluting each other."

After a while, the old man waved over the woman who had admitted Donovan. Looking in the direction of the Mercedes, he spoke for a moment.

The lady disappeared and soon reappeared at the front door. With a broad smile, she walked down the steps and up to the car. "Welcome to Two Apple Ranch. I am Kiyoko McLean. My father would be most appreciative if you could all stay and join our family for dinner this evening."

"Dinner?" snapped Martha.

"Of course we would," said Diane. She stepped out and shook Kiyoko's hand. "I am Diane Donovan, Admiral Donovan's wife. And this is my son Walter and his fiancée, Martha."

Kiyoko bowed, then Diane awkwardly took her hand and they shook. Diane asked, "Er, excuse me, McLean?"

"My husband, Howard McLean," said Kiyoko with an easy laugh. She took Diane's arm in hers. "He's president of the bank's American division. He'll be down in a moment." She pointed to the courtyard. "Those are our children out there. You should meet them."

"I'd love to." They walked up the steps.

Walt watched them go. "I'll be damned."

"But—" said Martha.

"But what?" growled Walt.

"What about Jerry Kingsley? And Marty Savedra needs an answer right now."

"Screw Marty Savedra. And screw Jerry Kingsley and screw you, too," Walt said. "Come on. You might learn something. If not, here's your cab fare." He opened his wallet, dropped a hundred-dollar bill in her lap, and got out. "Wait up, Mom."

ACKNOWLEDGMENTS

This work, somewhat larger than my previous novels, is a composite of some very capable organizations, fine friends, and close family. In particular, I would like to thank Mike Amick, railroad engineer extraordinaire, for his friendship and compelling commentary on railroad operations; Dr. Robert L. Jones for his thoughtful and enthusiastic help in medical areas; my old friend Jim Dale, who was there when I needed him on questions about the Far East; and Michael R. Fisher, lieutenant commander, USN (ret), who rendered fantastic assistance in naval matters. Other friends making phenomenal repeat performances are: Dr. Frederick J. Milford, Dr. Russell J. Striff, MD, and George A. Wallace, Commander, USN (ret). Patricia C. Hass was helpful in getting me over some bumps in the road. Appreciation goes to Ron Doering, my editor at Presidio Press, for taking on this project. In particular, my thanks go to Shawn Coyne, another old friend, who really pitched in when it mattered. I would also like to thank my agent, E. J. McCarthy, for his expertise and encouragement.

Helpful also have been my readers who, over the years, have sent great feedback and encouragement. I've learned a lot from you and look forward to continued exchanges via my website at www.johnjgobbell.com.

Finally, to my wife, Janine, who has been there through this one, plus five others, plus raising a fine family, my love and appreciation.

John J. Gobbell
Laguna Niguel, California
March 15, 2006
John@johnjgobbell.com

NOTES

One

1. 01 Level—First deck above the main deck; 02 level is above that, etc.

Two

2. SHO-GO—Victory Operation

Six

3. TBS—Talk between ships, line of sight radio gear
4. CIC—Combat Information Center
5. gouge—slang for agenda

Eight

6. cold iron—no boilers lighted, all power drawn from shore facilities
7. third substitute pennant—indicates the captain is not aboard

Twelve

8. butt kit—slang for ashtray
9. EOD—Explosive Ordnance Disposal; ammunition and bomb expert

Fourteen

10. SHO-GO—Victory Operation
11. *Seppuku*—a ritualistic form of suicide to save honor
12. *Jushin Kaigi*—former prime ministers who became consulting elder statesmen
13. *Kono BaDianearo*—damned fool
14. *Miso*—a bean paste
15. *Toho*—Toho Motion Picture Company
16. *Dai Nippon Teikoku*—the Great Japanese Empire

Sixteen

17. MOS—Military Occupation Specialty

Twenty

18. R4D—Navy version of the venerable DC-3 or C-47
19. block—a section of track varying in length from a few hundred feet to a number of miles set aside to be occupied by just one train. Block entrances were guarded by block signals consisting of a system of colored lights or semaphore arm signals.

Twenty-one

20. Hogger; Hoghead—railroad engineer

Twenty-two

21. Big Blue—Halsey's Third Fleet, a striking force composed of fast carriers (33 kt.) and fast battleships
22. special sea detail—an evolution for leaving or entering port where the ship's best sailors are assigned to the pilothouse for steering and navigation; to the engineering spaces for proper throttle control; to the navigation spaces for precise plotting of the ship's position; and to the deck force for line handling or anchoring

Twenty-three

23. 1 MC—ship's PA system
24. JOOD—Junior Officer of the Deck

Twenty-seven

25. PRITAC (*Pri*mary *Tac*tical circuit)—TBS (talk between ships; line of sight) radio circuit used on bridge, monitored in CIC

Thirty-one

26. Ulithi—The few remaining Japanese escaped by canoe and paddled one hundred miles southwest to Yap Island, which was bypassed by American forces.
27. sea cabin—closet-sized stateroom on the bridge deck behind the pilothouse. With just a bunk, washbasin, and toilet, the captain sleeps here while the ship's at sea, giving him quick access to the bridge in emergency.
28. putting on my crow—passed the test for third-class gunner's mate and will sew on an arm patch
29. TINS message—"This is no shit."

Thirty-five

30. fast battleship—Such as the *Iowa* class, could achieve fleet speeds of over thirty knots, thus keeping up with the carriers and destroyers. Older battleships, like those sunk at Pearl Harbor, were rated at only twenty-one knots
31. Sergio Osmeña—Manuel L. Quezon was president of the Philippines

when war broke out. With MacArthur, he escaped Corregidor by PT boat in 1942 and lived in exile in the United States while awaiting his return. Tragically, Quezon died of tuberculosis in July 1944 in Sarnac, New York, the day after MacArthur returned from his Hawaii Conference with FDR. Thus Sergio Osmeña became president.

32. atabrine tablets—malaria protection

Thirty-eight

33. five bells—six thirty
34. *Kishinami*—IJN destroyer
35. *Isokaze*—IJN destroyer

Thirty-nine

36. DJ—Dear John letter. A letter received in a combat zone from a girlfriend or wife announcing her decision to leave or divorce him

Forty

37. CAP—combat air patrol. Fighters assigned to protect airspace over the ships
38. Kate—Allied code name for the Nakajima B5N2 single-engine torpedo bomber
39. DRT—Dead Reckoning Tracer. An electro-mechanical plotting and navigation device mounted in a large table

Forty-one

40. Fukudome—Vice Admiral Shigeru Fukudome, commander Sixth Base Air Force and Second Air Fleet, Clark Field, Luzon
41. *Tone*—IJN heavy cruiser
42. *Myoko*—IJN heavy cruiser

Forty-three

43. cap the T—a classic naval maneuver, predating Lord Nelson, in which a column of ships sails perpendicular to an opponent; the advantage being that all his guns are unmasked to one side while the opponent, steaming in a column, can only fire forward

Forty-eight

44. Arleigh—a name invented by Arleigh Burke's mother, most likely derived from the Raleigh of Sir Walter Raleigh
45. six fast battleships—Admiral Halsey, commander of the Third Fleet and Mitscher's superior officer, flew his flag in the fast battleship USS *New Jersey* (BB 62)
46. Task Force 38—Task Force 58 became Task Force 38 when Admiral Raymond A. Spruance turned the reins over to Admiral Halsey

47. Pearl Harbor veterans: *Maryland* (BB 46), *West Virginia* (BB 48), *Tennessee* (BB 43), *California* (BB 41), *Pennsylvania* (BB 38)

Fifty-one

48. 29 MC—intercom system connecting key parts of the ship.
49. USS *St. Lo* (CVE 63), one of the six escort carriers of Taffy 3. Sunk by kamikazes in the late morning of 25 October 1944
50. SecTac—Secondary (supplementary) Tactical TBS radio circuit, as compared to PriTac (primary tactical circuit)

Fifty-three

51. *Baltimore*-class cruisers—the Japanese compounded their woes by misidentifying *Fletcher*-class destroyers as *Baltimore*-class cruisers.
52. Takao—major Japanese naval port and communications center on Formosa during World War II, now Kaohsiung on Taiwan. Also *Takao,* an IJN heavy cruiser

Fifty-six

53. USS *Vulcan* (AR 5)—a repair ship
54. USS *Princeton* (CVL 23)—light carrier lost to bombing attack 24 October 1944